Juror 55

CHRIS ZIMMERMAN *Summer '12*

ISBN: 978-1-935356-16-5

Cover photo: Courtesy of Amish Country Images, Wade Wilcox

Second edition, published by Joker's Conundrum LLC

Chris Zimmerman
P.O. Box 180
Shepherd, MI 48883
E-mail: setterindebtor@yahoo.com
Website: www.authorchriszimmerman.com

Printed in the United States of America

Juror 55

Also by Chris Zimmerman:

INTENTIONAL ACTS
THE SECRET-KEEPER
THE COVENANT FIELD
FORTY MILE POINT

One

IT WAS A RATHER CHILLY EVENING for April's standards, not that April was a real person, but rather my second favorite month of the year. The season's last snow squall had deposited a vast collection of flakes on the grass, the sidewalk, and the parking lot, which was teeming with cars, visitors, and concerned citizens from all over northern Michigan.

At nearly seven, I nodded to a pair of state troopers, then sliced past the folks who were puffing cigarettes near the entryway into the Standish high school gymnasium. Inside, the place was packed with people abuzz in chatter about the person they were anxious to see. I saw men wearing their over-sized, fleece-lined, lumberjack shirts; their spouses wore silky nylon jackets embroidered with either union badges or various excavation-company logos. This was the heart of the Democrats' stronghold; every one of them had come to the high school that April evening to hear the man they had elected and re-elected over and over again.

Both sets of bleachers had been pulled out of the side walls, and the basketball court was covered by rows of metal folding chairs. There were people in every chair on the floor and on most of the bleachers, too. The crowd was restless and their babble reverberated against the metal barriers, the basketball hoops, and the wide, formal stage. A podium stood all by itself in the middle of the stage, two paces away from the backs of four or five members of a private security team who wore cheap navy blazers adorned with gold badges on their breasts.

I pulled my camera out of my bag, screwed on a wide-angle lens, and got ready for the man of the hour. He was going to walk right past me on his way to the podium; my pictures would tell a thousand words in tomorrow's paper. I am, after all, executive reporter and chief correspondent for my own newspaper, the *Gratiot County Recorder.*

We were all waiting for Congressman Floyd Capp, who was making his first town hall meeting since his controversial deciding vote to overhaul the nation's health care system. He called the vote "the toughest of his career," but in reality it shouldn't have been that difficult. Nobody wanted the bill passed. Not the American public. Not the people of northern Michigan. Nobody.

But Congress passed it anyway—without knowing what was in it, without the public's support, and without even considering whether or not it was constitutional.

Floyd Capp's vote made his constituents angry, but it delighted two of his largest campaign contributors: the trial lawyers and the pharmaceutical companies who both loved him. Those two groups wanted to see the bill passed, because it preserved the lawyers' right to sue for malpractice, and gave the pharmaceutical companies an enormous pool of Americans who had just been given "free" health insurance.

Congressman Capp turned his back on the people who elected him in favor of the special interest groups he swore to disavow. His constituents weren't the least bit afraid to tell him that he had betrayed their trust. I looked up at the top row of the rafters. The people held banners that read, *Traitor!* and *We Shall Remember Come November.*

Mr. Capp was flying into a hornets' nest and he didn't even know it.

A shouting match erupted in the fourth or fifth row of the folding chairs. Two men stood up and pointed their fingers at each other, puffing their chests in the process. I couldn't understand what they were saying, but the fracas was quickly suppressed by an approaching deputy who left his post at the side door of the gym.

Holy hell, I thought, *this is going to get very interesting.*

Something felt odd. I counted cops: two state troopers at the front door, and two deputies at both side doors of the gym. That was it. The guards at the stage were little more than window dressing. In the grand scheme of things, security seemed a little light for a congressman who was embroiled in so much controversy. If Capp could turn his back on his constituents, he certainly was capable of underestimating their umbrage toward him too.

In all reality, if elected officials are doing their jobs, they shouldn't have to worry about their safety. There shouldn't be any reason to have a police presence in your own district.

Everyone in the gymnasium knew why the police were there.

Capp wasn't doing his job, because he wasn't representing the people. First, he voted for the stimulus program that proved to be a disaster, then he opposed the extension of middle-income tax cuts. The vast majority of people in our district didn't want the government spending all that money, and they certainly didn't want to pay higher taxes. Capp ignored them all.

When the health-care bill came up for discussion, he disgraced us all when he agreed with the foolishness of "we have to pass the bill to find out what's in it." After he cast the deciding vote, he admitted to the commentators of *Fox News* and *Meet the Press* that he never even read the bill before he voted for it. What's worse, he told talk-show hosts that the reason it would take four years for the effects of the law to be implemented was "to control the people."

Control the people, Congressman?

Not in America, and certainly not in Michigan.

All over the North Country, groups of concerned citizens pooled their money and bought billboards with disparaging remarks on them about Capp's betrayal. On I-75, near the Pinconning exit, a giant brick American flag was covered with a banner that read: *Dump the Chump*. Pictured next to those words was an image of Floyd Capp. Up the Lake Huron coastline, near the little town of Ossineke, the owner of a fleet of semi trucks parked one of his idle trailers on the edge of US-23. Taped to the side of a boxy, enclosed trailer were three or four giant Capp campaign signs. In big, bold letters, were the words: *Liar!* On the east side of I-75 near the Indian River exit, there is a small billboard with the words *Jesus, come into my heart* written on it. It's been there for years, and is written in a fancy font. After Capp's vote, the sign now has an accompanying request: *and give Floyd Capp a hearing aid.*

I had never seen such outrage directed at an elected official. Newspapers and media outlets from all over the state covered the angst of the citizens who threatened to recall the man if he wasn't killed first.

Deep down, though, I suppose Capp believed that he had his backers. Maybe he did.

As I glanced at the front row of folding chairs, I took special notice of two men sitting closest to me: clean cut, wearing baggy windbreakers over their crisp oxfords. One was nonchalantly reading a folded newspaper, the other fiddling with his BlackBerry. They looked slightly out of place, maybe a bit too clean cut for the occasion. One of them had a little ear bud jammed in the side of his head, and I wasn't sure if he was listening to music or orders from some sort of central command post.

Those two must be the capitol police—all the way from DC, I thought. *I bet they're packing a handgun under their baggy jackets.*

Hard to say how many other undercover police officers might have been there. They have a way of making themselves small in the most obvious of situations.

I didn't have much time to wonder; a dark black Suburban screeched to a halt outside the gym doors. A couple of staffers jumped out of the back seat and acknowledged the troopers at the door. They didn't exactly shake hands, and it appeared to be a rather informal greeting. I eased toward the door, maybe thirty feet away, and took several pictures. It was eight minutes after seven and the good congressman didn't seem to care that there were hundreds of people waiting for him inside. How rude. After thirty or forty seconds of waiting for the congressman to finish his phone call, one of the staffers opened the passenger side door of the Suburban. Congressman Capp snapped his phone shut, stuffed it into a pocket, and put on his fake, immovable smile.

I took several shots of him as he buttoned the top button of his sport coat and shook his host's hand. Both gentlemen laughed smugly as if everything in the world was carefree and la-de-da.

As they came at me, I clicked more photos. Mr. Capp didn't look as tan or as polished as he did on television. Makeup must have hidden his age spots, the wrinkles around his eyes, and the sheen atop his perfectly bald head. I hid behind the lens as the little group meandered past, oblivious to the firestorm that was about to be unleashed. It was tricky shooting both men because they were so much shorter than the troopers behind them. As we neared the entryway to the gym, I heard the host ask, "Anything you want me to say for your introduction?"

Capp laughed, "As the great Malcolm X would say, '*make it plain.*'"

The great Malcolm X? I thought, *this guy really is out of touch.*

The host laughed aloud, but I figured that anything the congressman said would have elicited a similar response.

Brown-nosers and butt-kissers have the same traits no matter what the setting: laugh at your boss's jokes regardless of how bad they are.

The noise level inside the gym had grown to an idling snarl, and when the dignitary tapped on the business end of the microphone with his index finger, the masses eased off the throttle.

"Ladies and gentlemen," he pleaded. "Ladies and gentlemen. As mayor of Standish, it is my pleasure to introduce Congressman Floyd Capp."

Faint applause was drowned by the chants of "Trai-tor! Trai-tor!"

I slipped behind the staffers and heard them say, "This is not going to be pretty," as the congressman confidently marched up the stairs toward the podium.

They were right.

As Capp raised his hands to the crowd, urging them to settle down, someone in the back of the gymnasium lit a pack of firecrackers; at least that's what it sounded like to me. The state police didn't know if it was firecrackers or a machine gun, so they drew their side arms and raced farther inside. That must have been the cue for more mayhem, because almost immediately the gym began to fill with silky, white smoke. Screams of panic swept over the crowd, and I figured that the smoke was actually tear gas. The people trampled each other on the way to the side doors, but for some reason they couldn't get out.

The troopers who rushed inside were caught out of position and were swarmed by the mass of riled guests.

Capp ducked like a coward behind the podium. The staffers raced up the stairs, waving their arms, yelling at him to get up. Capp did get up, just in time to see his two aides get throttled by the two undercover fellows in the front row. A couple of swift kicks and three punches later, the staffers were sent flailing into the security team at the front of the stage.

Those DC boys are serious, I remember thinking, *but why would they beat up two of their own? Didn't they know who was guarding the congressman?*

The scene became a wild mass of people rushing for the only open door. Chaos erupted and the shouts of protest turned into cries of fear and panic. The two undercover guys took hold of the terrified congressman and whisked him out of the gym. By then, I had put away my camera, and the tear gas was stinging my eyes. The crowd was running past me: choking, wailing, clutching handkerchiefs to their faces, and cursing the chemicals that were wreaking havoc on their senses. A man pushing a wheelchair slowed the stampede, so many of us dashed around the obstruction on our way to freedom.

I've never been so happy to feel the snow as I was on that April evening in Standish. It soothed my eyes and those of all the other attendees who made it outside. They coughed and heaved and bent at the waist in an effort to relieve themselves of the stinging pain. The images were incredible, but they were tailor made for a devoted newspaperman like me. And, as far as I could tell, I was the only journalist there.

The people used Capp's Suburban for a crutch as they caught their breath. No one cared who was inside the vehicle, or if it was needed for a quick getaway. We were all concerned with our own safety, and the safety of others, when the private security team escorted the two staffers outside. One of them had an enormous shiner under his eye, the other, a ripped shirt.

"Congressman!" they yelled in unison.

And then it dawned on us. *Where was the congressman?*

Someone in the Suburban rolled down the tinted windows and yelled from the driver's seat, "Everything's fine. He's in the back of the state police cruiser."

"What?"

"They just left," he smiled, "Floyd and the two undercover officers."

I moved closer to the conversation. "Why didn't you stop him? Why didn't you do something?"

"Because you told me to wait right here."

The staffer with a shiner had lost his cool. "Damn it, Rusty, you friggin' jack wagon!"

Rusty, the driver, yelled back, "What?!?"

"Where are the police?" the staffer demanded, rhetorically. Instead of two cruisers behind the Suburban, there was only one.

"Congressman!" the second staffer yelled again, as if his dog's name was *Congressman* and it had run away from home.

Swarms of people surrounded the Suburban and poured into the parking lot. When the state police troopers made their way outside, the plot thickened even more.

"I told you not to leave your engine running," the second trooper coughed in the direction of the first. "Wait till the captain hears about this."

Just then, a sheriff's cruiser sounded its siren and took off down the driveway, between the rows of cars. Several seconds later, the first cruiser was joined by a second, then the remaining state police sedan. None of the cruisers made it very far; they all ran over a spike strip near the end of the driveway.

I looked at the congressional staffers' faces as reality painted a fantastic picture: their grim charade was over. They weren't going to hoodwink their constituents any longer. The lies, the deception, the grand-standing on television had come back to haunt them.

Congressman Capp was gone.

An hour after Capp's disappearance, the authorities found the missing state police cruiser parked in a secluded, wooded area west of Standish. Even though there weren't any boot tracks in the mud and snow, the police called in tracking dogs to search the area for any sign of Capp. They came up empty.

A little more than an hour after that, a satellite tracking device was used to help locate Capp's phone. It was found all right, in a rest-area dumpster just south of Grayling, on I-75. In the same dumpster was a standard-issue bullet-proof vest that Capp wore under his sport coat.

To complicate matters, the authorities responded to a tip from a motel manager in downtown Standish who saw several people leading a man into one of the rooms. One of the men was wearing a suit and tie, and a pillowcase over his head. After word got out that the congressman had been kidnapped, the motel manager called the authorities, who swarmed the motel. There were four men and one woman inside the room: the man under the hood was getting married soon, and the hood-stunt was nothing but bachelor-party mischief. The woman was a dancer at *Deja Vu* in Saginaw who performed at private parties on her days off.

The villains used the distraction at the motel in Standish to whisk Capp away to a secluded location in northern Michigan. Once there, they used a cheap video camera to film Capp's final moments. Bound to a straight-backed chair, and completely naked, Capp read a two-sentence statement about the mistakes he had made in Congress. "I never meant to cause the people of northern Michigan any pain. It was wrong of me to vote for that health bill, to ignore my constituents, and to listen to my biggest campaign contributors instead of the people who elected me."

Capp had tears in his eyes and he talked like he had been drugged or been forced to swallow a barrel of alcohol. He shivered almost uncontrollably, and with each sentence he uttered, a small plume of steam pursed his lips. Wherever Capp was, it was cold and damp.

The entire country watched in horror as a man wearing a black hood over his head moved the congressman from an upright position to the floor. Capp was still seated, but his head was on the ground. The camera jiggled slightly as the man in the hood stepped back to adjust the camera's point of view.

Chubby little Congressman Capp looked at the camera and pleaded for his life. "Please don't do this! We can work this out! I've got money! Lots of money!"

But the man wearing a hood would have none of it.

He returned to Capp, carrying a large block of wood in one hand, and a mammoth, imposing battle axe in the other. The blade on the axe must have been eight inches across, and I could tell by looking at it that it would pack quite a wallop.

"How much do you want?" Capp demanded.

Hooded man didn't say a word as he placed the block of wood under Capp's neck.

Capp squirmed, so the man made a fist and buried it in the center of Capp's face with a tremendous wallop.

"Shut up, you friggin liar," he growled.

Blood spurted from Capp's nose. He cried the cries of a child.

The man picked up his axe, held it to Capp's throat, and said. "Congressman Capp, your life is now over. In one minute thy judgment come."

With that pronouncement, the man in the hood raised his axe over his head, and slammed it into the block of wood, Paul Bunyan style.

The scene was remarkably despicable and fortunately, ended five seconds after the hooded man's deathly blow.

YouTube pulled the video an hour or two after it was posted, thank heavens, but television stations all over the country picked it up and the story spread like wildfire. Several federal law enforcement agencies were involved in the investigation, naturally, and it didn't take long for them to cast a net across the breadth of Michigan's Lower Peninsula.

A week later, the police centered their investigation on a twenty-seven-year-old man from the little town of Meredith on the edge of Gladwin County. Marshall Yandle was the leader of an ultra-right-wing religious group called the

Heretic Fringe—the group that claimed responsibility for the kidnapping and beheading.

The authorities almost caught him several times throughout the weeks that followed, but Yandle managed to stay one step ahead of them by utilizing his superior woodsmanship and survival skills he learned in the military. The authorities had a hard time getting close to Yandle because he installed an elaborate system of police scanners and global positioning systems to track their whereabouts. What's more, he had intimate knowledge of the north woods and knew which homes were occupied and those that were merely hunting camps. The police said that he wouldn't stay in one place for more than twenty-four hours at a time, and took pride in leaving his favorite Bible verses etched into the kitchen tables of the cabins where he had spent the night.

Residents in the North Country were on edge. Sporting-goods stores sold loads of ammunition and tons of new firearms. Sales for security systems soared, and neighborhood watch groups sprang up overnight. *America's Most Wanted* visited Gladwin, Standish, and Meredith, and stoked the fires of fear. Pawn shops were advised to be on the lookout for a man the authorities called, "Little Rambo." Yandle's picture and story became the lead news item on the evening news broadcasts and front-page headlines from Detroit to Houghton, Manhattan to San Diego.

The manhunt was underway.

If I had known that the two clean-cut dudes inside the gymnasium were bad guys, I might have stuck out my foot as they rushed past me with Capp in their possession. Tripping them would have foiled the Heretic Fringe's plans and saved the congressman's life.

As it stood, I knew who Marshall Yandle was, and I had a hunch where he might go next.

Two

ALMOST FOUR WEEKS HAD PASSED, and Marshall Yandle was still at large. Every other member of the Heretic Fringe who was involved in Capp's kidnapping and murder had been captured, arraigned, refused bail, and awaited the prosecutor's next move.

Even though the manhunt for Yandle was still in full swing, I wasn't about to let turkey season pass without trying to kill a beautiful white tom that lived behind an Amish farm in Gladwin County.

Early one morning I made the drive from Alma to the North Country, parked the truck behind a one-room schoolhouse, and began the long walk across a cultivated field of planted corn.

I love this time of year when everything on the farm is lush and green: growing by the hour, reaching for the sun, clawing for the warmth it would soon deliver. The earth on that early May morning was soft and fertile, the rows and rows of corn sprouts only a day or two old. A heavy dew had settled on the land, and it gathered in tiny beads of sweat that dripped seductively from the edge of every leaf.

The world was anything but quiet. I heard the satisfying pluck of frogs peeping in a nearby swamp, and smelled the fragrant roar of fresh pollen. The robins, the geese, the cardinals—

everything—had a song to sing. The creatures of the world greeted the rising sun with a glorious serenade on a cloudless dawn in the heart of mid-Michigan.

For man and beast, it felt good to stretch the legs, to tune up the vocal cords and embrace the warmest season ahead. After a long Michigan winter, it was great to be outside, to be free of the confining weather, to dip a toe into spring's tepid water and have it please the soul. I was happy. The birds were happy. The world was a peaceful place.

The white gobbler was a real trophy, not just because of his peculiar genetic makeup, but because he had not just one "beard" protruding from his chest, but rather two that I figured were at least ten inches long. Two beards are a rarity, which made "my" bird a real trophy.

I spotted him several times throughout the spring where a long, hilly pasture melted into a lovely woodlot of oaks and maples. It was easy to see him out there. He was the shape of a giant snowball, the way his feathers were all puffed up, his tail fanned like an enormous hand of playing cards. He acted more like a dancer, or a matador, the way he stepped this way and that, posturing for the ladies, swishing his tail to the left, to the right, to anyone who would watch.

The hens in his harem hardly seemed to care. They kept their noses in the pasture—looking for bits of food, perusing the stash of produce as if it were a farmers' market on a care-free Saturday morning. They all seemed oblivious to the maestro in their midst. When the hens actually submit themselves to the toms, it must be a small miracle, because I've never seen it happen. But I know it does, because year after year, there seem to be more wild turkeys.

None, though, like the albino-white monster that I guessed would weigh more than twenty-five pounds. He was broad across his back, and tall; two attributes that add heft to the scales. If the hunt came together as I thought it would, I was going to have the tom stuffed by a taxidermist and mounted on the wall. Which wall, I didn't care.

My wife, Colleen, probably wouldn't care, just as long as it was somewhere in the attic or the garage.

My partner at the newspaper, Walter Claety, wouldn't care either, provided that it was out of sight from the public eye.

I laughed to myself.

Who am I kidding? A mounted turkey means more to me than to anyone else. It would be a conversation piece, but that's about it.

First things first, Derrick, I reminded myself, *close the deal, then worry about getting it mounted.*

Before I knew it, I was at the fencerow that separated the rows of corn plants from the green, flowered pasture. I found an oak tree that was wide and tall, its bark flecked with moss. There was just enough clutter at the foot of the oak to obscure my outline. Turkeys have excellent vision. Superb hearing. It is often said that if they could smell, they would be impossible to kill because they could see danger, hear trouble, and smell it coming.

To offset their excellent vision, I wore camouflage from head to toe. Facemask. Gloves. Even my shotgun was cloaked in a brown and green sheath that the people at the sporting goods store nicknamed "a sock."

I had an excellent view of the surroundings. The pasture. The woodlot at the far end. The sun creeping out of the horizon. I placed my padded seat-cushion at the base of the tree, melted into the trunk, and absorbed the majesty that is springtime in mid-Michigan.

The stage was set.

Battlefield ready.

The tom fired the first volley, and was gobbling up a storm. He filled the spring air with the rebel yell of courtship. I guessed that he was a hundred and fifty yards away, perched on a tree limb, teetering on the notion of calling a mate, yet ever watchful of danger that might be lurking.

Somehow, the tom survived the first three weeks of turkey season. He had made it through the gauntlet of perils that reduces a turkey's life span to a little more than eighteen months.

In a way, I felt bad for hunting turkeys after they survived the long Michigan winter. If they haven't starved or frozen to death, been hit by cars, or eaten by a host of predators that are much better at hunting than me, why should I be so lucky as to shoot one that strolls into shotgun range?

On the other hand, when a male turkey responds to my female impersonation and comes waltzing in to the setup, it is a thrilling sight to be sure. And it doesn't always work out. A lot of times, the toms listen to my hen calls, but choose not to come in. It's like they understand the concept of playing "hard to get," or are able to decipher the real hens from the phonies.

I'm always a bit reluctant to start calling first thing in the morning. Start too soon and he might get bored. Start too late and he already might have flown out of the roost and set his itinerary for the day. The best time to call a tom still on the roost, is to do it when he's just about to fly down. With a little coaxing and cooing on the call, I could convince the tom that some good loving is only a few steps away.

Dawn stood still. It hung tentatively in the growing radiance. A group of crows drifted overhead but didn't say a word. Somewhere off in the distance a train whistled, and it made me realize I wasn't the only person alive.

After fifteen minutes of waiting, I put the turkey call in my mouth and uttered a few subtle yelps. The tom responded with a gobble. We were connected by the sounds of love. It was amusing to talk like a hen and have a tom think I was real. It was seduction of a perverted kind. Instead of wooing a woman, I was pursuing a turkey with the x-rated pillow talk of a bird.

Ah, spring.

Brings out the lover in me.

Seduction is so much fun, no matter what the game, no matter what the season.

Two minutes later, the tom dipped off his perch, flapped his wings a few times and made a graceful landing in the field. Through my binoculars, I saw him shake the dust from his feathers, the sleepers from his eyes. He turned his head and scratched an itch on his shoulder, oblivious to the danger lurking a hundred yards away.

It was the closest I had been to the tom all season. He was bigger than I thought. Twenty-five pounds for certain. Maybe thirty. He would make a fine spectacle on the wall, a conversation piece that, someday, I would pass on to my grandsons, who would take it off to college and hang it on their dorm-room walls.

But there was still work to do. Mr. Tom was still seventy yards out of range, and by his actions, I knew there must have been at least one hen nearby. Hens usually take their time getting out of bed in the morning. They let the toms fly out of the roost first, and I'm not sure if that's because they want the toms to make sure the coast is clear, or if they just like the idea of sleeping in. Either way, the tom kept cocking his head this way and that, looking up in the trees, strutting his stuff and gobbling to all that would listen.

Tom gobbled at my lonesome hen calls, but he also gobbled at a crow that reappeared and barked a "caw-caw-caw-caw!" The honk from a Canada goose was just as worthy of a gobble, and so were the intermittent blasts from the train that was headed in our direction. The romantic bond I thought the tom and I had forged only a few minutes previously was nothing more than a delusion. My hen calls were just another noise in the woods that deserved a robust yodel.

But I wasn't completely out of the game. It's not like tom ran the other way when I tried my best to sound like a hen. He was now sixty yards out and joined by a svelte, little hen that was maybe half his size.

His gobbling worked; and he had called in a mate.

If only the cardinal overhead had the same luck. He was trying his hardest to pull an acquaintance out of the surroundings with his soulful whistles. Slowly, I looked up and saw the ball of red feathers sitting on the oak's outstretched arm—a cleft baby finger—singing its little heart out.

Where's your congregation, Cardinal?

Answer my prayers, will you?

The hen was leading the tom away from me and I knew that he'd never leave her side. My heart sank. The hunt I had imagined was crumbling before my eyes. Drastic measures were a necessity now. I tried a different kind of call—one made out of wood—and shaped like an overgrown matchbox. When I scraped the top of a wooden box on the bottom, it made a raspy, whine-like sound that grabbed the hen's attention. She snapped her head high and I wasn't sure if that meant that I was busted or if she took exception to what I had said. She dared me to repeat myself.

So I did.

The hen cocked her head, propped her hand on a hip, and yelled back at me.

Now we were getting into it.

Whatever I said didn't sit well with Miss Moffett.

I yelled at her.

She yelled at me.

The tom, well, he was caught in the cross-fire. He continued to stand there in the flowered pasture, feathers fluffed wide, tail fanned wider. He seemed to say, "Ladies, please, there's plenty enough to go around."

I really didn't care about the tom, however, because I knew that the key to the hunt had settled on the hen's shoulders. If I could draw her in to investigate me, the tom wouldn't be far behind.

We continued our bickering. The hen. Me. I was yelping and clucking. She was clucking and yelping. With every verbal jab, she stepped my way. When she dipped below the hill, I raised my shotgun to my shoulder and balanced the forearm on my knee. At any moment, she'd come trotting up the hill, a chip on her shoulder, ready to teach the loudmouth on her turf a lesson about who was boss.

Tom was with her, a step or two behind. He was watching every move, drooling at the prospects of courting two hens for the price of one.

I was soaking it up. The trickery. The spring hunt. What was falling apart only a few minutes previously was now coming together as if I had drawn up a back-door play in a basketball game. Even though I couldn't call in the tom, I sure had his girlfriend riled up.

Hey, all's fair in love and war.

As long as the tom made it into shotgun range, I wasn't about to ask him if he felt betrayed by the hen.

And then I noticed my labored breathing. The adrenalin was kicking in and having its way with my heart, my lungs, my jittering hands. It was an intoxicating potion and one that I never experience in the pheasant fields or grouse woods. Then again, pheasants and grouse are all about snap shooting at quick targets. Turkey hunting swirls around the buildup, the anticipation, the gutsy utterances on a box made of wood or a call inserted into the roof of my mouth. It's the hunt, rather than the kill, that makes turkey hunting so much fun.

Shooting a turkey is relatively easy; aim at its head and let 'er rip. The part that leads up to that instant is what makes it such a gas.

I became one with the tree trunk. A limb of ancient oak. My eyes were glued to the gun barrel, the curve of the land, to the trophy that was marching to his death.

I ignored my fanny and the way it had fallen asleep. The tingling in my leg would eventually go away once I stood up and retrieved my trophy.

I knew that my bird would be along at any moment.

My ears were glued to the surroundings. No more frogs peeping. No more red birds singing. The robins, the crows, the geese were smothered by my own concentration. All I could do was listen for the rustling feathers of a tom turkey strutting into range.

Just as I wondered if the hunt was going to turn into a kill, the hen reappeared. She almost overran the brow of the hill, ten paces from the end of my gun barrel. I didn't dare blink, but kept my focus on the slope behind her.

And gloriously, he appeared.

A knight in shining armor.

His majesty, the king.

I caught a glimmer of the beard. A pair. A sight to behold.

The hen knew something was wrong. She realized that I wasn't a tree limb, but rather a ruse of the human kind. I heard her sound the warning call—a subtle "putt" mumbled under her breath—so I knew I had to act fast.

In that crucial instant, I peered down the gun barrel and saw a mosquito perched on the peep sight at the end.

The hen was in the way of the tom, and the mosquito made everything more complicated. We were locked in a standoff. The hen sounding the alarm. The tom, holding court. I couldn't shoot. Then I could. With each passing second the tom slipped farther and farther down the hill. At first I could see his chest. Then his shoulders. Then his neck. It was now or never.

I shot.

And what a shot it was! The recoil feels like a kick from a mule, as two ounces of birdshot fired in the tom's direction.

The hen ran away. Or flew. I didn't care. All my attention was on the hillside, twenty yards away.

No bird.

On legs still asleep—I stood—which allowed me to see five feet farther down the hill.

No bird.

This is bad.

I stepped away from the ancient oak and still couldn't find him. *Oh, no.*

My heart was still racing as I made it to the brow and scanned the down slope. He was gone. He had melted into thin air, or at least May's version of it.

How could I miss?

I looked back to the oak tree and imagined my sitting there, shotgun pointed in this direction.

He must have ducked my shot exactly when I squeezed the trigger.

I looked down and tried to find a white turkey feather, or a drop of blood.

None.

There were no turkey tracks for me to follow, just a faint wake through the dewy grass. He had come up the hill and then he ran away towards the woods. No blood. No feathers. No sign of struggle.

A clean miss.

My hearing came back to me. I looked back towards the barn and noticed the tinkling sounds of a Swiss cow bell. Dairy cattle were making their way down the lane, swishing their tails behind them.

I heard the laughter of children as they rode their bicycles down the street.

The sounds of birds filled my ears again.

The marsh was alive.

The train had come and gone.

I had missed the tom completely.

How could it have happened?

I dismissed the miss as a stroke of bad luck. The giant tom was fortunate; I was not. It had been a long time since I missed a turkey, and I must have been overdue for a whiff.

Things happen.

Life goes on.

It just wasn't my day.

I took my time getting back to my old Suburban. The beautiful spring morning captured me, and I wasn't quite ready to get on with things. The morel mushrooms were popping, and I picked a couple dozen in the woods at the end of the pasture. They filled my camouflage headnet and were just big enough that they didn't fall through the slits for my eyes.

The clang from a school bell distracted my attention for an instant.

I found the tree where the tom had spent the night, and by the number of droppings underneath the branches he may have spent a number of evenings in that location. It didn't take much imagination to see him perched up there—those nasty, clawed feet wrapped tightly around a limb.

I couldn't believe that I had missed that bird. It wasn't a tricky shot by any stretch; he wasn't a moving target and he wasn't too far away. At twenty yards, the bundle of bb's from my shotgun must have been about the width of a pie plate when they whistled past his ear. He must have ducked at the same instant that I shot.

On the long walk back to the truck, I heard another tom gobble across the street. It was slightly muffled in the gathering breeze. He was a long way away and I wondered if it was the tom I had just missed.

No way.

My tom was probably on his knees somewhere, thanking God for the chance to live another day. It would be a long time until he'd gobble again. It would be forever until he'd return to that roosting tree and the evil fenceline not far away.

I really blew a golden opportunity at a fantastic tom, but somehow I was okay with it. I'd get up early the next morning, drive up to the Amish farm, and listen for other gobblers in the area. With any luck, I'd fill my tag with a normal, dark-colored bird by the end of the season. With one exception, there is hardly any prettier time of year, no better time of day, than to be outside in early morning in the middle of May. That exception, of course, is the entire month of October.

My eyes were glued to the crumbly fine earth and the tiny sprouts of corn. I noticed my boot tracks from a few hours previous and how they were headed in the opposite direction. They seemed lighter than the tracks I was making now, and I figured it was because of the hope that was lifting my steps.

I still had my shotgun slung over one shoulder, a padded seat-cushion draped over the other. As I rounded the edge of the woods and pulled the truck keys from my pocket, I heard horrible shrieks and cries coming from the one-room schoolhouse on the edge of the property. The terrible noise stopped me dead in my tracks.

The sounds weren't like a fire drill or a game.

They were horrible.

Pure torture.

A violent, grisly voice and the piteous howls of the children.

It was way beyond horrible.

It was orchestrated mayhem.

Something was terribly wrong.

I stepped toward the schoolhouse, sixty yards away, not thinking about the shotgun still in my hands.

"God's word says to lay down your life as a living sacrifice!" the voice growled in the springtime still. "Don't you know the Bible says that the perfect love casts out all fear?"

I ran to the corner of the school.

"For in one hour, thy judgment come!" the voice growled.

The children cried.

"I'm going to shoot every one of you!"

They cried even louder.

I wasn't sure what to do. My phone was back at the truck and it would have taken too long for help to arrive. The neighbors were too far away. There were bicycles parked in metal racks, and a stanchion for the horses on the edge of the gravel driveway. A pair of robins paraded through the bulbous glade of dandelion flowers.

Pow!

Glass spattered all over the drive, sending the robins racing for cover.

I couldn't move.

I was paralyzed by the quandary of what I should do.

I didn't ask for this.

The Amish elders who gave me permission to hunt had never told me there'd be this kind of trouble.

"Fear not. The Holy Spirit controls his people. Do you believe?"

The cries turned into howls.

I wasn't a believer. In fact, I couldn't believe that I was about to witness a mass murder and it was happening here and now.

I thought about making my way to the front door and negotiating with the madman.

"You owe me!"

The voice was gravelly. Angry. It was on the far side of the school, but it was loud and clear.

I crouched around the corner, ducking beneath the window sill, slightly higher than my shoulder. The windows were open and I could hear the children crying, the terror in their sniffles.

"Which one of you kids belongs to the Beilers?"

The voice was in the front of the school, near the door.

"Round 'em up," he said, "stand on your seats. I want a good look at you."

"In one hour—in one minute—thy judgment come."

I looked up through the open window at the rough-sawn planks on the ceiling. My heart was racing again. Like it had never raced before.

"Who's going to die first?"

Shrieks of torture.

Pow!

He shot, but I'm not sure if he actually killed someone or if he shot through the open window on the opposite side of the school. The bottom of the window was over my head, so I couldn't see what was going on inside.

"I'm going to start with your teacher."

The voice was getting louder. He was coming at me. I wanted to hide. To run. To get the hell out of there.

The teacher never said a word, and I wondered if she was bound to a chair, a length of duct tape stretched across her lips. I smelled the smoke from the shot and it made me cringe with disgust.

How could someone be so cruel?

He had to be stopped.

I heard his footsteps on the hardwood floor inside. They were heavy and getting louder.

He stopped in front of the open window, three feet away.

By the tightness in his skin, I figured that he was twenty-five, or thirty. Sideburns above a deep, discolored scar. There was no negotiating with this fool. He was the madman everyone was looking for, Marshall Yandle.

"Your last lesson, Teacher, is to tell us that smokin' ain't no good for us."

A cigarette dangled from the corner of his mouth, another tucked behind his ear.

When the flame from his lighter sparked the end of his smoke, I raised my shotgun to the base of his jaw. The gun barrel trembled slightly, just like it always does when I'm turkey hunting and the moment of truth is close at hand. The bead at the end of the barrel swayed from his ear to his eye, then back to his ear.

I flipped the safety off; it made the slightest "click."

Yandle turned his head and looked right at me. I saw the

same hopeless expression on his face that I have often seen on a wild turkey when it strolls into range and realizes that something isn't quite right. They know when something is awry, and the game, its life, is finally over.

The cigarette drooped slightly between his lips.

The gun barrel was the last thing he ever saw.

I never felt the recoil, heard the sound, or smelled the burnt gunpowder. All I could say was that I didn't miss. Yandle's head exploded all over the rough-sawn ceiling.

I dropped the gun and collapsed against the wall. My knees gave way and I slithered to the ground. The sounds of wailing children filled my ears.

I felt the May sun warming my face and wondered if it was the hands of God.

The angels were singing. They sounded like robins, and cardinals, and cute little warblers that have no names.

Whether my tears were from relief or sadness, stress or sorrow, I'll never know. They poured from my eyes like a warm, May rain.

The only thing I've been told is that I spent a week in the hospital, balled up like a baby, never speaking a word. Never taking a bite of food.

I never thought that blowing a man's head off would send me clattering on a rollercoaster ride of emotions. Even though my actions were warranted, it wasn't an easy thing to get over. The children I saved, the nightmares I prevented, should have been salve to my feelings, but it wasn't. The man I killed and the investigation that ensued would take me across the heart and soul of Michigan's Lower Peninsula and alter me in ways that weren't so honorable. The people I would meet, the soul-searching I endured, were only part of the adventure that would change my life forever.

Three

STRANGE WHERE MY MIND TOOK ME in that hospital room. It wasn't a dream, but it wasn't reality, either. I floated across the Milky Way of my distant past and relived the events that shaped who I am today.

Wherever my mental travels took me, the sounds of screaming children overwhelmed me. In torrents. In buckets and bushels. In giant waves and runaway tsunamis.

Although I couldn't see the children's faces inside that schoolhouse, I knew that they must have borne the horrific expressions of fear. I mean, it's one thing if they had never played video games where the object is to kill as many villains as possible; it's a whole other matter when the children have probably never laid eyes on a television.

They're so sheltered. So innocent. So trusting, those Amish kids. They've had no exposure to the nightly news, to drugs, to the things that make everyone else in the world cynical.

I have always had a fascination with the Amish. It's like they're some sort of secret society that nobody wants to join, but hardly anyone chooses to escape.

Collectively, they remind me of the days of Abe Lincoln, Lewis and Clark, or Thomas Edison. Individually, I wonder about their daily routine. What's it really like to live without electricity? Why, in God's name, would they want to shun modern conveniences?

I know exactly why.

Modern convenience, greed and anger all played a part in the trauma for those children. I couldn't blame the parents from sheltering their kids to the ways of the world. I heard their sniffles and their tiny, wholesome prayers.

God heard them, too. He must have.

It's almost as if he called me to be their guardian angel. I was in the right spot at the right time. Then again, maybe I wasn't. Taking a life is a tragedy that can scar a life forever. Without a doubt, it can wreck a man and kill a childhood.

I was a mess. Even though I was somewhat oblivious to my surroundings, I could feel people touching my hands, and sensed a bright light in my eyes. Was it the heartless probe of the doctor's stethoscope, or the illuminated welcome sign to heaven? I couldn't wince or flinch. I was paralyzed by the image of the exploding head and the weeping children.

Hunger eluded me. Thirst came and went. I slept the big sleep, over and over again. I heard voices, but I couldn't tell if it was reality or a dream. Regardless, I couldn't tell who they were or what they were saying. I was drifting through grade school and the formative years of my life.

Elementary school was where I learned to stick up for myself. When I was young, I understood that it's not always best to deal with your rivals head on, but get even with them in underhanded ways. Early in life I learned that revenge can be a very satisfying feeling.

I got a taste for revenge on the farm, when I explored my dad's stash of farm implements. He had a whole wall of them in the tool shed that was devoted to torturing the cattle herd. There were clamps for castration, de-horners that could have doubled as pruning shears, brass nose rings, and ear-tag pliers. My favorite implement, though, was the cattle prod, which my dad called the "hotshot." Only eighteen inches long, the hotshot looked like a nightstick with two small metal probes at the end. Whatever touched the metal probes got a whale of a shock.

Even though I had delusions of taking the hotshot to school and torturing my enemies, I decided not to. Instead, I discovered that it was an excellent tool for drawing earthworms out of the ground. Those big nightcrawlers couldn't help but slither their way out of their holes and into my hands when the prod was underground and shocking them into oblivion. Once in school, those worms ended up in the most bizarre places. I'll never forget the look of horror on his face when the class bully chomped into his lunch only to discover that he had taken a bite of ham and cheese and earthworm sandwich. When he washed it down with a gulp of milk, he realized that there were a dozen worms in the bottom of the carton, too.

Even though the charade gave me great joy, I didn't gloat about it to my buddies. I took solace in knowing that I got even with my enemy without having to pay the price for my part in it.

Over time, I set my goals on bigger fish—the teachers. I liked some of them. Most of them. But there were a few who played favorites, or were mean, or didn't care. My earthworm treatment was given to them, too. In their desk drawers, book bags, and coffee cups. I even typed envelopes with their names and addresses on them, and mailed each of them an "earthworm sampler" consisting of blood worms, nightcrawlers, and the slimy green ones that smell like a bag of rotten potatoes.

I got even with the teachers, the bullies—anyone who had wronged me—in sneaky, conniving ways, while at the same time avoiding physical confrontation.

Relatively early in my grade-school experience I realized that the world wasn't always a kind place. All in all, the "unfair" things in life kept me awake at night, and I had a hard time letting "them" go.

My dad told me it wasn't healthy to keep stewing about things. I got in trouble at school for the earthworm incidents, and Dad used analogies such as "life isn't fair, Son, you have to shed unfairness like water off a duck's back" to help me get over the mean notions in my head. Nothing seemed to work. I worried about things. The teachers. My grades. The next test in school. The stress of middle school was an excuse for anxiety, and cause for concern.

My mom said my spiteful streak was a sign that I had "passive-aggressive" tendencies. Although I really didn't understand what she meant, she only needed a few more troublesome events in class before she took me to the school psychologist.

I can't remember the psychologist's name, but I recall what she looked like. Skinny and frail. She had bone-thin wrists and knobby, protruding knee caps. Her hair was straight and lifeless, but she smiled a lot and had pleasant, trusting eyes. We played a lot of games during our appointments. Not mind games, but card games and silly stuff like hangman and "football" from a piece of paper folded into a triangle. She showed me how to do "cat's cradle" and a "witch's broomstick" from a loop of string. We practiced shooting baskets with a Nerf basketball hoop she had mounted on the back of her office door. The two of us laughed and giggled a lot, and I quickly thought of her as one of my friends.

In an unintended kind of way, the psychologist and I made a connection. Before too many sessions, I was telling her about the jerk in my class, the bully on the playground, the tough guy on the bus, the mean teacher, everybody. Looking back, the game playing was the doctor's way of breaking the ice between us. It worked. The counseling. The personal conversations. Her advice.

As a somewhat misguided young man determined not to let anyone get inside his head, I let the school psychologist do exactly that. She helped me understand that even though I had thoughts about "getting even," I didn't need to act on those urges. Over time, I learned to channel the negative energy into something more productive.

The incident inside that Amish schoolhouse wasn't exactly a spate of retribution; after all, the madman hadn't done anything to hurt me. I just happened to be at the wrong place at the right time. Maybe it was the right place at the right time. Because of the shooting, I couldn't move. Or talk. Or feel. My limbs were numb. My mind drifted to some of the things I had written since college. My latest kick was to write letters to businesses located throughout the country. Little companies and big companies. I wrote dozens of letters to tell the managers what great employees they had. And I didn't need much of a reason to fire up the word processor and type away at the keyboard. People who simply do their job are a rare commodity. I've always liked helping the little guys. The underdogs. I know a lot of folks who get paid by the hour and whose annual raises are determined by positive, unbiased feedback like mine. Good karma, I thought, was something worth spreading around.

Not all the letters were positive, however. I didn't hesitate to complain about the poor service I had received, or an item I had purchased that didn't meet my expectations. I wrote one of the big-box stores to complain that their oil changes took too long to finish. Letter writing took hold of me. When I couldn't get one of those fake logs to light in the fireplace, I wrote the manufacturer in Georgia. They sent me a brand new package of logs and a check for the money I had spent for the first bundle. I didn't have the heart to tell them that the second parcel was just as bad as the first. Because of the letters I had written, I never knew what I'd receive in the mail. The coupons, the letters, the vouchers for oil changes, a box of rice, a jar of salsa, frozen pizzas, and a night's stay at a hotel chain kept rolling in.

Letter writing was a mildly amusing activity, and proof that sometimes "the squeaky wheel gets the grease."

The letter I would write to the manufacturer of the shotgun shells would be a good one, especially when I got to the part about "what a nice job it did on a person's head."

I thought about the turkey that I somehow missed and what it must have been like to have a wicked load of bb's whistling past your ear. My mind was racing. My feelings thrown to the wind. Why was I here, so confused? My mind flashed to the first time I saw a dead body and how the sight of it sent me reeling. Working as a reporter, my assignment was to go to Iowa to cover the presidential caucuses. Instead of just covering the caucuses, I brought my dog on the trip so I could go pheasant hunting. On one of those pheasant hunts, I found an abandoned semi-trailer in a barn. When I opened the trailer's door, the driver was dead behind the wheel. I still remember the man's gimlet stare and the way his blood was caked to his neck beneath a perfect, cleft slit. The sight of death made me sick, but I was still intrigued with the surroundings. I took dozens of photographs. The images sizzled into my memory and helped make a whale of a story.

I relived the panic, the determination, and occasionally the exhilaration I felt when I was digging into a newspaper article, and it paid off with a great story. I couldn't just let a story go. I had to keep digging, searching, sniffing after the truth. My dad's advice about letting my problems roll like "water off a duck's back" was still in my head, but so hard to accept. There was no denying that I did have trouble letting things go. Once a story took hold of me, I was possessed by it. It would keep me up at night and churn butter into buttermilk during the day.

My mind revisited the day I saved a man from the frigid waters of northern Lake Huron. He was wanted for murder and had jumped off the ferry that he had hoped would take him from Mackinac Island to St. Ignace for his escape. Even though I had every reason not to save him, I just couldn't let him drown. The guy was floundering in front of me, and I had to help.

And yet, I hesitated for half a second.

After all, he was considered a very dangerous man—much

larger than I—and he was facing a very long jail sentence. Some people think that murderers and rapists deserve to die; I couldn't let him suffer. Instead, I dove into the harbor, pulled him from the lake, and rolled him on his side. When I did, a dribble of Lake Huron poured from his lips. A mental image came to mind of the bully in school and the way he threw up after he swallowed the earthworms in his milk. Now the earthworms were crawling in the fugitive's mouth.

He was cold, but I found a pulse beneath his dark, curly whiskers.

I tilted his head back and pinched his nose.

A crowd had gathered on the pier where the ferry had departed only a few minutes earlier. They were watching me under the cold, heartless pool of the mercury lights. I noticed the flash from the cameras and remembered that I wasn't the only journalist on the island. As much as I tried to avoid the limelight, I wasn't going to let that discourage me from saving a man's life.

I took a puff of air and pressed my lips against his. His chest rose slightly and I knew that oxygen was filling his lungs. I did it again, and again, and again.

I wanted to tell him to "Wake up."

Wake up?

"Wake up."

Me?

I opened my eyes, slowly. The light seemed strong, and it stung my eyes.

I thought for sure it was the end of my life and the Lord had sent a shining chariot to take me away.

Instead of the Lord, it was my daughter, Elizabeth, only a few inches away from the end of my nose. Colleen, my beautiful wife, was by her side.

Elizabeth's dainty, loving lips were pressed against mine.

Her graceful little voice spoke to me, saying "Wake up."

There were no more stories to cover, no more earthworms slithering through my head, or wailing kids in the Amish schoolhouse. The exploding head was gone for now. At last, the nightmare was over. I was back in the real world. All three of us shed tears of joy.

"It's so good to see you again," Colleen whispered.

"We missed you, Daddy," Elizabeth added, softly.

I felt their heads resting on my shoulders and the tears streaming down my face.

I looked around and realized I was in the hospital. *How weird is that?*

Where have I been?

"Derrick, the whole world wants to talk to you," Colleen proclaimed.

"The world?" I asked. "Me?" It felt odd, finally, to talk, to string my thoughts into perceptive sentences.

"The television stations. Radio. All your colleagues in the newspaper world." She was smiling. The familiar dimples under her eyes were beaming with pride.

"Why?"

Elizabeth put her hand on my cheek.

"Daddy, you're a hero."

"Why?" I asked.

"The man you killed," Colleen whispered, "those children you saved…"

I looked into the beautiful eyes of my wife as she searched for the right words.

"Oh, Derrick," she sighed. "I'll tell you all about it."

"Let's go home," her smile pursed her face. "Home where you belong."

Four

HOME SWEET HOME didn't have the soothing effect that I hoped it would. Our house was a lively place, full of distractions and music, television programs and flickering candles. There were meals to be made and laundry to do, errands to run and groceries to get. Colleen was really good about letting me take on as much or as little responsibility as I wanted. She gave me space to tinker and piddle around the house. There were times when the house was especially turbulent when I wished for the peaceful tranquility of the hospital room, where I could hide from reality, if only for a while. Before I left the hospital, the doctors gave me a prescription for some mood-altering drugs. They told me to take them if I had any more bouts of anxiety. I was never really sure what anxiety felt like, but the memories of the screaming kids and the exploding head were always simmering just below the surface.

After two or three days of popping the pills with very little effect, I decided to wash them down with alcohol.

I never really thought of myself as a drinker, but the combination of booze and drugs gave me a rather enjoyable buzz that helped me forget about what had happened at the schoolhouse. And while I was loopy, Elizabeth didn't seem quite so needy, and Jacque, my dog, not so demanding.

As hard as it was to admit, prescription drugs and alcohol became my way of escaping reality. It was easier to forget about the incident at the schoolhouse when I was floating on the numbing effects of the chemicals coursing through my veins.

Colleen noticed my increased intake of booze and I could tell that it bothered her. After a few years of knowing her, it's pretty easy to tell, just from the way she crosses her arms, that she doesn't like what's going on. Despite the doctors' advisements to the contrary, I think she believed that once I opened my eyes at the hospital and snapped out of my state of shock, everything would be back to normal. From her point of view, I think she thought I would shake off the episode in the schoolhouse and be my old productive self again, none the worse for wear.

All of a sudden, though, I liked drinking. I enjoyed the flavor of it and the ritual of making a cocktail. It smelled perfectly intoxicating, if not combustible when I took a heady whiff. After the ice had softened the alcohol's edge, it tasted good, too, whether it was rum and Coke, a Manhattan, or a gin and tonic. I felt like a grown man—an adult—when I had a tumbler full of ice and booze in my hands. It was neat to hold a glass of spirits and see the embalming fluids dancing in the light. I liked the side effects, too. The combination of ingredients desensitized the pain, and blurred the memories from my head. And I didn't just stick with the same old beer or my favorite brand of liquor. I whipped up all kinds of cocktails with bizarre names and unique ingredients. Happy hour was initiated earlier and earlier every day, but in all reality, happy hour was beginning to be not so happy.

Colleen tried a number of things in an effort to help me snap out of my funk. She always had an upbeat, cheery kind of outlook on life. I was certain that if she had kept a daily diary she would write in it that "somehow, some way, we would find a way to get through this troubled time in our lives." Instead of confronting me about my drinking, she came up with creative ways to keep my mind off the bottle. In the late afternoons—before happy hour—we went for long walks with Jacque. Colleen bought me a gift certificate for a half-hour massage at a local spa and a membership at a health club down the street. Her thinking was that a little aerobic activity and some healthy stimulation would stir something positive inside me. We took in a Detroit Tigers game at Comerica Park, and went on a sunset dinner-cruise to the Charity Islands in the middle of Saginaw Bay. Her idea for a feint didn't work because I kept relapsing into the need for booze and the desperate desire to escape reality.

One morning in June—after a big breakfast—she sat me down in front of the television and asked me to pay attention.

"Derrick, I want you to watch this."

I could tell that she meant business. My mom was there, too, sitting upright in the recliner beside me. Even Jacque lifted his head off his little doggie pillow and looked at us like it was serious.

After Colleen loaded a DVD into the player, and pressed the buttons on the remote, the television screen came to life. I recognized the urgent, melodic introduction of Channel 3's nightly news broadcast and the familiar face as our local news anchor started reading the lead story.

> *"Good evening ladies and gentlemen; a northern Michigan man is dead, but another tragedy may have been averted at a Gladwin County schoolhouse late this morning. Marshall Yandle, twenty-seven, was fatally shot in the head as he held seventeen Amish children hostage."*

The view on the television shifted slightly to the left, and an image of a horse and buggy appeared over the broadcaster's right shoulder.

> *"The shooter, Derrick Twitchell—a reporter from Alma—was in the area hunting wild turkeys when he heard the children screaming inside the schoolhouse."*

I noticed the way the broadcaster raised his eyebrows and smirked slightly at the prospect of hunting wild turkeys. It's like I was some sort of deviant Pilgrim for hunting wild turkeys when there are plenty of tasty, chemically fattened birds resting comfortably in the freezer at the grocery store.

> *"Yandle is said to have been the leader of the Christian militia group, Heretic Fringe, which has claimed responsibility for the murder of Congressman Floyd Capp. Since late April, Yandle was the subject of a massive manhunt, involving several law enforcement agencies. Police also say that Yandle was on the Amish farm to avenge an unsuccessful attempt to sue one of the Amish families."*

Colleen pushed pause on the remote, and my attention turned in her direction. She was almost crying. "Derrick, you're a hero. You killed the guy who did this to our congressman."

Her comment barely registered.

"You helped save all those kids," she tried again.

I looked away, to the backyard. Elizabeth and a friend were on the swing set, underneath a handsome white pine. They were laughing and smiling, like children do on a beautiful day in June.

I didn't ask any questions or acknowledge her pleas.

"Derrick, we're worried about you." Mom finally broke her silence.

"Don't you want to know about this guy Yandle?" Colleen countered.

I didn't want to think.

That question didn't spark any interest.

They looked at each other, resigned to the fact that I really wasn't myself. Both Mom and Colleen seemed to know that I was using alcohol to dull my anger.

"You're a reporter, Derrick," Colleen offered, tearfully. She wasn't cheery after all. "Don't you want to find out more about this guy?"

I sat on the edge of the couch, ready to get up.

Just then, Elizabeth and her friend came crashing through the back door. They screamed the sounds of delight, but when they slammed the door—"Pow!"—I went berserk.

"Stop it, you two!" I yelled at the top of my lungs, unable to control myself. The noise they made—the sounds they created—triggered a drastic reaction in my head. I ripped my hands through my scalp, sorry for the outburst, but helpless to the cause.

They ran away. Both of them.

Colleen ran down the hall after them, and Jacque ran after Colleen. Mom stayed in her recliner, the queen matriarch.

A second or two passed, awkwardly.

I gathered myself slightly. "I'm sorry you had to see that, Mom."

She reached for the wooden lever on the side of the chair, extending the footrest.

"I am too, Derrick."

I heard Elizabeth crying and it hardly fazed me.

Before the incident at the schoolhouse, I would do anything to protect my child from traumas that could have soiled her childhood. Now, I was the source of her angst.

"I never thought I'd see the day when you would yell at your own child, Derrick. Something isn't right with you," Mom said.

She was always the master of the obvious.

Colleen reappeared from the hallway and added her two cents.

"You can't go around yelling at Elizabeth, Derrick," she said.

Maybe it was more than two cents.

"Nobody yells at my kid and gets away with it."

She was defending her family, sticking up for what was right. I noticed her hand on her hip. She looked like the hen turkey in that Amish pasture, madder than mad.

"Even the dog is on pins and needles because you've yelled at him so much. He's not sure if you're going to whack him with a newspaper, or pat him on the head."

"I'm sorry, Colleen," I stammered for just a second, "I can't help it." I didn't know what else to say. A sincere apology hardly seems sincere when it's followed by an explanation of my behavior.

"We've made an appointment, Derrick," Mom announced.

"For what? Obedience school? Jacque's not a bad dog, just a little hyper, that's all."

"No, no, Derrick," Mom smiled, warmly. "I'm not talking about obedience school; it's for you, Derrick. We've made an appointment with a psychologist."

Mom was serious. They both were.

"Oh, great." I sighed.

Their idea reminded me of middle school and the woman psychologist with the lifeless hair and the Nerf basketball hoop taped to the back of her office door.

"What if I don't go?" I asked.

"You're going, Derrick," Colleen said. "Mom's right. You need some help. Before the shooting you never would have yelled at Elizabeth. Jacque's never been kicked by you, either." Colleen held a tissue to her nose. "I'm kinda at my wits end with you, Derrick," she said. "I don't know whether to hug you or slap you."

Mom had her opening. "You can't go around drinking all the time, either, Son."

I didn't know what to say, but I knew that I was ashamed of my conduct.

This was their little intervention. They seemed sincere in their intent and used examples of my conduct to cement their resolve. And what the heck, I knew better than to drink myself silly. The drugs only masked the pain I was feeling. Nothing in my life seemed to make me happy. I was in a dreary kind of dismal haze that I couldn't shake. It clung to my head like a turban.

The women in my life had me outnumbered three to one. They were determined to get me some help, which was an honorable and loving thing to do. And really, maybe deep down, I was crying for it all along.

Five

O N THE AFTERNOON of my first appointment with the psychologist, Colleen and I played golf. Even though the
warning label on the bottle of my prescription drugs said that I
shouldn't operate heavy equipment, I drove the golf cart without smashing it into a tree, a sand trap, or any other golfers.
In a loving, playful way, Colleen said that I was just as bad a
golfer when I was on the medication as I was without it. She
beat me in golf, as usual, thanks to her booming drives off the
tee and her wonderful touch around the green. I don't think
there's anything more beautiful than a woman with a pretty
golf swing, and the competitive fire in her belly.

Before I had the chance to tee up happy hour that afternoon, I drove Dad's old Harley a half hour north to the St. Jean
Centre in Mount Pleasant. Built way back in the teens, the
Centre is anchored in a rolling, wooded enclave on the outskirts
of Mount Pleasant. Most of the trees on campus are antiquated,
their lower limbs cracked and mangled, or lying lifelessly on
the leaf-strewn forest floor. It must have been perfect squirrel habitat because the giant rodents owned the place. I saw
close to a dozen of them, loping from tree trunk to tree trunk
or chasing each other in a frenetic game of tag. The buildings
looked like they could have been an army barracks at one time,
but the military chose to discard eons ago. Three stories tall, the

structures were square and boxy and made of cold, depressing blocks and steep-angled slate roofs. It was half prison, half asylum and the bars across the windows made me wonder if their intent was to keep the lunatics from getting out, or the ghosts and satanic spirits from getting in.

It had been probably ten years since I had been to the Centre, and that wasn't long enough. The setting gave me the creeps, the inhabitants a bad case of the willies. There were murderers and rapists behind those bars, all of whom were incarcerated because of the crimes they had committed and the mental illnesses they had endured.

My appointment was in building G, which was easy enough to find. I parked Dad's bike far away from the building, just like he used to do. Dad hated the idea of getting door dings on the side of his vehicles, and he always parked beyond the most popular spaces. And what the heck, a few extra steps weren't going to kill me.

Once inside the building, suite five was down the hall, on the right. I nodded to an elderly man polishing the floors with a mechanized buffer the size of a push lawn mower. I wondered if he was one of the patients on work-leave, or if he was simply an elderly man with a second job. In either case, the tile floor didn't need waxing or polishing; it had a hue on it that could have passed for a fresh sheet of ice.

Miss Peacock, the receptionist, was pleasant enough. I tried to make small talk with her about the nice weather we had been having. She made eye contact with me, and I noticed the headset crimped around her ears. We traded my insurance card for a one-page questionnaire about my family history, medication, and whether or not I had tried to harm myself. I had to roll my eyes at almost every question; it seemed like an invasion of my privacy.

I didn't really feel like talking to anybody about what was banging around my head.

It happened. It was over. It was time to move on with my life, somehow, some way. In time, I knew that the memory of what happened would eventually fade and everything would return to normal. Until then, I was perfectly content to wallow in alcohol and drugs. What could a psychologist possibly help me with? In my head, I was ready to dig in my heels and try to block anything he or she said. I wasn't going to listen, or offer information, or—

"Derrick?"

I looked up from my chair and saw a man looking down at me.

"Yes."

"Nice to meet you. My name is James Ong."

We shook hands and he asked me into his office, his den, or whatever you want to call it. A brown leather couch was against the partially drawn shades; a pair of matching armchairs flanked the coffee table in the center. I noticed two boxes of cream-colored tissue on the coffee table and a dainty woven wastebasket underneath. His office was warm and cozy, and I heard the tick-tock of a grandfather clock in the corner of the room. Dr. Ong sat on a swivel chair across from me, pulled out a white legal pad of paper and a pen. He scribbled something on the paper, crossed one leg over the other, and asked, "Your wife tells me that you've got some coping issues. Is that right?"

I laughed.

"Nothing like laying it all out there, Doc."

"Please, call me Jim."

"Okay, Jim. She must have told you about what happened at the schoolhouse, right?"

"Yeah, she told me about it, and I saw it on the news, too." He was smiling. "Read about it in the paper. It was a big deal."

I had to remind myself not to cooperate. It seemed like it was my turn to say something but I refused.

Jim picked up on my reluctance and added more to the story.

"I can't imagine shooting someone's head off." He shrugged his shoulders until they nearly touched his ears. "It's no wonder you're not the same person."

I agreed with him.

"You don't think I'm a nut case, do you?" I asked.

"Of course not," he shook his head. "Sometimes bad things happen to good people."

He made sense, but I quickly found myself sizing him up. He was a little younger than me. Wedding ring. Handsome, despite his wide nose. He looked rather comfortable sitting there in his swivel chair, a red sweater vest over a faded tattersall oxford.

I didn't feel quite right about talking to the guy, even though I knew that was why we were there. The competitive spirit swelled inside me. I felt a little insecure, perhaps vulnerable, for being on the patient-side of the coffee table instead of the other way around. I was usually the guy to fix things, not the person who needed to be fixed.

There was no way I was going to open up to him. Heck, I didn't even know how. If the coffee table served as a divider between us, I added brick after imaginary brick to the wall until I couldn't see Jim and Jim couldn't see me. I crossed one arm over the other in an effort to block whatever the agenda was. We could talk all day long about the weather, my daughter, my wife, my hobbies, the dog, bird hunting, whatever, but I wasn't going to tell him how I felt. What I saw. What I remember. What I forgot.

Jim must have picked up on my reluctance, because we sat there in a boisterous silence. It felt like we were getting dressed in the men's locker room after a rigorous game of racquetball and a quick shower. I didn't want to look at him and he didn't want to stare at me and all my deformities and imperfections. Instead, he scratched at his notepad, and it made me wonder if it was a diversionary tactic.

I put my elbow on the armrest of the couch and took note of a small bronze plaque on the back of the lamp. Inscribed on a bronze-looking plate were the words, *Thanks for everything. Steve & Susan.*

"So, you do a lot of marriage counseling?" I asked.

"Sure. We treat the general public and the residents who live in the Centre. Do you and you wife need some counseling?"

I laughed. "No, no. I don't even like it here."

"What do you mean?"

"It's nothing personal." I was backpedaling. "This place gives me the creeps."

"Why?"

"The last time I was in here I interviewed one of Michigan's most notorious serial killers."

"Who was it?" he asked.

"Atari Bigby."

Jim nodded. "The Oakland County killer?"

"Yes," I said. "I interviewed him for the paper."

"The guy had a giant mole between his eyebrows," he remembered, "with long gray and black hair growing out of it."

I nodded my head, but it occurred to me that the man seated across from me seemed to have an answer for every topic I brought up. "How did you know about him?"

"Everybody in southeast Michigan knew about him," he said; "he killed all those children in the late seventies, and the *Detroit News* offered a reward of a hundred grand for his arrest."

James Ong knew his stuff, but since I brought it up, I wasn't about to let him steal my thunder. "Remember everyone telling their kids about 'stranger danger,' and how they were supposed to stay away from people they didn't know?"

"Heck yeah," he said. "The nightly news had stories about how nobody would let their kids ride the bus because they were so afraid they would get kidnapped. Had angry parents taking their kids to school, and creating all those traffic jams."

I thought that maybe Dr. Jim had lost his sense of who was supposed to be talking, me or him.

"What happened in the interview?"

I sighed. "They took me into the bowels of the Centre, I remember that. I had to walk past a long row of other jail cells, or whatever you want to call them. Guys were swearing at me and speaking in tongues. I think some of them must have thought I was the devil or something. It wasn't a padded cell they took me to, but it must have been some kind of retaining room."

Jim nodded, as though he knew what I was talking about.

"Did it smell really bad?" He asked.

"Oh yeah, like a locker room. Had a picnic table in the center."

"They probably handcuffed him to a metal ring on the underside of the table."

"You're right, Jim," I said, "not his hands, but his belly chains."

"Keep going."

"He didn't need to be cuffed—that was for sure."

"Why do you say that? I mean the guy killed four children. Left their bodies in view of the police stations in Birmingham and Livonia—"

"Because he was on his last legs," I interrupted, "had prostate cancer that spread to his liver and kidneys."

"Is that why you were interviewing him?"

"Yes. I thought that maybe he would want to clear the air after his life sentences."

Jim nodded and inched forward in his chair.

"It wasn't really a life sentence," I corrected myself. "He had been declared criminally insane. That's why he was kept here all those years."

"We've got a whole complex full of them," Jim said. "What did he say?"

"He didn't admit to anything. It was like talking to Saddam

Hussein. The murders, the grief he caused, the shoddy detective work was everyone else's problem."

"How did that make you feel?"

I knew that question was coming. Shrinks always ask that.

I hesitated. "It was frustrating, that's for sure, but I almost expected it. I imagine that a lot of those guys believe that the system is out to get them."

"No doubt," Jim said. "It's like every day the world opens up and poops on their parade. Most of the criminally insane at the facility have no sense of remorse, or guilt."

"I didn't let him squirm away from me, however. I kept bringing up those kids he murdered. How a day doesn't go by that those parents don't miss their children."

Jim nodded. He was right there with me in the interview.

"I told him how sad birthdays had become for those parents," I said, "how they couldn't drive past the police stations without feeling a twinge of sorrow, or how Memorial Day takes on a whole new meaning."

Jim leaned back in his chair and tapped his pad of paper with the pen.

"Derrick, I think I understand a little bit of what's going on with you and your situation. You really have a caring side to your personality, which is precisely why you know about those children who were murdered thirty years ago. That same kind of tenderness stirring within you that makes it so hard to deal with what happened at the Amish schoolhouse."

He got me.

It was an excellent commentary.

I didn't know what to think, or how to answer.

My eyes fell to the floor and the wicker wastebasket beneath the oak coffee table. I noticed the plastic rim inside and the wadded up tissues. He had brought someone to tears in a previous appointment, and the tissues became the tears' downy nest of sorrow.

This guy was good.

What seemed like an innocent conversation about an innocuous topic had me reeling in double takes and second thoughts. The longer I said nothing, the more poignant his observation appeared.

And of course, Jim said nothing.

A pro knows when to shut up and let the inquisition fester.

"You mean, there's nothing wrong with feeling the way I do?" I asked.

"That's right, Derrick. There's really no correct or incorrect way to feel."

"How should I feel?" I asked, rather insecurely.

"That's a good question. There's really no right or wrong answer."

I was floundering with things to say, but I'm glad I kept them to myself.

When was the last time you shot a guy's head off?

Have you ever seen someone's brains splattered all over the ceiling?

"What's a normal way to act in that case?"

"Derrick, there isn't really a proper way to act." Apparently my line of questioning was getting a little redundant. "I'm just trying to understand your behavior at home."

"What else has Colleen told you?"

"That you like to drink. That you like to yell and you're short tempered. And that you've lost your interest in writing newspaper stories…"

Round and round we went on the merry-go-round of dialogue. It seemed like our conversation didn't have much direction until Dr. Jim revealed his prescription for my recovery.

"She also told me that you get a lot of joy out of driving your late father's motorcycle."

I nodded.

"What kind is it?"

"Harley."

"That's cool. I've always wanted one."

I smiled for a second or two, and thought about giving him some advice about which one to buy.

"I think you ought to jump on Dad's bike and go back to the schoolhouse. Spend some time there alone," he said. "Confront the memories head-on. It might help you realize that whatever took place there is over, and it's time to move on with your life."

Although I could think of a lot better ways to spend an hour, it wasn't that bad meeting with him. He seemed like a nice fellow and he had a genuine concern for me and my mental health. I never caught him glancing at the clock or staring at me with the glassy eyes of boredom. We agreed to meet a week later at the same time, same place.

Instead of walking out the same door I came in, Jim directed me to the side door of his office, which opened into the courtyard of building G. I noticed last year's acorn caps resting on the edge of the sidewalk and how the fox squirrels seemed abnormally fat. Once I cleared the edge of the building, the footway split into two directions: the parking lot and to a quaint little house sleeping amongst an elegant stand of pines.

Dad's Harley wasn't parked that far away, and after a few minutes I had unlocked my helmet, pulled out the gloves from the inside and put everything on, slowly but surely. It was the nicest of early summer afternoons as I swung one leg over the saddle of the bike and sat there checking my e-mail.

James Ong walked past, not forty feet away. I thought about saying something friendly but decided not to; I had said my piece inside. He walked past me towards the house. An elderly English setter walked out to meet him with a friendly, swishing tail that bobbed up and down and left to right like a conductor's wand. Dr. Jim gave him a pat on the head, a scratch under the ear and called him "Toby." The dog walked away, stiff-legged and sore, but the second member of Jim's welcoming committee was already tugging on his leg. It was a girl. A young girl. Jim reached down and picked her up. She gave him a kiss on the cheek and said, "Look Daddy, I'm helping Mommy dry the lettuce."

"You are?" Jim asked, gushing with pride.

"Look and see," the girl said, pointing at a clothesline not far away.

There, in the dim of late afternoon, amidst the sheets and towels, washcloths and dishrags, the girl had a dozen or more pieces of Romaine lettuce hanging by clothespins.

I laughed. The guy had a great life.

Outside his office, he seemed to have a great family. Inside his office he was professional and understanding.

Although he opened our appointment with an inquiry about my coping skills, it seemed like we never really got around to diving into the topic. Maybe it was his way of building rapport. Perhaps a light and fluffy conversation was his way of breaking the ice. The only thing I was sure of is that Dr. Jim had become so small that he fit between my ears.

He was inside my head.

Six

Colleen never did say much about my appointment with Dr. Ong. We had dinner, cleaned up the kitchen, and folded the laundry without as much as a passing mention. I think she thought it was my business, not hers. Even after all the years of being married, we both observed each other's boundaries.

After putting Elizabeth to bed, I was ready to talk. Colleen had just gotten out of the shower and had slipped into a pair of khaki pants, a tee shirt, and a thin denim blouse. She was blow-drying her hair in the bathroom so I had to raise my voice just to be heard.

"Do you think I should care about the guy I killed?" I yelled, hoping not to wake Elizabeth.

"What makes you say that?" she countered.

"I don't know. That's kinda what the doctor said."

Colleen bent at the waist and directed the warm air to the back of her head. It may have been her way of thinking about her answer, so I waited for her response.

"Yeah, I think you should care. I mean, every life is sacred, right?"

She finally turned off the dryer, and we didn't have to yell.

"The important thing is that you don't let the incident ruin your life," she added. "If you try to hide the pain by drowning your sorrows in alcohol, I don't think that's a good idea and I think that you know it too."

I didn't say anything.

"I mean," she sighed. "I understand why you would want to drink, but I don't think it's a good idea."

Colleen's toenails were painted a brilliant red, so cute and petite beneath the hem of her pants.

"Thank you for saying that," I confessed. "It makes me feel like you're in my corner."

"Never, ever doubt that, okay?" she pleaded.

I followed Colleen to the walk-in closet. She pulled a pair of cowboy boots from the rack, and then sauntered across the bedroom to the dresser. A second later, she had a pair of white tube-socks in her hands.

"The thing that's really been bugging me," I said, "is that it seems like most members of Congress should have loads of security, but there really wasn't much at the high school."

"You're right, Derrick. Hardly anybody knows this, but most congressmen don't have much security detail when they're in DC or when they're home, unless they're like the Speaker of the House or something like that. There's no Secret Service guarding them like there are for the President. A lot of times they rely on local agencies when they're home on recess."

She sat on the edge of the bed and pushed her toes into her socks.

"In Capp's case, however," she continued, "he had one capitol police officer with him and Capp was wearing a bulletproof vest. The guys who wanted Capp dead really had every detail worked out."

I was listening to her every word.

"The congressman was escorted to the high school by several aides, one from his Midland office and the other from Cadillac. The driver was an intern from Onaway."

"What about the capitol police?" I asked.

"There really aren't enough of them to go around, from what I've been able to find out," she said. "They escort congressmen back to their home districts only if there's a credible threat to their safety."

"Was there a threat against him?"

"Yeah. Capp had some elderly guy from Frankenmuth say that he was going to hang him from the Mackinac Bridge. That was the threat, and that's why there was a capitol police officer with him."

"What happened to him?" I asked.

"Nothing, really. They said on the news that a capitol officer was on the backside of the gym, and wrote down the license plate numbers of the guys who tossed in the tear gas and chained the doors shut."

Colleen was on the bed next to me. She put her arm around my back and gave me a half hug. It felt nice and reassuring.

"I gotta go," she said as she slipped into her boots.

"Where?" I asked, somewhat surprised.

"To the bar."

"The bar?" I was shocked.

"I'm working, Derrick. I'm trying to infiltrate the Heretic Fringe."

"Where?" I asked.

"At the VFW in Houghton Lake."

"That's more than an hour away."

"I know," she sighed, "but this is going to make a really great story, if I can get in with them."

"Yeah, but…"

"You have to trust me on this one, Derrick. It's going to make a heck of a story."

Colleen made it back to her jewelry box and picked out a pair of earrings. They were buffalo nickels, and rather sexy in a tough-girl kind of way. As she put them in her ear lobes, she pulled the nightstand drawer open and handed me a folder.

"Here," she said. "Take a look at the file. These are some of the news reports I recorded while you were in the hospital. See if it stirs your journalistic juices like it did mine. I'll be home late."

She kissed me on the lips, said "Love you," and started down the hall. I watched her go. It was a nice view.

"Wish me luck," she said.

Just like that, Colleen was gone.

It is often said that there are two things you never want to witness being made: sausage and laws.

Having never seen sausage being made, I can only imagine what goes into it.

Literally.

On the legislative side, I envision the recipe to include handshakes and winks, favors and pressure from a litany of lobbyists, constituents, and special-interest groups from every conceivable angle on a particular issue. They all want what's best for themselves, for each other, the country, everything. As a legislator, it must be difficult to take campaign contributions from a certain group, then maintain a neutral outlook when it comes to voting on a particular bill. Conflict of interest has become a way of life in Washington and it must be one of the seedy things that makes young congressmen think, 'Gee, this really doesn't sit well with me.'

Colleen had scores of newspaper clippings regarding the Capp case: they detailed the turmoil leading up to the health-care vote; and an eight-hundred-thousand-dollar grant for three bridges in his district. Capp's critics said that the money for the bridges appeared to be a bribe for his 'yes' vote on the health care. Of course, Capp denied all of it, but the fallout after his vote included death threats against his family and acts of vandalism at his offices located across the district. Only the legislators who voted for the health care got death threats. The ones who voted against it didn't have to apologize or make amends for the vote they had cast.

But I had to hand it to Capp. Instead of cowering in his DC apartment, or in his mansion at Harbor Springs, he was willing to go to the voters to explain his position. If his own constituents were going to harm him, he was going to let them have the chance. If pigs are needed to make sausage, Capp was going to be first in line.

And slaughter him they did.

Colleen had a DVD in the folder she'd given me. When I loaded the disc into my laptop computer, news broadcasts came at me in waves: first the kidnapping, then the stolen police cruiser. The standoff at the motel added a bit of a twist, before the macabre visual of Capp's beheading. There was plenty of drama and suspense as the manhunt got organized, reorganized, then failed again.

Yandle's final act was to go berserk in an Amish schoolhouse. That was the last thing he did, and the last thing I remember.

Seven

THE FOLLOWING MORNING, I woke up early and drove the old Suburban into Amish country. As I approached a stop sign on one of the crumbly blacktop roads, a young robin scrambled in front of the truck. Try as I might to stop, I couldn't. Instead, I swerved to straddle it. When I looked in the rearview mirror a second or two later, there was the little guy, rolling on the pavement, flapping his wings aimlessly. It's like he bumped his head on the undercarriage and didn't know his fanny from deep center field.

He was joined by his anxious mother, who seemed to say, "Come on, Robin, pull yourself together."

But Robin didn't pull himself together.

He lay there flopping near the yellow center line until the vehicle behind me squished him flat.

I couldn't imagine the grief that must have poured over mother bird. Her baby—sluiced down as a toddler—would never have the chance to enjoy the rest of the warm season in Michigan, a leisurely winter down south with all the other snowbirds, or an adventuresome return trip to God's country.

There wasn't anything I could have done to prevent the accident. The mother wasn't to blame, either. It was just an unfortunate fact of life that sometimes happens with youthful carelessness.

It seemed odd that I should care so much about a dead little bird. After all, I was willing to kill a turkey one hundred times bigger than the baby robin and that didn't bother me one little bit. Regardless, turkey season was officially over and for the first time in umpteen years, I didn't get a bird. I really didn't stew about it, but then again I really missed having a wild turkey dinner. What's more, I missed that exhilarating relief that comes from killing a big gobbler.

In my head, Dr. Ong was with me on this little adventure. He'd have one leg propped over the other, fiddling with the seat belt, his mobile phone, the window, whatever he could get his hands on. In a nonchalant kind of way, he'd ask harmless little questions that would eventually form the noose around my neck. I hated the way he had painted me into a corner at his office. It's like we were playing a game of chess, and I had been snared by his strategic methods. My pawns fell during the early moves of harmless questions. My rooks, my knights, my bishops—they all toppled as Dr. Ong and I jostled during the meatiest part of our meeting. Just before the appointment ended, he boxed me into a corner, where he lowered the boom with the inquiry about the serial killer and the kids who were murdered thirty years ago. I don't know why I cared so much about the murdered kids from way back then, nor the Amish kids now. It's like I couldn't let it go. The Amish kids' voices and ghastly images were still inside my head, but they weren't as vivid as they once were. I battled those thoughts every waking hour, while at the same time I was learning to cope with them one day at a time. In my own private little way, I thought maybe if I had a bigger role in the kids' lives maybe it would help us all get over the trauma.

I took Dr. Ong's advice and made the drive back into Amish country. As I neared the Amish schoolhouse, I noticed a large billow of smoke billowing into the bright, June sky. A minute or so later, I realized that *it was the schoolhouse* that was the cause of all the smoke.

A group of somber looking Amish men looked in my direction as I pulled into the parking lot. Instead of jumping out of the truck and initiating contact, I sat in the driver's seat for a moment as the truck caught its breath. The men were gathered around a fire that had reduced the schoolhouse to a half its normal size. Instead of standing a story and a half in height, the schoolhouse was a seething pile of glowing ash and intermittent flames. The last thing to burn was the cupola—old and weathered and missing its bell.

I put the vehicle in park and made my way to the men who were supervising the burn. All four of the men were wearing homemade jeans and paper-thin, short-sleeved oxfords. I knew one of them as Eli Beiler, the man who had let me hunt his farm. The other three I figured were elders because their beards were long and gray. The elders had their gloves on the polished handles of their shovels; Beiler, a garden rake.

I wanted to say something about it being a strange time of day for a bonfire, but I decided to bite my tongue. A simple "Morning" worked just fine.

They nodded back at me.

I watched the flames eat through the shingles and the two-by-six rafters that had collapsed and were exposed like the remains of a trout dinner. The fire hissed and popped as it gnawed a nightmare's memory.

The elders didn't ask why I was there, but they all seemed to know who I was. They didn't ask me to leave, either. It was like they were thankful I stopped by, but they weren't going to come out and say, "You saved our children's lives."

A subtle clang of a bell distracted my attention. It was in the back of a buggy, parked fifty yards from the fire. The horse pulling the buggy must have shifted its weight and made the clapper thump the edge of the bell. The sound of the ringing bell made me think about the days of my youth, when the ice cream man used to ring the sleigh bells on his mobile concession stand. I wondered if the Amish elder would have the same effect on the neighborhood kids as he and his horse clip-clopped their way down the road, bell-in-the-back clanging away.

For whatever reason, I was in a good mood.

"What happened?" I asked one of them. "Did it get hit by lightning?"

"Noo," one of the elders answered. "Ever since dah shooting, we thought it best to tear down dah building."

The wind changed direction slightly, and we all had to turn our heads to escape the sting of wood smoke. It wasn't quite as bad as the tear gas from the gymnasium.

"We are thankful that you saved our children, but we can't expose dem to you and dah ways of dah English."

I nodded my head and chose my words carefully. "I'm thankful that you let me hunt turkeys on the property, and that things worked out the way that they did. You'll never know what might have happened if you didn't have an albino turkey on the back of your property or if you hadn't given me permission to hunt."

It felt a little odd. I mean, I showed up at the schoolhouse because I wanted to come to grips with the shooting. They, on the other hand had destroyed every earthly reminder. I wondered what Dr. Ong would think of their style of closure.

"God verks in mysterious vays," the elder responded.

"We feel that it's spelled out in dah Bible," the middle elder added. "Romans chapter twelve, verse two: 'We shalt not conform to dah outside world.' Dah shooting is an example of why."

"I understand," I said.

The wind picked up again and the flames roared in earnest.

"So what are you going to do about a school?" I asked.

"We'll build a new one dis summer, after dah second cutting."

I wasn't sure what he meant by 'second cutting,' but I figured that he was referring to either his beard, his mullet haircut, or the field of alfalfa across the street. It really wasn't any of my business and it felt like it was time for me to leave. My ten-minute mental-health visit was plenty. They were having their own little exorcism and I wasn't a member of the clan.

I turned to the truck and started to walk away. "I'll get out of your hair, gentlemen. Good luck."

Eli Beiler finally opened his mouth, "Mr. Twitchell?"

He came at me with his rake in hand.

"Could yah give me a ride up to the hardware store?"

I hesitated for a second, "Sure, which one?"

"Come on, I'll show you."

Eli walked past the elders who raised their eyebrows incredulously.

Looks like this Roman would rather get a ride in a gas-powered chariot, I thought.

We walked to the truck, and Eli took off his straw hat momentarily and wiped his brow against his shirt sleeves. He spit. "Thank you, Mr. Twitchell."

"For what, Eli? And call me Derrick." I extended a hand Eli's way, but he didn't shake it. Instead, he glanced over his shoulder toward the elders.

"They kinda frown on us getting too close with the English. Especially the guy in the middle."

"I noticed. What's his name?"

"Ivan Petershwim. He lives around the corner, three farms down. He's a smart man, but wants to control everybody's lives."

Eli opened the back door of the Suburban and slid his rake inside. A second later, he was on the seat next to me.

"Thank you for saving my kids' lives."

I smiled; his gratitude warmed my heart. "You're welcome, Eli."

Now it was his hand that stretched my way. We shook on it, but instead of the old, "Howdy Doody" kind of grip, Eli wrapped his fingers around my palm, then he did the old finger clasp that I've seen NBA players use on the sidelines after a big game.

This can't be the secret Amish handshake, I thought.

"Where are we going?" I asked.

"Go up to the corner and turn right."

"Whose idea was it to burn down the school?" I asked.

"The elders, who else?"

Eli took off his straw hat and draped it over his bent knee. He looked to be balding fast, and his hair hung at his sideburns like a pair of goat's ears. But despite his beefy, thick physique, he was a sensitive man with an independent streak.

"We can't even wipe our ass without asking permission from the elders," he said.

I couldn't believe my ears. Or my nose. The smell of sweaty man filled the truck.

His hand turned the knobs on the dashboard air conditioner and the old truck created a spring breeze.

I turned the corner and asked if he had seen the big white gobbler behind the farm.

Eli draped an index finger over his shaved upper lip. "Oh, yah, he's around. I thought about taking him out with my two-seventy."

"Don't do that."

"Why not?" he asked.

"It's not turkey season, that's why. You could lose your hunting license, and besides it'll cost you a lot of money if you get caught."

Eli chewed on my warning. While he did, I reeled in the view of the countryside. It was a beautiful early summer morning in the northern part of mid-Michigan. We drove beneath the outstretched limbs of maples and oaks that formed a tunnel over the road. A fieldstone wall on the side of the blacktop framed the setting. It was a glorious sight, and one that I hoped to revisit in the fall when the leaves were aflame in color.

My reverie was interrupted by an oncoming buggy. Eli ducked beneath the dashboard. His head was at my knee, his beard nearly touching my jeans. I sailed toward the occupants of the buggy and raised an index finger off the steering wheel. The couple in the buggy waived back modestly, just like the folks in Iowa while they're driving their pickups.

"What are you doing?" I asked him.

Eli peeked over the top of the dashboard, then over the bench seat towards the rear windows as if he were a fugitive from the law.

"Oh that's Ivan Hooley, his wife, Sarah, and their prized Chestnut mare."

"She looked like a nice one."

"Sarah?" he asked. "She's not very nice. In fact she's kinda nosy."

Eli missed my point so I switched gears and fed into his trepidation.

"Aren't you supposed to be getting a ride from the English?"

"They frown on it, you know, Romans chapter twelve."

"How old are you, Eli?"

"Oh, I'm thirty-five."

"How many kids?"

"Six, so far," he said, sitting back in the seat.

"How many were in the schoolhouse?"

"Three," he said. "I got one that's graduated, another who was home with ah fever and a toddler."

"So your oldest is eighteen or so?"

"No, no, about fifteen. We only go to eighth grade, then dah children help around dah farm."

We had pulled into the west end of downtown Gladwin, but the town wasn't exactly a blur of activity. Instead of heading for the hardware store, Eli told me to pull over. He jumped out of the truck and walked into a print shop, homemade jeans and all. The lady behind the counter presented him with a box the size of a microwave oven. Eli opened his wallet and handed her the money.

A second later he was in the truck, the box of printing between us.

"Thanks," he said, "you saved me a trip to town."

"No problem."

I was about ready to turn the truck around, when Eli interrupted me, "Dah co-op is just up dah street."

I nodded, put the truck in gear, and we were off again. All of a sudden, the hardware store seemed like a ruse.

"When we get there, just pull around to dah grain elevator in back."

Seemed like Eli had a routine.

Before he slammed the truck door, he said, "Door number three."

He did have a routine.

I dropped Eli off at the front door of the co-op, and I drove around back to door number three. While I waited, I looked at the box of material Eli had picked up from the print shop. He had printing all right, but not on plain old paper. They were paper bags—larger than a lunch sack but smaller than a grocery bag. The image seemed wholesome enough: a bundle of wheat tied at the midriff and the words *Thy Daily Bread* printed across the top.

That was all I could read before a man in coveralls tapped on the window.

I put Eli's material away and explained to the man that we'd have an order for him to fill. We made small talk until Eli appeared from around the corner.

Eli handed the man his paperwork, and the man disappeared into the caverns of the elevator.

I waited there for a minute or two, thinking that at any time the man would appear with a sack full of oats, or barley, or some other wholesome grain used to fatten Eli's farm animals.

Not even close.

The man reappeared, driving a forklift truck carrying a pallet-full of sacks stitched across the top with a cotton string.

"Here's your wheat flour."

I jumped out of the driver's door and removed Eli's rake from the back of the truck. The sacks were heavy—maybe fifty or seventy pounds apiece—and with every sack they tossed inside, the old Suburban groaned in protest.

I don't know how many sacks there were, but it seemed like there were at least twenty. My truck looked like it had lead in its pants.

"All set?" I asked Eli.

"Almost," he said. "There's another load coming."

"What? Eli, I, ah…"

"It'll be just fine, Mr. Twitchell."

"I'm not so sure about that. This truck's got like a million miles on it. Last week I had to put new wheel bearings in it, and I think the shocks are starting to go."

Eli just stared at me.

"Shocks are the things on the undercarriage that keep you from feeling every little bump." I crouched at the rear tire and tried to point them out. "Some people call them 'shock absorbers' because they absorb all the shock."

Eli glanced behind the rear wheel well, but I wasn't sure if he did that to be nice or if he remotely cared.

"Don't worry about it, Mr. Twitchell. God will take care of us," he said with such certainty that I knew he believed it. I looked at him a little skeptically; after all, it wasn't his truck that was groaning under the stress.

The man on the forklift reappeared. "Here's your rye and the white."

"What about dah malted barley?" Eli asked.

"Got it."

We loaded five or six bags into the back seat, and Eli's order was complete. He waved at the man in the coveralls and that was that.

I put the truck in gear and pulled away from the loading dock. My Suburban handled like a yacht in rough seas. It floated over the potholes and warped lanes but it certainly wasn't in the mood for quick turns.

"All set?" I asked.

"Yah, that'll do'er," he said.

"So you really didn't need to go to the hardware store?"

"Naw. That was just a way to get past dah elders."

I nodded my head and we turned west out of downtown Gladwin.

Eli and I sat there in relative silence.

Finally, I had to say something.

"Looks like your baking business has really taken off, Eli."

"Yah."

His one-word answer kept me off kilter.

I told him about my mom's Belgian waffles and what a wonderful cook she is. The topic seemed to quell Eli's resistance and he proceeded to tell me about the growth of the family's sideline business.

"We only bake sourdough now. Got our own secret recipe and as soon as we get some money around we'll upgrade dah ovens."

"What's wrong with the ovens you have now?"

"Nothing really. They're just old and tired. Not very efficient."

"It's been a while since I've had any of your bread," I said. "Does it still have the real thick crust?"

"Oh, yah. It's good."

"What do you do, sell it off the farm?"

"Oh, yah. It's really my wife's deal; I just get all dah supplies."

"That's neat, Eli," I said as kindly as I possibly could, "it warms my heart to hear stories like that, especially in today's tough economic conditions. And to think that it all started because of the lawsuit against you."

Eli acted like he really didn't want to talk about it any longer. We were still a mile or two away from his farm when we passed beneath the maple-forest tunnel once again. Eli didn't have to hide from any of his neighbors and he finally seemed to be at ease. I was thinking about his sideline business and whether the elders approved. Just as the notion pursed my lips, I looked at Eli who had a terrified look on his face. He yelled, "Look out!"

My head snapped to the road ahead. The giant white gobbler was facing the truck, less than fifty yards away. It's like he had started across the aging blacktop, but changed his mind. I swerved to the left, but the Suburban responded like a thirty-foot cabin cruiser in three-foot waves. Instead, I cranked the wheel to the right—all the while my foot slammed on the brakes. The tom finally made up his mind and trotted to the left, flapping his wings. I swerved more to the right, but temporarily lost control in the loose gravel on the shoulder. The front right tire careened off a pothole and we skittered to a screeching halt.

The rake in the back must have ripped across the top of the flour bags on the way to the dashboard because my truck was engulfed in a cloud of powder.

"I told you I should have taken him out with my two-seventy," Eli said.

I laughed and waved my hand back and forth to clear the dust. When I rolled down the truck windows, the flour billowed into the summer air, Cheech and Chong style.

We were stuck.

I put the old Suburban in four-wheel drive and tried to back it out, but it just seemed to make matters worse. Only three of the four wheels were on the pavement. The fourth was halfway down the ditch.

We were stuck.

"Let me get out and push," Eli said.

We both got out of the truck and looked things over. My truck was resting on its front axle. Eli walked to the rear of the Suburban and shook his head. "This doesn't look good. Let me check inside."

He opened the back doors of the Suburban and examined the cargo.

"I tink we lost one bag of wheat when it slid from dah back."

I looked at my Suburban and the sorry state it was in. In my head, I was already thinking about calling a tow truck, what kind of damage I might have done. Eli didn't seem to mind our predicament at all. For him, it seemed, it was just another one of life's little challenges.

"What do you think we should do?" I asked him.

"Well, I don't tink pushing's going to help."

"You're right, Eli. We're stuck."

I opened the double doors in the back of the vehicle and sat down on the bumper. Eli sat on the edge of the road, picked a blade of grass and put it in his mouth. It was a calm, summery, early afternoon in mid-Michigan. A gentle breeze stirred the cottonwood trees, sending millions of their tiny fluff particles adrift.

I thought more seriously about calling a tow truck, but then I wondered what was stirring in Eli's mind. I liked the guy and his simplicity. Nothing seemed to rattle him. Nothing seemed to make him worry. Eli gave the impression that he was adrift in the breeze as well. He was helpless to the fate of God's plan. He had nowhere to go. No place to be. His wife's bread would get made. The chores would get done. Somehow. Some way, the kids would grow up and life would go on.

For a few pensive seconds, I wished my life was that way. The Amish way. Instead of deadlines and commitments, I would have effervescent faith and a never-ending supply of blessings.

"What do you think we should do?" I asked him again.

Eli pulled the blade of grass from the corner of his mouth. He spit. "You got a cell phone don't yah?"

I nodded.

"Why don't I call the Yoders and see if dey can't bring their team of Belgians up here?"

"That would be good."

"Then again, the Ivan Petershwim's kids aren't far from here. Dey got four or five Percherons that I'm sure could pull dis ting out."

"So the Petershwims have Percherons?"

"Yah. They're really good horses. Not quite as big as dah Belgians, but just as nice and almost as powerful."

"Do you know their phone number?"

"Yah."

I handed him the phone, and he dialed the number. A few seconds later, Eli began speaking. His inquiry was friendly enough and filled with references about the weather and how the crops were doing. He was a master at small talk and I appreciated the way he tactfully danced up to the favor.

A car zoomed past us and we waved.

After a few minutes of explaining the situation and where we were, Eli finally said, "Great den. We'll see yah in a little while."

He handed me the phone and we were in business.

"We were lucky to catch Mr. Yoder," he said. "Most people are outside doing work on a nice day like today."

"Don't the Amish have phones outside their houses anyway?"

"Yah, dey got little phone booths outside, but what a lot of elders don't know is that many of the Amish got cell phones. They won't take out the phones in their names, but add a phone onto the English's plan. Some got phones inside our houses, too."

"Oh?" I was leading him on.

"We keep it in a closet or in dah cellar. We just gotta remember to turn off dah ringer when company comes over."

"Sure. You wouldn't want the elders to find out about it, right?"

"Right," he said dismissively. "Dah elders got a problem with electricity too, so we use hydraulic power instead." Eli clasped the whiskers on his chin, then added, "I tink we ought to jack up your truck. It'll make it better for the team to pull out and with a little nudge we can get dah truck rocking."

"That makes sense, but the jack's buried under all the flour."

"I can get it."

Eli never hesitated. In the blink of an eye he had the first sack of flour flung on his shoulder. He crossed the road, took a step or two over the ditch, and dropped his load on a sandy spot near an oak tree. I was still struggling with the first bag when Eli returned for a second.

"Here let me get it," he said.

He lunged at the bag and gave it a yank. The momentum he garnered from its descent quickly became the force which took the sack over his shoulder. He did it in one fluid motion and I had to marvel at the exhibition. Eli wasn't a big guy, but he sure was powerful. He made the massive load look like a lunch sack full of sandwiches. The Belgians and the Percherons had nothing on him.

After the fifth or sixth bag I was able to get at the jack from behind the wheel well. I took the opportunity to ask Eli about his kids and how they were doing.

"You mean since the deal at dah schoolhouse?"

"Well, yeah."

"Dey are not doing so great."

I took the jack and made my way to the front of the truck. Eli followed me, but he didn't offer any more information. Finally, I said something that I hoped would pique his need to talk. "I'm sorry about that."

I crouched beneath the front bumper, found a level place for the jack and started plunging away with the little crowbar. Gradually, the truck inched its way off the pavement.

Another car slowly passed us, and I heard Eli tell the folks inside that help was on the way. He repeated the words "tank you" over and over again.

"What's wrong with your kids?" I asked him.

Eli didn't say anything until I reappeared from beneath the vehicle.

"Dey cry in their sleep. I got one son dat wets his bed now and my older son quit doing the tings he loves."

"What a shame."

"Yah, it is, but I tink that everything will work out. The younger boy loves to hunt, so we'll see what he'll be like after dis fall. Maybe he'll quit wetting dah bed."

"What kind of hunting?"

Eli smiled, harmlessly. "Squirrels and rabbits. Sometimes partridge, but they're hard to get."

"How neat. What about turkey?"

Eli shook his head, no. "Never done dat. Says he wants to but I haven't had dah time to take him."

"Would you mind if I took him sometime next spring?"

"No, I don't mind. Let's see how he's doing, maybe by then he'll be ready."

"Great, I'd be happy to," I said smiling. "What was it that your older son quit doing?"

"Oh…" Eli responded, "He was into carving and wood-working. Made his own bows and arrows."

"That's neat."

"Dey were beautiful. He used red oak and hickory for dah bows, and cedar and birch for dah arrows. He even had turkey feathers for dah fletching."

"How old is he?"

"He's almost twelve."

"So he's in seventh grade?"

"Yah. He's a real craftsman, or at least he was before dah shooting," Eli said.

"What a shame," I added. "Have you tried talking to him?"

"Yah."

"How did that go?" I asked.

"Fine, I tink. I always try to tell my kids to keep looking ahead. There's hope for dah future."

"Anything else?"

"Yah. I told my son that after graduation next year, and with dah woodworking skills he has, he could pretty much write his own ticket."

"What do you mean, Eli?"

"As a woodcraftsman, he could go pretty much wherever he wanted, and make a darn good living."

Eli was like the rest of us who wanted what's best for our kids. On one hand, I felt sorry for Eli's sons, but on the other hand I really wanted all of us to get over our own mental anguish.

So, from one father to another it seemed appropriate to say, "Today's kids don't listen to their parents."

Eight

B Y EARLY AFTERNOON, Mr. Yoder showed up with his team of Belgians, named Buster and Billy. They were covered in frothy white sweat that changed their honey-colored coat to a deeper shade of brown. Mr. Yoder appeared to be a kind and gentle man, with his silver-gray hair contrasting his bright, blue eyes. He was rather short, perhaps a bit too young to be an elder, but he had a way about him that commanded attention. Maybe it was his confidence, or his no-nonsense demeanor.

Yoder and his team seemed to have a little ESP thing going on when it came to the task at hand: he'd back the boys to the rear of the Suburban and they would pull it out of the ditch. Just to be safe, Eli would hold the harnesses and tackle out of the way so that neither Mr. Yoder, nor the boys would trip over it. It was a rather big deal, and it wasn't long before a handful of cars had stopped to watch our undertaking. Some of the people whipped out their cameras and snapped a few pictures.

"Steady now," Mr. Yoder said as he eased the mammoths in reverse. He looked rather uncomfortable behind his two work-horses. The way he guarded his private parts, it was almost as if he had been kicked before.

"Easy, Buster."

Buster was on the ditch-side of the road and he flirted with the same demise that had claimed the Suburban. He was oblivious to the loose footing and seemed to be more concerned with the horsefly that was perched on his flank. He twitched the tiniest of muscles, trying his best to shoo it away. It seemed odd that such a powerful beast could control his muscles in the nimblest of ways.

I could hardly watch. All I could imagine was Buster losing his footing in the loose gravel, stumbling down the incline, and dragging old Billy down with him. They'd get caught up in the rigging, pinched under each other's weight, and end up with broken limbs. There is nothing worse than the hideous wails of injured horses.

On second thought, the wailing of an injured horse couldn't compare to the kids in the schoolhouse.

At the very last second, I decided to jump back in the truck to make sure it was in neutral. It was. I heard Eli wrap the chains around Suburban's chassis. *Eli had better find a decent place to anchor those chains*, I thought. *Buster and Billy are massive beasts and it seemed like they could draw and quarter my truck if Mr. Yoder asked them to.*

"Steady now," Mr. Yoder commanded.

Eli gave the thumbs up signal. The stage was set.

Mr. Yoder placed his palm on Billy's massive hip. The scene reminded me of a high school football game and the way the coach puts his hand on a player's shoulder pad.

"Gentlemen," Mr. Yoder announced confidently, "step up, please."

Buster and Billy leaned into the sweat-stained rigging, and I felt the Suburban flinch. A second or two later, the jack gave way and the tire was set free. Billy temporarily lost his footing on the pavement, but he regrouped.

"Come on, boys," Mr. Yoder encouraged.

The boys listened.

Inch by inch they made progress, until miraculously my truck was safely on the blacktop.

"You got it," Eli cried. "Great job."

Both Eli and Mr. Yoder were elated. It's like they took extra pride in using their team on such an exotic project as my Suburban. This wasn't the old honey wagon they were pulling away from the barn, but rather, a motorized contraption that didn't eat bales of hay and create bushels of manure.

I started the Suburban and waited while Eli removed the rigging from the rear of the truck.

The cars that had stopped to watch us started their engines and drove off. Most of them waved when they passed, as if they were appreciative of the show. Eli and Mr. Yoder didn't even acknowledge them. They were merely a distraction.

While Eli and Mr. Yoder hooked the rigging up to the wagon, I crossed the blacktop and grabbed a sack of flour. It wasn't *that* heavy—just really bulky.

I finished my task at the same time that Eli and Mr. Yoder had said their goodbyes. I thanked Mr. Yoder for his help, Eli jumped in the truck and, thankfully, we were on our way.

"Whew," Eli said, smiling, "I didn't think that was going to work."

I smiled and nodded my head.

"Did you see that when old Billy lost his footing?" Eli was almost giddy—like he was recanting the action at a tractor pull.

I didn't answer; Eli's question was rhetorical.

My mind wasn't engaged in what just happened, but rather what was going on beneath the truck.

The steering was all wrong. Or at least the tire. It felt wobbly. Rather weird.

Eli felt it too and suggested that he take a look at it once we arrived at his farm.

"Besides," he said, merrily, "I'm getting hungry."

He did have a point; it was well past lunchtime.

The old Suburban limped into Eli's driveway, scattering a handful of chickens in the process.

"Anywhere's fine," Eli said. "We'll take a look at it after lunch. Come inside, won't you?"

"Sure, I will. I'm hungry too."

I stepped out of the truck and reeled in the surroundings. Eli's farm wasn't neat and tidy, but I could tell that it was a working operation. At least a half-dozen bed sheets, in various colors, hung on a giant clothesline that stretched between the corner of the garage and the top of a silo, seventy feet away. A bike-tire rim at either end of the line made for a pulley system, which made it easy to stand in one spot and take care of business. No dryer sheets necessary: the dust, the grain chaff, the smell of a working farm took care of that.

Between the hen house and the barn, I heard the clang of a Swiss bell. The sound came from the lead cow in Eli's dairy herd, who wore the bell like a pendant around her neck. She and the rest of her lady friends were draped in the shade of a large oak tree on the edge of the pasture. What a great way to while away the June afternoon: swishing flies with your tail and chewing your cud, while in the company of your fellow beasts.

Eli had it made. He had a decent house and plenty of fresh food to eat. His garden was lush and green, and promised a bountiful harvest in the coming weeks. He and his son would always have a place to hunt, and when it was time for bed, his sheets would smell like *the fresh dairy-air.*

He had children, too. They rushed to greet him—dressed in their homemade clothes—as if he had just returned home from a foreign war. They were amazingly happy, it seemed. They hugged him and squeezed him and called him "papa." It was a cheerful reunion, a joyous occasion, and Eli had only been gone for half a day. I hadn't seen that kind of affection in forever.

"Are you coming inside, Mr. Twitchell?" he asked.

"Yeah."

"We'll unload dah truck after lunch."

"And take a look at the undercarriage," I reminded him.

He nodded. "Come on."

The children led the way through the open garage door and up three or four stairs to the back door. A handful of cats tried to nose their way inside, but the boys pushed them away.

"Come on," Eli said again. "Don't worry about your shoes. My wife will take care of everything."

I'm not sure who was more proud—the children of their mother, or Eli of his wife.

"Dis is Rebecca," Eli said, beaming.

My hand reached to shake hers, but she lead with her left.

"Nice to meet you, Rebecca," I said.

"You too, Mr. Twitchell."

"Rebecca lost her hand in a corn picker when she was a child," Eli mentioned.

Oh gosh, I thought. I had to look. It was gone.

"They tried to rush her to dah hospital, but you can't exactly hurry when you're driving a horse and buggy," he said, laughing half-heartedly.

Rebecca gave him a playful slap as if to say, "Be quiet, will you."

Eli gave her arm a squeeze and he smiled slightly. "She never realized dat not having a hand would be dah perfect tool for kneading all dis bread." He swung his arm to the countertops. It looked like nap-time in a nursery at a hospital. Each mound of dough was snuggled under a dishtowel. There were rows and rows of it, gestating in the moist, June air.

"Not before lunch, will you?" she scolded him.

He shrugged his shoulders and asked what was for lunch.

"Chicken salad," she said. "Have a seat, Mr. Twitchell." Rebecca gestured to the other end of the kitchen to a long, wooden table. It didn't take much imagination to picture Jim Bob, Mary Ellen, and the rest of *The Waltons* crowded around a table just like it.

The Beiler kids were still in the kitchen: the girls in Eli's brood were carrying faceless dolls; the boys, wooden tractors. Rebecca said something to the children in a foreign language. They shuffled out of the kitchen and went outside.

None of the kids said anything to me and barely acknowledged my presence. It's like they had been told or taught or brainwashed into believing that the English weren't to be trusted. I didn't mind their shyness because I know that sometimes it takes a while for the bonds of trust to be forged.

"Did you want buttermilk or lemonade to drink, Mr. Twitchell?"

My mind flashed back to the time I ate at a jazz club in Detroit and ordered collard greens and chitterlings. Back then, I thought I should experience all that the culture had to offer. I didn't care for either side dish then, and I wasn't about to embarrass myself by trying to choke down a glass of buttermilk now.

"Lemonade would be fine, thank you."

She nodded, and Eli told her all about the episode with Mr. Yoder and my truck. She seemed to appreciate all the extra effort Eli went through, just to get her baking supplies.

Lemonade never tasted so good, guzzled right out of a tinted Mason jar.

We both watched Rebecca float around the kitchen and the way she sliced the bread, chopped up the chicken, the onion, and the celery. I never thought about her club for an arm. She was busy and oh-so-happy doing it. Despite the dreadful outfit she was wearing, she was rather pretty in a natural kind of way.

The kitchen had a functional quality to it. A pair of massive, old stoves framed one side of the room, a giant, hydraulic-powered mixer and a stack of frail metal grates on the other. No pictures on the walls, granite countertops, or fancy cupboards. The only thing out of the ordinary was a wooden bin that had a potato carved into the front. Above and below the potato were the words, *Eli Beiler, Potato Peeler.*

When lunch was finally served, Rebecca's sourdough didn't disappoint me. It had a wonderfully thick crust and a tangy, lip-smacking kind of flavor. I'm not sure what made the bread taste so good—if it was the fact that I was terribly hungry, or that the setting was perfectly wholesome. No matter what the case, I loved it. I really, really loved it.

What's more, I loved the surroundings. The kitchen didn't have a dishwasher, a microwave, buzzers, coffee pots or electric can openers. But that all seemed okay—with life's conveniences come complications and clutter. Rebecca's kitchen was the hub of her bread-making enterprise and the centerpiece of the family gatherings. Eli and Rebecca seemed content with the life they had made, and the lifestyle they had chosen. They smiled a lot and laughed at themselves in harmless little ways. Their conversation was meaningful, lighthearted, and borne of the compassion between them. I could tell that Eli really loved his woman and Rebecca took great pride in taking care of her man.

After lunch, Eli and I got back to work. We unloaded the truck, and drove it to a shady spot in the barnyard. He helped me ease the front end onto a pair of ancient cinderblocks. It looked slightly precarious sitting there, but Eli thought nothing of climbing under the motor with his pocket flashlight. A couple of his boys were the same way, only they were small enough to sit up under the motor, straw hats and all. The situation made me a little uneasy as I stood there and analyzed what was going on. If it were my kids, I certainly wouldn't let them sit up under the vehicle. If the cinderblocks were to give way, all three of them could be injured. After a few minutes of inspection, Eli asked for his box of wrenches. I handed him the set and heard the ratchets doing their thing. The truck heaved with every turn, and I hoped that the blocks would stay intact.

There was a lot going on at Eli's farm. The starlings overhead distracted my attention. They were arguing over something important at the threshold of a purple martin complex. The Guernseys and a couple of red angus were fussing on one side of the barnyard and I figured they were anxious to be fed and the cows relieved of their cargo. I heard some giggling at the other end of the barnyard and saw Eli's daughters playing in the pasture near a couple of massive horses. His youngest—maybe four years of age—was on her older sister's shoulders, bare feet pressed against her sister's back. She reached for the halter of her dad's Belgian and grabbed it. I watched her dangle from the massive beast, who tried to free himself of the encumbrance by shaking his head back and forth. Eli's daughter swung wildly—her dress flailing in the breeze—until the older daughter smacked the Belgian on the rear which made the horse lurch into the open door of the barn. The kid could have broken a limb or been trampled by the hooves. It was dangerously crazy and I wished I hadn't witnessed it.

"You're done driving for dah day," Eli said.

"Oh?" I countered.

"Look at this," Eli said as he reappeared from beneath the vehicle. He held a metal rod in his hand that was flattened and forked at either end. "This ting goes between dah housing for your tire and the steering mechanism on dah axle," he said.

"Looks like it's bent," I suggested.

The rod was only eighteen inches long, but it had a major bow in the center.

"Yah, it's almost broken," Eli nodded. "But I tink we can fix it. Come on."

I followed Eli to the garage, where we found a couple of bicycles.

"You can use my bike, Mr. Twitchell. I'll use Rebecca's."

"Doesn't matter to me," I said. "Where are we going?"

"The Yoder's farm. Dey got a welder and all the tools. We'll heat this thing up and get it back to normal."

He whistled the theme song from *I Dream of Jeannie*, which seemed a little out of place. After all, how could he know about a television show, if he wasn't supposed to be watching it?

Eli took a length of bailer's twine and wrapped it around the rod and the bike's handlebars. When it was securely fastened, we rode down the driveway to the blacktop. Eli didn't seem like he was in a hurry, but he carried a pace that was rather quick. I didn't have a hard time keeping up with him, but it wasn't easy either. We drove past the old schoolhouse, which was still smoldering in the searing afternoon sun. Eli didn't even acknowledge its presence.

The fuzz from the cottonwoods was more noticeable as we coasted down a large hill. Their tiny puffs came at me like the mini-clips of a dream. I felt the joy of riding a bike again, and held my arms at my side. It made me feel like a kid.

For Eli, it was old hat, or in his case, old straw hat. He never even smiled, and looked absolutely ridiculous with the fuzz trapped in his beard.

About a mile later we pulled into another Amish farm. Like Eli's, it wasn't necessarily neat and tidy.

Eli rapped on the side door of the house, but nobody answered. He came back to his wife's bike and propped his hand on his chin. His fingers raked his beard, burying the fuzz farther and farther into his copse of whiskers.

We both heard a pig squeal in the barn and headed in that direction. It wasn't really a squeal like "Feed me! Feed me!" but rather a guttural plea for its life. I've spent enough time in the farm country of Iowa to know the difference between the two sounds.

Eli made it to the barn first. He knocked on the door, then proceeded inside, the same way a doctor enters an examination room. The squealing was louder now. Terrifyingly so. We walked through the milk house, past the empty stanchions in the main part of the barn, to a small room at the rear. There, in the spider-web-infested, dimly-lit confines, was a pig hanging from its back legs. Dripping wet, the pig swayed gently back and forth as if it had run out of steam in a neighborhood swing set. An Amish man wearing a long, plastic apron and a pair of rubber boots held a garden hose. He was watching a second man as he scrubbed the pig with a soapy brush. Mr. Yoder nodded in my direction from across the room.

"Be sure to get behind his ears," the man with the garden hose said. He had a bit of a hair lip, and his teeth were dirty and crooked.

With that, Mr. Pig got an earful of suds, which sent him into another swaying tizzy.

Eli nodded at one of the men's wives. She held a galvanized pail in her hands, and I noticed the way her hands and chin had a slight tremor. It looked like she could have had Parkinson's.

I heard the trickle of water as it ran through a metal grate on the floor, and I smelled the stench of death in the air.

The pig was exhausted; its chest was heaving in earnest.

Eli turned to me and whispered that maybe I should wait outside.

I shrugged my shoulders as if to send a message of "It'll be okay."

Eli nodded.

I inched my way farther into the room and saw the tools of torture mounted on the far wall. De-horning devices. Castration pliers. Cattle prods. Small tools and large. My dad would have approved.

At last, the knife.

The Amish man with the garden hose gave the pig one last spray. It squirmed in protest, but was exhausted and had lost all desire to squeal. I watched it sway back and forth, eyes blinking continuously, a tendril of drool hanging from its face.

"All set?" he asked.

The man put the brush in the bucket of soapy water, and nodded. His wife handed him the metal pail.

If Colleen were present, she'd have said a prayer for the pig's soul.

There really wasn't any spiritual anointment involved with what came next. The man with the tall boots put on a pair of giant rubber gloves, fiddled with a machine in the corner of the room and approached the pig with a couple of metal spikes. He touched the spikes together, and an arc of electricity jumped between the two. It was the pig's final moment. The man drove the stakes into its ears and the electricity delivered the brutality. After ten seconds, the spikes were removed, and the man with the bucket grabbed the pig by its ears. He pulled the knife from the wall, and in one decisive stroke cut the pig's neck wide open. The blood spurted all over, most of it into the metal pail.

I had to gasp at the scene. It was a powerful display and one that I had never seen before.

Eli and I left the room and we walked back outside. He wasn't whistling any longer.

I felt a sudden urge for a drink, or some other drug to burn the image of the murdered pig from my mind. It was the second trying experience since the horror at the schoolhouse, and I wanted to blot it from my thoughts.

The killing seemed so violent, so personal. It was way different than shooting a turkey or a pheasant, because there was no sport involved. No fair chase, either. I don't know if I could kill a pig like that, unless it was torturing my daughter or ravishing my vegetable garden.

In a merciful kind of way, I felt sorry for the pig, but understood the necessity.

My urge for a drink was washed away in conversation.

"Mrs. Hooley was the one with the pail in her hands. She tinks that everyone loves her blutwurst, but it's terrible," Eli said, privately.

"What's blutwurst?" I asked.

"It's sausage made with pig's blood."

"Whoa," I said. "I don't know if I could eat that either."

"We've got church here tomorrow and dat's why she's making it."

I nodded.

"After the service, we all share a meal."

"Well, Eli, good luck with that."

"Yeah, I tink they're going to be a while butchering that pig, so I think you're going to be out of luck as far as getting your truck fixed."

Eli had stated the obvious.

"That's okay, Eli, I understand." I hesitated for a second or two. "I'll call my wife and see if she'll come up to get me."

Eli nodded.

"Tomorrow's Sunday," he said. "We won't do any work on it then, but I'll have your truck fixed by early next week."

"Thanks, Eli."

Nine

WALTER CLAETY, at the newspaper, wasn't exactly the most patient man in the world. He liked to make things happen, get to the bottom line, and meet deadline after deadline. He wasn't one to hem or haw, but I wouldn't put it past him to think that I had been nursing my mental anguish a little too long. Several weeks had passed since I had set foot in the office; so I knew that Walter must have been getting a little perturbed. What's more, I knew that he usually went on an extended vacation in the summer, which meant that I would have to hold down the fort.

In other words, it was time for me to get my act in gear.

Walter knew it.

Colleen knew it.

Everybody did.

The newspaper was my career, my chosen profession. It had consumed my life in a lot of ways, but at the end of the day, I really believed that I was good at it.

Or at least that's what I thought.

Because of my mental-health holiday, it had been weeks since I contributed anything worthwhile to the paper. I may have developed a big head about the value of my writing, but

I think the subscribers missed reading my columns. What the heck, I missed reading my columns too. They were fun and lighthearted, and, in a lot of ways, shed a glimpse into the human condition.

I don't know if I had writer's block or if it was my diminished mental stability that kept me from making a contribution. I'd hate to ever think that I was lazy.

Colleen would never accuse me of being lazy. And frankly, I don't think she'd ever dream up saying something so callous. She was entrenched in the matter of the Heretic Fringe and couldn't wait to tell me about it, on that late Saturday afternoon in Amish country.

"They don't know who I am or what I'm doing, Derrick," she said. "It's like I'm undercover."

"What do you mean?" I asked. "Isn't that what you said you were going to do?"

"Well, yeah, but so far I've just kinda skirted around the edges. Now I've got a chance to really get inside this group."

"Colleen," I said, somewhat concerned, "are you sure you want to do that?"

"Oh, Derrick, I don't know. I feel like the story has taken hold of me. It's like I'm on the boat crossing the Delaware with Washington himself. These people are extremely angry at the government."

"So they're planning a revolution?"

"I don't know if I'd say that. They're just really, really concerned with what is taking place."

"Why are you staying with it?" I asked.

She hesitated for a second. "This is the kind of story that could win awards, and how often do you get a chance to do that?"

"Hardly ever," I shrugged.

We drove past a topless club east of Harrison. There were a couple of cars in the parking lot, and I figured

that it was the manager and the cook who were reporting for work an hour or two before the entertainers had
to arrive. For a second there, I imagined the smell of diced
onions in the kitchen mixed with the pungent snarl of
Pine Sol in the lounge. Before the sun would set, the onions
would be chili and the Pine Sol would be replaced by perfume
and spilt beer.

"Why don't you just tell me what's going on?" I asked.

Colleen hesitated for a second.

I waited patiently and Colleen started in, "I'm at the VFW
in Houghton Lake."

"Last night?"

"Right. And I'm not really doing much, just kinda hanging
out at the bar."

"Was it busy?"

"It was busy, but it wasn't packed."

"Did you leave your wedding ring on?"

"Derrick!" she frowned. "Of course I did."

"Sorry. I just think you're really good looking and I wouldn't
want some guy to get the wrong idea."

Colleen shrugged off my inquiry.

"There's like six or eight people who are in jail."

"What do you mean?" I asked.

"Part of the group, they're charged with conspiracy to harm
a federal official. They're being investigated by a grand jury."

"You mean on the Capp murder?"

"Right," she said "they were denied bail."

"So who's remaining?"

"I don't know for sure, Derrick, but the bartender seemed
to know a lot about it."

"Keep going."

"We were kinda chitchatting throughout the night. I played
the part of being an angry American and dropped little hints
about the country going to hell in a handbasket. He liked what I

had to say, so I really poured it on thick. I said something about the liberals destroying the fabric of our country, the conservatives getting soft around the middle, and the Tea Party being a band of do-gooders."

I nodded, then noticed a spotted fawn lying dead on the shoulder of the road. The thing couldn't have been a day or two old and weighed less than my Brittany. *What a terrible thing to lose your baby like that.*

"Feeding the bartender's fire was easy," Colleen chuckled. "He quoted a verse from Ecclesiastes: 'The heart of the wise inclines to the right; the heart of the fool to the left.'"

I laughed. "No kidding. What happened next?" I asked.

"At the end of the night, he told me to check out *The Turner Diaries.*"

"What's that?"

"The FBI calls it the 'Bible of the radical right,' but it's really just a novel."

"Never heard of it."

"Well, it was published more than thirty years ago. I already looked into it."

"What's it about?"

"A modern-day revolution in the United States."

"Seriously?" I doubted her facts.

"Oh, yeah. Timothy McVeigh promoted the book before he bombed the federal building in Oklahoma City."

"That's just great," I said sarcastically. "Sounds like some light reading."

"I haven't even started it yet, but I know you can buy it at gun-and-knife shows and through members of the neo-Nazis."

"Holy hell."

Colleen winced when I swore, but she let it pass this time. "They're extremists, Derrick."

"Who?" I asked.

"The people who killed Capp, that's who. The Heretic

Fringe." I listened to her talk, but what she told me wasn't the most pleasant thing in the world. "They had newspaper clippings framed and on the walls," she said.

"What do you mean?"

"Remember that guy in Texas who flew his airplane into the IRS building?"

"Vaguely, I guess. It was shortly after nine-eleven; why?"

"Well, the folks in Houghton Lake sure haven't forgotten about what happened. They've got clippings on the walls leading to the restrooms and they all deal with Americans trying to get even with the government." She took a breath and asked me, "You know who Patrick Henry is, right?"

"Help me out."

"He was the patriot who said, 'Give me liberty, or give me death,' way back in the late seventeen hundreds."

"What about him?"

"They've got pictures of him in the hallway, too. He was the one who urged the American colonies to revolt against the British."

"Weren't you the least bit afraid?" I asked her.

"No, Derrick. I wasn't afraid, but I feel like the VFW in Houghton Lake is the center of the whole thing. The trouble was that I had a hard time getting anyone to talk to me about it."

I thought for a second or two about what she had said. It didn't make much sense. "Why do you think it's at the center of something big if nobody will talk to you?"

"The hall is where they arrested five or six of the conspirators. I overheard some people talking. They were laughing and saying things like 'You'd better be quiet. Big Brother has this place bugged.'"

"I wouldn't doubt that, if they've bugged it. That's what they do."

"I checked out who was arrested. Two of the guys were from South Haven."

"Way down on Lake Michigan?"

"Yeah. The Ivey brothers. They were the ones who booby-trapped the road with spike strips and blew out the cops' tires."

"Allegedly," I reminded her.

"Right, right," she smiled. "There was a guy from Plymouth who threw the cans of tear gas inside the gymnasium and locked the back doors," she said. "The guy who pepper-sprayed the troopers was from Kalkaska."

"Quite an operation," I said.

Colleen bit her lip. Her eyebrows pinched together as if she were concentrating really hard.

"Oh," she said somewhat relieved, "The guys who chained the troopers' cars together were from Lansing and Alpena."

It was rather amusing to see her try to keep it all straight in her head. The men they arrested were from every corner of the Lower Peninsula.

"I think that's everybody, except for the ringleader."

"Who's that?"

"You don't remember?" she asked me.

"No, who is it?"

Colleen put her hand on my knee.

"It's okay."

We rolled into the driveway. Home at last.

Elizabeth was riding her bike around a chalk racetrack she had drawn on the concrete. Mom was sitting in a lawn chair, a glass of iced tea on a TV tray next to her. Jacque, our dog, was proud to greet us—a dead fox squirrel dangling from his freckled jowls.

"I want to know, Colleen. Can you tell me?"

Before she pulled on the door handle, she looked in my direction.

"Derrick, honey," she said. "I'll tell you anything you want to know. It was Marshall Yandle. You killed the ringleader of the group. He was from Gladwin."

Her hand patted my knee again.

"You're a hero, Derrick."

I nodded.

"I don't feel like a hero. I feel like I'm hungry. What's for dinner, by the way?"

Colleen jumped out of the driver's side door and gave Elizabeth a big squeeze.

Mom looked over her reading glasses and the newspaper and smiled, warmly.

The dog wagged his tail egg-beater style, but he wasn't about to let me take away his limp prize. He undoubtedly put a lot of thought, not to mention a good bit of stalking, into capturing the squirrel.

All the world seemed like a peaceful place.

I caught a whiff of something delicious. The plume of scent must have started in the kitchen and had drifted through the garage and onto the driveway. It was now tapping on my shoulder like a friendly neighbor.

"What's for dinner?" I asked again.

Mom didn't even hesitate.

"Pork roast," she said, smiling, "fresh from the crock pot."

"Lovely," I said with a sigh as my mind slipped back to the farm in Amish country. The ghastly image of the pig's demise made me think twice about rolling up my sleeves and diving into the main course. Then again, they are rather tasty and I was proud to be at the top of the food chain.

"Let's eat," I said. "It's great to be a carnivore."

Ten

D EAR OLD WALTER CLAETY was ready to go on vacation when we met at the newspaper early Sunday morning. His camper was wedged into the back of his pickup, and his border collie watched us intently through the passenger-side window. I had to wonder if his dog would eventually try to herd Walter back to the dashboard if he took too long chitchatting with me.

"Where are you headed?" I asked him.

"I'm going to catch the noon car-ferry in Ludington, and meet some family in Friendship, Wisconsin," he said enthusiastically. His false teeth made a whistle when he spoke. "I've got a coupla cases of Vernors for them to drink. They love that stuff. We'll have a big bonfire, eat some of that homemade sausage they sell over there, and drink ginger ale. Tomorrow, I'll get up and head west."

"What's your destination?"

"Yellowstone. Going to spend ten, fifteen days there. Maybe a month. I want to catch some cutthroats and see some wildlife. I thought about having a little section in the paper about my vacation diaries. Maybe I'll e-mail you some photos and copy."

"That will be great, Walter. Do you have your cell phone?"

"Oh, yeah, but you should be all set. I just placed an order for more paper. We've got tons of ink, and the press has been running like a charm. Payroll isn't until next week, and the accountant should be mailing our quarterly reports within the next day or two. There's ten, fifteen checks for you to sign, but you'd better get online and check our balance before you send them out."

I think he liked saying "ten, fifteen."

"That's great," I said. "Is the password for the bank still under the desk calendar?"

"Sure is. In red ink." Walter hesitated. "What about you?"

"What about me?" I asked.

"Are you sure you're up for this?"

Walter didn't beat around the bush. For the first time since I had returned to work, he acknowledged the eight-hundred-pound gorilla in the room.

"I'm on the mend, Walter," I lamented. "Work will be good for me. I just wonder if we'll have enough stories to fill up a paper."

"Yeah, well, there are a couple of journalism students here who are doing their best, but you gotta watch one of them. He's got a tendency to overexaggerate things."

"Hyperbole?"

"That's it," he said. "Extreme exaggeration. You'll know it when you read his stuff."

"Any stories I should be working on?" I asked him.

"Not really. You could probably fill some space if you covered the bank's renovation. They'll have a state-of-the-art alarm system, you know that."

"Sure."

"You could probably take on a political story if you wanted to."

"Oh?"

"Yeah, the governor has named Capp's replacement."

"Who's that?"

"Roy Mahoney, from Canadian Lakes."

"Wasn't he the state representative…?"

"Senator," Walter interrupted me.

"Right. Right. Wasn't he the guy who was protesting the water bottling plant in Mecosta?"

"That's him. Thought it would drain all the aquifers and lower the lake levels."

"Why would the governor tap Mahoney instead of someone else?" I asked.

"Cuz Mahoney is just as liberal as Capp used to be, and he can't run for re-election."

"Term-limited?"

"You got it, Derrick."

"I suppose it wouldn't make a bad story. We'll figure something out."

"I'm sure you will, Derrick."

Walter stuck out his hand and we shook on it. What the heck, we hugged half-heartedly. He was like an uncle to me, and I loved the guy in a platonic kind of way. Even though we were technically only co-workers, we were really close friends.

"Have a great trip, Walter," I said again.

He waved, but never looked back.

I watched him hop into the cab of his truck, give his dog a pat on the head, and start the engine. He put the truck in gear and off they went. I stood there for a minute or two and thought about their adventure ahead. They'd drive up the palm of Michigan's Lower Peninsula, turn left where the cornfields meet the cedar swamps of Clare, and across the heavenly, oak-covered hills of Nirvana, Scottville, and eventually, Ludington. It was a beautiful day for a ferry cruise across Lake Michigan and it made me wish I was along for the drive.

As much as I was intrigued with the notion of an extended holiday, I knew that it was time to button my chinstrap and get down to business.

I had a paper to publish, and it wasn't going to get done by me sitting there, dreaming about glorious Lake Michigan.

Eventually, I made my way to my office, not far from where Walter and I had spoken. It had been several weeks since I had set foot in the place, and Walter wasn't lying when he said there were 'ten, fifteen' checks for me to sign. They were laid out in rows like playing cards in a game of solitaire. The longest row was payroll for all the staff, including Walter, who must not have needed the money for his trip. The second row was our utilities, and last but not least was the lease payment from the newspaper to me, the landlord. I stacked the checks on top of one another, and stuffed them in a drawer. I'd get to all that during the week.

The inbox in my e-mail was overflowing with messages and forwarded jokes from an assortment of friends and relatives. They all had to wait for one e-mail that came from a complete stranger who wrote *Dear Mr. Twitchell* in the subject field.

Inside, it read:

My name is Henry Rush and I've read your articles many times. I'm writing you because I've been charged with conspiring to murder a United States official. This allegation stemmed from an anonymous letter I sent to Congressman Capp shortly before the health-care vote several months ago. I am out on bail, awaiting trial later this summer.

Mr. Twitchell, I am nearly eighty years of age and I don't want to spend what little time I have left in this world locked up in a jail cell. I sent the letter because I felt like there was no other choice. Mr. Capp didn't listen to his constituents; he didn't care what they thought. The polls showed that the vast majority of the people of northern Michigan didn't want government-run health care, but he voted for it anyway. My letter was a plea for him to listen to us; in other words, a last-ditch effort to change his position.

I am writing you with hopes that you will interview me and tell the citizens of Michigan that I'm really not a criminal, just an American citizen who's fed up with our elected officials. Please come to my cottage in Glennie and I'll tell you all about it.

I didn't know what to think. His name seemed remotely familiar, but I couldn't quite place him.

Instead of responding to his inquiry, I Googled his name and came up with several hits. The most reliable source was from the United States District Attorney's office, whose office posted a press release regarding the matter. It appeared as if Mr. Rush had given me only half the story. He was officially charged with "conspiring to assault, kidnap, or murder a U.S. Official." Of course, Rush didn't mince any words in his alleged letter to the late congressman: "You should be prepared for the consequences of a 'yes' vote. We will hang you and your family members from the catwalk of the Mackinac Bridge."

That seemed like fairly harsh language to me, even if Rush was an eighty-year-old man. I chose not to respond to his letter, but I didn't delete it from my inbox.

After a few minutes, I thought that maybe I should have responded. After all, he might try to hang me from the catwalk, too.

Then again, his e-mail was already ten days old. If he hadn't started any trouble yet, he might not after all.

I just wanted to avoid the whole business with Marshall Yandle, the conspiracy of the murdered congressman, and the Heretic Fringe.

All I wanted to do was slow down and chill out. Have a few drinks. Catch a little buzz and forget about all my troubles.

I sat at my desk for quite some time in the Sunday-morning silence, dreaming about Eli and Rebecca and their easy-going lifestyle. By now the whole Amish clan must have finished their church service and were enjoying Mrs. Hooley's homemade blutwurst. I bet it wasn't as bad as Eli made it out to be. Even if it was bad, I'd bet they'd have plenty of side dishes to pass around the table. I, for one, would be filling my face with Rebecca's sourdough, or maybe the Petershwims' purple cabbage.

Even though it was early in the day, I wished I was in Amish country.

Colleen and Elizabeth had gone to church. Jacque and I had gone for a long walk. There was still plenty of time to get Monday's newspaper together, but for some reason, I couldn't pull myself away from the notion of a Bloody Mary.

I could have a few drinks and still get some work done. It sounded simply marvelous.

Without a second thought, I got up from my desk and found the fifth of vodka on the top shelf of my closet, and the breakroom refrigerator still had an eight-pack of tomato juice on the bottom shelf. In just a few minutes, I was sprinkling salt and pepper on the first drink of the day. Nothing tastes better than the first sip of a cold Bloody Mary with all that pepper and flavor.

The sip was probably more like a gulp, but it tasted great.

I fired up the computer, opened a document, and sat there. The boiler made a hissing sound and the cat walked across the threshold of the office. There were distractions everywhere. I looked at the clock; fifteen minutes had come and gone and I still wasn't sure what to write. There was little doubt that I was rusty, so I poured another drink.

I bounced ideas around in my mind, but I couldn't seem to get them onto the computer screen. I felt like I had a loyal following in the paper who had undoubtedly heard about the incident at the schoolhouse. They were patiently waiting for me to write something. Anything.

And so, I just started writing, not necessarily for the people who would eventually read it, but for my own peace of mind.

I can't tell you where I've been, nor can I tell you what's going on inside my head. All I know is that I killed a man several weeks ago and I haven't been the same since.

Even though many creatures have fallen from the blast of my shotgun, the visual effects of the man's exploding head have given me nightmares. Most of you would have done the same thing that I did, but I have to tell you that it has taken its toll on me and my family. All I want to do is forget about the screams of horror, the gunfire, blood, and pretend that that horrible moment never happened. Of course, that's not how it works.

Time—I'm told—will help heal my wounds. I hope that you, the readers, understand that I may not write as frequently as I have. Please be patient as I work to heal myself through this difficult period.

Almost thirty minutes had passed and all I had to show for my efforts was a couple of rusty sentences. As much as the afternoon's deadline loomed over my head, I wasn't in any rush to make things happen. I was out of practice, and sometimes it takes a little while for the productive juices to start flowing.

I looked down at the ice in the bottom of the coffee cup, and noticed how the cubes were half the size they had been just half an hour ago. They looked porous, with a hint of red. *Why did I choose a Bloody Mary?* It seemed remarkably ironic.

I poured a third drink and called it "brain lubricant."

The office cat rubbed against my ankle, curling its tail against my calf. I swished him away, but he rolled on his back at the foot of my desk. My English springer, Synch, used to strike the same seductive pose when she wanted her belly scratched, but Jacque just jabs me with his nose until I massage his ears. Strange, how the smallest events can trigger such pleasant, vivid memories.

The Amish schoolhouse where the incident occurred has since been burned to the ground by the elders. The Amish children who witnessed the tragedy have scattered to the neighboring farms where they live. Although I don't know how all the children are dealing with the tragedy of that day, I understand that several of them are having a very difficult time coping with their emotions. And why wouldn't they have trouble? Their innocence was obliterated in one horrendous blast.

The sips kept coming my way. The vodka was kicking in. I was enjoying the blurred vision and mild incapacitation. All of a sudden there were two lines of copy on the computer screen for every sentence I had written.

Pleash don't feel sorry for me. Might need a little time before I figure shomething out.

I wasn't exactly sure what I meant by "figure *shomething* out," but it just seemed like the best thing to write.

My head was swimming in emotions, and reeling from the serum coursing through my veins. Bloody Mary had made a bloody mess of me.

I didn't know what to write and I didn't care who might read it. I just wrote.

The Amish have a very shpecial way of dealing with thingsh. They'll take the tragedy in shtride, regroup, and move ahead.
Ash for me, I'm not so sure.

Eleven

"So what happened?" Jim asked me, blunt as ever. I hesitated.

"Well," I said, recanting the incident at the newspaper's headquarters, "Colleen called the office on the way home from church and realized that I had been drinking. She could sense it in the way I slurred my speech."

"Was she mad at you?"

"Yeah, you could say that. She dropped our daughter off at a friend's house and came to see me."

"What did she say?"

"She thinks it's okay to get drunk if I'm at a wedding, or out with some friends, but that's about it."

"I see," Jim said, a twinge of sarcasm in his voice. "She doesn't think that it's a good idea to get smashed on Sunday mornings."

"Right."

"And Colleen didn't want your daughter to see you drunk, right?"

"That's it"

"What do you think?" Jim asked.

"What do you mean?" I batted the shuttlecock back at him. If we were verbalizing a game of badminton, I was prepared to volley back and forth.

101

Jim traced his thumb and finger across his chin and re-phrased his question. "Do you think it's a good idea getting smashed on a Sunday morning?"

"Well…no," I said, tentatively. "But I'm glad that she bailed me out."

Jim nodded. "Did Colleen do the right thing?"

"Of course she did. Somebody had to put Monday's news-paper together."

"She knows how to do that?"

"Yeah, she used to be my boss when I was a reporter at the other paper down the street. She knows all about the business."

"I see. That makes it handy." Jim scribbled on his note pad. He lifted a page in my file, and I saw his eyes dart back and forth. Finally, he asked, "Did you ever make it back to the schoolhouse?"

"Sure did."

Jim was a good listener. He didn't interrupt, nodded his head often and watched me talk through it all. When I got to the part about visiting the farm a second time, Jim sat on the edge of his seat.

"So, you went back to the farm to pick up your truck?"

"Right, just this week. Eli put everything back together and had it running like a charm."

"You went up there, picked up your truck and headed for home?"

"No. Not really."

"What happened?" Jim asked.

I wasn't exactly sure where to start, for fear that I'd bore him with useless details. Then again, I didn't mind telling Jim about Eli's farm because that setting made me feel so much at ease. And what the heck, Eli was an unusual guy and an excel-lent topic of conversation.

"Eli Beiler is his name. He's the guy who let me hunt tur-keys on the back of his farm. A bit of an odd-looking man with a peculiar-shaped mouth that curls up at the corners, as if he can't keep from smiling," I said. "He's growing bald, but has this dreadful long hair that sticks out from his straw hat."

Jim smiled.

"I think he's got LSD or something."

Jim laughed. "Don't you mean OCD?"

"Yeah, whatever. He's compulsive. Can't even eat like a normal person."

"What do you mean?" Jim crossed one leg over the other.

"He eats a sandwich while there's nothing else on the plate. When he's done with the sandwich, he gets a fresh plate and has some potato salad. When that's done, he gets a fresh plate and has some pie."

"Whoa."

"I know, it's weird," I said. "His poor kids have to wash all those plates by hand."

Jim nodded and seemed fascinated with an amateur's account of Eli's condition.

"His poor wife knows exactly how he likes things done. She doesn't think it's weird. At least that's the impression I get."

"What do you mean?"

"She kept bringing him his food, just like he wanted. And with every fresh plate, she gave him a fresh fork, too."

"Why do you think you feel so comfortable there?" he asked.

I hesitated again. Jim had a way of reducing questions into the fewest possible words.

"I'm not sure," I said. "It's the whole Amish lifestyle. The simplicity…the wholesomeness of it all. Eli takes great pleasure in doing things the old-fashioned way."

Jim nodded, but waited for a better explanation.

"Like how to chop wood. I never knew that you're supposed to snap your wrists just as the axe hits the log."

Jim raised his eyebrows.

"Most guys use a maul and try to overpower a log with brute force."

"Or," Jim said, "They hook a hydraulic splitter up to their tractor."

"Right, right. It's like they know that they're doing things the hard way, but they seem to relish in it. They appreciate the little things in life, like their children and their health."

"What else?"

"I don't know...like the timeliness of things. Like when to pick the strawberries, and how to make jam without adding lots of pectin. Eli's wife has a bread business and she knows exactly how long it should rise and how long to bake it."

"How does she run a bread business?"

"Eli and Rebecca are rebels, I think. He doesn't mind the Amish lifestyle, but he doesn't want his kids living in poverty, either. It's like he believes that certain modern conveniences are okay if it helps you to do God's work."

"Like what?"

"Like the other day a couple of his neighbors slaughtered a pig, but they didn't just slit its throat. Instead, they shocked it with this portable welder, and then knifed him wide open..."

"And Amish aren't supposed to use electricity, but it's okay if it merely stuns the pig."

"You got it," I said, "Eli's got a generator outside his home. It powers their computer, which is hooked up to the Internet. That's how they do their marketing, keep track of their books, everything."

"What's the name of their business?"

"Thy Daily Bread."

Jim snapped his fingers in delight, "I buy their bread all the time. That stuff is unbelievable."

"All they make is sourdough."

Jim was beaming. "That's all you need. I'm telling you, it's the best toasted and dipped in eggs."

"It's the crust. Or the flavor. It's just amazing."

"I buy it right here in Mt. Pleasant at Ric's Grocery Store."

"They told me that UPS delivers it to stores and restaurants twice a week." I said. "He made it sound like they've got accounts set up all over this part of the state."

"That must explain the cost. It's like six bucks a loaf, I think."

"You're right. And Eli and his wife sell it to Ric's for three."

"How do they make any money?" Jim asked.

"They just do. Eli said that they make about sixty-five loaves a day. Some stores pay them four and now they're selling it online directly to the public. They've got a website and they're hooked up with a credit card vendor."

"No kidding."

"I'm serious. Eli's wife, Rebecca, is in charge of it all. I don't know how she does it. She's an accountant and the marketing arm of the operation. Oh, and if you'll pardon the pun, she really doesn't have much for an arm. She lost her hand in a corn picker. Now there's just a stump."

"Whoa."

"You should see her too. She kneads the dough with her stub, and her elbow."

Jim was laughing. "I'm sorry. You've just spoiled my image of their kitchen."

"I know it."

Jim and I sat there for a second or two. Maybe eight or ten seconds. He uncrossed his legs and tugged his sock past his calf. He swept at his thighs as if he were swishing away bits of dog hair.

I didn't know what else to say.

Jim did.

"Life for the Amish isn't all a bowl of cherries, is it, Derrick?"

"What do you mean?"

"I mean, it sounds like you've spent a bit of time on the

farm. Have you seen, or witnessed, anything that might make it seem like it's not the good ship Lollipop?"

"Do you mean like an incident or something that would make me think that their lifestyle isn't a bed of roses?"

"Anything at all," he said, open-ended.

"Well, yeah."

"Like what, Derrick?"

"It's the kids. Eli told me about his son and the way he quit doing his woodworking since the shooting. He's got another little girl who wets the bed and has taken up sucking her thumb."

"What do you think?"

"I believe him, but I can't really tell for sure since I didn't know them before the shooting. All I can say is that the kids are painfully shy. They speak this funky language. I think it's German."

Jim nodded. It felt like he was sizing me up.

"So what do you want to do?"

"What do you mean?" I asked.

"I mean, this is our second session together, and I think I've got an understanding of what's going on. You feel great when you're dealing with the Amish, but you don't when you're at home or at work. That's when you do your drinking."

Now it was my turn to nod.

"When you drink, it upsets your wife, which only seems to make matters worse. Am I right?"

"Yes," I nodded some more.

"So from where I sit, you can either take up drinking full-time and make a career out of it, or, you can figure out a way to come to grips with what happened at the schoolhouse and somehow put it in your rearview window."

There it was, blunt as ever. He smashed the shuttlecock over the net and into the far corner of my court.

I squirmed in my chair as if I had a broken lightbulb in my boxers. Jim let the hemorrhoids of his statement fester. After what seemed like an eternity, he picked me up off the floor.

"Derrick, I think you're a really good guy," he continued, "You've got a lot going for you…"

The grandfather clock in the corner of his office was ticking, ticking, ticking. It made the setting especially sincere because nobody lies to a grandfather. Jim wouldn't lie to me and I hadn't lied to him. He really seemed to care about my progress, even though I wasn't sure why. I never thought about a shrink being a normal doctor; I just thought that they were a sounding board of sorts. Over the course of two or three appointments, Jim had become more than a sounding board. He had a way of taking a hatchet to the clutter in my head to reveal my inner feelings. I don't know how else to explain it. The advice he gave me came out of left field, but it would change my life forever.

"You've got a lot going for you, but at the moment, I think you're a loser."

I huffed.

"What!?"

"Yeah. You're a loser. Marshall Yandle might be dead, but he's got the better of you, Derrick."

Jim said it with a wry little smile, eyebrows lifted.

"Every time you take a drink, Marshall Yandle has a toast."

I shook my head no. Not because I disagreed with Jim, but because I didn't like the concept of getting beaten.

"What are you going to do about it?" he asked, "are you going to let the ghost of Marshall Yandle haunt you for the rest of your life, or are you going to man up and take control of the inner battle?"

"I…I…"

"Derrick, you killed the bastard who needed to be stopped. If it wasn't for your heroism, a lot of kids might have been murdered."

"I can't just forget about killing him."

"I know, I know," Jim nodded. "That's why you're here."

Jim was on the edge of his seat again.

"You need some help, Derrick and I'm here to help you. Do you understand?"

My eyes were blinking to the sounds of the clock. "Yes."

"Whatever you tell me stays between us."

"Right."

"I learned a long time ago that in everybody's life there are challenges to overcome and situations that present unique opportunities."

"So what are you trying to say, Jim?"

"That unless you stay in bed all day, good things and bad things happen to you. Ever hear the saying about 'turning lemons into lemonade'?"

"Sure. Hasn't everybody?"

"Of course they have. Don't let the bad parts of your life get you down. I don't know how to beat Marshall Yandle, but I know you're capable of it."

I was listening intently.

"Don't worry about beating him a month from now or a year from now. Beat him in this instant, in the next minute."

Jim acted like a cheerleader and I couldn't help but soak it all in.

"One day at a time, Derrick."

"And turn lemons into lemonade," I countered.

Jim nodded.

I laughed.

For now, at least, I could conquer the world.

Twelve

I WALKED OUT OF OUR APPOINTMENT feeling better about my-self, but not totally convinced of how I was going to turn lemons into lemonade when it came to Marshall Yandle. After all, it took some imagination to do the same on a living person, let alone someone who was pushing up daisies.

During our first session Jim suggested that I re-visit the schoolhouse; this time he was my cheerleader. It made me won-der what his strategy would be at our next appointment.

Jim's message continued to ping inside my head. It seemed like a good idea for pulling me out of this funk, but I wasn't quite sure how I was going to make it happen. Needless to say, I didn't want to let him down. I didn't want to let Col-leen, Elizabeth, my mom or Walter down either. They were all counting on me to get back to normal—to be my productive, normal self.

That's if I believed that I was normal.

I always thought that normal wasn't so normal.

I'd rather be a happy non-conformist than an unhappy, normal person any day.

Either way, after three or four days of handling the paper's business and successfully avoiding alcohol, I decided to take Dad's old Harley up the Lower Peninsula's east side to the cabin of Henry Rush.

I wanted to take my time and make the most of the afternoon. After all, it was nearing the end of June and the unofficial start of vacation season. I passed boat after boat coming from Saginaw Bay, and I figured that the walleyes must have been biting. In my head, I was aboard those boats with the fishermen as they bobbed along, miles offshore, waiting for the next bite and a ticket to a tasty dinner.

When I made it to Standish, I took a drive around the high school and tried to piece together Capp's kidnapping. It must have been quite an undertaking with all the assorted elements rolled into one enormous tragedy. I could almost smell the tear gas, hear the wailing sirens, and feel the rush of people all over again as they trampled from the gymnasium. It would be one of those events that people would talk about for years and years, if not generations.

The waitress in the diner down the street said that the incident caused quite a stir within the community. "We had cops all over the place. They must have been detectives, I guess. I seen more guys in suits that week than I have in years," she said. "Sometimes, they just ordered a dozen burgers and milkshakes and had us deliver it to the police post down the street."

I raised my eyebrows and listened politely to what she had to say.

"That Capp had it coming to him, though. He never listened to what we wanted."

She must have thought I was a sympathetic ear, because she'd wipe off a table, and skate past with another tidbit of information. I was beginning to regret bringing up the topic.

"Some of the regulars in here say that they want to help the guys who were arrested. They want to send them money for their defense or have a potluck fundraiser."

The bean soup was delicious; the fish sandwich smothered in tartar sauce was even better. My attention was divided between the food in my midst and the waitress's story that seemed to gallop along skeptically.

"They wouldn't never get a conviction here. Got too many people who are fed up with the government."

I smiled politely and laid my money clip on the table. The waitress picked up on my intentions and ripped a paper check from the pad.

"Course they can't help the one guy. He got his head—"

"Thank you for lunch," I interrupted. "The fish was excellent."

She backed off. Two fives and a dollar bill later, I saddled up the bike and was on my way up the coastline, through the little hamlets of Twining, Whittemore, Hale, and eventually, the wilderness inside the Huron National Forest.

Henry Rush's cabin wasn't much, but it seemed to suit him just fine. It was small and run-down; his was the-place-behind-the-cabin that sat on the water's edge. I knew that Hunters Lake was relatively deep and clear, and offered some decent fishing opportunities for bluegills and bass. Fishing and hunting are always decent ice-breakers, especially with the people who live in northern Michigan. If I tilted my head just right, I could see a sliver of water between the neighbor's Michigan State banner and the willow trees down the street. Except for Henry's back patio, which had a shingled roof and built-in screens, the cabin was made from burnished yellow logs that were peeling a previous year's shellac. As I approached the front door, I heard the raucous banter of children splashing in the lake down the street, and the nervous luff of an American flag overhead. Mr. Rush was a proud American.

He invited me inside, but instead of sitting in the living room, he took me to the kitchen in the rear of the cabin.

"Have a seat," he said, keeping a watchful eye on a metal contraption on the stove. "This is a Norwegian triple boiler. I put the strawberries in the top and boil the hell out of them. The juice is captured in the second pan. That, along with pectin and sugar will eventually become strawberry jelly."

Although I appreciated his hospitality, I was more impressed with his ability to multi-task. Anybody who can entertain company and whip up a batch of jelly at the same time is a very industrious fellow.

"I give the stuff away to all my clients at the holidays."

"Nice. I bet they appreciate it," I said. "What do you do for a living?"

"I'm a real-estate appraiser."

"Great."

Henry looked a lot closer to seventy than eighty. Even though his eyelids drooped over his lashes, his face was relatively wrinkle-free. His teeth were stained a bleak shade of gray, and I figured it was from the coffee that loitered around his kitchen in cups and cans, in plastic jars and little one-serving packets.

"Lately though, I haven't needed much jelly to give away," he said.

"Why's that, the economy?"

Henry stood at the stove and removed the lid from his contraption. When he did, a plume of steam rose into the metal hood.

"Heck yeah," he said. "That, and now the feds have added so much paperwork that it's hard to crank these appraisals out like I used to."

"Is that something new?"

"Sure it is. When Congress passed the banking overhaul, they added a bunch of red tape."

Henry retied his apron and wiped his hands on a dishcloth.

"They're crooks," he said. "Every last one of them."

I asked him if he was ready to go on the record.

"Yeah, I'm ready, but first I'd like to say that the federal prosecutor who's in charge of my case committed suicide."

I looked at him in disbelief, so he added more details.

"She worked out of the Bay City office. She was found asphyxiated in her garage."

"Wow," I stuttered, "how is that going to affect your case?"

"I don't know. My lawyer isn't the best about calling me back. It just happened the other day."

"So, the police say that it was a suicide?"

"That's right."

"Did she leave a note or anything?" I asked.

Henry shook his head. "Not that I'm aware of. You know the police don't really say a lot about stuff like that. Her funeral is tomorrow in Midland."

"Okay."

He unclipped a thin, plastic hose from the edge of the pot, took the stopper off the end, and the juice slithered into a bowl.

"I was thinking about going to the funeral," he said, "just to see what her personal life was like."

"Oh yeah?"

"I live in Frankenmuth, and Midland isn't that far out of the way."

"Is there any other reason why you'd like to go to her funeral?"

"No, why do you ask?"

I shrugged my shoulders. "Pissing someone off right now just doesn't seem like something you'd want to do."

"I don't care about that."

"Mr. Rush, do you like to stir things up?" I tried to come across as being very sincere.

He flashed his grim colored teeth and smiled, "Would you like a cup of coffee?"

I smiled back at him, picked up my pen and held it to the reporter's pad. "No, thank you, but you go ahead."

He turned the knob on the stove and I heard the igniter *click-click-click*. A second later the flames emerged next to his triple boiler and Henry was in business.

"Ever since I lost my wife, I've become very critical of the government," he said, sadly. "She was my pride and joy. In a lot of ways, she kept me on level ground."

"Congressman Capp's office said that you were one of their most vocal critics."

"I know, but they had it coming to them."

"They said that you had sent them something like fifty-eight e-mails in the last four years."

"Sounds about right. They never answered a one, which made it worse. So I sent some more."

I was scribbling away.

"Next thing you know, I'm writing them like it's a diary. Almost every day I'm reminding them of what it's like to be an American, how we all have to live by the Constitution, how the Founding Fathers wanted less government, not more."

"And that's how you came up with fifty-eight e-mails."

"That's right, but I don't think there's a jury in Michigan who will convict me."

"What are you charged with?"

"Conspiring to murder, or assault, a federal official, but there was only one piece of mail that was threatening. It's funny how you have to threaten someone in Washington before you get their attention."

"How did they know it was you?"

He laughed, "I put my name on the letter! I'm not afraid. And for the record, I never said that *I am going to hang you from the Mackinac Bridge*, I said, *I fear that you'll be hung from the Mackinac Bridge.*"

"Did your lawyer say that it makes a difference?"

"Yup."

"Then why did these prosecutors come after you?"

"I guess because they wanted to make an example of me."

I nodded.

"So, you sent the letter before the health-care vote?" I asked.

"Right. Capp eventually voted for the damn thing, which sealed his fate at the school in Standish. There are a lot of people out there who would have loved to see him hang from the

Mackinac Bridge if they had half the chance. He's dead now, so they missed out."

"Mr. Rush, does it make you happy that the congressman is dead?"

"Well, yeah. He, and all those other crooks down there, took an oath of office to represent the people. Nobody wanted this health-care thing, but they voted for it anyway."

"Somebody did; the polls showed that thirty percent were in favor of it."

"Those are the same people who're on food stamps, and welfare. The ones who want something for nothing."

Henry took the tea kettle from the stove, reached into the cupboard overhead and pulled out a jar of instant coffee. A second later, he was pouring hot water onto the bits of coffee inside his cup. *He did like to stir things up.*

"You know," he started again, "the health-care reform had very little to do with reform. Those congressmen take campaign donations from the trial lawyers, who make their living off suing doctors."

"What's that got to do with Capp?"

"The reason why health insurance is so high is that the doctors have to practice defensive medicine. They gotta run test after test for fear that they'll be sued."

"So it's all the lawyers' fault?" I asked.

"It's certainly not the insurance companies'," he sipped. "They pay the doctors' bills from the premiums they collect."

"What do you want me to write about you?" I asked.

He smiled.

"Just tell the truth, that's all. Look at all these letters I received."

He handed me a stack of envelopes bundled together with a thick red rubber band. There must have been twenty-five in various shapes and sizes.

"What do they say?" I asked.

"Most of them are from Michigan, Capp's district, but they

all support me. There's a lot of anger out there. America is fed up with the baloney in Washington."

"You mean there's a lot of people within the community who feel the same way you did?"

"Absolutely. The people in Congress can't keep ramming these social programs down our throats and tell us that it's good for us. We don't want that. They've awakened a sleeping giant."

"Who's that?"

Henry sipped. "The American electorate. They're tired of their representatives voting their own political ideology rather than the will of the people."

"Are you one of those right-wing extremists, Mr. Rush?"

He laughed, slightly.

"I'm an American," he said candidly. "I believe in eternal freedoms, not bailouts and free lunches."

I scribbled.

"I served in the military," he said, "I fought for my country, and I didn't do it for these flaming idiots who want the government to pay for everything."

"What was your take on the Capp murder?" I asked.

"As a military man or just a citizen?"

"Either…"

Henry pulled up a chair, flipped it so the back was against the edge of the table and sat down, saddle style. His hands cradled his cup as if the liquid inside was warming his fingers. An old, weathered watch wrapped around his wrist and his shirt was worn thin. He seemed like an honest man who just wanted to be heard. Frustration oozed from his pores, making it easy for me to understand his thoughts and feelings.

I imagined Henry on the stand during his trial. He was going to make a wonderful witness on his own behalf. The prosecution was going to have a tough time bagging this old bird, not just because Rush was so believable, but because the prosecutor and the good congressman were both dead.

"As a citizen, I was shocked at how that military group pulled it off. It's like they took their pent up anger and put it into action. I know exactly how they feel, but I would never have gone through with that."

My pen was in overdrive.

"As a military man," he continued, "I think the people who pulled off the mission did it with amazing precision. It's like they thought of every angle. I think that they must have had some military training to pull it off. Special operations maybe."

"What about the police?"

"What about them?"

"Do you think the police might have helped?" I asked.

"You never know. There's a lot of crooked cops out there."

"When does your trial start?" I asked.

"Next week. It was supposed to start this week, but the prosecutor killed herself the day before we were supposed to start." He raised his eyebrows and shrugged his shoulders. "Her replacement wanted at least a month to prepare but my lawyer argued against it and the judge agreed."

"Doesn't that sound fishy?" I asked.

"What? That she killed herself the day before my trial?"

"Yeah."

"I guess, but she had a lot of other trouble on her plate."

"Oh?"

Henry took a big swallow. "Keep in mind that a lot of federal laws are written so broadly that federal prosecutors can string up just about anybody they want. It creates a system that is driven by politics, not necessarily justice."

"How do you know all this?"

Henry laughed. "My lawyer told me, and I looked into it. I got nothing else to do, Derrick."

I was staring at him.

"This is my case," he said "I'm in the fight of my life. The prosecutor was Capp's hired goon. Three years ago she was

written up for withholding evidence. Eventually they trans-
ferred her to Bay City because of all the bad publicity. That was
the first thing my lawyer asked the Department of Justice at the
bond hearing."

"What did your lawyer ask?" I needed clarification.

"If the prosecutor was withholding evidence."

"Was she?"

"They wouldn't say anything about it."

Henry had all the answers.

"My lawyer also told me that most of those prosecutors
have incentives for the number of cases they prosecute, and
hardly any sanctions for crossing ethical boundaries."

"I know, but, Mr. Rush, *she killed herself the day before your
case went to trial?*"

"Don't look at me," he said defensively. "They looked into
it. The police. All their detectives. They didn't find anything
wrong."

All I could do was eye him up.

"I'm just a penny-ante kind of criminal," he said "I got on
the wrong side of Congressman Capp by hassling him the way
I did."

At nearly six o'clock that evening, I took a couple of pictures of Henry Rush on the driveway in front of his cabin. He
was leaning against the trunk of his old Buick, just above the
bumper sticker that read *you look like a sissy in your foreign car.*
He didn't smile for the lens, but that was okay; the wrinkled
American flag in the background provided a stark contrast to
his clear, honest face. The photos were worth a thousand words
apiece, which was all the help I needed to complete my story
for the paper.

Instead of driving home the same way I came, I decided to
tiptoe across the soul of Ogemaw County's farm country. The

barns, the fieldstone farmhouses—everything—seemed to glow
in the dinner-time calm of a late June evening. I noticed a couple
of farmers who were working their hayfields and I wasn't sure if
it was the first or second cutting. For a moment or two I thought
about Eli's operation and whether he was doing the same.

By the time I made it to the bar at the Willow Tree restaurant
just south of West Branch, I was ready for something to drink.
A beer sounded wonderful—then again, so did a vodka tonic. I
resisted the urge for both and ordered a glass of water instead.

"Very well," the bartender said. "Would you like a menu?"

"Yes."

"My name is Rochelle."

"Thank you."

A second or two later, Rochelle had my silverware and water on a paper placemat. I looked down and read the ads: lawyer
Jacob Chitwood had the center all to himself. Surrounding him
were the real estate, chiropractic centers, insurance agencies
and two or three dentists. Chitwood's ad was huge; he wasn't
afraid to flaunt his picture, and boasted about the locations of
his offices in Grand Rapids and Traverse City. I knew that he
had spent a small fortune on advertising, and I made a mental
note to call his office about placing an ad in our paper.

The Detroit Tigers were in the seventh inning of their ball
game against the Baltimore Orioles. I didn't care about listening
to the announcers on the television behind me; a black dude in a
polyester jump suit was belting out a variety of oldies not ten feet
away from me. The music was canned, but his voice was wonderful and the songs that he sang reminded me of the days when
Grandpa and Grandma used to dance at weddings and family re-
unions. For some reason, I couldn't forget the lyrics to *Wives and
Lovers: "Run to his arms whenever he comes home to you."* Ain't that
a fact, Jack. Whoever wrote that line knew what he were talking
about. It makes a man feel good to have his woman miss him.
And what the heck, I was missing my woman, too.

After placing my dinner order, I realized that someone had sent me an e-mail, *Where RU?*

Ever since Colleen had gotten involved with the Heretic Fringe, she used a variety of e-mail addresses. I didn't recognize the address on my mobile phone, so I typed, *is that u, queen M.I.L.F.?*

Yup, the Mom you'd Like to Fondle. Where RU?

W Branch, eating dinnR.

BummR. Got an early morning appointment in Houghton Lake, she typed. *Going to bed early and was hoping for a little ct.*

CT?

Cuddle time.

Rain check?

Sure.

Don't wait up. Lub you, I served.

Lub you more, she returned volley.

Her electronic company was the best I could muster, but it was better than dining alone. If Colleen couldn't join me, I'd just as soon be chitchatting with a perfect stranger. A good story and new friendship are only a handshake away. Everybody has a story to tell about the life they've lived. With a little spice and imagination, even the most mundane existence can be an entertaining affair.

When dinner and the ball game were finished, I jumped back on the bike and made my way south and west towards Gladwin. Even though it was quite dark, I decided to take a small detour and roll past Eli's farm. It seemed odd to check in on my Amish pals, especially at that time of night, but sometimes harmless urges turn into wondrous events.

At nearly ten-thirty that evening, I turned off the bike's motor a hundred yards before I reached Eli's farm. The bike's momentum carried me over a small hill near his house, past his long driveway, and onto the flat where his barn was built. I took off my helmet, kicked the stand into position on the shoulder of the road, and listened to the noise of mid-Michigan, well past sundown. Dad's bike was catching its breath, so I walked several steps closer to the barn.

The sounds of the night surrounded me. I heard the cattle not far away and the way they chewed their cud with that rhythmic clench. One of Eli's Guernsey's must have had a piece of grass stuck in its throat because it kept hacking, swallowing hard, then hacking some more.

A car, chattering along the side road some distance away, distracted my attention for several seconds. I watched its taillights roar past the burned-out schoolhouse about a half mile away and came to a rolling stop at the railroad tracks.

Except for the subtle hum from Eli's generator behind the farmhouse, mid-Michigan was deathly quiet. Aside from the light in Eli's basement, and the fireflies skating across the evening theater, it was completely dark.

I had to wonder what was going on in Eli's basement. Was Rebecca down there, pecking away one-handed at the keyboard, creating an invoice for one of the many grocery stores that carried her bread? Was she doing her bookkeeping and worrying about a certain store whose invoice was ninety days overdue? Perhaps she was doing her banking and taking pride in knowing that her balance had climbed into five digits. Maybe six.

I'm not sure why I stopped at Eli's farm. It's like I was drawn to it like a moth to a mercury light. There was no rhyme or reason. I just wanted to take a short break, and there's nothing wrong with that.

By the time I made it home an hour or so later, Colleen didn't exactly run into my arms like the song suggested, but that was okay. She was fast asleep and snoring, momma-bear style. When I crawled into bed, she placed her hand on my elbow and sighed "Good night, Baby."

"Good night. Colleen."

That was the end of my day.

Thirteen

THE FOLLOWING MORNING I woke up relatively early, had a quick breakfast with my daughter, and dropped her off at the sitter's house. From there, I made it to the newspaper and fleshed out the following day's edition. Walter Claety had submitted a bunch of photos and a story about an encounter with a grizzly bear out west. Even though Walter is a great editor and newspaperman, he's not the best writer in the world. I'd have to clean up his stuff when I returned to the office.

I'm not sure why I decided to drive to Midland to attend the funeral. After all, I never knew the now-deceased federal prosecutor, nor had any interest in the cases she was handling. The only reason I felt like I ought to go was to quench my investigative juices.

Arriving at the church forty minutes before the start of the service gave me plenty of time to stake out a place to photograph the attendees. That practice has become ritual for me ever since I had watched the first half hour of *The Godfather* and the way the FBI scratched the wedding guests' license plate numbers on their pocket notebooks. Why they needed that information was never really explained in the movie, but I figured that if that ploy was good enough for the FBI several decades ago, it was good enough for me, too.

Some churches lend themselves to such clandestine activities, while others have too many entrances and not enough "cover" in order to be effective. The church in Midland was almost perfect. I eased into the lot, cruised around the perimeter, then backed into a parking space in the shade of a massive white pine. The attendees would roll into the lot, find their place to park, then stroll past me forty yards away. I'd get a good look at their faces, and the camera would be in overdrive. In a lot of ways, the set up at the church was a lot like turkey hunting, when strategy is paramount to luck.

The funeral directors dallied outside the door of the church and held bundles of "funeral" flags in their hands. They never thought twice about me reading a newspaper in my car. I was just another out-of-town guest with a penchant for arriving early. Then again, I could have been an FBI agent, there on a hunch that maybe the decedent's suicide wasn't self-inflicted after all.

The driver's side window was down, and I had my sunglasses on. My car wasn't exactly square inside the parking place, but somewhat cockeyed so that the side-view mirror wouldn't obstruct my line of fire, so to speak. The hearse sat at the curb twenty yards away, and the attendees would have to walk around it on their way to the church doors.

July was almost here. The sun was warm and powerful, and it baked the asphalt parking lot into a gigantic, painted cookie sheet. The heat rose in undulating, silent waves.

A black Escalade pulled into the parking lot and I assumed it was the decedent's parents, husband, and two children. All five of them were dressed in black, even the little girl who couldn't have been more than four or five years old. The husband carried the grieving daughter in his arms; her dimpled hands were wrapped around her dad's neck and shoulders. The son—maybe twice his sister's age—was sandwiched between his grandparents, who held his hands in their own. As hard as it was to keep their heads held high, eventually the parents of the departed looked towards the sidewalk, tears rolling down their cheeks. It was painfully sad.

Eventually, all five of the prosecutor's family approached the front door of the church, which was held open by the funeral directors. When the family disappeared inside, the staff proceeded to walk down the sidewalk until they reached the parking lot. Once there, they adorned the family's Escalade with a funeral flag. That must have been the protocol for the funeral directors—wait until people had left their vehicles, then put the flag on the hood. As they approached my vehicle, I eased farther into my seat; the camera on my lap and my finger on the trigger.

Not long after, more people arrived. Neighbors, relatives, family friends, I guessed. I caught the men in focus as they pulled their sport coats from the hangers in the back seat, and the women touched up their makeup in the passenger-side mirrors. An elderly gentleman rolled past me in his Crown Victoria. He was barely able to see over the steering wheel, and parked five feet past the yellow dividing line, oblivious to the obstacle he had created.

It felt good to be on the front line of the action. Vehicles kept coming at me. The folks from the Department of Justice were easy to spot. Two sedans filled with men cruised into the parking lot. The "Government" license plate and the parking pass dangling from the rearview mirror were sure tipoffs to their employer. When the men poured out of their vehicles, it appeared as if they all bought their outfits from the same government-approved department store. Their suits were navy blue or a bland shade of gray; white, starched shirts and stiff, polished shoes. They turned off their cell phones and put away their sunglasses as they walked inside.

I didn't have to wait long for their female counterparts from the office to arrive. They were driving the same kind of sedan as the men, but instead of parking in the same vicinity, they decided to roll up next to me. I put the camera on the seat next to me and covered it up with a section of newspaper. Instead of glaring right at them, I pretended like I was talking on my cell phone.

"What's happening?" I asked myself.

"Wow," I said, amused with the charade.

The women primped themselves slightly before they stepped out of the car. Even though I didn't want to stare at the driver, I couldn't help but notice her. She had cinnamon red hair and a beautiful smile. I could tell she had a lot of confidence, charm and ambition, just like my wife. I was willing to bet that this woman, whoever she was, made people feel good about themselves, not because she was fake or patronizing, but because she genuinely cared. The other members of her group smiled a lot too, and I presumed that they were the type of folks who were there to celebrate the prosecutor's life, not mourn her passing.

When the redhead stepped out of the driver's side door, I had to take note of the goods she was packing. She was tall and athletic, dressed to the nines, with just a few golden accoutrements, and was quite an eyeful if not a *tall glass of water.*

And without batting an eye, she said, "Morning."

I never even thought about my make-believe phone call; the redhead had taken away my ability to think straight.

"Morning," I said apologetically, "beautiful day for a funeral."

"I suppose you're right. The heavens are smiling upon us."

That was about the end of our exchange. I never thought anything of it, but as she marched away with the other members of her well-dressed entourage, I remember what my dad used to tell me, "It's okay to window shop."

Henry Rush was the complete opposite of the agents when it came to his wardrobe. He really wasn't out to impress anybody when he shuffled inside the church wearing his red suspenders, white shirt, and blue Dickie pants. Maybe he was going for the patriotic look.

As I watched Henry head for the door of the church, I figured it was almost time for the service to start. There were lots of people inside the church and I thought about putting on my sport coat and following suit. I was glad I waited.

A newer cargo van approached. On the front bumper was a license plate that read *God is my co-pilot.* I nonchalantly lowered the camera, and eased into my seat. The van drifted past me, and I made eye contact with both the driver and his female passenger in the front seat. On the side of the van were the words *Darlington Bible Church, Houghton Lake, Michigan.* Everything about it seemed like a normal church van until I read the bumper sticker on the caboose: *Fire the Democrats.*

After parking ten or twelve spots away from me, six or seven men and four or five women piled outside. None of them were dressed up, but they weren't slobs either. The men looked like they were wearing Wrangler jeans and golf shirts you could buy off the rack at Kmart for five dollars apiece. All the women, except one, had on a dress of some sort. The woman who wasn't wearing a dress had on brown denim slacks and a black blouse. She crossed her arms as she walked behind the entourage, making me think that maybe she felt a little out of place. Her intriguing physique and stride seemed familiar to me. I zeroed in on her face, and clicked four or five images, bing, bang, boom. The more I looked at her, the more familiar she became. The red wig threw me, but there was no mistaking the slight dimples beneath her eyes, the curve of her cheeks, and those heavenly lips. It was Colleen!

All of a sudden, I felt my blood boil. It surged like lava through my veins. *What the hell are you doing, woman?*

As the group came closer, I lowered the camera.

My hand was on the door handle; I was ready to fling it open and run after my baby.

Step by step they came.

My heart raced and the adrenalin wrecked havoc with my breathing.

She didn't see me.

None of them did.

They were chatting, but I didn't listen to what they had to say.

They were two car lengths away, then one.

Colleen was still behind the mob when one of them said, "Looks like we've got company, gang," pointing toward one the sedans. "Let's send them a message."

The whole group turned their attention to the sedans. When they spun, Colleen stepped my way slightly and slammed an index finger to her lips as if to say "Be quiet! It'll be okay."

"Okay, okay!" I spoke to myself.

The entire group stood in front of my vehicle, facing the opposite direction.

"Hand me an ink pen," one of the men barked. Two of the three women opened their purses and rifled through the clutter. "And some paper."

"Come on," Colleen urged them, "Let's get going. We're already late."

The men ignored Colleen's request and took a pen and paper from one of the women. They were milling around in front of me and I had a hard time seeing exactly what was going on. The leader of the group was crouched by the front tire, then he leaned over the hood of the sedan. He scribbled something on the paper and stuffed it under the windshield wiper, laughing angrily. Colleen shook her head and they all shuffled toward the door of the church.

I was relieved in a way; concerned in another. It was hard to watch my wife hanging out with that crowd. They weren't exactly skuzzy, but the monotony of their outfits and the obedience of the women was rather disconcerting. The men had their hair trimmed military tight, and the women's clothes looked as if they could have been homemade. Although I had no proof of it, it seemed like they had a strict, regimented hierarchy that they all observed. The way the women dressed and acted, it was almost like they were part of a secret sect.

When they disappeared inside the church, and my heart rate returned to normal, I jumped out of my car and marched to the windshield of the sedan. After unfolding the piece of paper, I read the note's three little words: *The Turner Dairies.*

What the heck, I thought. *Why would a dairy farmer from Houghton Lake have a beef with the federal government?*

My eyes led my head from the piece of paper to the trees on the edge of the parking lot. The clouds in the sky had no answers, either. It was baffling. I was confused.

"Excuse me, sir."

My daydream was interrupted by a member of the funeral staff who slid between the two sedans. He placed a funeral flag on the right side of each hood and wiggled through the maze of bumpers.

"Of course," I said.

It felt rather weird to be stuck in the parking lot like that, thinking, thinking, thinking about the note in my hands. Instead of standing there, I decided to go back to my car and consult the Internet on my phone. *Turner Dairies* produced a couple of hits—an ice cream and cottage cheese company from Wisconsin, and a wholesale food outfit in Arizona.

That couldn't be it, I thought.

The note had me completely stumped.

I must have sat in my car for ten minutes, thinking about everything that had just transpired. My wife was inside the church, hanging out with a group of people who could have been part of a secret sect. There was no way I was going inside now, but I didn't want to leave without toying with the creeps from Houghton Lake, either. This was my golden opportunity.

In big black letters, I wrote on my reporter's pad: *We know you did it.*

If they had any guilty conscience at all, they'd be squirming in their seats.

'*Did it*' could have meant anything. All the penny-ante crimes they committed would have come flooding back to their collective consciences.

Then again, if they did have something to do with the prosecutor's suicide, they really would have been nervous.

Either way, the last thing I cared about was if I upset them.

The bums deserved some unnerving.

I looked around. The funeral directors had split up and were either at the back door of the church or had already gone indoors. My vehicle had a mini-flag on the hood as did the others. All was well with the world.

Pulling away from the parking space, I turned down the lane between the cars and stopped behind the van. A second later, I jumped out of my car and was at the van's driver side quarter panel. It took a little effort to slide my note under the windshield wiper, as it was tucked beneath the cowling of the hood and cluttered with the propeller-shaped seeds from the maples. For half a second, I realized that I really shouldn't be doing this. Knowing my luck, the owners would have some sort of security system mounted in their vehicle and my image would be plastered all over their hangouts in Houghton Lake.

Undaunted, I left the note anyway.

Colleen and I didn't exactly exchange pleasantries when we met at home later that day.

"Why didn't you tell me you were going to the funeral?" she demanded.

"I just found out about it yesterday!"

"You could have blown my cover, Derrick."

"I could have blown my top for seeing my wife with a gang of right-wing radicals."

"I, I—"

"Couldn't you have just met them at the funeral?" I interrupted.

"No! Derrick, you don't understand."

"You're right, I don't understand."

Elizabeth didn't like what was taking place. In her innocent little voice, she urged us, "Somebody needs a time out…"

It worked. Colleen and I both took a deep breath, and we laughed.

"You're right, Elizabeth," Colleen said as she bent to Elizabeth's eye level. "Now, come here and give Momma a hug."

They embraced, bear-hug style. When they did, Elizabeth said, "Momma smells like cat pee."

I bit my tongue.

"Let's get some dinner going, shall we?" I suggested.

They both nodded.

Nothing satisfies the craving for an argument like a full tummy. In no time at all, I had five or six pieces of chicken shakin' and bakin', the rice sautéing, and Elizabeth had the package of veggies in the microwave. Jacque was fed and watered and Elizabeth retrieved the mail. Colleen disappeared to the opposite end of the house and I presumed it was to take a quick shower.

A "time out" was exactly what we needed.

Colleen and I waited until the end of the day to sort out what had taken place, and when we did, our emotions were riled again.

"What the hell were you thinking?" she asked. "'*We know you did it*?"

"What?" I tried to play dumb, and then turn the tables on her: "Why would he leave a note about the Turner Dairies?"

"It's the friggin' *diaries*, Derrick, not the *dairies!*"

It took me a moment to realize the misunderstanding. "How was I supposed to know he didn't know how to spell?"

I wasn't exactly yelling, but I was a little anxious.

Colleen sighed.

We were on the deck, sitting around the patio table. Colleen had a glass of wine in hand. I had a lemonade.

It was like we both had a difficult time getting to the bottom of the issue.

She said it again, " 'We know you did it.' Why would you write that?"

"I had to think of something…they're just scary people, Colleen. I don't know how else to say it."

"I know, but what did they do to make you want to say that?"

"The prosecutor's suicide. I don't think she killed herself."

Colleen huffed. "That never entered their minds. They were more concerned with the tire that they slashed."

"They slashed a tire? When did they do that?"

"On the way out of the service. They were the first ones out of the funeral and realized that the note was gone."

"Were they mad?"

"Well, not really, because you never left your name," she sighed. "You really don't want to mess around with these people."

"Why not?"

"I told you before. *The Turner Diaries.* These people believe in it. They think of it as their modern-day Bible."

"And?" I wanted her to tell me more.

"And if they don't overthrow the government, it's not because they didn't try."

"What are you getting at?"

"They think the government's got way too much power, way too much control. We've drifted away from the Lord's will and away from what the framers of the Constitution wanted."

"And what does that all mean?"

"They answer only to God, and they hate the government."

"So that gives them the right to slash the agents' tires?" I asked.

"No," she said, sipping her wine, "heavens no, but they think they're at war."

"Why do you want to hang out with these people?"

"I'm not hanging out with them, Derrick; I'm trying to get the story. That's all."

"Who are you going to sell it to?"

"I don't know. Why does that matter?" She was reeling. "I'm not doing it for the money. It's exciting and a sign of the times."

"What do you mean?" I asked her.

"It's exciting and dangerous," she said. "This whole right-wing radical movement is a sign of the times. We've got high unemployment, record foreclosures, high gas prices, and out of control rage. There are lots of angry people out there. I happen to be tapped into it, that's all. Tomorrow they're going to pick up the Ivey brothers from South Haven."

"Spike strip Ivey brothers?"

"That's right. They posted bail a long time ago."

"I have a question, Colleen. How did those two brothers from South Haven find their way to Houghton Lake?"

"That's easy," she said. "They have a family cottage on Lake Margrethe, west of Grayling, and I understand that they've been up in the North Country finalizing plans to build or remodel a factory in Traverse City."

"What kind of factory?" I asked.

"Canning. Their family owns Continental Foods and now they're trying to expand their business from canned blueberries down south to cherries up here."

"Interesting," I nodded. "So somehow while they were up here scouting things out for the factory, they got hooked up with the guys from Houghton Lake?"

"You got it."

"So, they're in South Haven?"

"No, in Bay City at the federal court," she added. "The rest of the men are waiting for the results of the grand jury. Of course, the government is going to have to find a new prosecutor."

"Why's that?"

"She killed herself. We were at her funeral!"

I sighed.

"What?" she leaned on me.

Neither Colleen nor I had any idea why each other had attended the same funeral. We were working two sides of the same story, but arrived at the funeral from different directions. It was about time that we laid our cards on the table, so I told her all about Henry Rush. She absorbed everything I had to say and didn't try to minimize my worries when I said, "I don't know where this story is headed, but I can tell you the further I get into it, the less I like it."

"What do you mean?"

"I have to tell you that this Dr. Ong has really been helping me, but in an indirect way. He tells me that once I figure out how to put a positive spin on Marshall Yandle, it'll be easier to quit drinking once and for all."

"I'm listening."

I found myself rubbing my eyebrows with the tips of my fingers. It was a gut-wrenching kind of confession and one that left me completely vulnerable. "When I shot in the schoolhouse I thought it would be the end of the story."

Colleen didn't interrupt me, for which I was thankful. There's nothing worse than having a spouse tell you how you should feel.

"In reality, it was just the beginning," I said, softly.

She sipped her wine, but her eyes never wavered.

"I'm worried about you," I continued, "and I'd hate to see you get into trouble with that group up north. I don't want to talk you out of covering the case, but I don't want anything bad to happen to you, either. I love you, Babe."

Colleen smiled. "Bless you, Derrick. I'm a big girl and I know how to handle myself. Have you forgotten about that time down in St. Martin when I saved you from those goons?

Remember the way I hit that guy in the head with that minia-ture baseball bat?"

I laughed, "Oh yeah. I can still hear the sound of his skull mashing."

"Or how about the time I went undercover when you need-ed my help finding Capp's aide up north?" she asked.

"That's when you bought that red wig you had on today."

We were smiling in a tender kind of way.

"That's right," she said. "I can handle this."

I knew she was going to say that.

"Besides, this is going to get interesting."

"Why do you say that?"

"The trial is next week for the Ivey brothers."

"Their murder trial?"

"Conspiracy. Aiding and abetting, malicious destruction of public property, stuff like that. There will going to be reporters there from all over the country."

"Where?"

"Flint," she said, eyebrows raised.

"Not Bay City?"

"No. The lawyers already filed a change of venue because they couldn't get a fair trial so close to the incident in Standish."

"Whose lawyers?"

"Our government's lawyers, the U.S. Attorney's office. They have acknowledged through newspaper and television in-terviews with the press that the public outcry over the incident would keep them from getting a guilty verdict."

"So, the government likes their chances in Flint a lot better than they do up north."

"You got it. What do you think?"

It didn't take long to answer. "I'd say they're right."

Fourteen

I AM A LUCKY GUY to have Colleen in my life. She is a strong woman in every way: emotionally, spiritually, physically. She's a great mother, a decent cook, and above all else, my biggest fan. That's not to say that she's a pushover; she'd put me in my place if the situation called for it.

Her most admirable attribute is her ambition. She's constantly on the fly—getting things done, planning ahead, plotting a course, setting more goals, and crossing others off her list.

I often think of her as my best friend.

She loves me unconditionally, without prejudice; with humor and encouragement, and an unwavering commitment. There's nothing she wouldn't do for me, at least that's what I've often thought.

I have what every man wants in a woman and I don't know where I'd be without her.

Yeah, I do.

I'd be lost.

Incredibly lonely.

A fish out of water.

My fear of losing her fueled my anxiety.

As strong as my feelings were about the strength of our relationship, I hated seeing my girl hanging out with those people from Houghton Lake. I felt a twinge of jealousy and the slightest stab of insecurity. There would be no way that she'd ever leave me for one of those men, but she might end up in jail because she was a conspirator in their plot to overthrow the government. Colleen loves me and I love her; we have a nice little life together. On one hand, I was convinced that everything was okay, on the other hand my insecurities told me that maybe there were some fissures starting to develop in our relationship. Did I have anything to worry about? I don't know.

At our next session, Dr. Jim listened to me ramble about her for probably a half hour. Slowly, but surely, the guy was getting to know everything about me. I shared more about myself with him than I had with most of my friends, and that made me feel a little vulnerable, which made me even more insecure. It was a Catch-22 or a dog chasing its tail.

In a lot of ways I'm like most men—if something's broken, I want to fix it. If something isn't working, I want to change it. All I wanted to do was protect Colleen from danger, from temptation, from the trouble lurking like a snake in the grass. She was getting more and more involved with this Heretic Fringe, and it had made me quite worried.

Dr. Jim agreed with me. Or, at least he understood how I could be so concerned.

"You never really said what her political views are," he said. "Does she share the group's philosophy about politics or is she just along for the ride?"

"She's investigating them. It's work to her."

Jim nodded. "So she's really not a radical."

"That's right."

"What are they up to now?"

"I'm not entirely sure, but I haven't seen her much since the trial started this week."

"Whose trial?"

"Henry Rush."

"I know who he is. He's the guy from Frankenmuth who told Capp he should be hung from the Mackinac Bridge."

"You're right."

"She's covering the trial, is that right?" he asked.

"No, no, Jim, I'm the one who's been gone," I said. "I'm the one who's covering the trial, and she's taken over at the paper until our manager returns from vacation."

"I see. Didn't the case get sent to the jury today?"

"Yeah, it was. How'd you know?"

Jim shrugged his shoulders. "I follow this stuff too, you know. It's part of my job."

"What do you mean?"

"I'm a psychologist and a jury consultant. I do psychological analysis for defense attorneys or the prosecution."

"How does that work?"

"Sometimes I get involved with civil matters, too." Jim put the cap back on his pen and tugged at the top of his socks. "I don't get involved with the smaller cases; it's usually for the high-profile matters."

"So, you must have had a lot of training."

"Well, yeah. I've got master's in behavioral psychology and, of course, my Ph.D. to treat patients."

"What's your take on the outcome of the Rush matter?"

"I don't know, Derrick. I wasn't even there. What do you think?"

"Who knows? I liked Rush's attorney. Sharp guy. He's playing the sympathy card, because of Rush's age and his military service. Of course, the government had to put a new attorney on the case since the original prosecutor committed suicide."

Jim asked for more details, so I kept rambling.

"The government had a new chief prosecutor, who really didn't know what was going on, but they also kept the same cute redhead as his assistant."

"What do you mean?"

"The redhead was really good looking. Dressed up. High heels. The whole ball of—"

"No, no that's not what I meant," Jim said. "I was referring to the way they kept dropping the ball."

"Oh, yeah," I said. "He kept mispronouncing words."

"Seriously? Like what?"

"Like where Rush was from, Frankenmuth."

"What about it?" he asked.

"His Frankenmuth sounded like 'youth,' and every time he said it I could see the jurors shaking their heads. It's like they were wondering *Where'd they find this cupcake?*"

Jim laughed, "That's the kiss of death."

I laughed, too, even though I wasn't exactly sure what he was talking about.

"Any decent lawyer will tell you that you've got to be empathetic," he said. "You're not empathetic if you're mispronouncing words that are directly related to the case."

"Sounds like you think that the prosecution is going to have a hard time winning this one."

"Sure he is. And let me tell you something: federal prosecutors hate losing."

"Doesn't everybody?"

"Well, yeah, but if you're a defendant in federal court, you've broken some sort of federal law. That's called a felony— a lock-the-door-and-throw-away-the-key kind of offense. That kind of case usually means that there's a lot of media attention."

I nodded.

"Was the courtroom packed?"

"Of course."

"How'd you get in? I mean, aren't there strict rules about gaining access to federal trials?"

"Sure there are, but I still have my credentials from the Associated Press."

Now Jim was the one who was nodding.

"I suspect that Mr. Rush will be back to making jelly and jam in no time at all."

We were nearing the end of our session, I could tell. It just felt like an hour had elapsed. Dr. Jim always seemed to have an ace up his sleeve when it came to the last few minutes of our appointment. Getting in the last word wasn't Jim's goal, but I think that he liked to make sure that I had plenty to think about until our next appointment. Jim's grandfather clock in the corner was tick-tocking away, but I didn't dare glance its way.

"You haven't really mentioned if you've been drinking."

"Heck, I haven't had time for it."

"What about the pills?"

I shook my head.

"Ever think about it?"

"Sure. I'd be lying if I said no."

"Is it hard?"

"Yeah, it is, but I try to stay busy."

"Does Colleen help or hinder you?"

"She's a help, no question about it. I mean she likes to have a cocktail, a nightcap at the end of the day. By then I've pretty much lost my interest."

Jim leaned into his question; "Ever think about Marshall Yandle?"

I hesitated.

"I'm not really sure what you mean."

"The man you killed. Marshall Yandle."

"Well, I don't think about him personally, but I do think about the incident."

"So, you've separated the incident from the person."

"I guess I have. Marshall Yandle, the human being, the man is not on my mind. What I can't get out of my mind is his head exploding when I squeezed the trigger."

"Interesting. Why don't you think about the man?" he asked.

"I guess I don't want to know about him. He was about ready to murder those kids, and I had to do what I had to do."

"Was there any doubt in your mind what you should have done?"

"Not really. What are you getting at?" I asked him.

Jim shrugged his shoulders as if he was trying to deflect my glare. "What if the guy you shot was really one of the kids' parents? Or an unarmed citizen? You could have been in huge, huge trouble."

I sighed. *The guy's line of questioning really didn't help much.* "Well, Jim, it's really a moot point, isn't it?"

"You're right. You're right."

Jim closed his folder. I glanced at the clock. We had only a minute to go.

"One last thing," he said. "What *do you know* about Yandle?"

"Very little, other than he was the *head* of the militia group in Houghton Lake."

Jim acknowledged my little pun with a quick smile, but it didn't deter him from another inquiry.

"The thing that's really been stirring in my mind is why did Marshall Yandle end up at that Amish farm?"

I shrugged my shoulders.

"Of all the places you could have crossed his path, you had to have met him there." He smiled in a strange kind of way. "Why is that?"

"I give up," I said sheepishly. "But I'll look into it."

Fifteen

S UMMER HAD CAST ITS DREAMY SPELL ON THE LAND. Days were
hot and long, while evening seemed to languish for hours.
It was the time of year when the canoe liveries made their
money, campgrounds hung signs that read "all full" at park
headquarters, and golf courses offered "twilight rates" after six.
By then, the corn had sprouted tassels and its musky, pollen-
scent was nearly edible on the gravel roads and farm fields of
mid-Michigan. Summer was a time for getting things done; for
making things happen; for building a one-room schoolhouse
on the corner lot of Eli's farm.

At least a dozen Amish buggies were parked in the shade of
giant oak trees on the edge of the school property. Several hay
wagons—piled high with rough-hewn lumber—baked in the
sun next to the cinderblock foundation. There were children.
Lots and lots of children. They ran around the construction site
in grass so long that it nearly touched their pant hems. Neither
the boys nor the girls were noisy or mischievous, but full of
energy and that wholesome, care-free kind of propulsion associated with youth. One of the boys—perhaps four or five years
old—tugged at the apron of his mother and pointed to the
other boys in the group. She dismissed his tattling as frivolity,
patted him on the seat of his homemade jeans, and sent him on
his barefooted way. Her body language said it all, "Run along,
now. It'll be okay."

Besides, it seemed his mother had more important matters to attend. She was in the shade of a corner oak tree, and together with a handful of other women, was getting ready for the noon meal. Two of the huskier women were pushing wooden picnic tables together, while the youngsters adorned each end of the tablecloths with quart jars of pickled something. Whatever was inside the jars didn't matter; they kept the tablecloths from blowing away in the warm breeze. Eli's wife unwrapped a loaf of sourdough with her stub for an arm while Mrs. Hooley, The Pig Butcher, picked up a wicker basket from the back of a buggy and carried it to the picnic tables. Her Parkinson's didn't seem that bad.

It was anything but quiet. The men were hard at work, baking in the sun. Several were driving nails, while two younger men were bent over their hand saws, plowing though each board stroke by stroke. I noticed the backs of the men and the way the sweat had stained their shirts and the rim around their homemade jeans. Corn pollen wasn't the only palatable hormone swirling in the August breeze.

Everyone seemed to have a role. The elders did the measuring, the young men the sawing and the middle-aged men, the hammering. No blueprints or a set of plans; it was like they all were on the same mental page when it came to construction. A couple of younger women had a wooden tray loaded with glasses filled with what looked like iced tea. They carried it to the men who picked up a glass and poured the contents down their throats without saying "Thank you" or "Whew, that was great" or express any form of gratitude. In a way, the cold drinks were something that seemed to be expected. Not even the young men paid any attention to the young women; it was like they all knew there was work to do.

But it wasn't all serious. After parking the truck and approaching the building site, I heard whistling. The theme song from *Three's Company.*

It had to be Eli.

It was.

He was inside the foundation—between the rows of floor joists—white plastic pipes scattered near his feet.

"*Come on knock on our door. We've been waiting for you,*" I sang.

He laughed. "We don't exactly have a door for you to knock on. What are you doing here?"

"I want to help," I said, rather loudly.

One of the elders took off his straw hat, wiped his face with a hanky, and gave me the watchful eye.

"Good. Hand me dat glue," Eli said.

There were actually two, pint-sized cans on the edge of the foundation. I picked up the primer and handed it to Eli who was wedged between the joists.

"Thanks," Eli said, smiling.

"What are you making?" I asked.

"Well, in dah simplest of terms, indoor plumbing."

"Cool."

Eli held a piece of pipe that was maybe ten feet long and six inches in diameter. He had punched a hole through the cinder blocks, large enough for the pipe to pass. On the outside of the wall, he had dug a trench through the earth, which led to a giant underground vault.

"Let me guess: that's the pipe that will go from the toilet to the septic tank."

"Dat's right," Eli said, unscrewing the cap off the primer. "Dah kids have had to use the outhouse, but we plan on putting in a well. Might as well do dah bathroom now, as opposed to waiting until dah well has been dug."

Eli tamped the primer wand on the edge of the can, then scored the edge of the plastic pipe. He did the same routine on the inside of an elbow-shaped connector, before reaching for the glue. I handed him the can, and just like that, the elbow and the pipe were connected.

I didn't dare ask him what the elders thought of the concept of indoor plumbing. This probably wasn't the best time to stir the pot, so to speak.

Eli wrapped a wire coat-hanger around the pipe, then hung it from one of the floor joists. It seemed like for now his work underground was through.

When he stood, I asked him how he planned on getting the water from the well to the toilet without the use of electricity.

"Propane. You can do a lot of things with propane."

"Including heat, right?"

"That's right. Dah old school was poorly insulated and it only had a wood stove."

"So I take it you'll have a furnace in here too?"

"A small one. Here, give me a hand." I gave him a heave-ho, and he appeared topside.

Eli brushed the dirt from his jeans and he wiped his brow.

"Are you going to help us or what?" an elder asked.

Eli and I both looked at the elder, ten paces away. He and the others were lined up, ready to hoist a wall of studs. We grabbed hold of the monstrosity and gave it a shove. It was quite heavy. Up it went, perfectly straight, remarkably plumb with the foundation.

"Hold 'er there boys," the elder cried as he and another long beard rammed a two-by-six under the structure. "Okay, good. Steady now."

I looked to my right and recognized a blue-eyed Mr. Yoder. On my left were the two young men who were the brawn behind the saws. Both were stocky and round-shouldered and their thumbs seemed to grow out of their wrists. When they smiled I noticed the crooked teeth so small they looked like they could have been baby teeth.

"We got it," the elders said, "let 'er go."

We all backed away from the two-by-six studs and miraculously, the wall stayed right where it was. It looked rather precarious sitting there—all that weight supported by two boards.

"Now let's get this sidewall put together."

One by one, the middle-aged men moved the sawhorses to the rear of the foundation. They hauled the lumber from the wagons to the sawhorses in preparation of building another wall of studs.

"Twenty-four feet, six inches," the elders cried. "So cut the boards at four feet six."

"Got it."

The young men readied their saws. When the lines on the boards were scribed with a heavy carpenter's pencil, I realized that the two men were having a competition to see who could cut through the boards faster. In a country bumpkin kind of way, it was a mild amusement, and one that everyone in the group seemed to appreciate.

If had a gambling problem, instead of a plain old drinking problem, I might wager on who was going to cut through the boards faster.

As much as I wanted to say something along those lines, I knew that the decorum didn't call for it.

And when it came right down to it, the young men didn't need any added incentives for speed; they tore through the boards in no time at all. Each board would be used to make a double layer of two-by-eights for the top and bottom of the wall. The ten-foot sections of two-by-sixes would form the wall joists, to match the first wall already in place. When the young men finished cutting, the older men knew exactly what needed to be done. Every man but me was wearing a leather-bound carpenter's belt complete with a metal ring for his hammer handle to fit into. I wish I would have brought my belt so I would have fit in with the guys. Then again, if I had my own belt, they might have expected me to know which end of a hammer to pick up.

As busy the setting, I couldn't help but stop and think about what a nice undertaking this was. Everybody was merrily pitching in, in a communal kind of way.

Well, almost everybody. Despite the warm breeze and the occasional bellow from one of the cattle, I heard some commotion coming from the outhouse. Some of the older boys had barricaded the door, so whoever was inside couldn't get out. The person trapped within was banging on the door and screaming at the top of his lungs. His cries for help were drowned in the summer breeze. Nobody else seemed to care about what was taking place, and I really didn't feel right about bringing it to their attention. After all, I was an outsider.

And it's not like the men in the group didn't see what was going on. They looked at the boys and never even raised an eyebrow. Unless there was some sort of emergency, the men couldn't care less.

They would have cared if they had to ride home next to the child who was stuck inside. Even if it was the "off season" for the outhouse, it still must have reeked with all that heat, all that humidity.

I hate outhouses.

Doesn't everybody?

I didn't have much time to think about the poor waif inside the outhouse because the women said it was time for dinner. The men didn't exactly drop everything and run over to the picnic tables. They milled around the construction site until the bottom row of boards was completed. In a lot of ways the men acted like Eli's herd of Guernseys and the way they meander to the barn when they are good and ready. Food could wait until the timing was just right.

I didn't want to be the first one to the table. Fortunately, the women came to the men and pried them away from their work. They lassoed the boys from the outhouse, and urged the girls who were climbing a tree.

We all sat down at the tables, which were pushed together in sets of two. The elders never said a prayer, but everyone lowered their chin and remained silent for a moment.

It was an old-fashioned picnic with thermoses of lemonade, fried chicken, potato salad, and Rebecca's sourdough. The pickled asparagus was surprisingly delicious, even though I had had my doubts about it. The kids were at the table and they watched me intently, but really didn't say much. Nobody did. Eating couldn't be mixed with talking.

Eli's bizarre eating habits were in overdrive, but his wife had planned for it. She had stacked three or four paper plates at his place setting, one for each part of the meal. Eli took full advantage of her thoughtfulness and ate each course on a fresh, clean paper plate.

Even though I had only been helping for an hour or so, it felt good to kick up my heels and relax. The others in the group seemed just as willing as I was to let the noon meal linger. It was hot. And the lemonade tasted wonderful. The longer we sat there, the more conversation took place.

For the boys in the group, however, there was adventure to be had. They downed their drinks and drifted off to their bicycles parked against the fence.

One of the elders said that they ought to finish the framing by the end of the day. Another one said that the materials for the steel roof would be delivered the day after tomorrow. For several minutes the men talked about a big job they had to do up north: How they were going to get there, where they were going to stay, and who was going to stay home and do the chores. I didn't think it was my place to ask about the details. The men were all business and the women were barely a distraction. It made me think that the women really weren't held in very high regard.

Maybe not all the women. Twice I saw Eli wink at Rebecca. He complimented her on the bread she had made, and squeezed her wrist, which made her smile.

By then the boys had zoomed up and down the driveway several times and the girls went back to the climbing tree. The men finished their drinks and brushed the crumbs from their beards. A couple of them loosened their work belts a notch. The women began tidying up the picnic site and I heard them mention that they had brought the materials to work on a quilt.

Everything in the world seemed so content, the Amish lifestyle so rewarding.

Until utter disaster occurred.

As we walked back to the building site, the lead boy in the entourage of bike riders whistled past us. He gained speed and momentum as he zoomed around the wagon full of lumber toward the two-by-six braces for the wall of timbers. He took the corner too fast—too wide, in fact—because he caromed into the brace. When he did, the wall of joists heaved perfectly vertical for an instant, which sent both braces free. The wall had nothing to support it, and in the breeze, began its lethal fall.

"Look out!" we all screamed.

Too late.

The two bike riders behind the first never saw the falling guillotine. Both of them rode straight into the danger.

It was horrible. One kid took the brunt of the fall across his arms and thighs. The other boy took it in the head. The force knocked them backwards, sideways, rasp over teakettle. We all ran to their aid. Their bikes were mangled. I saw the youngest boy's femur protruding through his homemade jeans. Blood was everywhere. In spurts and spatters. On their straw hats and paper-thin shirts.

"Angus! Angus! Angus!" one of the dads screamed.

I thought for a second that one of the cows had gotten loose and was about ready to trample us.

"My son!" Eli cried.

Oh, duh. Angus is the name of your son, I thought. *Now I understand.*

Craziness ensued as the men lifted the wall and the women rushed underneath to retrieve their children.

"Oh, my god! My god! My god!"

The boys beneath didn't know what hit them. They were mangled and twisted and lying there woozy still. It was worse than the incident in turkey season. I squeezed my eyes until I saw stars and no matter how hard I tried to blot out the terror in the parents' cries, I couldn't. They were beyond horrific.

One of the elders took his place next to me on the wall of wood and began saying the Lord's Prayer. I jumped in with him. We all did, except those who were trying to take charge, "Get some water!"

"Somebody call dah police!"

"No, wait!" I yelled, "It'll take too long to get here. Come on, we'll take my truck and call them on the way."

With that proclamation, I sprinted to my Suburban, started the engine, and threw it in reverse.

Seconds later, the men flung open the back doors, and began the process of carefully loading the two injured boys. Instead of keeping my eyes on the back of the Suburban, I watched the elders take umbrage with the older boy who caused all the grief. He was the one who had pinned another kid inside the outhouse and now his carelessness caused the tragedy. Either way, it was his time to pay the piper. The elders had him cornered against the fence near the buggies and judging from their body language, weren't very happy. The boy reluctantly took off his shirt and put his hands on the top rail of the fence. One of the elders reached into the buggy and pulled out a whip that must have been six feet long. I knew what was coming next.

A few seconds later the old Suburban was loaded and drove like a boat again. Instead of a leisurely cruise—as was the case when we were hauling the grain—I knew that I had to hurry. The women in the very back resumed their Our Father, only this time it was in Pennsylvania Dutch. It looked like they were straddling their children, facing the front. Their thumbs were wedged in their eye sockets, their fingers outstretched to form a point. With all the heads and hats and bonnets in the way, it was hard to see who they were. Besides, I had to keep my eyes on the road, my fingers on the keys of my cell phone, "Nine-one-one. What is your emergency?"

"We're on our way to Gladwin hospital. You'd better have the surgeon ready, and put the helicopter on notice. I've got two little boys who are going to need a lot of attention."

"You're on your way now, sir?"

"Yes."

"Which direction will you be arriving?"

"West."

Eli was seated directly behind me, but for the entire ride, he was bent over the seat, facing the grave situation in back. Gone were the sweat stains, the hardened, no-nonsense traits of his culture. It was Rebecca and him fawning over their little boy in the gravest of settings. Their love for that child was oozing from their pores.

Mid-Michigan was a blur at seventy-five miles an hour. A sheriff's deputy was expecting us and ran interference at every intersection.

It was madness when we arrived, but I'm glad I made reservations.

A host of nurses met us at the entrance. They were already dressed in their scrubs and head caps.

We piled out of the truck and let the nurses do their job. They were careful and quick, but I heard one of them utter notice that things didn't look promising, "Good heavens."

Cries erupted. Not sobbing, grief-filled wailing, but a quiet, heartfelt release of emotion. I handed my passengers a bundle of paper napkins from the glove box. They were thankful for the gesture and for the ride to town.

When the nurses took the boys inside, I moved my truck to the parking lot, not far away.

After several minutes, I made it back to the waiting room, and saw several Amish glued to the television set. Fox News had a panel of blonde political experts on the screen, and as much fun as it was to see what they were saying, it was even more fun to watch the Amish watch the commentators. It's like they were witnessing Martians emerge from a space ship with all their makeup, coifed hair and remarkable wardrobes. I wasn't about to judge the Amish. If television and Fox News helped them forget about their fallen members, it was okay with me.

Instead of staying in the waiting room, I decided to step outside and get some fresh air. An ambulance parked in front of the hospital put an end to that notion, however, as its noxious diesel fumes nearly overtook the setting. Farther and farther away I moved. By then, it was the middle of the afternoon, and I thought about sending Colleen an e-mail. I really wasn't sure of where she was, or what she was doing, let alone what address I should have used. She's constantly changing her e-mail address in an effort to keep her identity a secret. Just like a lot of couples, we were both so busy that we saw each other only for a brief time every day. Colleen's ears must have been ringing because she sent me an e-mail from a bizarre address while I was standing there, phone in hand.

Itz me, Colleen. W's hapning? she asked, which was her way of saying, "What's happening?"

Plnty, I typed.

Me, 2.

Like w? I asked.

Jry's in.

Jerry who?

No, the jury, Silly.

My attention was diverted for a half second as a helicopter appeared in the sky. Amidst the clattering blades and hammering engine, it slowly began its descent towards the rear of the parking lot, where a half-dozen large pylons marked the edge of its landing pad. It seemed to struggle in the gusty breeze, but managed to land without incident.

I gotta run, Babe. Lub you.

The Amish were the first ones who poured out of the emergency-room doors, making way for the nurses and gurneys not far behind. One boy went into the back of the ambulance, the other raced past me on his way to the helicopter. Little Angus Beiler had both arms and a leg in inflatable casts. He was flanked again by his mother and father who both wore sad, concerned faces. Through all the mayhem, however, I realized that there was a glimmer of hope in the dire situation: both boys were still alive.

There was help to be given, but I wasn't quite certain how to go about giving it. If they needed a ride back to the farm, I'd be happy to give it to them. If they wanted to use my phone for whatever reason, that was fine too.

The ambulance squelched its siren and zoomed out of the parking lot. The helicopter revved its motor, gained momentum and climbed into the air. My head was on a swivel between the two distractions. An Amish man and woman waited near the entryway, where the ambulance had been. Eli and two nurses walked back from the helicopter pad. I hooked up with them and we all went back to the entryway.

"Mr. Beiler, your son has three severely broken limbs," a nurse said. "He's going to need surgery. We're not equipped here to perform the operation he needs. The hospital in Saginaw is fully capable. They've got a surgeon waiting for Angus to arrive."

Eli's voice crackled with fear. "He's going to be okay, yes?"

The older of the two nurses hesitated, "This is quite critical, Mr. Beiler. Multiple broken bones can be a serious, serious thing."

Eli shook his head.

I put my arm around his shoulder and he turned in my direction. My act of comfort turned into a full-fledged bear hug. The nurses waited several seconds, then suggested that we head to Saginaw.

"Come on, I'll give you a ride."

Eli wiped a tear from his eye. "Just a minute." He walked in the direction of his neighbors, while the nurses waved goodbye. "I've got to make sure dey can get a ride home, and somebody looks after my family."

Even in all that pain and emotional turmoil, Eli had enough sense to make sure that his remaining blessings would be well taken care of.

Five minutes later, we were south of Gladwin on M-30 and had raced through the little town of Winegars, the turnoff for Estey, and crossed a handful of creeks that eventually make their way into the Tittabawasee River. Eli placed his straw hat on the bench seat between us. He stared through the windshield and blinked the blinks of remorse. The permanent smile etched beneath his cheeks had evaporated into the somber circumstance; all that remained was the bleak facial expression of an optimistic man presented with life's dismal setbacks.

To help lighten the rather pensive, speechless situation, I told Eli that it should take only an hour to get to the hospital.

He nodded slightly, then watched me fiddle with the navigation system on the dashboard.

"Saginaw's hospital is a really good one," I said. "Angus will be well taken care of."

Eli bit his lower lip, and shook his head. When he did, the hair on either side of his bald spot swung back and forth.

Fidgeting and fussing seemed to be Eli's way of dealing with stress. He jammed the very end of his thumb to his front teeth and tore off a tiny piece of skin. A second later the piece of skin landed on the dashboard, which was followed by another, and a fair-sized sliver of fingernail. My poor dashboard was flecked with Amish crumbs.

I had a hard time dealing with that. Not that I take great

pride in the cleanliness of my truck, but with the window close at hand, why wouldn't he simply flick the particles outside? My dad, Chick Twitchell, used to tell me, "You don't want to handle things twice," every time we had the septic tank pumped. This was a prime example of it. Somebody had to wipe off the dashboard and vacuum the floor and it seemed that there was no good reason for it. I remained quiet as the fingernails, the cuticles, the bits of skin piled up on the dashboard, the windshield, the passenger-side window. They were all over the place.

After we made the sweeping left turn east of Midland, Eli finally piped up and said what was on his mind.

"I hate to sound ungrateful, but ever since you came into our lives, we've had some awful bad luck."

Instead of defending myself, I wanted to hear more about what he had to say.

"What do you mean?"

He sighed. "I appreciate you giving me a ride to dah hospital."

"No problem."

"No really, I know these trucks really burn dah gas," he said, wagging a thick pointer finger my way. Eli reached into his pocket and pulled out a black leather wallet. The guy had a wad of bills stuffed inside that must have been a half-inch thick. He thumbed through the stash until he found just the right one.

"Here you go."

He placed a ten-dollar bill under the lid of his hat.

Not wanting to sound unappreciative, I said, "Thanks, Eli. What did you mean about the bad luck?"

He propped his chin on the palm of his hand, wrapped a thumb around his jaw, and pointed his index finger next to his nose. For a second there, I thought he was going to take his freshly trimmed finger and start digging inside a nostril.

Thank goodness, it was just the posture Eli took while thinking.

"First it was dah lawsuit. Then, it was dah shooting, and

now dis." He wasn't overly accusatory, but merely stating what was on his mind.

"The lawsuit with that Marshall fella?"

"Yeah."

"What about it?"

"I knew we shouldn't have gotten a lawyer."

"Oh, Eli."

"What? Dah Lord giveth and dah Lord taketh away. He would have taken care of us without the expense of a lawyer. I should have listened to dah elders and turned dah other cheek."

I shook my head. "We've already been over this. The Lord helps those who help themselves, too."

"If we'd have lost dah lawsuit and had to give up dah farm, we could have been in Pennsylvania by now."

"Is that where you'd rather be, Pennsylvania?"

"Either dat, or Ohio."

"That's what you get for hiring a good lawyer, Eli. You won. You saved the farm."

Eli returned to his vigil out the window. I looked for geese on the pond near the Dow complex, but didn't see any.

"There's nothing wrong with winning," I suggested. "You had no idea he was going to go postal."

"I had no idea he was going to go berserk, either."

I couldn't help but raise my eyebrows and stare in his direction. "That means the same thing, Eli."

He frowned as if to say "Whatever," then added, "You didn't have to dig up all dat stuff on Yandle."

"That 'stuff' was what made the difference in the lawsuit. Aren't you glad the jury got to know about his involvement in the militia?"

"Well, yah."

"It showed that he wasn't a reputable guy."

Eli didn't say a word.

"When I got pictures of him hauling lumber into the VFW

in Houghton Lake and working on the foundation for their new bathroom, it showed that he really wasn't all that injured. In the judicial system, that's how you win, Eli."

"I know but I felt like he may have been entitled to someting."

"You tried to settle with him. And remember when the case went to a mediator?"

He nodded.

"Yandle and his lawyers rejected both the offer and the mediation," I reminded him.

"I know but dah guy had dat scar on his face."

"That's true, but it's not like you were the one who cut him. You showed him how to run that saw, Eli, but he was the one who was using it."

I think he was feeling guilty for defeating Marshall Yandle in court. It seemed to go against his nature, in that he believed that confrontations could be settled by a firm handshake and an old-fashioned apology. Surely, Eli's testimony at the trial helped his cause. He was magnificent on the stand, and was so sincere that the jury dismissed the case.

Eli's lawyer made the jury believe that the Beilers were being picked on by modern society. He presented a case that sympathized with the Beilers and made it appear that they were simple folks with wholesome ways.

After the lawsuit was finalized, the Beilers had more trouble with their former employee, Marshall Yandle.

"I should have given him more instruction with dah saw. Maybe den he wouldn't have sued us, poisoned our dog, or hung dat calf from dah rafters."

Eli shook his head again.

I didn't say anything. We had been over this before, and Eli had no proof that Yandle was the one behind the animal killings. Then again, Yandle was the only suspect who had the motive to do it.

"So, aren't you glad that you won the case?"

"Well, yah."

"It appears that this whole thing is over now."

By then we were on I-75, just north of Saginaw. The traffic raced past my old Suburban, which had long since given up the urge to keep pace.

"My boy is going to be okay. He has to."

"Have faith in the doctors and nurses, Eli. They'll take good care of him."

He crossed his arms as we exited the expressway and turned towards the hospital.

"I was going to ask you, Eli, of all the places where Yandle could have gone—could have hidden—why do you suppose he went back to the schoolhouse after he killed the congressman?"

Eli struck that thinking man's pose and said, "I always figured dat he had one last score to settle. Like he had an axe to grind with dah congressman, and he wanted to get even with us before he was caught."

He had it all figured out. He knew what Yandle was like in every way. From what I knew about the situation, Eli's logic—his theory—seemed to make sense. I was half-thinking about my next appointment with Jim when Eli threw something at me from the sky blue: "Me and my wife were talking, Derrick, about dah situation and we tink it's a little odd that you happen to be at dah right place at dah right time."

I turned the corner into the hospital, past the flower beds and the neatly trimmed shrubs.

"What do you mean?" I scoffed.

Eli shrugged his shoulders and unbuckled his seatbelt. "Don't take dis dah wrong way, but dah way you were out dere hunting day after day, and hanging around dah farm, it's almost like you were waiting for Yandle to show up."

Now I was getting defensive. "What are you trying to say, Eli?"

I slowed the Suburban to a crawl.

Eli furled his lips, picked up his straw hat and reached for the door handle. "After dah kids ran home from dah schoolhouse dat morning, I went to your Suburban before dah police arrived. Your turkey decoys were in dah back seat, but I also found your machine guns, all sorts of ammo, and a bulletproof vest."

I raised my eyebrows in disbelief.

"We didn't tink dat dah police would look too kindly on dat, besides me and Rebecca were tinking dat maybe you weren't necessarily hunting turkeys, but—"

Eli opened the door, and flung a leg outside.

I grabbed his left forearm and squeezed. It felt like a combination of sweat and hair. "But what?" I demanded.

Eli yanked his arm free, pulled a hanky from his back pocket, and began wiping down the dashboard. The cuticles, fingernail clippings and bits of skin made a nice little pile in the palm of his free hand.

"But what?" I asked again.

He tossed them outside, brushed one hand against the other and said calmly, "We were tinking dat maybe you moved on to bigger game."

His statement hit me right between the eyes.

Floored by the insinuation, I sat there with slack in my jaw and disbelief painted across my face.

"Remind me," he said, "I've got your guns and equipment back at dah farm. Tanks again for dah ride."

Sixteen

S EVERAL HOURS LATER, with Colleen, I had a hard time broaching the subject of my being a "big game hunter." Not that she would have passed judgment or necessarily agreed with Eli's theory; it just seemed like a rather odd topic to bring up over dinner. Besides, she had a very important announcement to make:

"Your buddy from Frankenmuth, Henry Rush, was acquitted."

I laughed. "I knew he wouldn't be convicted!"

"It was on the news this afternoon. That's when I texted you."

"Thanks, and I'm sorry I had to cut you off there…"

"I understand," she said, "you're a busy guy."

We were preparing a late dinner of grilled pork chops and fresh corn on the cob. On the way home from the hospital, I stopped at the grocery store in Mt. Pleasant for a loaf of Rebecca's sourdough bread. In a summer-time kind of way, it was a meal fit for a king.

"What's up with the gang from South Haven, are they out of jail now?" I asked her.

"Yup. The Ivey brothers posted bail a long time ago and they're preparing their defense."

"How do you know?" I asked.

"Their lawyers were at the VFW today and were outlining their case."

"They let anybody sit in on it?"

She nodded her head, and added, "it was open to everybody at the VFW. They want us to look into Congressman Capp."

"What about him?" I asked.

"His background. His pet projects and earmarks in the health-care bill."

"Why is that relevant?"

"They want to establish that Capp was a reckless spender and really didn't care about the people he was supposed to represent."

"So, what did the lawyers say?" I asked her.

"They said that Capp established the Michigan Maple Syrup Association in Cheboygan by giving them two and a half million dollars."

"What's wrong with that?"

"That was five years ago, and they've received a million dollars every year since. I hear that the founders have brand new barns and state-of-the-art equipment, compliments of the taxpayers. The association, in turn, has donated about a tenth of that money to the Committee to Elect Floyd Capp."

"Isn't that illegal?"

"Sure it is. It's a House ethics violation, too, but now that Capp's dead, it's like water under the bridge."

"I've never heard of the Syrup Association."

"Neither had I," Colleen admitted. "Their goal is to organize Michigan's sugar producers. Prices on the global market are through the roof, but Michigan only taps one percent of its maple trees. Apparently, the people in Quebec tap a third of its maple trees and are making all the profits."

"So, in this case, it sounds like Capp's intentions were good, but he kept pouring good money after bad?" I asked.

Colleen nodded, "Five years later, Michigan syrup makers are still really unorganized. It continues to be a bunch of mom-

and-pop producers who sell it at craft shows, Boy Scout camps and the local IGA."

She sent me to the deck with a stack of plates, silverware, and a platter half full of pork chops. Apparently, I was supposed to set the plates on the patio furniture on my way to the grill.

The window between the deck and the kitchen was open so we were able to continue our conversation through the screen.

"Sounds like the guys from South Haven have got quite a strategy and a huge defense budget," I implied. "Who is it?"

"Jacob Chitwood. Ever hear of him?"

"Well, yeah. I seen his ads all over."

"What's up with you and your grammar?" she asked, frowny-faced.

"Sorry," I lamented, "I've seen his ads and I'm sure he's a darn good attorney."

"You're right, he's got ads all over the north country. He's a member of the American Justice Association," she answered. "Ever hear of them?"

"No, why?"

"They're the trial lawyers I mentioned and were one of Capp's biggest campaign contributors," she said, shaking her head. "The trial lawyers lobbied Capp to make sure the health-care bill didn't have any tort reform in it, and now they're representing Capp's killers."

"Is that ironic, or just a tremendous conflict of interest?"

"I think it's the way business gets done in Washington. One hand scratches the other. You have to follow the money, Derrick. That health-care bill is the ultimate gravy train."

The pork chops sizzled when they hit the metal grate under the lid. A second later they were covered in spices that added a hint of aroma to the setting. I looked through the screen and saw Colleen dropping the ears of corn into boiling water. She poured the tea into ice-filled glasses and put a lemon wedge on the edge of each glass. Dinner was taking shape.

"Capp also gave a pile of money to the Department of Agriculture to help study bovine tuberculosis in the deer herd in northeast Michigan," she said.

"What's the big deal with funding the agriculture department?" I asked.

"If the deer give the tuberculosis to the cattle, you can't sell them on the open market."

"That sounds reasonable."

"Sure it does, until you find out that the Department of Agriculture doesn't do much of the testing themselves. Labs all across the Midwest are hired to do the testing."

"Let me guess," I suggested. "Those labs help Capp get elected by giving him campaign donations."

"Right again," Colleen affirmed. "Elizabeth, time for dinner."

The pork chops had been flipped, re-seasoned and were caramelizing gracefully under a tangy coating of barbeque sauce.

I thought for a moment or two about Capp and the way he used to operate. It was making me sick to my stomach, even though I wasn't sure if half the stuff Colleen had told me would be admissible during the trial. Still though, I remember Capp's off-color campaign slogan: *Cut the crap, elect Floyd Capp* at the end of his television commercials. He made me angry just thinking about the way he misled his constituents.

Colleen and Elizabeth slid open the screen door. One had a platter of fresh sourdough in her hands, the other a bowl of steaming-hot corn on the cob and a stick of butter.

"That's just disgusting," I blurted.

My wife and child stopped dead in their tracks, thinking that my *faux pas* was an insult to the food they were carrying.

"Daddy, you still have to try a bite," Elizabeth warned me.

I laughed at her innocence and budding confidence. She was going to make a wonderful mother some day.

"I'm sorry, Baby," I said.

She forgave me, I could tell.

Colleen called the house to order, Mother-Hen style. We knew what to do, what was next and what was after that. The Twitchell residence had a bit of a routine, but it was okay; it was far from boring. After praying for a child of our own—and eventually getting one—raising Elizabeth was a daily blessing.

There would be no more talk about Capp and his murder until our child went to bed. When Elizabeth did retire, I met Colleen in the bedroom, laundry basket in hands. She flipped my socks and underwear to my side of the bed, hers on the other. The garments were flailing so fast that she could have been a dealer at a blackjack table.

"Did Capp have any other earmarks?"

"In the health-care bill there were dozens; had them listed on his website and wasn't the least bit bashful about it. One of his former aides said that Capp used to call earmarks 'croutons on the salad.'"

"You've called Capp's office?" I asked her.

"Sure I did. I want to get to the bottom of how and why he spent so much money. Heck, I want to know why he voted yes for health care when nobody really wanted it. Plus, the wider we can make the circle of suspects, the better chance we have of creating reasonable doubt."

Colleen was hard to listen to. Rolling up your sleeves and diving into a group or organization is one thing; it's a whole other matter to engulf yourself in their culture and root for their acquittal despite so much evidence to the contrary.

"Colleen," I hesitated, "it sounds like you're actually rooting for Yandle's gang to be cleared of the charges. Have you lost your reporter's objectivity?"

She fell silent.

"Didn't you say that this group from South Haven put down the spike strips that blew out the police tires?" I asked, affirmatively.

"Well, yeah," she confessed.

I had to weigh my words carefully. "What could they possibly say or do at their trial that would change the jury's mind about their guilt?"

Colleen turned her head, almost shamefully.

Piling on the guilt was a temptation, but I resisted. Instead, I pulled a trick from Dr. Jim's playbook and let her squirm in her solitary silence.

"Oh, Derrick."

Her utterance lingered for as long as it took to play with her hair, her earrings, any number of items that would divert the spotlight from her conscience to something less disturbing.

Instead of a heartfelt confession or a poignant declaration, Colleen turned the tables on me.

"I don't think you should be the one to hand out advice," she said, painfully sincere.

"What do you mean?"

"This is a hard to say, Derrick, but I don't think you ought to be throwing stones in glass houses."

"Serious," I said.

"Serious-lee," she corrected me.

"What are you getting at?" Now I was the one getting defensive.

"I know you went through a lot at the schoolhouse, but there are a few things that don't really add up."

She had me stumped.

"A week before the shooting, you erased the files on your laptop and the memory in your iPad. The police said that you wiped out the recall feature from your GPS too."

I hemmed for half a second, "Th-th-that's just a coincidence."

"What were you afraid of, Derrick? Why would you do that?"

I shrugged, nonchalant.

"I took a lot of grief for you." Now it was her turn to crank up the full-court pressure.

"What do you mean?"

"I mean, I took some heat from the damn State Police. The FBI. Walter will tell you they were at the paper, too."

I shook my head.

"While you were in the hospital, I had all kinds of them traipsing around the house. The guys from Homeland Security wanted to know where you kept your friggin' machine gun."

"Homeland Security?"

"Heck yes, they were here. In case you've forgotten, Congressman Capp was a federal official. Those agencies had to check to make sure it wasn't a foreign nation or terrorists that kidnapped him. And just what was I supposed to tell them? I had no idea that you owned a machine gun, let alone where you kept it. They had a copy of the permit with your information and signature. It was attached to the search warrant."

Now it was my turn to squirm in silence.

Colleen set the laundry basket down and parked herself on the edge of the bed. We were side by side, arms folded across our chests.

"You don't hunt turkeys with a machine gun. That I know for certain," she said quietly.

I bowed my head and ran my fingers through my hair. The harder I pulled, the more it felt like the truth was lodged in the roots of my scalp.

Colleen put her arm around my side.

She made me feel loved and in a gentle kind of way I should reveal what was buried in my mind.

"Colleen, I bought that gun because I was scared."

Her hand moved from my flank to the inside of my knee.

"All I knew was that our congressman was dead and that they still hadn't caught the people responsible."

Somehow the corner of my lip became wedged under my teeth.

"I knew that Eli had some dealings with the Yandle, so I figured that it was worth staking out his farm. I didn't know what kind of weapons Yandle would have, so I figured better safe than sorry."

"Why didn't you tell me, Derrick?" she pleaded.

I looked in her direction and had a hard time being honest.

"Because I didn't want you to worry," I said, sheepishly.

Colleen raised her eyebrows and tilted her head skeptically.

"Because I didn't want anyone else to know the truth," I said quietly.

She patted my knee affectionately as if it were Jacque's head after he had done a glorious task.

"Tell me what's going on, Derrick. You can trust me with what's on your mind."

I couldn't look at her any longer. The secret that had been gnawing at my soul had finally torn loose.

"I've probably never told you this, but when I was a boy, my dad gave me a slingshot for my birthday. It was called a 'wrist rocket' because it had a strap that went around your forearm. It came with a canister of bb's that was so large I thought it would never run out."

Colleen didn't interrupt me, for which I was thankful.

"At first, I shot soup cans and paper plates with little bullseyes scribbled on them. Dad suggested that I thin out the flock of pigeons inside the barn, which introduced me to the concept of killing living creatures. It never really bothered me to kill those pigeons because I felt like I was doing my part around the farm. Dad told me that they pooped all over the place and were full of diseases and he paid me twenty-five cents a pigeon."

Colleen pulled herself away from the bed. Apparently, I was taking too long to get to the point.

"Anyway, one day I took the wrist rocket and went for a walk in the row of pine trees in front of the farm. A chickadee landed on a branch about ten feet from me. They're so trusting, so naïve. I remember thinking that it would be very easy to kill it."

Colleen had put away her underwear and socks and disappeared into our bathroom.

"Instead of leaving the chickadee alone, I killed it."

"Okay," she said.

"I didn't just kill it, Colleen. I murdered it. Decapitated it."

Her head popped through the open door, as if she was hiding the rest of her body. "What are you trying to say, Derrick?"

"When the thrill of killing the pigeons wore off, I wanted to expand my horizons," I said.

Colleen disappeared again, so I cut to the chase.

"I've had a lifetime of excitement in the outdoors. Birds are fun to hunt. Trout fishing's fine. Salmon are a ball. Never had much interest in deer hunting, or going out west on a big-game hunt. A safari seems a little too hoity."

I heard the shower starting. Colleen reappeared. She was wrapped in a thirsty towel that stretched from her arm pits to the top of her thighs.

"Derrick, please," she begged.

"Okay, okay," I said. "As gruesome as it is to say, I've always wondered what it would be like to try to kill somebody."

"Oh my God, Derrick."

"Legally," I said, "justifiably!" I almost shouted over the din of the shower.

"You really are sick," she said behind the glass door. "I guess you got your wish."

Colleen jumped in the shower and the sounds of splashing water filled the air. Instead of waiting for her to finish, I stood outside the shower door and completed my admission. "Even though it was technically okay for me to kill Yandle, the guilt I'm feeling now reminds me of the time I killed the chickadee."

Colleen didn't say a word.

I didn't expect that she would.

Seventeen

COLLEEN AND I NEVER DID TALK about my macabre admission, and I really can't blame her for not wanting to go there. Some things should be buried in the folds of your brain and hopefully never see the light of day. Honestly, I really don't make it a habit to present her with alarming secrets about my distant past. Colleen and I both agreed that we should both keep a few secrets from each other to preserve the veil of modesty between us. Mystery in a relationship isn't always bad; at least that's our thought on the matter. Fresh ideas, new experiences, and unfamiliar settings add traction to our marriage; what's more, it helps us steer clear of the ruts that could bog down our relationship.

For a while there, I struggled with whether I should have told her my little secret. On one hand, I felt I had to tell someone; the truth was weighing heavily around my neck. On the other hand, my admission could have been so devastating that she might have taken drastic action and pushed me away. My little secret was serious, and it could have wound up being a contentious caveat that could have lingered for as long as we were married.

If the shoe was on the other foot and she had a secret to tell me, I'm not so sure she would have spilled her beans. Colleen has always been extremely modest. She hides her eyes when I streak naked from the shower to the bedroom dresser, shouting "Have no fear, Genital Man is here!"

Conversely, I hardly ever saw her naked unless the shades were drawn, the candles were lit and she was in the mood for a little *tête-à-tête*. Undressing her in the seething calm of a romantic interlude was as much fun as pouring heated massage oil on her freckled back.

Colleen had a way of keeping me off balance. She'd leave me love notes etched into the skin of a banana or scribbled on the napkins tucked into my sack lunch. By lunchtime, the message scribbled in the banana peel would be gloriously obvious and was just as suggestive as the texts she sent me throughout the day. She must have at least a dozen different kinds of perfume, twenty varieties of outfits that scream "come love me," and an assortment of v-neck sweaters that made me wonder, *What's beneath that sheath?*

When it came to the newspaper and our careers as reporters, we were all business. She had her stories; I had mine. I helped her whenever she asked for it, and she helped me even when it wasn't painfully obvious that I needed it. We had a mutual commitment to the growth of our newspaper and the suitable upbringing of our daughter. Shared values and ideals helped us strike a nice balance between work and play.

My involvement in Marshall Yandle's death had several tentacles that could have pulled us apart in our professional and relational lives. Still though, I didn't press Colleen about the stories she was working on, and she didn't pry into what I had on my plate. We considered it a professional courtesy to allow each other a little breathing room.

Without a doubt, I didn't dare set foot in the VFW at Houghton Lake. Even though Colleen never said anything about it, I was certain that at least some of the members loathed me. After all, I killed the leader of their little group, and in the months previous, helped defeat him in court.

When I first heard the story about Marshall Yandle suing an Amish family from Gladwin, I really didn't give it a second thought.

I mean, as an editor and publisher of a newspaper, I get tons of requests to cover a litany of events, stories, and programs. My daily "in-box" at the paper is overloaded with information, pleas, and press releases. Sorting through the self-serving items to truly find what's newsworthy is the key to being a good newspaperman.

And I hate anonymous notes. If the writers don't have the guts to sign their name to a letter, they're really not deserving of the attention their issue allegedly deserves. I'm not sure who sent me the anonymous letter, but I had a sneaking suspicion that it was a clerk or a foreman at the courthouse. Either way, when the letter said, "An Amish family is going to lose all they got," I figured it might be worth investigating.

By the time I got involved in *Yandle v. Beiler,* the plaintiffs had already deposed Eli and had an understanding of his financial assets. Eli was one of four sons who each inherited a hundred-sixty acres from their father. Together with the barns, farmhouse, livestock and equipment, Eli's operation was appraised at just shy of a half-million dollars.

And Eli seemed okay with walking away from it all. I think he sincerely believed that God would take care of his family and him somehow, some way. Even though he didn't want to hire a lawyer, I urged him to consider it. Rebecca agreed with me, and after the initial legal consultation, started the baking business to help pay for her defense. Neither Rebecca nor Eli ever knew what the lawyer's actual hourly rate was because of the arrangement I had made with one of my father's former associates. When my dad died, he left his law practice to a younger colleague who reaped the benefits of Dad's oil-related income streams. Part of the terms they agreed upon was that he became the family's source for legal work. Since none of our family members had any legal work for him, the proverbial "clock" that Dad set up had quite a few credits on it.

The lawyer provided an ample defense and used the information I dug up on Yandle to help the Beiler's case.

Make no mistake, the more I looked into Marshall Yandle, the more I learned that he was full of contradictions and turmoil. He had blemishes on his record, before and after his other-than-honorable discharge from the Navy. His recruiting officer said that he got into trouble for not following orders, for rabble-rousing the ranks, and for "disturbing the peace" while on leave.

"Marshall had a hard time with authority," he told me. "He couldn't understand the concept of chain of command."

As far as his habits were concerned, Yandle liked to tip the bottle, or, as my dad used to say about heavy drinkers, "liked to pull on the cork." He got nailed for a minor in possession while in his senior year of high school, and a drunk-driving ticket a year before the work-site accident at Eli's farm.

For several months, he worked as a butcher at the IGA in the little town of Meredith, but his former boss said he had to fire Yandle because he couldn't get along with the other workers. "He was always bad-mouthing the union, and trying to recruit others to join his church," he said. "Finally, I just had to let him go because of all the trouble he caused."

The manager said that when he fired Yandle the two of them got into quite a skirmish. They never threw any punches, but there was plenty of pushing and shoving, yelling and threats.

"Yandle had a hard time taking criticism," the manager told me. "When I fired him, he said 'you'd better watch yourself' and stuff like that."

I never did ask how Marshall Yandle and Eli Beiler met, but I could see why the two of them might get along. Yandle had reliable transportation, was rather religious, and had a host of power tools that would make short work of the side jobs Eli took on during the summer months. Eli told me that Yandle was always really good about picking them up on the farm and driving them to and from the job site.

But, it wasn't always a pleasant experience. Eli said that Yandle liked to crack open the beers on the drive home from work and he listened to conservative-talk-radio shows any time he was near the vehicle.

"After a hard day of construction, Yandle used to come unglued listening to those guys on the radio," Eli said. "He hated the liberals in Congress. Called them 'socialists' and 'pinko communists.' I could see how he became involved with the militia."

If there was a recurring theme in the saga of Marshall Yandle, it was that the guy had a chip on his shoulder. It's like the police, the military, society and the Democrats had to be stopped. He was mid-Michigan's version of Timothy McVeigh—a menace to society and a tragedy waiting to happen.

The Heretic Fringe took him under its wing.

They made him their leader; he had found a home.

Yandle was the one who devised the two-part plan to kidnap and murder the congressman. The first half of the plan was carried out with military precision, the second half with spiteful vengeance.

Either way, the trial involving the Ivey brothers from South Haven was ready to start. Located in the heart of downtown Flint, the Federal Courthouse sits amongst a cluster of one-way streets and old, tired buildings. Flint, like most of America, would rather abandon its historic roots in favor of newer buildings far from the center of town. I parked my vehicle in the parking deck across the street and took notice of a man urinating behind a parked car in the corner of the stairwell. My street sense kicked in quickly as I walked briskly, eyes forward and focused. I knifed past the bums and panhandlers, toward the stoplight where I rubbed elbows with prosecutors Jack Jacobetti and his associate, the lovely Penelope Melton. Fresh off their defeat in the matter involving Henry Rush, neither barrister was in the best of moods.

As much as I tried to come up with a clever or witty ice-breaker, I totally struck out. Ever since I first saw her stroll up the sidewalk at the funeral of her colleague in Midland, I had developed a mild affinity for Ms. Melton.

Instead of coming up with a charming statement, or smiling meekly at Ms. Melton, I looked up at the trees on the courthouse lawn. It was a beautiful late summer morning. Locusts sizzled from the tree tops on the courthouse campus while cars whizzed past, sending six or eight house sparrows into the nooks of the parking garage behind me. I noticed the flattened pieces of chewing gum amidst the cigarette butts and dirty, neglected cracks of the sidewalk.

Jacobetti glanced at the spectacle across the street. A group of fifty or more protestors was lined up in front of the courthouse stairs, wearing a version of the patriots' garb from two hundred years ago. A couple of them started playing a perfect rendition of *Yankee Doodle Dandy* on their fife and drums. Five or six news-channel vehicles were lined up, satellite antennas protruding from their roofs.

"Look at this," Jacobetti lamented.

"May the circus begin," Melton moaned.

When the traffic light turned from green to yellow and the vehicles slowed to a stop, the sparrows in the parking deck flew out of their roost and onto the remains of cheeseburger that had been flattened into oblivion by the passing motorists. The sparrows surrounded the hamburger bun and were chirping merrily as if they were knights at a round table. Melton never noticed the birds as she entered the crosswalk, even though she could have injured three or four of them just by dropping her leather attaché.

About halfway across the street, the entourage of reporters came at us with their cameras, their microphones, and the urgency of a developing story. In a way, I felt sorry for their plight. They were all accountable to some boss, some media outlet, some looming deadline. Every day I thank my lucky stars to be my own boss, the publisher and chief reporter all rolled into one.

"Mr. Jacobetti! Mr. Jacobetti!"

Mr. Jacobetti smiled, raised his hand, Pope-style, and the reporters cleared a path. I noticed the ring on his right hand— gold and gaudy—a bold "S" on the face of the dark green stone.

The reporters back-pedaled while they barked questions.

"Why did you decide to prosecute the men from South Haven separately instead of with the others from Houghton Lake?"

"Is Congressman Capp's wife going to testify?"

"Do you like your chances in this case any better than the Rush matter?"

Jacobetti shook his head at the inquisition. He never stopped to address the crowd, but that didn't surprise me. Most attorneys are so geared up for the rigors of a trial that they very seldom stop to speak.

I followed Jacobetti and Melton through the maze of protestors and beneath a sign that read *Don't Tread on Me*. We skipped up ten or fifteen marble steps at the front door of the courthouse. Once there, Jacobetti said good morning to two state police officers—one male and another female—who proceeded to pat us down. After passing the pat-down, Jacobetti gave the massive door a tug and both Melton and I slid inside.

Waiting for us near a metal detector were two more guards, each sporting massive beer bellies and pencil-thin mustaches. Instead of saying "good morning," they asked us to empty our pockets into the little plastic container on the conveyor belt.

When I dropped my possessions into the bin, they asked me, "Are you an attorney?"

"No, I'm not," I admitted.

"Well then," one of them said, "you can't have your cell phone on the premises. You can't even have a camera."

"Serious," I said, incredulously.

"Serious-lee," Melton corrected me. Looking over my shoulder, I saw her nod in my direction, just as cool as the other side of the pillow. "I'd have thought you would have known that by now," she stated, facetiously.

"Known what?" I asked. "That only attorneys can have cell phones inside the courthouse, or that it should have been 'seriously' instead of just plain 'serious?'"

"Either, or," she grimaced, unzipping her attaché and putting her phone and car keys in the basket directly upstream of mine.

I gathered my phone, loose change, and car keys and backed out of her way.

Ms. Melton took off her sport coat and laid it across her belongings. She must have known that the three or four metallic buttons on the cuffs of her navy suit would set off the metal detector. I tried to come up with a pertinent comeback, but my mind was somewhere between Melton's cute smile and her delicious figure. The girl had all kinds of charm, sex appeal, and confidence—three ingredients that are worth savoring. The more I looked at her, the more she seemed familiar.

"Have we met?" I asked.

"Not officially," she said, "But I've heard about you. You are the person who shot Marshall Yandle."

I nodded in her direction.

"I've seen you around and read your stories," she said charmingly. "You're a good reporter."

She passed through the metal detector without a hitch. One of the guards took an extra long look at the faint black line that crept up the back of her stockings.

"Derrick Twitchell." I said, extending my hand. "Good luck today."

"Nice to meet you, Derrick," she said, squeezing my hand.

"If you ever want to go on the record, here's my contact info," I said, partially stuttering. She pulled the business card from my fingers and stuffed it into the front pocket of her navy blazer. Jacobetti gathered his belongings, while Melton slid into her blazer. Both the guards and I watched as Ms. Melton clip-clopped across the polished marble floor to the courtroom of the Honorable Steven Brewer.

About an hour later, one of three law clerks cleared her throat and said, "All rise. The Honorable Steven Brewer in Federal Court presiding."

The judge opened the side door behind his bench and seven or eight steps later, was seated on his throne. Judge Brewer was mostly bald, and the top of his head shimmered in the overhead lights. Everyone sat down, and five or six people in the gallery took the opportunity to clear their throats and cough.

I noticed that the government had spared little cost in building the courtroom. The ceilings were at least twelve feet high, and the pillars between each window were made from some sort of marble or granite. Everything else, including the gallery benches, was made from either cherry wood or mahogany.

One side of the courtroom was packed with the pool of jurors; each was wearing a red-and-white badge on their clothing. On the other side of the aisle, a litany of reporters, professional artists, observers, Tea Party associates, and members of the Heretic Fringe were present. My wife was in the middle of the group, wearing her familiar red wig. Dr. James Ong sat directly behind the defense, but for all I knew he could have been spying on them for the prosecution. Either way, he didn't see me, which was okay.

When everyone was seated, the bailiff read the docket number and announced the case of *United States of America vs. Peter and Russell Ivey*. The bailiff also read the list of charges against the defendants, who both pleaded not guilty.

Just as His Honor explained the ground rules to the pool of

jurors—and set the stage for their selection—Jacobetti brought a motion to dismiss thirteen of the ninety jurors.

"On what basis?" Judge Brewer asked.

"May I approach?" Jacobetti asked.

"You may." His Honor waved both defense lawyers toward the bench along with Mr. Jacobetti and Ms. Melton, who brought along her yellow legal pad.

The courtroom erupted in restless chatter, most of it conjecture—I suspected—of why the prosecution would want to axe thirteen jurors. The longer they discussed the matter, the louder the gallery became.

I had already scribbled a half page of notes. In my head, I was thinking about how I was going to concoct a lead for tomorrow's newspaper.

After a minute or two of arguing back and forth, the four lawyers and the judge disappeared into the chambers, behind closed doors. The court reporter stood, adjusted her skirt slightly, and took her coffee cup behind the same closed door. She reappeared a minute or so later, carefully holding her cup, along with one for the clerk.

The Ivey brothers turned their chairs slightly, and chitchatted with what could have been their family members in the front row of the gallery. Both brothers were dressed in a suit and tie. They looked to be in their late twenties or early thirties. Both wore pensive, worrisome faces.

I was in the back row of the courtroom near the window. All the action was ahead of me and to the left. A man and two women from my side of the courtroom got up from their seats and exited through the heavy wooden doors at the rear. The man had on a patriotic outfit that included a triangle-shaped hat, a buckskin vest and pants. The women were just as festive, just as convinced that the trial of the Ivey brothers was an assault on the American way of life. One man even wore an old-fashioned gray wig and a pair of Ben Franklin-style eyeglasses. It was quite a spectacle.

In the absence of any appreciable entertainment, someone in the gallery started humming *My Country, 'Tis of Thee*. After a few bars, he was joined by scores of others, including the members of Colleen's clan who provided the lyrics. They were loud and patriotic—their chance to tarnish the jury pool in their own little way.

Although they were slightly off key, their singing bounced around the courtroom, *"Sweet land of liberty, of thee I sing."*

Some of the jurors got up and left.

The armed guards stepped toward the fray and demanded that they stop.

"Screw you," one of them shouted, "it's our First Amendment right!"

"Land where my fathers died, land of the pilgrims' pride."

Both guards zeroed in on the troublemaker and yelled in his direction, "Stop it now, I tell you."

Half of the group put their hands over their hearts, the other half raised their fists in defiance.

"From every mountainside, let freedom ring."

The guards charged into the mob, batons clenched in their fists. The women screeched in terror, but didn't exactly get out of the way.

The singing, humming, and gleeful chorus had turned to swearing, the chaotic raucous of shuffling feet, and mad punches.

"Grab him!"

They fought.

"Officer down!"

"Get the gun!"

I wished I had my camera. A video camera. It was wonderfully poignant and barbaric; the kind of action that television stations crave.

People were running for safety and slamming into the state police who had burst open the courtroom doors and whipped out their tasers. Most of the women shrieked and ducked behind the pews. Not Colleen. She was in the middle of the madness, and judging by her actions, it appeared as if she was trying to help calm the storm.

"Hold it right there!" the cops shouted.

Some of the mob froze in their tracks. Others were so engaged in fisticuffs that they wanted to get in one last poke. The guards were on the floor between the pews, pushing and shoving, batting arms and kicking legs.

"Stop or I'll shoot," one of the troopers yelled, pointing his taser right and left. Instead of getting up, the men continued their brawl, which made the use of a taser unlikely. It was like a scrum in a hockey game, where the best remedy was to roll up your sleeves and start peeling bodies from the floor. Just like that, the trooper holstered his taser and joined two or three others who leaped into the fracas and attempted to pull the combatants apart.

"Knock it off!" they yelled.

"Quit."

After a minute or two of brutality, the troopers gained the upper hand. The guards wheeled to their feet and tried to compose themselves. They tucked in their shirts, checked for blood on their fingers, and tried to fix their hair with their hands.

One of the guards found his baton on the floor and pointed it at one of the Tea Party members whose wrists were stuffed in handcuffs behind his back. "How do you like them apples!?"

"Knock it off," the troopers chided.

I wasn't sure if the troopers were going to arrest the combatants, or if their objective was to escort them out of the building. Either way, the troopers had at least one Tea Party member on each arm as they exited the courtroom.

"There's nothing quite like a little fireworks at the start of a trial to get the juices flowing, huh Twitchell?"

I looked ahead. It was Henry Rush.

"What are you doing here?"

"Same as you; I'm just a casual observer."

"Congratulations; I heard about your acquittal."

"Thank you. I gotta tell you I was a little nervous about it."

"I bet you were. You were looking at a lot of time behind bars."

"Yeah, basically the rest of my life," he said. "I want to thank you for writing that story. You never know how it may have affected the jurors in my case."

"What do you mean?" I asked.

"Just what I said. You never know how or what a jury will think."

We both looked to the commotion at the door. The troopers were removing the last of the troublemakers.

I didn't really want to hear any more of Henry's theories, for fear that maybe he'd admit he was using me to gain his acquittal.

"It's the same thing as what just took place here," he said. "I'd be willing to bet that the Ivey brothers' strategy is to create some sort of diversion, a patriotic exhibition."

"That may be the case, but why did the defense want to eliminate thirteen jurors?"

"I'm not sure, but you watch, they'll get something on the record when the trial resumes."

Henry was an odd bird. He couldn't just stand in front of me like most people; he had to shuffle off to one side or the other. When I pivoted to keep him in front of me, it felt like we were just an embrace away from doing a waltz. If I didn't pivot with him I felt like I had to talk to him over my shoulder. I don't know what was worse—the shuffle thing, or his dangerously apparent knowledge of the legal system.

"Mind if I sit here?" he asked.

"No, no," I said, somewhat reluctantly, "have a seat."

Henry wiggled past me and took a seat. I sat next to him and traced the outline of the graffiti carved into the pew ahead of me.

"Look at that," Henry said, "Punks today don't have any respect for property or the value of a dollar."

"It looks like it's been here a while, since the days when you could still bring a pocketknife to your hearing."

"The government is wasting our money installing those metal detectors. Judge Brewer doesn't need protecting. He's supposed to be a real tough cookie." Henry looked towards the front of the courtroom and said, "You watch, Judge Brewer will come out of chambers and will want to clear the air. He'll temporarily dismiss the entire jury panel and put something on the record. After about ten minutes, he'll bring them back in and boot the thirteen without any reason at all."

"Want to bet?"

"What do you mean, 'Do I want to bet?'"

"You sound rather confident, that's all."

Henry thumbed his suspenders. They were striped red, white and blue. "I don't want to bet, but I think that's what will happen. It's like these lawyers stole a page from my attorney's game plan. Don't you remember?"

I nodded my head, slightly, and said, "Kind of."

"My lawyer found out something on every one of the jury members," he said. "He knew what kind of person would make a favorable juror."

"Oh?"

"We wanted educated males. White guys. The people who are sick of the government's intervention and high taxes, while at the same time sympathetic to my cause."

"I remember. You had a bunch of them on the panel. How did you know who was going to be in the jury pool before the trial even started?"

"Well, you know," he said, quietly.

"No, I don't," I said even quieter.

"You gotta watch it, Derrick. The U.S. Marshal's office might be listening."

"The what?"

Henry gestured for me to keep my voice down, adding "The marshals. They're involved in high-profile court cases to protect federal judges."

"I thought they were only into tracking down fugitives."

"Heaven's no, Derrick. They're on our southern border and fighting the battle against illegal aliens," he said. "They investigate terrorists who are on trial. They do all kinds of neat stuff that you never really hear about."

I looked around the courtroom. Things were beginning to settle down.

"They're sneaky quiet, too. You never really know, but there might be three or four of them in this courtroom. Most of the time, they're dressed in plain clothes."

I looked up again and made a quick assessment of my surroundings. There could have been twenty marshals on my side of the aisle, slightly less amongst the jurors.

Henry picked up on my wariness.

"In my case, the lawyer I hired had a nephew who was dating a girl who worked in the court system," he whispered. "In a roundabout way, we were able to get the list."

"Holy hell, Henry. Is that legal?"

"Probably not, but I don't go around telling everybody about it."

I shook my head. "Do you think that's happening here?"

"You never know. It's not something that you go around asking. All I know is that it can be done."

My mind flashed to Dr. James Ong, and the jury consulting part of his practice. It made me wonder what he was doing here, whom he was working for, and what their strategy might have been. He wasn't seated very far from all the action.

"I'm going to grab a cup of coffee from the vending machines downstairs. It's probably not the most flavorful brew you've ever had, but it might not be bad. You want one?"

"No thanks, Henry."

"Save my seat, okay? There's something else I want to tell you."

Henry waved slightly, slid down the aisle between the two rows of seats, and disappeared behind the courtroom doors.

Eighteen

A S PREDICTED, Judge Brewer called the courtroom to order and temporarily dismissed the entire jury panel.

Henry Rush tapped me on the forearm and whispered a coffee-smelling crow, "I told you so."

Judge Brewer approved the prosecutors' motion to dismiss thirteen jurors. The reason for their dismissal was that they had been in contact with and unduly influenced by the members of the Tea Party.

Brewer almost growled when he spoke, and when he cocked the microphone under his nose, his voice bellowed in stereo. He had a thick, burly mustache, and his necktie was the size of a clenched fist beneath his black robe.

"I would also like to remind dah visitors of dis court that we will not tolerate any more shenanigans," he said.

A former resident of Negaunee, in the Upper Peninsula, his heavy Finnish accent served him well when dealing with the Yoopers in Marquette's Federal Court; now his pronunciation of certain words was a source of amusement for nearly everybody in the courtroom. The more Brewer spoke, the more people looked at each other and snickered. While preparing for the case, I discovered that Brewer had been run out of Marquette five years ago. He ruled in favor of the DNR when it prosecuted a landowner for shooting a wolf. Although the landowner had every right to protect his sheep from imminent danger, he didn't have the right to bait the wolves in the area with deer carcasses that were killed by vehicles. Since wolves are protected federally by the Endangered Species Act, the case wound up in Brewer's court. The locals were outraged by his decision, which eventually warranted his transfer to Flint.

"If I hear any more disturbances from dah jury or dah members of dah audience, so help me Lord, I will hold you all in contempt," he said. "Now, bailiff, please bring dah jury back inside. I gotta docket to keep."

The panel moseyed inside and Judge Brewer rattled off the thirteen names and their respective jury numbers. "Thank you for your service to dah community," he said, "but we won't need you any longer. Make sure you call dah jury hotline on Sunday night to find out when you report for dah next trial."

He didn't give the thirteen any reason for their dismissal. Apparently, they couldn't ask, and the judge didn't bother to tell them.

When the dust settled on the jurors' removal, His Honor introduced himself and gave a brief description of his career on the bench. He glossed over his time in the Upper Peninsula, but didn't spare any detail when it came to the seriousness of what was at stake. He told the jury the ground rules for what was ahead and emphasized the importance of using only the evidence presented in court to make their decision as to the defendants' guilt or innocence. Jacobetti spoke next, and eventually, the lead defense attorney, Jacob Chitwood. Judge Brewer's spiel took the longest; Chitwood's was the most impassioned, and Jacobetti's emphasized the "black and white nature of the facts."

Finally, the court clerk pulled fourteen numbered ping-pong balls from a metal drum. After all the buildup, dismissals, and eventual reconvening, we could almost hear the panel exhale a sigh of relief when the first number was drawn.

One by one, the chosen jurors found their seats in the jury box. When the fourteenth juror was called, the bailiff asked them all to stand and be sworn in. Jacobetti had the first swing at interrogating the jury members and he started with juror number fifty-seven, Nola Kaiser, who was assigned juror number one. She was from the little town of Chesaning, in Saginaw County, and was the manager at the Broken Bell Inn for the last seventeen years. Jacobetti asked her if she had heard about the murder of Congressman Capp. Kaiser said that she had heard about it, but felt that she could be a fair and impartial juror. I noticed the way she squirmed in her chair and never really looked up when she answered the questions. Dressed in blue jeans and a silly-looking pink sweatshirt, Kaiser had a massive gray stripe in the part of her hair that made her look like she was part skunk.

"Nothing further, Your Honor," Jacobetti said.

"Mr. Chitwood?"

Everyone's eyes turned to Chitwood. He was tall, white, close to fifty-five, and like most lawyers in federal court, dressed to the nines. Instead of standing up, he glanced over his shoulder towards Dr. Jim, who tugged on his right ear lobe. Without batting an eye, Chitwood dismissed Kaiser "for cause."

Judge Brewer thanked her for appearing and reminded her to call the jury hotline on Sunday evening.

Another ping-pong ball later, and the clerk cried, "Number seventy-six, Margaret Nestle."

As Nestle waddled up to the jury box and raised her right hand, Henry Rush thought I should know what "cause" meant.

"They can dismiss any number of jurors without a good reason," he said, "no questions asked."

"Got it," I whispered.

"They can also have something like a dozen peremptory

challenges," he said. "They save those for people who might have an unfavorable bias."

"What happens if they can't come up with fourteen impartial jurors?" I whispered.

"Don't worry about that. They will."

Mr. Jacobetti started all over again with his line of questioning. Ms. Nestle was from AuGres, on the north shore of Saginaw Bay, and worked as a clerk at the Dollar General store. She never saw the need to go to college and spent most of her career working in various diners across the northeast side of the state. When Jacobetti got around to asking Nestle about Capp and whether she had heard of the case, she spared him any further questioning, "I'm glad Capp is dead. As far as I'm concerned, that bastard had it coming-"

"Next!" Jacobetti interrupted. "Strike for cause."

"Thank you for your service to the community, Ms. Nestle," Judge Brewer said, regrettably. "Members of the jury will disregard the statements made by juror Nestle."

Ms. Nestle never missed a beat, "You're welcome, Judge. I'll be expecting my check from you right away."

The clerk pulled another number from the barrel "Juror fifty-five, Zachariah P. Yoder."

Nearly everybody in the courtroom looked up to see Mr. Yoder standing in the middle of the jury pool, straw hat in hand, shuffling past the bent knees of his peers. There was no mistaking his snow-white beard and riveting blue eyes: it was the same Mr. Yoder who pulled me and my Suburban out of the ditch earlier in the summer. He looked downright respectable in his homemade jeans and pressed short-sleeve shirt. When Mr. Yoder found his way to the juror's box, he put on his denim overcoat, raised his right hand and swore to tell the truth.

As Jacobetti approached the jury box, Mr. Yoder sat down, back erect, elbows perched on the rests.

When Jacobetti asked Mr. Yoder about Capp's murder, Mr. Yoder said he was aware of it.

"Do you vote?" Jacobetti asked.

"Occasionally, if I can get a ride to the polls."

"How did you get here today?"

"I got a ride from my neighbor."

"Do you own a car, Mr. Yoder?"

"No."

"How do you get around?"

"We do our best. I own a couple of horses and a carriage or two. There's a few bicycles in the drive shed."

Jacobetti smiled, "You don't plan on commuting back and forth?"

"No."

"Mr. Yoder, this trial might go on for a week. Where are you going to stay? What are you going to do?"

"I don't know, yet. I've got a cell phone and a credit card. That means I can take care of myself."

"I didn't think that the Amish were supposed to have a cell phone?"

Mr. Yoder nodded. "We're not supposed to have it in our name. I added this one onto my neighbor's account."

"I see," Jacobetti said. "What do you do for a living?"

"I'm a farmer."

"Do you have animals?"

"Yes."

"Who's going to take care of them if you're gone for a week?"

"The Lord will provide. I've got a big family with plenty of children down the street. They will help."

Judge Brewer removed his index finger from his upper lip. "Mr. Jacobetti, can we stay on the topic, please?"

"Yes, we can Your Honor," Jacobetti said. "Mr. Yoder, have you ever served on a jury before?"

"Have not."

"How much education do you have?"

"I went to school through grade eight."

"Would you be able to convict a man and send him to prison for the rest of—"

"Objection," Chitwood interrupted, "Leading."

"Sustained," Brewer affirmed.

Jacobetti dropped his question and sauntered off to his side of the courtroom.

"Mr. Chitwood?" the judge asked, addressing the defense.

Even though the courtroom was crowded, I watched Mr. Chitwood look over his shoulder at Dr. Jim, who tugged at his left ear lobe. It appeared to be some sort of signal that the two of them had set up ahead of time. Chitwood eased toward the podium. When he arrived, he fastened the top button of his double-breasted suit, seemingly striking a pose for the colored-pencil artists in the front row of the gallery. If the artists were any good, they wouldn't miss the intensity etched across his face. "Mr. Yoder, there are some people who would say that you live a simple life, without the clutter of modern conveniences."

"Yes, that's the Amish way," Mr. Yoder said, a hint of Europe in his speech.

"We're going to throw a lot at you this week," Chitwood said, half-smiling. "You're a smart man, I can tell, but do you think your lack of understanding about modern conveniences will prevent you from keeping up with the testimony?"

"I can keep up. And I know right from wrong."

"What does that mean?" Chitwood asked.

Mr. Yoder wrapped his fingers around his chin and tugged at his graying beard. "People tell me that I'm honest and fair. Even though I don't know a lot about the ways of the English, I still am a good judge of character."

"Have you ever met the defendants?"

"Never."

"Did you know Floyd Capp?"

"No."

"Ever hear of him?"

"I guess."

"Why do you say that?"

"Because I always voted for his opponent."

"I thought you said that you didn't always get to the polls."

"That's true. I should have said, 'When I got a chance to vote I always voted for his opponent.'"

"Why didn't you vote for Capp?"

"Mmmm," Yoder hesitated—as if we were to expect a kernel of wisdom. "I didn't like the way he combed his hair."

The gallery huffed.

"I see," Chitwood said, scribbling a brief note on his pad of paper. "Isn't it a tremendous burden on you and your family for you to be a juror?"

"Yes."

"Why are you here?" Chitwood asked.

"The court sent me a letter that said I had to."

"I know," Chitwood said, observantly. "All these folks got the same letter you did, but aren't there some religious reasons why you shouldn't be here?"

Mr. Yoder pressed his lips together and made a frown. "It's my patriotic duty," he said confidently. "I'm an American first and foremost. The freedoms afforded to me and all Americans under the constitution allow us to practice whatever religion we want. I choose to be Amish. Even though our religion says that we shall not swear or judge others, I'm still an American and this is my patriotic duty."

"I understand," Chitwood nodded. "Nothing further, Your Honor."

Nineteen

IT TOOK ALMOST NINETY MINUTES for the entire jury panel to be selected and approved. Mr. Yoder was one bookend of the front row; at the other end was Oscar Haynes, a farmer from the little town of Vassar. Between the two men were five women, three of whom were white and two were black. One of the white women lived on the north side of Flint; the other two knew each other, but hadn't made contact since they went to grammar school together in Grand Blanc. The two black women came from totally different backgrounds: one was the dean at Saginaw Valley State University; the other "served a spell in jail" for a drug-related crime back in the nineties.

Jacobetti and Chitwood whistled through six peremptory challenges apiece before they settled on juror number eight— a retired librarian from Caro, who ended up sitting next to a former right-winger for the Flint Generals Hockey Club. Robert Gilbert (he pronounced it "Jill-bare") said he was born in French Canada, but became a United States citizen fifteen years ago. At least six-feet-four and two-hundred-thirty pounds in his prime, Gilbert was an imposing figure on and off the ice. He sat in the jurors' area as if it was the penalty box and trimmed his fingernails in the same nervous way that Eli did when we were on the way to the hospital. Even from the back row of the courtroom, I could see that the knuckles on his right hand were knotted and scarred. Chitwood noticed it too and asked him to explain why they were in the condition they were. Gilbert testified that he "had got in a few scraps in his day" and the doctors told him that his hand probably would never be the same.

Although I'm not a big hockey fan, I was familiar with Gilbert and his reputation as an enforcer on the ice. I remember that he occasionally was called up to the National Hockey League—for the sole purpose of protecting the best players on his team from the opposition's version of himself. Three or four times a game, the coach would tap Gilbert on the shoulder, which meant that it was his turn to take the ice and find someone to blast into the boards or challenge to a fight. When Gilbert fought, it brought the entire stadium to their feet, and more often than not, changed the momentum of the game.

Most of the time, Gilbert won the fights he was in. And he didn't just win; he pummeled his opponents with jackhammer right hands, and left roundhouses that connected with his opponent's face, his helmet, or the back of his head. With each victory, Gilbert skated off the ice, gesturing to the masses that he wore the belt of a heavyweight champion.

Judge Brewer had to corral Chitwood's fascination with Gilbert, and urged him "to either take care of business or leave the outhouse." In a Yooper kind of way, Brewer's message was loud and clear: Move it along, partner.

The five people on Gilbert's left worked once in some capacity of the automobile industry. Four of the five were laid off from various plants along I-75; the fifth was an executive at GM's Truck and Bus Plant in Flint. Most of the members in the back row had ethnic-sounding last names: Swatosh, Tsoukalas, Rychlinski, and Sarti. All but the executive were dressed in blue jeans and either t-shirts or golf shirts. A couple of them had facial hair, and tattoos on their forearms.

At nearly eleven-thirty opening morning, the jury panel

was finally set. Judge Brewer introduced the Ivey brothers and asked the panel one more time if they were kin to or knew either one. When nobody answered, Brewer took several minutes to explain the charges: Aiding and abetting, and murder of a federal official. His Honor further explained that the law didn't apply just to members of Congress; the Ivey boys could have been charged with the same crime if they were involved with the murder of a cabinet member or a federal judge. Judge Brewer seemed to take pride in being the center of attention and he re-introduced the four lawyers as if they were the starting lineup in a baseball game. I half expected each attorney to tip his or her hat and spit tobacco juice when His Honor explained what each lawyer's job entailed. Some of what Brewer said seemed to be statutorily required; the remainder of his talk was his commentary on how the trial was about to unfold.

When His Honor dismissed the court for lunch, he reminded the panel that they shouldn't talk to anyone, including each other, about the case until the trial was over and it was time for deliberation. "Moreover," he said, "the clerk will be taking your lunch order. You'll be eating in the deliberation room. Mr. Williams, the bailiff, will take you to and from the washroom across the hall."

"For those remaining members who appeared for jury duty, I want to thank you for your service to your community. You are free to go. As for the rest of you, we'll convene at one-thirty, sharp," he said.

The bailiff asked us to rise again. When we did, the jury disappeared behind the door opposite the judge's chambers.

When the gallery filed out of the courtroom, I hoped to make contact with Colleen. As much as I wanted to preserve her cover, I still wanted to make sure she was okay. There must have been at least twenty-five members of her group in the courtroom. When she shuffled out of her pew ten rows ahead of me, she secretly winked in my direction. I smiled slightly, but my heart sank when the burly man behind her gave me the old "We're watching you" sign with his index finger and middle finger pointed to his eyes.

I was busted. The guy knew that I was the person who killed Yandle, and judging by his demeanor, had some unsettled issues with me. He was a rather roly-poly fellow who had a drip or two of food on the front of his shirt. He had a thick, black beard and his head was nearly shaved. I suppose I should have been intimidated. Although I'm not a little guy, I wish that I was the size of Bob Gilbert. I'd have gestured back to the bruiser as if to say, "Wanna go?"

Instead, I cowered slightly and tuned into Henry's ramblings as if he was Uncle Remus at story time. "Those judges must blot out an entire week for a trial," he said. "But most of the time, they only last two or three days. A lot of prosecutors don't have the stones to take their case to the jury so they offer plea bargains well before that."

"No kidding?" I said facetiously.

Henry's redundancy was getting on my nerves, but in the grand scheme of things, he wasn't a bad guy. After all, if the goons in Colleen's gang wanted to pound the piss out of me, they might think twice if I wasn't all by myself.

"Did you want to go to lunch?" I asked him.

"Sure, where?"

"Let's check things out." As we approached the doors in Brewer's court, I looked toward the defense table. Dr. Ong was huddled with Chitwood and his associate. They were engulfed in some sort of strategy session, I was sure of that.

For a few worrisome seconds, I thought that the goons in Colleen's group would be waiting for me outside the courtroom doors. Instead of barging through the threshold, I let Henry go first. He made it through without incident and never quit talking. I sped up, did a mini-pirouette over the threshold, and resumed our conversation.

We walked past the office door of the Honorable Steven Brewer, the restrooms across the hall, and the metal detectors downstairs. When we made it to the front of the courthouse, the television crews were all lined up, doing their own unique version of an "exclusive" coverage of the Ivey trial. I looked at my watch and realized that it was shortly after noon. The reporters were giving the lead story for the lunchtime news broadcast.

"The trial of the Ivey brothers from South Haven got off to a rocky start," one of them said, clutching her notebook in one hand, the microphone in the other. "Members of the Tea Party started a brawl inside the courtroom that resulted in several members being thrown out of the proceedings. As you know, the victim in this case was the late Congressman Floyd Capp, who cast the deciding vote on the health-care bill. That vote landed him in hot water with the Tea Party and thousands of conservatives across the country…"

Henry and I skated past the diversion and onto the side-walk. Colleen's gang went one way, the Tea Partiers another. The sidewalks were relatively crowded with the bustle of office workers headed for lunch. In a way, I felt a twinge of regret about not having a work schedule like most people. It might be fun to be a part of a big team with a common goal.

Henry suggested a deli next door to the parking garage.

"That would be fine, Henry," I said, handing him a ten-dollar bill. "I'll have corned beef on rye. If they don't have pickled asparagus, how about a bag of chips? Would you mind placing my order? I'm going to grab my phone and see if I have any messages."

Henry nodded. "Anything to drink?"

"Yeah. An Arnold Palmer."

"A what?" he grimaced.

"They'll know what it is, Henry, trust me. Don't worry about a thing. I'll see you in a few minutes."

Henry waved, as if to say, "No problem."

I looked around. Everything seemed to be okay. Nobody was following me. The entrance to the parking garage was enclosed in glass, and I didn't see any bums crouched behind the stairwell. For some reason, paranoia kept coursing through my veins. I felt like I had made a hundred enemies when I killed Marshall Yandle, and they were all in the courtroom, ready to lynch me.

Dr. Jim would have a field day treating me and my suspicion. I'm sure we could fill up a couple sessions sorting out the feelings in my head. For a second there, I wanted to speak with him about his take on the jury. It would be fun to listen to him and understand his logic for approving each one of the jurors.

The sparrows brought me out of my daydream. They were on the ledge of the parking garage, looking down at me, chirping away. I looked up and saw a couple of them scratching an itch on their heads with their toes. One or two others wiped their beaks on the edge of the concrete barrier, and I wasn't sure if it was their way of sharpening their bills or brushing the cheeseburger crumbs from their faces. Sparrows be damned, I decided to make a mad dash for the car, up two flights of stairs and beyond the stream of people urine.

Thank goodness, my car was still there. I unlocked it and jumped inside. My phone was on the seat next to me with nineteen new e-mails waiting to be opened.

Some of the messages I didn't even want. Why the banks figure that I'll start a credit card from a mass e-mail is beyond my comprehension. Macy's sent me a personal message just to let me know that there were only two hours left of a ninety-nine cent shipping special they were running. How I ever got on the mailing list for male potency drugs I'll never know. On second thought, maybe I did.

Advertisements aside, I thumbed past the list of e-mails to one I didn't recognize. The subject line read: *Innocent.* The body of the e-mail: *Ivey brothers*. I looked at the e-mail address and didn't recognize it at all: doodledandy@gmail.com and it was sent fifteen minutes ago.

I sat there for a moment or two and stared at the tiny screen.

For heaven's sake, I thought. Somebody *knew who I was, had my e-mail address, and thought that by hook or by crook I could influence the proceedings inside.*

My eyes darted to the rearview mirror—no stalker on my tail and nobody crouched in the back seat of the car. I glanced through the windshield, spattered with bug juice, and let the blue, August sky pour into my head. *Who could it be?*

I was thinking a million miles an hour.

Who could it be?

Halfway between the blue August sky and the car's dashboard, I saw an orange sheet of paper tucked under my windshield wiper. Without a second thought, I opened the car door, expecting a dollar-off coupon at the deli next door. In my mind, I hoped that I might catch Henry before he placed our order and I'd be a hundred pennies richer for the trouble.

Not even close.

I grabbed the paper, unfolded it and saw a caricature of attorney Jacobetti complete with the gaudy, gold ring on his hand. Whoever made the drawing was a good artist. Mr. Jacobetti had an enormous balding head on the body of a stick figure. In big, bold letters were the words: *The Iveys are not guilty!*

It looked like it could have been made by an amateur. Maybe an amateur with an artist's talent.

I got out of the car and looked around. The fliers were stuck to every other windshield in the lot.

My mind flashed back to the funeral of the federal prosecutor in Midland. It was the Heretic Fringe who put a note under the windshield-wiper of the government vehicle. Could it be them again? Of course it could.

I slid my phone and the flier into the breast pocket of my

sport coat, locked the car and trotted downstairs. Henry Rush was waiting for me at a corner table, not far from the door, even closer to the pickup counter. It looked like an old-fashioned butcher shop. There must have been ten or twelve people behind the counter, each wearing a pointy paper hat and a white apron smeared with fresh blood. The place was super busy, and the staff members were shouting the numbers for the next person in line, and confirming orders to the sandwich-makers at the counter behind them.

"I gotta pepperoni on wheat with cheddar. Hot mustard on the side!"

"That'll be six seventy-five."

The *ding* from the cash register was drowned by the bustle of conversation, the tear of waxed paper, and the non-stop squeak from the door hinges behind me.

I joined Henry in the corner, at a small metal table that was more than a little wobbly. A book of matches was on the floor, next to one of the legs, and I tried my best to jam it under the leg.

"They told me what an Arnold Palmer was," Henry said, smiling from ear to ear. "After all those years of watching him advertise for Pennzoil on TV, I thought that maybe you wanted a quart on the rocks."

"Very funny, Henry."

"What can I say? I'm in a good mood."

"Why? Because of your acquittal?"

"Yes. Heck yes. Everything's going our way."

"Everything?"

"Yeah. Let me tell you about the jury today. Remember when I told you that I had white males at my trial."

"Yes."

"There's only one thing better: *unemployed* white males, and we got three or four in the back row."

I noticed that all of a sudden he was referring to the defendants as "we," just like Colleen did a few days previous. Not only was Henry rooting for the Ivey brothers, it was like he was part of the defense team.

"What about the librarian, or the lady in front with the drug conviction?"

Henry took a bite of his egg salad and when he spoke, it reminded me of Eli's Guernseys and the way they chew their cud. I saw the mess in his mouth, and it really grossed me out. "Women as a rule are more sympathetic then men," he mooed. "The librarian was a government employee, so she understands that you don't bite the hand that feeds you. The drug addict in the front row and the hockey player in the back row aren't really leaders. They'll just follow along with the crowd."

"Why would you say that about the hockey player?"

"You don't remember?"

"No, what?"

"Gilbert had a bit of a drug problem. It was in the *Flint Journal* many times. He liked cocaine and had a drunken-driving arrest, too."

"Why does that mean that he's a follower?"

"Because that's what drug users do. They're easily influenced by people in their surroundings. Insecure people feel better about themselves when they're in the company of their friends. They're more prone to succumb to peer pressure."

"I never thought of that, but it makes sense."

Henry took the last bite of his sandwich, wiped his lips with a napkin, and balled up the waxed paper in the palm of his hand.

"There's the guy you want to talk to," Henry said, nodding toward the cash register.

I looked over my shoulder, and saw James Ong, fiddling with the napkin holder at the counter.

"His name is James Ong and he's one of the best jury consultants there is."

"Are you serious?"

"Oh, yeah. The guy really knows his stuff. I've seen him in action. He'll have something on every single juror: how many times they voted and their political affiliation. He'll know all about their family members, what kind of pets they have, everything. He knows quirky stuff about people, too."

"Like what?"

"I don't know, like how businessmen have little tolerance for ineptitude and can smell a line of baloney from a mile away. Union members like to be a part of a team."

"Why is that relevant?"

"You'd have to ask him, but I'd be willing to bet that he graded every one of those potential jurors on whether they'll deliver the verdict the defense wants. He knows all about the judge, too: what he'll allow, what he won't tolerate, and how he rules on certain procedural matters."

I looked over my shoulder and Jim was still at the counter, four people ahead of the clerk.

"I'd be willing to bet that he knows this is where the jury will have their lunch order placed."

"That's cool, but please don't say anything to him, okay, Henry?"

"Oh, I won't. I don't even know him. We'll just let him get his sandwich and be on his way."

"Why do you know so much about this stuff? Did you used to be an attorney or something?" I asked.

"No, I just have always had an interest in politics. That's what got me in trouble. Before my trial started, I wanted to explore every avenue that would help my defense. Dr. Ong has a great reputation and has a list on his website where his clients were successful."

"Doesn't he do work for the prosecution, too?"

Henry laughed. "Oh yeah; he's a switch hitter. He's got testimonials from prosecutors and DAs from all over the country, vouching for what a great job he did."

Dr. Jim passed by the window, white paper sack in hand.

"So, why didn't you hire him?"

Henry laughed. "Couldn't afford him. That guy gets big bucks."

"Really?"

"Oh, yeah. He gets paid by the day, the size of the jury pool, and he gets a bonus if he wins. He'll even set up a mock trial ahead of time, so that the fake jury will let the lawyers know which parts of their arguments were most effective."

"Sounds like you've really looked into this guy."

Henry took a big gulp of water, swished it around his mouth, and swallowed. Instead of answering my question, he reached into the front pocket of his shirt and pulled out a floss-pick.

"I think his wife is a lawyer or something, because his contract was spelled out in every detail on his website."

While Henry was digging for debris in his mouth, I pulled out the flier that had been tucked under the windshield wiper.

"Do you think he would pull a stunt like this?" I asked, handing it to Henry.

Henry pulled the paper out of my hand and put his tongue next to his teeth. He squinted, and tried his best to get a piece of food that was wedged between his cuspid and an incisor. The sound he made reminded me of the chirp from a house sparrow.

"Dr. Ong? No, he wouldn't do anything like that. This is the work of the Tea Partiers, or more likely, the associates of the Ivey brothers."

Henry made sense.

"There are lots of people who feel helpless," he said; "they look to the government to take care of all their worries, but really the government is the reason for their worries."

"What does that have to do with this?"

"Eventually that helplessness turns into frustration, and frustration turns into resentment, which leads to desperation."

I waited for Henry to finish his train of thought.

"These fliers...the...the letter I sent to Capp," he stuttered, "they're acts of desperation."

"I know, but the jury probably will never see these fliers. The guards inside the court will have them removed."

"That really doesn't matter, Derrick. The fliers were put together to ease their own anxiety. And you never know, if a jury sees them it could influence them somehow."

Henry was digging at his molars. I couldn't look. "You never really know what the Tea Partiers did to influence the thirteen jurors who were excused," he said. "It could have been an event like putting fliers under their windshields or something much more egregious."

"Henry, you make it sound like you've had some experience with jury tampering."

"Not really. I just know that you can go to jail for an awful long time if you're caught."

Twenty

A T A QUARTER TO TWO, Judge Brewer rapped his gavel, and the bread-and-butter portion of the trial was underway. The number of people in the courtroom had thinned slightly, since forty members of the jury pool had been excused. What was once "standing room only" had turned into a courtroom filled with interested spectators and members of the media. Instead of letting Mr. Jacobetti give his opening remarks, Judge Brewer held a paper napkin in his hand.

"I would like to remind dah members of dah jury, and dah people in attendance, dat dis is dah second and final warning I'm issuing regarding dah integrity of dah jury. It is my job to make sure dat dey remain fair and impartial. If I find out about another incident like dis, we will lock dah door and have dah trial all by ourselves."

Everyone seemed to be confused by his warning.

"May dah record show dat clerk Johnson took dah jury's lunch order, and called it into Abrihim's Delicatessen across dah street. When she brought dah food back to dah deliberation room, dah napkins had dah words *acquit Ivey* written on dem."

A gasp arose from the gallery.

Judge Brewer reminded the jury that the message on the napkin ought to be disregarded and that they should report any other suspicious activity to the court. Instead of introducing the prosecuting attorney and letting him give his opening remarks, Judge Brewer reminded the jury that whatever Mr. Jacobetti and Mr. Chitwood said wasn't the witnesses' testimony. "It's merely a summation of what dey believe dah facts will prove."

With the warning out of the way, Jack Jacobetti was given the okay to speak. He stood, fastened the top button of his suit coat, and wheeled the small, mobile podium so he was directly in front of the jury box. Instead of diving into his speech, Mr. Jacobetti seemed to relish the fact that everyone was watching him. He pulled out a short stack of note cards from his pocket, placed them on the podium, and started in.

"Ladies and gentlemen, on behalf of my associate, Ms. Melton, the government of the United States, and concerned citizens everywhere, thank you for doing your part today. I am the people's attorney, and like it or not, you have hired me to put Peter and Russell Ivey behind bars."

The Ivey boys sat in their chairs like good little boys, even though they were close to thirty years of age. They seemed slightly out of sorts, with their ties and their new dress shirts. The collars and sleeves on those shirts must have been at least a half or three quarters of an inch too big; their necks and arms were swimming in excess. In a strange kind of way, I felt a little sorry for them. They had boyish kind of traits and a perceptible innocence that hovered around their heads like a halo.

After speaking to Henry about Dr. Jim's expertise, I wouldn't have put it past the defense team to dress their clients with traditional, new clothing, just in time for the trial. Who knows, maybe Jim bought the boys their shirts and ties with the intent of making them extra roomy, extra childlike. *Could Dr. Jim be capable of such devious details?* I wondered for a half-second if Jim's clients were female would he have them wear dresses and make it look like they just stepped off the set of *Little House on the Prairie*, just to give them a wholesome, innocent look?

Regardless of the Iveys' appearance, Mr. Jacobetti rambled on and on about the juror's patriotic duty, his commitment to discovering the truth, and made biblical references to "an eye for an eye." Henry tucked his chin into the fat on his neck, and proceeded to drift off. The guard took off his glasses multiple times, held them up to the light and wiped them down with a handkerchief. I noticed a couple of jurors glanced at their watches, as if to say, "Come on, Man. Get on with it."

As I sat there and listened to Mr. Jacobetti, I reviewed the circumstances of Capp's kidnapping and murder. Chronologically, Capp voted for the health bill in March, came back to his district in April and was murdered in the days after that. The Ivey boys were arrested, charged, and freed on bond a week after the incident in Standish.

"The people who organized the killing of Congressman Capp are going to be charged separately," Jacobetti said, thumbing his note cards. "For now, they're being investigated by a grand jury."

I looked around at the other journalists in the courtroom. They were scratching their notepads feverishly. Perhaps I should have been more diligent. Instead, I was taken with the words coming from Jacobetti's mouth. He was in the meat-and-potatoes portion of his presentation. Even though he kept banging away at the defendants' guilt, the words were pouring from his mouth with great rhythm.

"We will prove to you beyond a shadow of a doubt that the Ivey brothers played a role in the murder of Congressman Capp. They're just as guilty as the man who chopped off his head with the battleaxe."

Colleen couldn't exactly take notes, but she was rather engaged in what was taking place. I was watching her about five rows ahead.

"What happened at the Standish High School wasn't an accident or a misunderstanding," Jacobetti emphasized over and over. "The men who killed our congressman need to be punished. We need to lock them up and throw away the key."

Henry snorted.

I looked at my watch. Jacobetti had been up there for nearly fifty minutes, and if he wasn't so repetitive, he could have done it in half the time.

Finally, he stopped, and the courtroom breathed a heavy sigh.

At nearly three thirty, the prosecution called their first witness: Nelson LeBeuf, a deputy with the Arenac County sheriff's department. LeBeuf was driving the patrol car when the tires were allegedly blown out by the defendants.

After asking LeBeuf about his tenure with the department, and where he lived, Jacobetti asked him about the year, make, model of his police cruiser, as well as its mileage. LeBeuf answered all his questions and provided two receipts—one, for the set that were blown out, and the second for what it cost to replace them. Both receipts were entered into evidence. In a nutshell, the tires that were ruined had fifty-five hundred miles on them, and it cost six hundred dollars to replace.

LeBeuf went on to testify that on the date in question, the sheriff gave the staff a briefing about Congressman Capp appearing at the high school.

"We didn't think it was that big of a deal," LeBeuf said. He was a rather lanky fellow, with an oversized Adam's apple and an enormous cleft in his chin that would have made a Royal Canadian Mountie proud. "Keep in mind that this was before the shooting of the congresswoman in New Mexico or whatever."

"Why is that relevant?" Jacobetti asked.

"Because after what happened in Standish, then out west, we realized that there are a lot of mentally deranged people out there who want to make a name for themselves by killing a person with a high profile."

"Keep going."

"I don't know if there is much more to say. You'd think that a sitting congressman would be safe in his own district, but now I'm not so sure."

Jacobetti asked him to tell the jury about the day Capp was kidnapped.

"Shortly after our shift started, the sheriff gave us our assignments. We had four deputies guarding two sets of back doors at the gymnasium; it was my job to patrol the rest of the county."

"So in any normal shift, you have five patrolmen on duty?"

"That's right, four officers and a sergeant."

"So what happened?" Jacobetti asked.

"About six-thirty I received a call of a single-car accident near Alger in the northeast part of the county. Apparently someone had hit a deer and wound up in the ditch."

"So what happened?"

"Oh, I forgot to say that there were injuries involved."

"Right."

The guard wiped his eyeglasses again, Gilbert yawned, and the former addict in the front row looked at her watch.

"What happened?" Jacobetti asked.

"When I showed up at where the accident was supposed to have taken place, I couldn't find anyone."

"Is that unusual?"

"Yes."

"Why?" Jacobetti asked.

"It's almost like it was a setup."

"Can you explain?"

"It's like someone wanted to make sure that I wouldn't be near the high school."

"Who was that?"

"I'm not sure."

"Did you have the phone number from where the call was made?"

"Well, the detective said—"

"Objection," Chitwood interrupted. "Hearsay."

"Sustained," Brewer agreed.

Jacobetti seemed to be put out by the interruption. He sighed and rolled his eyes slightly as if an extra layer of theatrics would help sway the jury in his favor.

"Deputy LeBeuf, will you please tell the court where the call originated?" Jacobetti asked.

"At a pay phone in the area."

"Which area?"

"Near Alger," he said. "Near the exit off I-75. There are a couple of gas stations that sell jerky. They got pay phones—"

"What happened next?"

"Central dispatch told me to report to the high school. They said that a riot had broken—"

"Objection—"

"Sustained."

"Why were you called to the school?"

"They told me to report to the high school in Standish."

"So did you?"

"Sure did; when I arrived it was shortly after seven. There were people and cars all over the place. The area was quite congested. I've never been in a riot before but it sure seemed like it then."

"Why?"

"At first I thought that everything was cool. There were two state cruisers at the front door of the gym and the sheriff had two or three vehicles at the side doors. All of a sudden I saw three or four men acting suspiciously by the doors. When I turned on my lights they all took off running."

"What happened next?"

"Instead of chasing them, I looked at the doors and realized that they were chained shut. Inside, I could see people choking and realized that I had better free the people inside rather than chase after the suspects."

"Okay," Jacobetti gestured with his hands to keep going.

"Everyone was yelling and screaming. Half of the people I saw were bent over, choking. They banged on the glass door but they couldn't get out."

"So, what did you do?"

"I was trying to find the commanding officer to try to find out what we were supposed to be doing," LeBeuf said. "At that point I didn't even know that the congressman had been kidnapped."

"Keep going."

"I went back to the patrol car and grabbed the snips. It only took me a minute or two, but I cut the chain and freed the people inside."

It seemed that everyone was on the edge of their seats, waiting for the next bit of information.

"They all charged out of the gym, choking and clenching their throats. Finally, it seemed, I got a call on the radio that the congressman had been kidnapped."

"What were the details?" Jacobetti asked.

"The only thing they said was that he was in the back seat of a police car. They didn't say what kind or which department it belonged to."

"So what did you do?"

"I jumped in my car, turned on the sirens, and took off down the driveway. I never seen the spike strips on the road, but they got me real good. Blew out all four tires."

"How far did you make it?"

"Not very far at all. Maybe a quarter mile."

"What happened next?"

"I called in to dispatch that my tires were blown out and that I was ten-sevened."

"Deputy, for the benefit of the jury, can you please explain what ten-seven means?"

"Sorry; it means that I was in flatulence."

"It's okay, Deputy LeBeuf," Jacobetti promised. "Does ten-seven mean 'flatulence,' as in, having a flat tire, you like to pass gas, or does it mean that you're incapacitated?"

"Incapacitated."

"Okay, good. What did you do next?"

"I parked the cruiser on the side of the road with the flash-ers on and hustled back to the end of the school's driveway."

Jacobetti nodded.

"By the time I got there, the suspects responsible for my tires being blown out had claimed three other police vehicles, so I arrested them. There were cars parked up and down both sides of the school's driveway. They had the ideal place for an ambush and had set the perfect trap."

"Objection, Your Honor," Chitwood interrupted. "Will you please remind the witness that he should answer the ques-tion and not give his opinion of the alleged infraction?"

Judge Brewer sat up in his chair and placed both elbows on his desk. He looked at Chitwood, blinked, then Jacobetti, and finally LeBeuf. "Mr. Jacobetti, would you like to rephrase your question?" He asked.

"If it pleases the court, Your Honor," Jacobetti said, almost as if he was going out of his way to be a friendly, courteous barrister. "How many years have you been a member of the law enforcement community?"

"Sixteen."

Jacobetti cleared his throat and with an extra bit of mustard fired a fastball at his witness: "In your sixteen years of being a law man, have you ever seen a plot like this?"

"Objection! Your Honor—"

"Never mind," Jacobetti acquiesced. "I have nothing fur-ther."

By then it was almost four-fifteen, and I could see the wheels spinning in Judge Brewer's head.

Chitwood must have seen it too, because he spoke up and said that he only needed a few minutes to complete his cross examination.

"Very well," Brewer said, leaning back in his chair. "Your witness."

Chitwood strolled up to the podium again, bent his knee slightly and tapped the tip of his loafer against the polished marble floor. "Mr. LeBeuf, can you tell the court about the time you were arrested for drunk driving?"

"Objection!" Jacobetti scowled.

"Sustained!" Judge Brewer was upright in his chair again, peeved at Chitwood's audacity.

For the first time all afternoon, Mr. Yoder showed some emotion; he cracked a smile. It seemed like an odd occasion to find amusement.

"Your Honor, I think it's important that the jury knows about the witness' prior conviction of drunk driving," Chitwood insisted.

"Your Honor!"

"That's okay, Your Honor," Chitwood said, voice trailing off, slightly. "I'll withdraw that question. Better yet, let me rephrase it. Were you drinking at the time you made the arrest?"

"Mr. Chitwood," His Honor scolded. "I don't know what you're trying to get at, but you're skating on very thin ice."

Chitwood propped his hand on his hip. He smiled and said "Very well, Your Honor. I just have a few more questions."

"Carry on, Counselor."

"Deputy LeBeuf, you mentioned that there were five officers on duty on the evening in question, is that correct?"

"Yes."

"That's normal for your department?"

"Yes."

"Your Honor, I'd like to have the court reporter read Officer LeBeuf's testimony."

Judge Brewer shook his head. "The whole thing?"

"No, no, Your Honor, from the top…just the part about the normal day."

"Very well."

The court reporter pulled at a coiled-up piece of paper from the back of her machine, thumbed the inscription until she read aloud, "Witness: 'Shortly after our shift started, the sheriff gave us our assignments. We had four deputies guarding two sets of back doors at the gymnasium; it was my job to patrol the rest of the county.' Prosecutor: 'So in any normal shift, you have five patrolmen on duty?' Witness: Yes.'"

"Thank you. Thank you for your trouble," Chitwood said, gushing with courtesy. Without missing a beat, he turned his attention back to the witness. "Isn't that your testimony, Deputy LeBeuf?"

"Yes it is."

"Why don't you tell the court how you can explain the fact that you were working overtime on the day in question, and that on any given shift there are in fact four patrolmen on duty."

"Objection!" Ms. Melton finally got involved. "This line of questioning is irrelevant."

"Overruled," Brewer decided. "Mr. Chitwood, that doesn't mean that you've got a long leash."

Melton slumped slightly, bending the corner of her lip. She was called out on strikes.

"Were you or were you not on overtime on the day in question?" Chitwood demanded.

"Yes, I was," LeBeuf said. "There are four of us on patrol, normally, but the Captain authorized a half shift of overtime on account of the congressman's visit."

Chitwood saw him back pedaling. He let him twist in the breeze, Adam's apple and all. The courtroom was deathly silent, the jury on the edge of their seats. Colleen, Dr. Jim, everybody was waiting for the next question.

In a calm, dramatic kind of way Chitwood asked, "Why would you lie?" He whispered. "Why would you fail to tell the truth?"

Henry couldn't hear him. He nudged me on the forearm and asked, "What did he say?"

I held up a finger for him to wait.

The blood climbed up the deputy's neck; he was blushing a vine of ivy that engulfed his ears, his cheeks, patches of his forehead.

"I'm...I'm..." LeBeuf stammered. "I don't always have the best memory," he pleaded.

Chitwood had command of the stage. The silence he had orchestrated said volumes about the tack he was taking. It was, after all, the complete opposite strategy that his nemesis had devised: Jacobetti liked to hear himself speak, was redundant as a broken record, and carried a plume of arrogance that was more than palpable. Chitwood—despite his tailored suit, slicked back hair, and three-hundred-dollar loafers—understood the notion that what you don't say is just as powerful as what you do say.

If silence is golden, Chitwood wore it around his neck like a medallion.

"You don't always have the best memory?" Chitwood asked, especially doubtful.

LeBeuf just sat there.

"Do you remember saying that Alger is in the northeast part of the county?"

"Yes."

"And is Alger in the northeast part of the county?"

LeBeuf sat there, thinking.

Somebody in the gallery cleared his throat. Another sneezed.

"It's in the northwest," he lamented.

"You're right. It is," Chitwood whispered, as he abandoned the podium and strolled dramatically toward the witnesses' box. His steps were loud and deliberate; it sounded like maybe he had a pebble ground into the heel of his alligator-skin loafers. I heard it mash and wince against the marble floor.

"Mr. LeBeuf, how would you like it if you were sitting over there," he said, pointing to the defendants, "and the lead witness for the prosecution admitted on the stand that 'I don't always have the best memory?'"

"Objection, Your Honor!" Jacobetti and Melton howled in unison.

"Never mind. Never mind," Chitwood insisted. "I'm just trying to prove a point, Your Honor, that what the witness says and what took place could be two entirely different things."

Brewer shook his head, "Do you have any further questions, Mr. Chitwood?"

"No, Your Honor. That is all."

"Before we adjourn," His Honor said, gavel in hand, "I'd like to remind dah members of dah jury that they're not supposed to talk to anybody or each other about this case. The clerk will escort you to the deliberation room where you will have a chance to call your loved ones, who will bring a change of clothes and your toiletries. Due to the severity of the case and its massive media appeal, you will be sequestered in a motel until the trial is finished."

A groan arose from the jury box.

Mr. Yoder smiled from ear to ear; he had hit the lottery.

"You cannot watch television, or read the newspapers, but your meals will be paid for by the court. Have a good evening. We will convene tomorrow morning at eight o'clock sharp."

His Honor rapped the gavel, stood up, and was already at the touch-pad for his chamber door when the clerk cleared her throat and said, "All rise."

Twenty-One

MY HEAD WAS SPINNING IN DETAILS, thoughts and revelations when I ducked out of the courtroom and made it to the parking garage. In my mind, I was already into the story about the first day of the Ivey trial. How was I going to summarize it all into one lead paragraph? Should the fireworks with the armed guards be the lead, or something a little more salacious? The jury-tampering angle had a lot of sizzle, and the subsequent warning from Judge Brewer seemed to validate that fact. What about LeBeuf's testimony and the way Chitwood grilled him? It seemed like great courtroom drama any way I sliced it.

And that was before I made it to the car and my cell phone, at slightly after five in the afternoon. Thank goodness nobody had slipped another flier under my windshield, or sent me any more mysterious e-mails. My plan was get out of Flint as quickly as possible and zip up I-75 to the Clio exit. Once there, I'd turn left on M-37 and whistle through Montrose and Chesaning on my way to US-27. It was a pleasant, late afternoon for a drive, and I thought for a minute or two about buying some fresh veggies from one of the roadside stands I was sure to encounter. I was craving those fresh, plump tomatoes of August, or the snappy, flavorful cucumbers, sliced and marinated in mayonnaise. Add a few rings of onions, maybe bits of fresh chopped chives, and I could be in flavor heaven.

Strange though, how everyone, it seems, is in a rush to get someplace. The drivers in Flint were tailgating, and the speeders on I-75 roared past me even though I was traveling five miles over the limit.

About the time I made it to the Clio exit, I got a new e-mail.

I didn't recognize the address: *39andholding*, but I certainly was fascinated by the short, but intriguing subject line: *Hi.*

It had to be Colleen.

The body of the text was just as inviting: *Wanna talk?*

I looked out the window and made sure there weren't any cops following me or lurking in the shadows of the overpasses. The last thing I needed was a ticket for driving while texting. Although it was a little difficult to keep the car between the dotted lines at seventy-five miles per hour, and still hide my cell phone behind the wheel, I managed to answer her invitation. *Sure,* I typed. *Where?*

There's a corner bar in Montrose.

Cool, I typed. *I'm almost there.*

I breathed a sigh of relief—knowing that she was okay—while at the same time I looked forward to the opportunity to game-plan for tomorrow's newspaper story. As my former editor, she'd help me sort out the details of the trial that belonged at the top and prioritize the chain of events that should be buried in the ensuing paragraphs. In my head, I pictured her waltzing into the bar with her laptop computer-case slung over her shoulder, sunglasses tamped against her red wig. She'd order a tall Stoli's and tonic and have it half gone by the time her laptop came to life. Our meeting wouldn't be a booze fest, however, on account of the looming deadline hanging over our heads. We'd have to finish the story tonight and get it into Walter Claety's hands first thing in the morning.

For a few minutes I even entertained the thought of Colleen riding home with me, where we could continue our discussions about the trial and even work on the story as we rolled along. It had been forever since I had picked someone up from the bar—let alone my wife—and for a brief time I thought about the line I might use when presented with the opportunity: *Come on, Baby, I need your help with this. Why don't I take you home? Your car will be okay until morning.*

Instead of dreaming about Colleen and our chance to work together, I turned on the radio with hopes of catching what other reporters were saying about the first day of the trial. Instead of finding the news, I discovered a local talk-radio show whose host was blasting the liberals for ramming the health-care debacle down our throats. He even cited polling data that suggested the country was against the bill by a sixty-three to sixteen percent margin. *"It's no wonder they killed that socialist who voted yes,"* he yelled, the angst exploding from the speakers. *"He wasn't listening to the people who elected him. I'm here to tell you that in every revolution, blood has got to be spilled. Congressman Capp got the message; now tell me who's next in line?"*

I turned off the radio and finished the drive to Montrose in silence.

When I found a corner table at the bar, it occurred to me that I really hadn't had a drink in quite some time. As much as I wanted to have one now, I was really proud of the winning streak I had put together. It seemed that I had turned the corner on my cravings; now all I had to conquer was social situations like this. This would be one of those settings where a beer would taste wonderful, a vodka tonic even better, and a Manhattan better yet. Heck, a tall glass of hardened lemonade would be appropriate, if not downright tasty. The possibilities were endless, and with each passing second, my winning streak was in question.

Colleen would help me out. She'd be the one who'd lend a hand when it came to quelling my urges, even though it seemed a little strange that she'd suggest an establishment like this.

When the waitress asked me what I wanted to drink, I never thought twice about ordering an Arnold Palmer.

"You want a menu too, Hun?" she asked.

"Sure, Darlin' Any specials tonight?"

"We got a fourteen-ounce sirloin for eight ninety-five. Comes with your choice of potato and cole slaw."

"Sounds good. Why don't you give me a minute. I'm supposed to be meeting someone."

"Suit yourself," she said as she pulled a pencil from behind her ear and scratched something on the notepad. "My name's Candy."

"Thank you."

It looked like maybe Candy had eaten her share of candy over her fifty or so years. She had what Dad used to call summer teeth: some were there, some were not.

I missed my dad. A twinge of melancholy nibbled at my heart as I fiddled with my cell phone for several minutes. Walter Claety was expecting a story about the trial and I let him know that it would be there later today.

I caught a glimpse of the television hovering over the bar, and heard the reporter saying something about "tuning into TV 3's Twitter account for instant updates on all the fireworks in the Ivey trial." For some strange reason, I really didn't care about the trial any longer. All the sordid details seemed so irrelevant, so unfortunate after all.

And then, all of a sudden, things changed.

The People's favorite assistant prosecutor, Ms. Melton rolled inside. While she stood there in the doorway, letting her eyes adjust to the darkened atmosphere, I hid behind the menu and snickered to myself.

Colleen was going to laugh her head off when she saw who was here. This would be a golden opportunity to get the inside scoop about the prosecution's take on how the case was going.

Ms. Melton caught the eye of a couple of regulars at the bar. I heard one of them say, "You can sit next to me, Honey."

She brushed off his invitation, if not the drooling glare, and strolled to the other side of the building. When she did, I noticed that she wasn't wearing the blazer from the trial, nor the stockings that garnered so much attention. And she couldn't just walk the usual way; she had to take baby steps on account of the skirt wrapped around her thighs. The way her head moved to the right and left, I could have sworn she was looking for someone. Maybe a key witness? Her husband? A jury consultant of her own?

Gone were the dreary thoughts rushing through my head; now I was tuned into this lovely woman and who she might be meeting.

It seemed that half the bar was watching her as she paraded past the front door and directly towards me. I tried slouching farther into my chair, but there was no escaping her happy glare.

"Is that you, Derrick?"

"Oh, yes, hi, Ms. Melton." I tried to act like she had startled me as I stood up and shook her hand.

"Please, please. Sit down," she said.

We both kind of laughed for a second, although I'm not certain why. I tried to play it off like it was some sort of amazing coincidence that we should happen to bump into each other at such an obscure location. I was partially laughing at the thought of Colleen rolling in at any moment and finding me in a one-on-one with the prosecution's second in command.

Candy reappeared with my drink and took Miss Melton's order: a Bloody Mary.

"Are you hungry, Ms. Melton?"

"Please, call me Penny," she said, as she stuffed her sunglasses into her purse.

"Very well, Penny."

"Heck yeah, I'm hungry. We had to work through lunch, trying to get ready for the afternoon's grilling."

"How do you think it went?" I asked.

"The grilling?" she huffed. "That went great. We got our butts fried, that's what I think." She was still riled, and I noticed the crease between her eyebrows looked like it had been chiseled with a one-bottom plow. "Just let me tell you something, Derrick; I don't want any of this on the record."

"Any of what?" I asked, wryly.

She tucked her hair behind her ear, but her fingers loitered at the base of her jaw.

"Any of this."

"Oh," I said.

Candy brought her Bloody Mary, and I caught myself staring at it. The celery stalk looked absolutely wonderful, stuffed like a ladder in a pool of intoxicants.

"What are you having, Derrick?"

"An Arnold Palmer. Iced tea and lemonade."

Penny clenched her eyebrows, and the furrow became even more obvious.

"You want a menu?" Candy asked, stabbing her pencil in Penny's direction.

"Um, ah," she stammered.

"They have a sixteen-ounce ribeye for seven ninety-five."

"It's only fourteen-ounce, Hun," Candy interrupted, flashing the vacancies in her gums, "and it ain't no ribeye. It's a sirloin."

Penny must have felt like she was getting tag-teamed.

"I do recall that it comes with your choice of potato, and cole slaw," I said, smiling.

"Can you give me a minute?" Penny asked.

"Suit yourself," Candy said, prancing back to her hideout.

"I've made enough decisions today," Penny said, a bit exhausted. "Sometimes I wish I had someone to make me dinner. It would be nice to just come home from work and have someone tell me, 'We're having spaghetti.'"

"Hmm," I uttered, "that would be nice, wouldn't it?"

She smiled, and raised her glass.

"Sure would," she said. "Here's to a better day tomorrow."

"And to the people who cover it," I smiled.

We chinked our glasses and had a little sip. Instead of concentrating on the drink in my hand, I watched Penny and the way she opened her lips to take in Mary's juices. She had a rather intriguing mouth, and her teeth were so white they had to have been bleached. The longer I stared at her mouth and thought about what was being poured inside it, I could almost taste the vodka, feel the tomato juice, and smell the hint of pepper as it crossed the threshold of her palate.

Colleen would be along at any moment, I was certain of that, and all those unwholesome visions would be purged from my mind.

"So, where is the jury staying?" I asked.

"Who knows. Brewer's got a couple of favorites. There's a Comfort Inn and a Sleep Inn near Miller Road and I-75, and there are plenty of restaurants in the area to feed the jurors."

Penny took another sip, and I stole a glance down the cleft of her shirt. She had a small scar on the top of her chest, about half an inch long. On either side of the scar were the footprints left behind by the stitches made by her dermatologist. If I had to guess, Miss Melton's sun worship in her younger years had metastasized into a tiny centipede today.

"Eating is about the only fun thing they'll be able to do."

"Why's that?" I asked.

"'Cause they take the television sets out of their rooms."

"Aw."

"Yeah, they're not allowed to have Internet or newspapers, either."

"What do they do all night?"

"Let's see. Not too much, I guess. The loners will read books, but the socialites will get together in one of their rooms and play cards."

"Don't the jurors complain about that arrangement?"

"Sure they do, but at the end of the day, Judge Brewer has to walk a fine line between preserving their integrity and being frugal with the People's money." She sipped. "When he was in the U.P., he got in trouble for bussing the jury panel to one of his relative's motels."

"What's wrong with that?"

"The courthouse was in Marquette, and his family's motel was almost to Houghton, ninety minutes away."

I laughed.

She smiled.

We both tipped our glasses.

"Did you see the reaction of the Amish guy in the front row, when he realized that the court would be paying for his room and board?" I joked.

Now I had her laughing. And drinking.

"I was going to ask you about the dismissal of the thirteen jurors. What was that all about?" I asked.

She shrugged. "Oh, geez, that was a goat circus. Jacobetti had a list of people who were threatened by the Tea Baggers, or Partiers, whatever you want to call them."

"What kind of threats?"

"I thought it was kind of penny-ante kind of stuff. All thirteen got anonymous notes at their houses."

"What's wrong with that?" I asked facetiously.

She chuckled, "The notes were attached to bricks. And the bricks were thrown through their windows."

Now, I was the one laughing.

The men at the bar glanced over their shoulders. Apparently I interrupted their afternoon board meeting, as in *bored* meeting.

"Why do you suppose there were only thirteen people who got the notes and not the whole jury pool?"

"Who knows?" she quipped. "Maybe they ran out of bricks."

"What did the notes say?" I asked.

Penny raised her hand toward the bar and jingled the ice in her glass. Candy saw her request and nodded her head.

Out of nowhere, I raised my fingers, forming the universal sign for peace. Candy nodded again, and my winning streak was over. I wasn't wishing her peace, but rather two drinks instead of one.

It's not the end of the world, I thought. It's only one drink. Tomorrow I'll start another streak.

"I didn't think the note was all that threatening, but my boss sure did."

"What did it say?"

"Just that the Ivey boys were innocent."

"Are they?"

She laughed. "That's the sixty-four-dollar question, isn't it?"

"Well, yeah. Don't take this the wrong way, but I think that Chitwood has already established cause for reasonable doubt, don't you?"

She hesitated and bobbed her head from side to side as if she was dodging punches. "Yeah, I have some real problems with LeBeuf. There was no doubt that he wasn't very convincing."

Candy interrupted our conversation. She placed a drink in front of Penny and another in front of me. "You ready to order?"

I extended my palm to Penny, who nodded her head approvingly. She said that she'd like the special, cooked medium rare.

"You get your choice of potato."

"I'll have scalloped."

"Don't have that."

"Sweet potato?"

"Sorry, Hun, we got baked or fries."

"Oh, okay. Baked would be fine."

I ordered just about the same thing—to keep things simple—then took a sip from Mary's cup. It was wonderful. Beyond what I was expecting.

Candy disappeared.

"I guess if I were on the jury," I said, "I might question the deputy's testimony."

Penny nodded.

"How did Chitwood know about the drunk driving?"

"Chitwood is always prepared. He convinced his clients to hire a jury consultant named James Ong who's even more thorough."

"Oh yeah?"

"He's honestly a shrink from Mt. Pleasant and has a practice at the St. Jean Centre up there. Does this jury consulting business on the side."

I was tuned into her story.

"I went to law school with his wife, Rachel," she said. "I think they have one or two kids together."

"That's cool."

"He's really a nice guy, and I'd be willing to bet he's got the dirt and skinny on every one of those jurors. He's probably got some on me and Jacobetti, too."

We drank.

All of a sudden our pleasant conversation had turned somewhat cheerless.

"I think that's half the reason why Fayette killed herself."

"Who?"

"Fayette Pappas. The prosecutor in Midland."

I nodded, but didn't say much. This wasn't a time to be talkative.

"That's when I first met you," she said, "in the church

parking lot. You were in your car, with your sunglasses on. Everybody in my vehicle thought you were a private investigator. I thought you were," she paused, "I just thought you were…"

It seemed like maybe Penny caught herself. I was rather glad that she did.

I never thought that we met; I just saw her at the funeral.

"I don't know what the heck was wrong with her," she said, "but it must have been something pretty bad for her to want to kill herself."

We kept drinking.

"Have you looked through her caseload?" I asked.

"Well, yeah, and the only thing remotely sensitive was an allegation made by a group of constituents up north."

"What's that?" I asked.

"They had a complaint that the unions were the only ones allowed to bid on government-subsidized construction projects."

"And that's wrong?"

"Well yeah. Just because the government is involved in the financing of a project doesn't mean that it has to go to the unions."

"What did she find out?"

"That the congressman might have been pushing contracts the unions' way." She looked at her watch and added, "I haven't really had time to look into it all."

Candy picked up our empty glasses, and brought two more. "Your dinner will be right up."

I had forgotten all about Colleen at least for the moment. Penny had all my attention.

"I heard that Pappas was run out of Grand Rapids because she withheld evidence," I suggested.

"Well yeah, three years ago, but that wouldn't be reason to kill yourself now." Penny's eyebrows were in overdrive. She made them ebb and flow with every swing of emotion. "I mean, you can't be a federal prosecutor and not expect to ruffle some feathers throughout your career. We aren't dealing with jaywalkers and purse thieves. We're dealing with high-profile cases: major, major felonies, and most of the time we're prosecuting people who are well connected."

"What do you mean?" I asked her.

"The defendants are buddies with congressmen or politicians. They're ingrained into their communities and have multiple business partners. Most of the time, it's complicated."

"Is that why you decided to try the Ivey brothers separately from the rest of the Heretic Fringe?"

"It wasn't my decision, but yeah, that was our strategy. I'm not so sure I agree with it now."

"Are you complaining, Penny?"

She smiled. And sipped her drink. Maybe it was more like a gulp. Either way, it appeared as if the alcohol gave her some liquid courage.

Her hand squeezed my wrist. It caught me a little off guard.

Don't even think about it, Derrick. It was just a harmless little gesture, I thought.

"Does it sound like I'm complaining?" She stared right through me.

"No," I lied, sincerely. "I heard that Pappas was a bit of a hired gun for the departed congressman."

"Who told you that?"

"Was she?" I shrugged, taking a drink, which thwarted her question in the process.

"I think, to some extent, we all have our marching orders."

Candy arrived with our plates full of food. For bar food, I'd say it looked rather tasty and smelled simply wonderful. I got my wish and had a slice of tomato on my plate, next to the steak.

"Thank you," we said in unison.

Penny reached for the salt and pepper, while I unfurled the napkin and silverware.

"Does your steak look okay?" I asked her.

"Looks fine. How about yours?"

"Well, it's a little rare. I think it's still bellowing."

Penny smiled.

I glanced at the television, and saw sketches of her on the screen. She looked a little like a red-haired Barbie, instead of the mature woman that she was. The men at the bar didn't realize that the woman on the television was the person sitting next to me.

"I don't think a congressman would ever call up a prosecutor and say 'Hey do this or do that,' but you never know."

We dove into our meals and the television showed a live shot of the jury pool boarding a van. All but Mr. Yoder had an overnight bag on their shoulders; he carried his belongings in a pillowcase.

"I always thought that those kinds of things from Washington ran downhill," she chewed. "The congressman might be behind the scenes, but it's the cronies that make things happen."

Candy brought us another drink, but I'm not so sure I needed it. The vodka was chewing a hole in my senses and I was starting to lose touch of the reason why I was even there. It was my hope that Penny would go on the record and I could get a whole bunch of useful quotes about the case, but I'm not so sure that's what was on her mind. She seemed to think that maybe I would be a good companion for dinner. What's more, she never really answered my question about Ms. Pappas being a hired gun for the late congressman, so I tried to rephrase it, back-door style.

"How many of Pappas' files are you handling?"

"This is the second."

All of a sudden, I noticed my tongue felt a little thick, and my vision a little blurred. There was no mistaking that I was getting mildly intoxicated. "Anything out of the ordinary?"

"No. Other than every case seems to be a little out of the ordinary. They're all interesting."

"What about Pappash's e-mail or phone recordsh? Do you ever look into those?"

"Not really, Derrick. I've got a lot on my plate right now." I wasn't sure if she was talking about the work she needed to do, or the half-eaten piece of cow still sleeping on her plate.

One thing was for certain, since I hadn't had a drink in so long, my tolerance for alcohol wasn't very high.

"What about the Tea Party?" I asked.

"What about them?" she countered.

"How about the H-H-Heretic Fringe, ever look into what they're doing?"

"Are you okay, Derrick?"

"Yesh."

She glanced my way and suddenly had four eyebrows instead of two. The two on the right side of her face were raised somewhat higher than the ones on her left, and I believe it was her way of being skeptical. Either way, I felt a little tipsy.

"We rarely get personally involved with the investigation. It has to be something huge. Besides, I just was assigned to the case."

"I she."

The buzz had eclipsed me.

I wasn't able to concentrate.

And I missed my wife. My daughter. And my dog.

Despite the longing in my heart, the world was a beautiful place. Good old Bloody Mary had tinted my outlook on life in a glorious way. I wore rose-colored glasses and was at the helm of the Good Ship Lollipop. Everything that popped into my head came spewing out of my lips:

"Did your parents hate you?" I asked.

"Why would you ask that?" she looked at me, rather mad.

"'Cause of your name, Penny Melton."

She didn't respond.

"Do you melt a lot of penniesh?"

"Ha, ha," she said sarcastically, "that was my married name."

"Will you excush me? The rent's up on my Arnold Palmer."

"Go right ahead."

I pushed the chair away from the table and drifted slowly to the men's room. When I arrived, I noticed that the bar owner had a cork board mounted on the wall behind the urinal; tacked to its face was today's edition of the *Flint Journal*.

What a great idea, I thought. I can catch up on the day's reading, and go potty all at the same time. It's like killing two birds with one stone.

But I couldn't just stand there and read the paper. Even in my debilitated mental state, I still had the ability to think about killing *three* things with one stone.

I whipped out my cell phone and quickly realized that Colleen had not called.

She hadn't e-mailed either.

I was rather bummed.

It's not like her to stand me up.

Colleen's mysterious e-mail address was staring at me: *39andholding*. Without as much as a second thought, I managed to type five little words: *Can u pick me up?*

My attention turned to the headline on the front page: *Trial Starts in Capp Slaying.*

The story's lead was a dandy, and it was one that I wished I had written. It was clean and "punchy" as Colleen would say: *The nation's attention will be turned to Flint this week as two South Haven residents will be charged as conspirators in the murder of a northern Michigan congressman.*

Colleen responded: *I'm not that kind of girl.*

With so much attention focused on the proceedings, the stakes for the attorneys involved couldn't be higher.

I love it when Colleen plays hard to get. It's one of the sexiest things she does. *What kind of girl R U?* I typed.

The defense has hired flamboyant jetsetter Jacob Chitwood, who brings a ninety-seven percent acquittal rating into the trial.

The prosecution has had a bit of a shake up after the suicide of Fayette Pappas—the lead attorney for the government.

Before I had time to digest what I was reading in the article, Colleen sent me a response that was a little confusing, not to mention slightly terse: *I'm a friggin' busy girl, that's what.*

Pappas' replacements, Jack Jacobetti and Penny Melton, failed to successfully prosecute Henry Rush—the man accused of sending Congressman Capp a threatening letter in the weeks before his death.

Instead of responding negatively to Colleen's e-mail, I typed: *I need you.*

She didn't reply immediately, so I zipped up my fly, and read one last paragraph: *The defense has hired jury consultant James Ong from Mt. Pleasant, who says that the anti-government climate in today's society has increased the odds of getting an acquittal. "Even with the government changing the venue from Bay City to Flint," Ong said, "I still believe that the prosecution has a tough road to hoe."*

That James Ong is everywhere, I thought. *I would have never guessed he was such an influential person.*

I turned on the faucet and lathered my hands with soap. The door to the bathroom opened wide and a man wearing a UAW cap waltzed inside. We nodded to each other slightly the way men do when they want to say 'How's it going,' without actually saying 'How's it going.' I dried my hands on a coarse, brown paper towel and walked towards the table.

When I arrived, Penny was gone. She left twenty-five dollars tucked under the salt shaker, even though I didn't see a check.

I looked around. She wasn't at the bar, or mingling with the folks at the other tables. I peeked outside to the parking lot, but wouldn't recognize her vehicle if I tried.

It seemed rather odd for her to leave the way she did. I finished my meal in peace, and cut up the scraps of steak for my dog. Jacque was going to love what I was going to bring home, and wouldn't know the difference in taste between my steak and Penny's.

Of course, that's if I made it home.

Despite my feeling of invincibility that often comes with a snoot-full of spirits, I still had enough common sense to realize that I was in no condition to drive.

Instead of fiddling with secret e-mails, and all that clandestine electronic correspondence, I decided to call Colleen. She was, after all, my wife, and every once in a while a man's got to put down his foot and say exactly what's on his mind.

"If it's not too much trouble, can you please pick me up?" I asked.

"Of course, I can," she said, pleasantly. "I was just about to call you. Where are you, anyway?"

I wasn't exactly sure how to answer that question. It seemed that she should have known.

"I'm in downtown Montrose," I said, not especially proud of myself, "and I had a few drinks."

"Oh, Derrick," she sighed. "I was just about to call you. Did you have too many?"

"Yeah, probably. Where are *you*?"

"I'm on my way. I'll be there in a little while."

Twenty-Two

AFTER SETTLING MY BILL WITH CANDY, I decided to wait for Colleen at the intersection of the main streets in town, rather than in the bar's parking lot. There was no sense in rubbing Colleen's nose in the fact that her husband had been drinking when he should have been covering the trial and writing a great story about it.

If I were serious about having fun and drinking myself silly, I would have invited her inside and bought her a round or two of whatever she wanted. Sure, I was enjoying the little buzz, but in all reality, I felt a little foolish for getting that tipsy. The longer I sat there on a bench under the main street lamp in town, the angrier I became at myself. The booze had quelled my enthusiasm for writing the story and I totally missed out on a golden opportunity with Ms. Melton. She really seemed like she wanted to talk about the case, but I chased her off, like a total imbecile.

She seemed to be "a friggin' busy girl," just like Colleen.

As I watched the cars whiz past me and sobered up somewhat, I realized that Montrose had become little more than a place to take your foot off the gas. It's small town America—like downtown Flint—where the buildings are old and tired, but still relatively useful. Sure, there were new strip malls on the outskirts of town, but downtown Montrose has a bit of charm that reminded me of days gone by. Montrose—like every town in America—must have had a diner that served slices of pie and a cup of coffee for two forty-five. It didn't take much imagination to picture the morning coffee club, where eight or ten white-haired men gathered to chat about the world's problems. Most of the men missed their calling in politics, in athletics, in fishing tournaments, and in a lot of cases, in settling down with the right woman. But if misery loves company, then the men at the diners across America have plenty of companionship, laughs and complaints about their plight in life.

Montrose reminds me of some of the small towns in parts of Iowa, where the backbone of the community's economy is connected to agriculture, but the heart and soul of its younger generation has turned to more glamorous careers in technology, health care, and engineering. The days of making a living on a two-hundred-acre farm are long gone. Now, it seems, a farm of that size is merely a hobby, if not a source for write-offs during tax time.

Colleen didn't seem to want to know about Montrose, farming, why I couldn't drive, or why I was even there. And since she didn't want to know, I wasn't about to volunteer. My beloved wife acted like a really busy girl, who had a lot on her mind. She offered no kisses, hugs, any form of affection, and didn't see me when I tossed the doggie bag under the passenger seat. All she did was jump into the day's events with the intent of reviewing it all.

"How about that trial today?" she asked me.

"Yeah."

"Did you see that Tea Partier's face after the police picked him up off the floor?"

"Oh, yeah," I lied.

"How about that Chitwood? He's slicker than advertised."

"No kidding."

"I have to show you something."

She reached into her purse and pulled out a camera the size of a matchbox.

"Holy cow, Colleen. Where'd you buy this cute little thing?"

"The Internet. I'm dying to see how the pictures turned out; can you reach in the back and pull out my laptop?" she asked.

"Sure."

After a minute or two, I had Colleen's camera hooked up to the computer and the images flashing across the screen.

Some pictures were blurry, others were taken too far away, or the subjects weren't centered in the frame. She had one really, really good shot of the guard pointing his nightstick at the Tea Partier. It was like she had been standing over the guard's shoulder, and was looking down the barrel of his arm. Both troopers had grimaces on their faces, and yes, the Tea Partier had a trickle of blood down the side of his chin.

We both uttered a "Wow," which was followed by a miniature high five above the console.

After about fifteen seconds of ogling, it occurred to me that cameras weren't allowed inside the courtroom.

"How'd you take these?"

She raised her eyebrows mischievously, "Very carefully."

"What does that mean?"

"I never let anyone see it, that's all," she smiled naughtily.

"Wow."

"I never even raised it to my eye," she continued, half-laughing, "maybe that's why most of them are off center, or out of focus, or not worth a hill of beans."

"How'd you sneak it into the courthouse to begin with?"

She giggled. "I stuffed it in my bra. You should have seen the look on the guard's face when he waved that wand across the girls."

I was smiling in a boyish kind of way. Colleen's "girls" have been a great source of joy for me for many years. They're so hefty and round that she usually has them hoisted with enough under-wires and clasps that they would make any metal detector squelch.

"What happened when you failed the metal-detector test? Didn't the guard get suspicious?" I asked.

"My pat-down was routine at first, but when he waved the wand across my chest, it made a terrific buzzing sound. It's like I looked at him and he looked at me and was rather embarrassed."

"What did you do?" I asked again.

"Just shook it off like it was no big deal and kept right on walking to the courtroom."

"Worked, huh?"

"Oh yeah," she said, smiling; "what about you?"

"Haven't worn a bra in years."

"Ha, ha, Derrick. Did you have any trouble getting past the guards?"

"Oh, that," I said facetiously. "The first time I did. Never realized that phones weren't allowed inside."

"It's been a while since I've been involved with a court case," she said. "It was exciting. Plenty of fireworks. Did you finish your story?"

"No, haven't even started it."

"Derrick!"

"I know, I know. I've got the motivation now with these pictures you took today."

"Good. We just have to come up with a way to get them published without getting into trouble," she said.

"Well yeah. Don't want that. How do you suppose we make that happen?" I asked.

Colleen raised her eyebrows and bit the corner of her lip. Her mind was racing a million miles an hour as she clutched the steering wheel and negotiated traffic. I noticed, however, that she wasn't driving into the sun, but away from it. Instead of heading west on M-37 towards home, we were headed east, back to I-75.

"Where are we going?" I asked her.

"Oh, I forgot to tell you—Frankenmuth."

"Frankenmuth? Why?"

"I'm following a hunch, Derrick."

"What about Elizabeth...tomorrow's paper...our responsibilities at home?"

"Don't worry about a thing, Derrick. I've got it all taken care of."

"I don't have any clothes, or anything."

"Got it, Derrick."

"Why Frankenmuth?" I asked.

"The jury. They're staying at the Bavarian Inn. The German place."

"How do you know?" I asked. "I heard they were staying south of Flint."

"No, they're not. I know exactly where they are. I followed them."

"Serious."

"Serious-lee, Derrick. It wasn't that hard."

"Are we just going to hang out in the lobby or are we staying there, too?"

"We're staying. And we're on the same floor as the jury pool. I already checked in, and had our luggage hauled up to the room."

"How'd you swing that?"

She bobbed her head the same way Penny did when I asked a question that she didn't want to answer. "I know how to get things done."

I smiled. She was exactly right, and not the least bit afraid to admit it. "What about the group you're working with?"

"They're camping in Byron at a Methodist campground on Myers Lake. It's south and a little west of Flint. They wanted me to come with them but I told them I had to go."

"I don't think they like me," I said, frowning.

"I think you're right about that, but they don't know that we're married. Heck, I'm still using my maiden name with them."

I smiled. Colleen seemed to relish the idea of living on the edge, of being undercover.

"I have to tell you about them, but not right now."

"Why not?" I asked.

"It's kind of a long story," she sighed; "it'd be good dinner conversation."

I nodded.

"What do you have in mind?" I asked.

"I feel like getting out of this wig, going with you out for dinner, taking a long, warm shower, and jumping in bed with you. How does that sound?"

I smiled, but I didn't have the courage to tell her that my belly was temporarily full.

"Sounds great," I said, enthusiastically.

About thirty minutes later we were seated in the main dining room of Zehnder's Restaurant in downtown Frankenmuth. It wasn't especially busy, but that stood to reason as it was a Monday, well past dinnertime. The dining hall was huge, and what it lacked in intimacy, it certainly had a lot of charm. The tables were neat and orderly, the floors meticulously groomed and vacuumed clean. Our waitress was decked out in a German outfit; all she needed was a be-bopper-style curtsy, a name like "Olga," and a heavy European accent and her ensemble would have been complete.

Instead, we got a "Tammy."

She rattled off the night's special: wiener schnitzel, purple cabbage and spaetzle. Even though I had just eaten ninety minutes previous, the thought of a second meal complete with the German's version of messed up little pasta was another temptation I couldn't resist. Besides, if I wanted to hide the fact that I was having dinner with another woman, I thought I should at least pretend like I was hungry. And really, I couldn't spoil the occasion. Colleen was great company and she had put a lot of effort into planning a date for the two of us even though it was a spur-of-the-moment kind of occasion.

I don't know what it is about German food that makes me feel so German. It's like the smell of sausages and grilled pig makes me want to strap on a set of lederhosen and call every woman "Frauline." All that allspice and vinegar should be drowned by mugs of beer and the pleasing melody of Edelweiss. I don't feel Asian when I go out for Chinese food, nor do I feel like wearing a sombrero after a plate full of wet burritos. German food stirs my soul, and the tangy, bittersweet flavor tugs at the strings of my heritage. For some people, food is food; it's the means to an end. For me, food is a flavor-filled adventure, and every once in a while, German food really hits the spot.

Colleen ordered the chicken and a glass of white wine. I ordered the special and a glass of water.

Even though we were both warm and strung out from the day's events, it felt good to kick up our heels and relax. For at least one night, the responsibilities of life could be put on hold.

And relax we did.

After our drinks were served, Colleen eased into the business of what was taking place inside the Heretic Fringe.

"I'm just about ready to quit this whole thing, Derrick," she sighed. "They're over the top."

"What do you mean?" I asked.

"Remember that David Koresh dude and the Branch Davidians down in Texas?"

"Kind of," I said.

"He was really messed up, Derrick. Anytime a couple joined the cult, he annulled their marriage, which gave him permission to have relations with the woman. He did terrible,

terrible things to the children and you know it didn't have a happy ending."

I didn't interrupt her.

"These people in Houghton Lake aren't that far from Koresh."

"What do you mean?" I asked quietly.

"They're masters of psychological punishment," she said, sipping her wine. "They use certain verses in the Bible to demoralize their women. They demand that they are subservient, and even though I haven't seen any signs of physical abuse, I have a sneaking suspicion that it's going on."

A family two tables away distracted my attention for a moment. There must have been ten or eleven of them seated there, and it appeared as if there was a mom and dad in their late sixties and their two kids who each had a spouse. The grandkids were sandwiched between the parents, leaving one of the dads closest to me. The guy didn't join in on the conversation, or even pretend he was at all interested in what was going on around him. All he could do was type on his phone that he kept on his thigh beneath the linen table cloth. I thought it was exceptionally rude of him to be carrying on like that, no matter what the reason. I felt like saying something to him, but I'm glad I didn't.

"About a month ago I went to one of their cookouts, way out in the sticks. I think they called it Dead Man's Swamp, south of Houghton Lake. Have you ever been there?" she asked, almost rhetorically.

"Yes, years ago," I said. "We went up there mushroom picking as a family."

"Right. Then you know what it's like. It's isolated; two-track roads and miles and miles of woods and swamps. That's where they decided to camp out, in the middle of nowhere. They had eight or ten little campers, and tents set up. A couple of them brought propane grills and folding tables for the coolers of lemonade and iced tea, hamburgers and hot dogs. The kids were running around, playing games and having fun. I thought everything was cool until supper ended, and they lit a bonfire." She shook her head and squirmed slightly in her chair. "Some of the women started talking about Marshall Yandle, so I listened in and pretended like I really wasn't acquainted with who he was."

The son or son-in-law couldn't be up to any good, I thought. Even your wife knows what's going on.

The wife—a blonde thirty-something wearing an orangey gingham sundress—couldn't look the husband's way. She kept her attention towards the other end of the table, and it didn't take too much deductive reasoning to understand that she and her husband had been fighting. Their expressions and body language said it all.

"The women said that Yandle never knew his father and was raised by his grandparents near Grand Rapids."

"I love Grand Rapids."

"Me too, but if you never knew your dad and your grandparents were working all the time, I'm not so sure you'd turn out the way you did."

"What did the grandparents do?"

"Apparently, Grandma worked at Wal-Mart as a greeter, and Grandpa was a bellhop at the Amway Grand."

I smiled. "That's not what I meant, Colleen."

She smiled even more and suddenly my query was lost in the swirling aroma of exotic plenty. Tammy arrived with the first round of food: warmed potato salad, purple cabbage, spaetzle, and sliced bread. I noticed Tammy's wrist and the way the ruffles of her shirt were snow white and coifed like meringue. It seemed that Zehnder's and all their employees had taken care of every detail.

"They said he was dyslexic and took so much abuse when he was young that he never finished high school."

I was admiring the spread on the table. It looked wonderful.

"That was the weird part about Yandle," she said; "he was allegedly a poor student but he was able to memorize vast passages of the Bible, could recite the Constitution and name all thirty-nine dignitaries who signed it."

"I'd say that's a little unusual."

"It gets worse. About once a month the group had 'spiritual retreats' at people's cabins or in the church basement. They said that one time they went up to someone's cabin near Atlanta, and Yandle preached to them for hours on end. He would always tie in his teaching with the Constitution and illustrate how today's Congress is violating it."

I absorbed everything she was telling me, and told her about Yandle's appetite for alcohol.

"That's true. He drank quite often, but he didn't want any members of the church to drink. He was full of contradictions."

"What about the murder of the congressman? Did they talk about that?"

"Yeah, they did," she said, just as Tammy brought our entrees, chicken and schnitzel, which was resting on a leaf of Romaine lettuce. We both smiled approvingly and Tammy went on her way.

Colleen lowered her head, closed her eyes solemnly, and said a little prayer.

I was thankful for the food, for all my blessings, but was distracted by the commotion coming from the table next to us. The father raised his voice and suggested that everyone at the table should communicate by cell phone instead of conversing like most families.

"Wouldn't that be pleasant?" he asked. "Then we wouldn't have to speak at all."

They all glared at the man at my end of the table.

"Daddy, please," the blonde begged her father.

"What?" the dad asked. "It seems that your husband has more important matters to attend to."

The children stuck in the middle put down their forks and looked up at him disappointedly. The family on the other side of the table did the same.

"You're right," the son-in-law said, wiping his chin with his napkin and storming away from the table, "I'm so outta here."

"Wait!" the blonde cried, as she followed him outside.

"What?" the dad questioned the rest of the family. "If the bastard's going to sit there and converse with someone else, while he's with us, then hell, yes, I'm going to call him out."

It was a little more drama than I had cared for during dinner.

Colleen looked over her shoulder and tried to shake it off like it was no big deal. "Where were we?"

I sighed.

"You were going to tell me what happened with the murder of the congressman."

"Oh yeah," she said, cutting a bite of chicken, "I really don't know if a lot of the women knew much about it. I suppose some of them really didn't want to know."

"Wait a second," I said, "Last time I knew you were going to the VFW up there, and now it's a church?"

"You're right, I was at the VFW, but then I learned that Yandle was part of the Darlington Bible Church, so I started going there. That's how I was invited to the camp out."

"What did they tell you?"

"They said that Yandle was going to tap five or six disciples for a secret mission. They said he touted it as a mission of 'extraordinary importance.'"

"Holy hell."

"Don't say that, Derrick," she said, rather motherly.

"Why not?"

"It's unbecoming."

"Sorry. I'm just getting caught up with all this craziness," I said, taking a bite of bread. It was wonderful, smeared with whipped butter from a golf-ball-sized jar; it had to be Eli's sourdough.

"Was the mission to murder the congressman?"

"Sure was."

"How did Yandle choose the people who were going to be on the mission?"

Colleen looked out the window and said that she could see the blonde and her husband arguing in the parking lot. I took the opportunity to eat.

"The women weren't really forthcoming—I'm not sure they were supposed to know any of it—but I did hear them say that the people who were chosen would be receiving a dead dove."

"A dead dove? I thought that doves are supposed to be a bird of peace?"

"You're right," Colleen nodded, "and I don't think it was a dove. It was probably a pigeon. We're still in mid-Michigan, you know."

I laughed, "So if someone received a dead pigeon, he knew that they were going to be part of the mission?"

"That was my understanding."

"What did they do, just mail it to them?"

"No, no, Derrick. It wound up on their doorstep, in their mailbox, or on the front seat of their car."

"Nice."

"Yeah, that's not all. The doves all had a note tied to one of their legs that said, 'In one hour, thy judgment come.'"

My mind flashed to the Amish schoolhouse and what Yandle had said to those kids. Even though my mind was clouded by time, prescription drugs, and a good bit of alcohol, 'thy judgment come' had a familiar ring to it.

Colleen picked up on my hesitation. "What's wrong?"

"That Bible verse," I said, "that was one of the last things Marshall Yandle uttered before I…"

Colleen reached across the table and took hold of my hands. "I'm sorry, Babe. This must not be pleasant for you. We can talk about something else, if you want."

"No, no, that's okay," I said somewhat reflectively, squeezing her hands. "I might need a little time to figure it all out. Did you look up where the verse was from?"

"I didn't have to. They said it was from the book of Revelations and has to do with the end of the world."

Colleen had me on the edge of my seat. I was listening to what she said; thinking about what she had witnessed, and wondering what kind of trouble she might be in.

"With all that secrecy, planning, and intention, doesn't that make the members of the Darlington Bible Church accomplices to Capp's murder?" I asked.

"I have no idea."

"Have they been called before the Grand Jury?" I asked.

"I don't think so, but it makes me wonder if they will." Colleen had a rather worrisome look on her face.

"What about you?" I asked.

"What about me?" she turned the tables on me.

"I wonder if you'll be forced to testify because of what they told you."

She huffed, "Don't think so. I didn't even get involved until after Capp's murder."

I nodded my head, but continued to wonder about her situation.

Apparently, it must have been on Colleen's mind too.

"You don't think I have anything to worry about, do you?" she asked.

"I don't know," I said; "I doubt it."

Colleen sighed, but then lunged into her meal as if it were the last repast she'd have as a free woman.

"Is there anything else you want to tell me?" I asked.

"I don't know," she whispered. "I'm not so sure I should be admitting the things I might have seen, for fear that I'll be taken into custody or forced to testify."

"Don't worry about it," I said; "your secrets are safe with me."

Colleen sipped her wine.

"You understand that I'm a religious woman, right?"

"Of course," I said; "why do you ask?"

"Because you know how hard it is for me to criticize some-one else's religious practices."

It wasn't like Colleen to apologize for something that hadn't taken place yet. Her eyes darted from mine to the items on the table, as if she was trying to figure out a good place to start.

"What is it?" I asked.

"What I saw at the cookout…I witnessed a disturbing kind of ritual, if you can call it that."

I felt my eyebrows climb across my forehead.

"After supper they lit a bonfire. It was a giant one, too. The original stack of wood must have been five or six feet high." She was almost whispering when she told me about the crackling of the campfire and the whippoorwills' lonesome wailing in the background. "One of the members pulled out his guitar and started playing all sorts of different songs. We sang along with him for about an hour and not all of them were hymns, either. The kids and pets stayed up for quite a while, but about ten-thirty, they all went to bed."

"The pets?" I asked.

"Yeah, it was almost embarrassing," she said. "They had a snaggle-toothed-looking pit bull named 'Peanut,' and they must have had cats, too, because the kids smelled like they had been sprayed with urine."

Tammy came back to the table, filled our glasses with wa-ter, and cleared my plate. Colleen was "still working on hers."

"By then the fire had ebbed somewhat and it was pitch dark. The women kept shushing their husbands so they wouldn't wake the kids. So in a quiet voice one of the guys raised his cup and said, 'to Marshall. May he rest in peace.'"

Colleen raised her glass to go along with her story.

"Then he said, 'He'd want us to repent for our sins…to be self-mortified.'"

"Holy…what does that mean?"

"I wasn't sure at first, but then they said it had to do with shame. We needed to be ashamed of our sins." I watched her gather her thoughts. She was spilling her beans; figuratively speaking, they ran all over the linen tablecloth and the clean, vacuumed floor. "One of the men took off his shirt and recited another verse from the Bible."

"What did you do?"

"I just went along with it. The women weren't offended by it, but then things got really interesting."

I couldn't imagine.

"Do you know what a *discipline* is?"

"No," I said reluctantly.

"Neither did I," she said, finishing the last of her meal. "It's like a whip. About that long." Her hands were about eighteen inches apart. "It's made of leather. Has a little handle on it, but instead of one strand at the end there's a whole bunch of them. Each leather strand has beads on the end that are about the size of a pea."

The blonde returned to the table next to us, nose and eyes glowing red. Her mom reached for her hand, which seemed to make the tears in her eyes prosper.

"Anyway, the man fell to his knees, and faced the fire. Someone handed him this discipline and he started flailing it over his left shoulder, then his right. It wasn't long before his bare back had red stripes across it."

"Gee whiz."

"He was chanting something in Latin."

"Good heavens! What did you do?"

"I was just stunned. The others in the group had the verse memorized and joined the man in his spell. At first, it was like a whisper but it became louder and louder. It was like creepy spooky."

"I guess so."

"Yeah, but then the other men took off their shirts and knelt at the fire. They all had those disciplines. They looked like a herd of cows the way they encircle a round bale of hay, and swish the flies away with their tails."

"Only it wasn't their tails, but this whip thing, right?"

"Right."

I thought about complimenting her on the description, but decided not to.

"The disciplines on their backs made a rhythmic, chanting beat and it wasn't long before the women knelt at the fire and did the same thing."

"Topless?" I almost exploded. "I'd liked to have seen that!"

Colleen looked at me like I was an impish child. "No, Derrick, you pervert."

"Sorry," I smirked; "what did you do?"

"I got the heck out of there."

"How? Did you run?"

"No, no. I just left. Told them I had to go."

"A couple of my lady friends waved to me like it was no big deal, but none of the men did. They were so caught up in their chanting that they never knew I was missing until I started my car and sped away."

"Don't you wish you had a camera?"

"Oh, I know it. It would have been great. After that incident, I decided that I should never be without a camera, even if it was a tiny one. The next day, I ordered that little camera I took into the courthouse."

"Makes sense."

Tammy arrived with our check, and a half-hearted pitch for dessert. Neither of us nibbled on her offer. "Thank you very much."

"So, some of the people who were at the courthouse today were at the campout earlier this summer?"

"Yes," she said, pulling a credit card out of her wallet, "most of them in fact."

"I'll pay for it, Babe," I pleaded, hand on hers.

"Not today, you're not. This was my idea," she said.

"Thank you," I said, "I'm glad you caught me before I was all the way home."

"Me, too," she smiled. "I was just about to call you when you called me. You would have driven back to see me if I didn't, right?"

"Probably," I snickered.

Tammy picked up Colleen's credit card, and we were alone again. The blonde at the table next door collected herself somewhat, and tried to salvage what was left of the dinnertime conversation.

"What's the significance of the discipline?" I asked Colleen.

"I can't figure that out," she said, dabbing the tablecloth for bread crumbs with the end of her pointer finger. "I did a little research and found out that they were used by Catholics years ago and by some religious group out of Tibet. How the Darlington Bible Church in Houghton Lake incorporated it into their worship service is a mystery to me."

"You'd think that with Yandle out of the picture, they would have abandoned some of his extremist practices."

"I suppose you're right," she said. "That just sounds like something he would have had them do."

Tammy returned with Colleen's credit card and a slip of paper for her to sign. When they finished their transaction, I was ready to go.

Colleen wasn't quite there yet. Instead of sliding out of her seat, she remained planted.

"I would have thought that after the campout you might have quit following the Fringe."

"It crossed my mind," she said. "Now I've had just about enough of them."

"If I can be perfectly honest, Colleen, it wouldn't break my heart if you severed your ties with them. It's hard for me to see my girl spend so much time with other men."

"I know. I hear you, Derrick."

"I'm getting tired of all the secrecy, too." Colleen nodded her head and listened to my gentle plea. "You've come at me with so many different e-mail addresses, that I'm not sure which one I should use."

"I'm sorry," she said, never explaining which e-mail address I should use for future correspondence. As long as it takes to stuff a credit card and receipt inside a purse, I had forgotten all about what e-mail address she'd like me to use.

The folks at the next table got up to leave, and the father put his arm around his blonde daughter. Grandma picked out a grandchild and placed her open hand on his face. She stroked his cheek and smiled pleasantly, as if she was taking stock in his future. I'm not sure why I took so much interest in what was taking place with the family next door. It's almost as if I was curious about the fact that almost every family has a little drama in it. Very seldom does it unfold in a public place.

As for me and Colleen, we couldn't be happier.

At least that's what I thought.

"Oh, Geez," Colleen uttered.

I looked across the table and there was Colleen, clutching her phone, shaking her head from side to side.

"What is it?" I asked.

She sighed.

"Look," she said, turning her cellphone in my direction.

I glared at the little screen she held in her hand. There—on the first night of the biggest trial in mid-Michigan's history— were five little words: *Every verdict has a price.*

I looked up at Colleen. She was smiling enough to make the dimples under her eyes appear.

"Who is this from?"

"The television station. Channel 3. I signed up on their Twitter account to get instant updates."

"So, it's not the television station that says 'Every verdict has a price,' but someone associated with the jury?"

"Yes," she said, fiddling with the phone again. "They say they received it anonymously."

We both sat there for a moment and let the gravity of the situation pour over us. It was one more wrinkle for the judge to harp on; one more factor for the lawyers to consider.

Even though it was only the first day of the trial, I was really fed up with what was taking place. It was just too much everything. Too much Judge Brewer and his empty threats. Too much Jake Chitwood and his polished routine. I was tired of listening to Jack Jacobetti, and his redundant, windy speeches; seeing Mr. Yoder's crooked smile; and the nervous way Bob Gilbert trimmed his fingernails inside the jury box.

A trial of this size really wasn't my cup of tea. I had made my career out of covering the little parts of a big picture. In this case, the trial was the big picture, and it had already received a whole lot of attention from my colleagues in the media. What's worse, the clock was ticking on the timeliness of whatever story I hoped to write. Clearly the television stations were ahead of me; so were the radio outlets across the state. If I had to bet, the bosses at the Associated Press had already divvied up the facets of the first day of the trial to the reporters on staff.

After seeing all the drama of opening day in the trial, and now hearing *every verdict has a price,* I felt a little like the trial was getting away from me. It's not as if I had a burning desire to write story after story, when there were so many other reporters doing the same thing.

As Colleen and I left the restaurant, and walked to the parking lot, I had to tell her that I really wasn't all that interested in covering the nuts and bolts of the trial.

"It just isn't my thing," I said.

She put her hand in the crook of my arm, and gave it a squeeze. "It's okay, Derrick. I'm proud of you for realizing that."

I smiled. There's nothing better than having a spouse understand what's going on inside your head and have her not pass judgment on it. If I had disappointed her, she wasn't going to let me know.

"Why don't you write a story about the Amish guy on the jury, or take some time off and find out what happened to the injured Amish children?"

I smiled. She had read my mind. "There are lots of little things I could cover, but I'm not sure which direction I should go."

"Come on," she said, getting into the car. "I know just what you need to clear your head."

Twenty-Three

COLLEEN AND I HAD A RATHER SHORT NIGHT in the Bavarian Inn. While she took a shower, I caught my second wind and wrapped up a short but thorough article about the trial's first day. While I was in the shower, Colleen revamped the photo of the guard and Tea Party member so it looked like it could have been an artist's rendition instead of an actual photo. Together, the story and image made a nice little insert into the morning edition of the *Gratiot County Review*.

I think we both felt a sense of accomplishment having achieved our objective for the day. This wasn't our first collaborative effort when it came to covering a story, and I hoped it wouldn't be our last. I'm not sure what Colleen felt about the arrangement of working together, but as far as I was concerned, it gave me a sense of pride, companionship, and teamwork.

And when Colleen asked for a bottle of soda and a bucket full of ice, it was my pleasure to walk down the hall and get it for her.

After all, she had packed my bathrobe, slippers and a new pair of silk pajamas. All I needed was a bowl-full of Borkum Riff stuffed into a straight-stemmed pipe, and Hugh Hefner himself would have been jealous.

The guard at the end of the hallway wasn't as impressed as

I was when it came to my sleeping attire. She was staked out maybe twenty feet from the ice and pop machines, and when I sauntered up to make nice with her, she glanced up at me from behind a pair of rather hairy eyebrows.

"You're not going to arrest me if I steal some of this ice, are you?" I asked.

"No," she smiled, folding her newspaper in half lengthwise.

"What's going on?" I questioned her.

"Oh, not much," she tried to deflect my question.

Instead of giving up, I asked the same thing a different way.

"If Humphrey Bogart were here, he'd say 'what's a nice girl like you doing in a place like this?'"

"Yeah, really," she smiled half-heartedly, then glanced down the hall to her colleague, near the stairwell seventy yards away.

"You don't want to tell me, do you?"

"I'm not supposed to say anything," she said. I noticed the Federal Court patch on the sleeve of her uniform; the handgun, taser, and a host of other implements riveted to her belt.

"The patches on your sleeve have blown your cover," I smiled. "You're with the court."

She couldn't deny it.

"There must be a big trial going on, is that correct?"

"I'm really not supposed to say."

"You don't have to say much. It's been all over the news."

She didn't respond, so I looked past her, through the bank of windows, and down to the parking lot, which wasn't exactly full. Parked all by itself under a streetlight was a rather elderly white cargo van, the federal court logo on its flanks. It seemed that the court guards had to babysit the jurors and the van all at the same time.

"What's the deal with those fliers under the windshield wipers of the cars in the parking garage?" She shrugged her shoulders, so I came at her from another angle. "Does the judge know about them?"

"Oh yeah," she finally admitted. "It's a five-year felony, too."

"What about the tweet from someone on the jury pool?"

She shook her head.

"You haven't heard about that?"

"No, I haven't."

"Yeah, TV3 reported on their Twitter account that one of the jurors said that 'Every verdict has a price.'"

The guard shook her head as I opened a little plastic bag and stuffed it into the ice bucket.

"It's probably the lead story on the news, if you want to catch it."

She glanced at her watch. It was just about eleven.

I heard some laughter coming from one of the rooms. It seemed like the jury pool wasn't going to let the trial get in the way of a good time.

"Can I buy you a pop?"

"No, thank you."

"Sounds like the jury's having fun down there?"

"Oh, yeah, that's the men on the panel. One of them brought in a poker set and now they're playing Texas Hold'em," she said. "That's about the extent of their fun. They ain't got no TVs or clock radios in the room so there's not much to do."

"So no Internet, either?"

"No. We took away their cell phones, laptops, everything."

"What time is lights out?"

"About a half an hour."

"That's cool. Hey, nice talking with you. Have a good night."

She nodded in my direction and I thought that was the end of our dealings.

I entered the little room with the machines inside and filled the bucket of ice. Two dollars later, I was wrestling with the trap door at the bottom of the pop machine. I'll never know why the machine makers make it so hard to retrieve your refreshment.

When I was finished with the vending machines, I heard laughter and commotion. Coming at me in full stride down the hallway was Mr. Yoder, dressed in a wrinkly white nightshirt that hung to his knees. White beard flowing, bare feet flailing, he was the spitting image of Rip Van Winkle upon his awakening.

"I wanna go swimming!" he shouted as he wheeled past me. "I wanna go swimming! Yahoooooo!"

The guard whipped out her baton and shouted right back at him. "Mr. Yoder! Mr. Yoder! Stop it right now."

Robert Gilbert stepped out of the open door of his room and started laughing. "There goes Yoder, over center ice! He's got a head of steam…go, man, go!"

More jurors spilled into the hallway and looked at the spectacle.

Mr. Yoder tried the old fashioned "Okey-doak" move of faking-right-then-spinning-left to get past the guard, but it didn't work. She probably outweighed him by thirty or forty pounds and was able to snatch him up before he reached the doors that lead to the swimming pool.

"Two minutes for holding!" Gilbert shouted.

Mr. Yoder squirmed somewhat, but the guard possessed a deadly combination of grace and power.

"You're not going swimming, Mr. Yoder. The pool is closed."

He muttered something in a foreign language.

"Say what?" she asked, ghetto style.

"Can we gooo swimming tomorrow?"

"We'll see about that. You've got a big day ahead of you."

They turned to where he had come.

"Have you been drinking, Mr. Yoder?"

"Nooo. Never touched tha stuff."

"You sure smell like it. Now come on, it's almost time for lights out."

Mr. Yoder looked somewhat disappointed in what had taken place, and his steps were rather wobbly as he walked back to his room.

"Gilbert, you know anything about Mr. Yoder's condition?" she yelled.

"No," Gilbert said.

"I told you that Jell-Ooo tasted funny," Mr. Yoder slurred.

"Mr. Gilbert, you know you're not supposed to be doing stuff like that," she announced. "Jell-O shots are not one of the approved snacks; now hand it over."

I watched the guard take control of the situation.

She ordered the other male jurors loitering in the hallway to go back to their rooms. "Come on, the party's over. It's almost time for lights out."

They groaned.

The guard at the opposite end of the hall joined the conflict, and together they managed to subdue the uprising. I bet they were flushing the remaining Jell-O shots down the toilet and would be tucking Mr. Yoder into bed with a couple of aspirin and tall glass of water.

I'm not sure who made the roommate arrangements, but it seemed like Yoder and Gilbert presented the most unusual pairing. Gilbert was huge; Yoder, quite small. On paper, at least, they had nothing in common, but it wasn't like they really needed a lot in familiar traits to be good jurors. All that was required was a clear head and an open mind, however dim or naive that mind may have been.

When I returned to our room, poured Colleen a soft drink, and explained why I had taken so long, she thought that the added mischief was par for the course. "At least when it comes to this trial. It seems like there's been a number of things happen that nobody saw coming."

"The scary thing is that it's just the first day," I confessed.

"Well, yeah," she said. "I don't think there's a person in that courthouse who thought that the prosecution won today."

"I think you're right. And I think they know it too."

"Why would you say that?" she sipped.

I hesitated. Colleen had lit the candles, had music play-ing and the lights turned off. No television. No distractions. It was just the two of us all alone inside that tiny cubicle. The sweet smell of spring filled the room and it made me wonder if it was lilac or lavender burning the wax. Both scents were at odds with the gruff-pleading Ray Charles who was performing somewhere inside her laptop computer. She had a thigh draped over the pulled-down bed sheet and was wrapped in scrump-tious little red teddy that barely corralled her goods. The stage was set; the setting so right. I didn't want to mess things up, but sometimes it's hard for me to think things through. I've goofed up many a romantic encounter by saying the wrong things at the right time or the right things at the wrong time. Tonight's encounter was just as tenuous, and reliant upon my smart-thinking and proper answers to make the romantic set-ting become a glorious reality.

"I ran into Penny Melton at the bar in Montrose," I said.

"Oh?" she sounded surprised.

"Yeah. I think that they know the first day didn't go very well."

"Why didn't you put any of that in the article?"

"She didn't want to go on the record."

"Oh. I see." She watched me take off my robe and sit on the edge of the bed. Colleen's attention casually turned to the gossip magazine in her midst. "What else did she say...off the record?"

"All kinds of things."

"Like what?"

I was beginning to feel like a rendezvous with Colleen was slipping away as the tone in her voice became more and more terse.

"Well," I hesitated. "She thought I was wrong about federal prosecutors being pawns for their congressmen."

Colleen waited.

"I don't really remember everything, Sweetheart," I said, as I placed my hand on the covers, near her knee. "It doesn't really matter now, does it?"

She raised an eyebrow and looked at me rather skeptically. It seemed like as long as she was asking the questions and I was doing the answering, I was skating on increasingly thin ice. Instead of waiting for the next inquiry, I decided to go on the offensive and take charge of the situation, "The most important thing is that I love you, and you love me and that we can finally see the light at the end of the tunnel."

"Aw, that's so nice," she glimmered, "but sweetheart, we still have many more years till Elizabeth goes off to college."

I smiled back at her and shook my head slightly. Colleen's innocence and naiveté were priceless.

"That's not what I meant, Colleen."

"You do love me, don't you?" Her hand reached for mine.

"Of course, I do." We touched. "I was thinking that we can see the light at the end of the tunnel when it comes to the trial."

"Oh, duh," she smiled. We both laughed momentarily.

"Sometimes I wish it wouldn't end," she lamented.

"What do you mean?"

"I kinda like this reporting thing."

"You always have, Colleen. And you're good at it too."

"Thanks," she sipped. "You know, I love being a mom and taking care of Elizabeth, but there's something rather captivating about rolling up your sleeves and diving into a story like this one."

"Oh, I know. And make no mistake, this one's a beauty."

"What do you think is going to happen?" she asked.

"You mean like, guilty, innocent or they'll cop a plea?" I asked, sliding under the covers.

"Exactly."

"I'm not sure. Look at the defense team. They're really, really good at what they do."

"See," she countered, "I look at the prosecution and believe that they can't end up losing. They already lost the case with Henry Rush. To me, the Ivey trial is like a pre-season football game. The real trial starts when they go after the Fringe and they can't go into that batting oh-for-two."

"I agree, but if they strike a plea bargain, and the Iveys go to jail, that still counts as a success."

"That won't happen, Derrick. That Chitwood's got an ego the size of the Upper Peninsula. He'll advise his clients that they've got a great chance of being free men."

"I know, I know," I agreed. "So you're saying it'll be all or nothing?"

"Yes," she whispered. "I don't think there's any doubt about it."

Her assessment made sense.

It seemed like we had temporarily run out of things to talk about. Colleen filled her glass with ice and more pop, rolled my way in the bed, and gave me a kiss on the lips. It was a pleasant way to end the day.

"Can you do me one more favor?" she pleaded, quietly.

"Sure, whatever you want," I whispered.

Her hand was on my cheek, my earlobe sandwiched between two fingers.

"I want you to take off your pajamas and roll on your tummy."

I smiled, slightly.

"My, my, aren't you forward?" I suggested. "What did you have in mind?"

"Oh, you'll see," she purred. "And I hope you enjoy it as much as I do."

Twenty-Four

Colleen's grand finale consisted of a glorious neck and back massage that lasted almost thirty minutes. While Ray Charles poured his heart out and the little red bulbs on our cell phones pulsed on the ceiling, Colleen fulfilled an exotic fantasy involving scented massage oil. And she didn't just slop it on me like it was red paint on a weathered barn; she heated the oil in the microwave to within a few degrees of scalding, then kneaded it into my skin with deft hands and enough pressure that she had me wondering if I had been a naughty, naughty boy. Although I was extremely grateful for the massage, I thought that Colleen walked a fine line between delivering a heaping helping of pleasure and a teaspoon full of pain. I never really verbalized my curiosity about her penchant for masochism, for fear that if I did, she might take offense at my comment and quit doing it all together.

And what the heck, I didn't want to complain. If a woman is going to go through the forethought and planning it takes to set up a romantic evening with her man, then take charge of the intimacy when the time is right, who am I to complain? I kept my mouth shut and a smile on my face through all the glorious events.

There's nothing quite like drifting off to sleep after a satisfying encounter with your mate. Instead of stewing about what's in store for tomorrow, a soulful kindling is a wonderful way to end the day. After enjoying the curves of her body, the flavors of her skin and joy that she brings, I couldn't help but say, "I love you," one more time. If Colleen and I are silverware, and we happen to be jammed into a kitchen drawer, Colleen wants to spoon; I love to fork.

A little before three, I was sleeping the big sleep when we were awakened by a horrific buzzing sound. After I untangled myself from the c-pap machine, I thought the noise was from the alarm clock on the nightstand. I banged on the buttons and twisted the knobs in a stupefied effort to stop the racket. In the process, I sent Colleen's plastic cup of melted ice and soda pop splashing all over the floor.

Colleen turned on the nightlight and wondered out loud, "What the heck is going on?"

Little did she realize that her "hunch" about spending the night in the same hotel as the jury was going to pay off handsomely. At first, though, she wasn't sure what hit her. She grabbed her cell phone. I found mine. Neither one of us had set our alarm.

We both realized it at about the same time: the buzzing sound was the fire alarm in the hall. I heard yelling and screaming outside our door, so I jumped out of bed and rummaged the floor for my clothes. Colleen did the same thing. We must have looked like a couple of startled nudists, with our boobs and daddy parts wagging to the pandemonium. We bumped into each other more than once—apologizing in the process—and realized that our pajamas were soaked by the ice and soda concoction.

"Come on, hurry!" she urged me.

"I'm hurrying, I'm hurrying!"

"Do you smell smoke?" she asked.

"No, but I'm not taking any chances."

"You grab the suitcase," she ordered, "I'll get the camera."

We tossed open our door and ran hurriedly into the hall.

The guards weren't far away, and had six or seven jurors lined up against the bank of windows. Some of them held their open palms to their ears in an effort to shield themselves from the blinding noise. Dressed in our pajamas and nightgowns, we raced past the guards and jurors, down the stairs and outside. The wail of the approaching sirens almost drowned the chit-chat from the motel guests who were standing around in varied reams of clothing.

"There's no fire," one of them said.

"It's a friggin' false alarm."

Ever since my house fire several years ago, I'm very leery of fires. For Colleen, the urgency of a pulled fire alarm was secondary to the opportunity to get the scoop.

Almost on cue, the guard opened the door of the inn and a parade of jurors poured outside.

Colleen's camera flashed and flashed, as she took shot after shot. The best picture of the night was going to be the one of Mr. Yoder in front of a shirtless, muscle-bound, Bob Gilbert. The look on Mr. Yoder's face was priceless. I knew that he was betrayed by the aftereffects of the vodka. His slack-jawed frown and watery eyes were a testament to the violence that must have been taking place inside his gullet.

Colleen couldn't just stand back and take pictures. She drifted towards the jury pool and asked nonchalantly if they were prisoners, or key witnesses in an important trial.

"Move it along," the guard warned her.

"Can't I ask why they're here?" Colleen didn't back down, "what they thought of LeBeuf's testimony?"

The guard kept the entourage moving away from the back door, the scrupulous eyes of my wife, and anything that might tarnish their objectivity.

After about ten minutes of the guests milling around the parking lot, and jury panel sequestered under the watchful eyes of the guards, the night manager announced that there really wasn't a fire. "The coast is clear and you can all go back to your rooms."

A Bronx cheer followed her proclamation.

Instead of hopping back in bed, Colleen said she was going to upload the photos she had just taken and submit them to the Associated Press. "I bet they'll pay me enough to cover our room," she said, a smile beaming across her face. She was happy and proud of her accomplishments. So was I.

Early the next morning, we checked out of our room, grabbed a coffee and a diet Coke, and were headed south on I-75. We were rather sleepy, but we noticed the court's van parked on the side of the freeway, its emergency flashers blinking in the morning fog. The bushy-browed guard was on the shoulder, talking into her cell phone, but I saw enough people heads inside the van to realize that the entire panel was still intact.

I took my foot off the gas and looked at Colleen. "Think we ought to stop?" I asked, almost rhetorically. "Mr. Yoder might be throwing up inside."

"No, no. Let's keep going. They've probably got a flat tire and they're calling a tow truck."

I looked in her direction. Colleen was undoubtedly correct.

"Besides," she said, "it'll give me time to snoop around the courtroom before the trial starts."

She was always planning ahead, anticipating the next move, and making the most out of the situation at hand.

"You know what I think?" I baited her.

"What?" she asked.

"I think you ought to talk to James Ong."

"Why?" she asked.

"I don't know if you picked up on him or not, but he was giving signals to team Chitwood about the viability of each juror."

"No, I didn't see that." She acted surprised.

"He seems like the kind of guy who might talk."

Colleen clenched her eyebrows. "Really, why do you say that?"

"I just have a feeling. You've never met him, right?"

"Right. I just talked to him on the phone, and that was under my real last name, not my pen name."

"There you go. I think you'll be fine."

"What do you want me to ask him?"

"Not sure," I said, struggling momentarily. "He'll presume that you know he's a trial consultant. Ask him about the makeup of the jury and which member might be tweeting Channel 3."

"Oh, is that all?" she asked facetiously. "Like that'll happen."

I wasn't sure what to say.

"You know, I've been thinking about that whole thing," she said, "and I'm really having a hard time believing that someone on the jury would do that."

"Why?"

"It seems like they wouldn't have the wherewithal. You know, the court's taken away their phones and computers."

She did make a good point.

"Maybe it's not an actual member of the jury, but one of their friends or associates," I said.

Colleen didn't acknowledge my statement, but added, "I wouldn't put it past Channel 3 to post something like that just because of the buzz it would create."

I had to listen as she made her third valid point in a row. "The other thing is, why would the government entertain an offer to pay for a verdict?"

"Exactly," I agreed, but I wasn't *exactly* sure why.

"It might happen in a civil matter, when either party could bid against the other, but there would be no way the government would pay for a conviction in a criminal case."

By then, we had taken the exit for I-475 and could see downtown Flint on the horizon. The tires of Colleen's car banged over every seam of concrete; it felt like we were galloping along like a train on its tracks. The radio was off; we sipped our drinks in silence, and played the different scenarios in our heads.

"If I know the government wouldn't pay for a verdict, and you know that, then you can bet that the prosecution does too, right?" I suggested.

"Correct," she agreed, but then she countered, "we may have overlooked one thing: The tweet Channel 3 sent out really didn't say that they wanted money."

"Right again, Babe. It said 'Every verdict has a price.'"

Colleen raised her eyebrows, "That's got a totally different connotation."

"It could mean anything," I said.

"What would be the price of a guilty verdict?" she asked.

"Or a *not guilty* verdict?" I countered.

We were deep in thought, and weighing the gravity of the situation. There were so many angles to the Twitter story that I felt a little overwhelmed by it all. And honestly, I really didn't want to believe that a verdict had a price. Maybe it was my own naiveté, but I truly thought that the court system was free of the questionable dealings that plagued other areas of government.

Juries can't be bought or sold, I thought. *Leave the bribery up to the politicians.*

I voiced my thoughts out loud. "I know that Congressman Capp had a lot of campaign contributors who expected him to vote certain ways."

"Right," Colleen acknowledged, "but he's dead now."

"I know, but he wasn't dead when he cast the deciding vote."

"So what are you saying, Derrick?" she asked, sifting through her purse.

I sat there for quite a few seconds, sorting my thoughts. All the action seemed to be at the courthouse. The obvious stories were being covered by a passel of reporters from across the country. I really didn't want to get involved with all that.

There was too much pressure, too much closeness, too much humanity. I wanted to cover a story like the one Colleen had with the jury in the motel. That was unusual, out of the ordinary, and extremely relevant. As usual, Colleen got the better of me. She beats me in golf, in reporting, and she has a gutsy streak inside her that would make the most experienced foreign correspondent envious. For a moment there, I felt a twinge of insecurity. She had taken the case to new heights, while I was the one dragging us down.

As Colleen pulled the mini-camera out of her purse and stuffed it into her cleavage, I remembered that she told me not to cover the trial if I didn't want to.

"I hope you're not disappointed, Colleen, but I don't think I'm going to go to the trial today."

She nodded.

"There's really no sense in both of us going," I said.

She shrugged her shoulders, as if she approved of my logic.

"Why don't I drop you off in front of the courthouse, leave the car in the parking deck, and leave the keys in the gas tank?" I suggested.

She didn't say a thing.

"Better yet, I'll drop you off a block away from the courthouse, park on the roof of the parking deck, and take the keys with me," I tried again. "You probably have an extra set in your purse, right?"

"Um..." Colleen hesitated.

"Aren't you going to say something?"

"I think you're forgetting something, Derrick."

"What's that?"

"Where you left your car."

Now it was my turn to feel silly. "Oh duh. It's still in Montrose."

I shook my head and laughed. "How could I forget?"

She raised her eyebrows and looked in my direction as if I was really weird. What the heck, I am weird.

"I guess I'm going to the trial after all."

"Yes, you are, unless you promise to have my vehicle back here by five this afternoon."

I shook my head. "No, that's okay. Knowing my luck, Judge Brewer would cancel the afternoon's session, and you'd be stranded. Worse yet, I'd get into some sort of pickle, and you'd be high and dry. I don't mind sitting in. If today's testimony is anything like the day before, there's bound to be some fireworks."

"Okay then," she ordered, "let's stick to our plan and I'll meet you afterwards."

It felt like we should have put our hands together like they do in the huddle of a football game. Instead, she unbuckled her seat belt and spun around on her knees. While I was driving forward, she was looking backward.

"What are you doing?" I asked politely.

I heard the luggage zippers zipping.

"Almost forgot my wig," she said, sitting next to me again. "I'd hate to blow my cover now."

While Colleen wrapped her blonde hair in a bun and covered it all with red, I noticed her outfit and how she looked perfectly boring. Plain skirt, plain blouse, and flats on her feet—if she was going after the subservient look, she certainly had it mastered. As she flicked and flitted with her crimson bangs, I noticed that she hardly had on any makeup.

It occurred to me that the she was going to look exactly like the other women in her group. No style, no pizzazz, and very little individuality.

My beautiful, dynamic wife had become a reflection of the Heretic Fringe.

Twenty-Five

It was about seven forty-five when I dropped Colleen off a block away from the federal courthouse in downtown Flint. As much as I dreaded the thought of abandoning her in the worst part of town, I figured that it was early enough in the morning that the thugs who might harm her would still be in bed. I learned a long time ago that if I was going to do business in the 'hood, I had better do it before noon.

Colleen would be okay because help wasn't that far away.

As I drove past the courthouse, I guessed that there were twice as many cops patrolling outside on the second day of the trial as there were on the first. Three or four patrolmen dawdled at the front steps, another two or three on the sidewalks. Near the intersection of the two busiest roads, a couple of mounted police surveyed their surroundings from atop their quarter horses. One of the beasts took a liking to the shrubbery and with oversized lips tugged at the leaves. I've never understood the effectiveness of mounted police in this setting, other than it seems like a symbolic deterrent rather than an effective tool against civil disobedience.

The entire crowd—the horses, the cops, scores of onlookers, Tea Party members, and the Heretic Fringe all stood behind the metal barriers on the grounds of the courthouse in the gathering heat and dwindling shadows. The Tea Party members must have been the warmest in their exorbitant outfits and historic, white wigs. Those garments, their fife and drums, the music they played, and the images they created were going to make the reporters and correspondents happy. It was, after all, high drama.

I parked Colleen's vehicle on the deck of the parking garage and made it to the stairwell without incident. Members of a private security firm were patrolling every floor of the parking deck, which must have been in response to the fliers that were placed under the windshield wipers the day before.

When I crossed the street from the parking garage toward the courthouse, I noticed the way the reporters almost had to yell into their microphones because of the commotion behind them. The Tea Party folks were singing *My Country, 'Tis of Thee.*

A boy about ten years old rode his bike between the reporters, toward the entryway of the courthouse. He pulled a newspaper from his shoulder sack and yelled in a very girlish voice, "Newspapers! Hot off the press!"

A man in a short-sleeved, button-down shirt raised his hand, a dollar bill or two flapping between his fingers. The boy kicked the stand on his bike, skipped in the man's direction, and made a sale. I thought for a second or two that the man could have been part of the Fringe, or an understated member of the Tea Party.

With all the people I hoped to avoid, I wasn't really sure where I should wait for the trial to begin. The police weren't letting anyone inside, and aside from the paper boy, wouldn't let anyone linger between the metal barriers in front of the courthouse. Penny Melton would be along at any moment, and as much as I wanted to talk to her about why she left so abruptly the evening before, this wasn't the time or the place to do it. If I knew anything about lawyers, it's that they were wound up during a trial. The Tea Party members would have accepted me into their crowd, but I really didn't relish the thought of rubbing elbows with the Heretic Fringe. The defense team was there, and Mr. Chitwood was giving an interview with a reporter from the *Saginaw News*. Instead of wandering around aimlessly, I bellied up to a mobile concession stand and ordered a cup of coffee and a warmed cinnamon roll. When the woman behind the counter put both items in front of me and said, "That'll be three twenty-five," I heard a voice behind me announce, "I'll take care of that."

I spun around and saw Dr. James Ong standing there, a smile warming his face. "How's it going?" he asked, passing a five across the counter.

"Not bad," I winked; "just looking for a little Irish whiskey for my coffee."

"A little hair of the dog?"

"Something like that. How are you?" I asked.

"Doing well," he said, ordering a coffee of his own.

"It looks like security has tightened up somewhat since yesterday."

"Yeah, it has," he said, "and now the jury's running late."

I thanked him for the breakfast and told him about seeing the van parked on the shoulder of I-75. Jim paid for his coffee and wondered if it had any police escorts.

"None; why?"

"I'm surprised by that. Usually, a marshal is sent along with the guards for cases like this," he stated, plucking cream and sugar packets from a plastic basket.

"What would the court be afraid of?" I asked.

"All sorts of things," Jim suggested. "Threats and intimidation. Suggestive material that might sway the jury's impression of what's taking place. Heck, even a newspaper headline can be a detriment."

He glanced toward the kid on the bike and shook his head. "Look at that," he said. "That kid's selling papers right where the jury's going to be arriving. If I were the judge, I wouldn't allow it."

"What about the bystanders?"

"I'd push them back, too. They have every right to assemble, just not right here."

"So, do you like the jury?"

Jim ripped the tops off his creamer and sugar packets, dumped them into his cup, and stirred it all together. Even though he wore a navy-blue blazer and sipped a warm drink on a hot summer morning, he was cool. It's like he didn't get distracted or nervous, flustered or riled. He was like a grizzled football coach who never shows any emotion whether the team was winning or losing. "You know, Derrick, it's not a perfect jury, but I think we can live with the hand we've been dealt." He shuffled out of the stream of foot traffic and added, "There's a couple of wildcards up there."

"The drug addict?"

"Former drug addict," he corrected me, "she's been clean for quite some time."

"Oh yeah?"

He nodded. "I talked to her parole officer, and he couldn't say enough good things about her. Her preacher said the same thing."

"Why does that make her a wildcard?"

"I never said that she was," he smirked.

He was right; it was my idea.

"You're not going to tell me, are you?"

"That's right."

"After the verdict's in, will you?"

"Maybe," he smiled, half-heartedly, "some day."

I got the feeling that Jim really didn't want to talk much about the jury or the trial. Perhaps it was bad luck, or bad karma, or it was just plain unprofessional to speculate. Maybe all that warmth he showed during our appointments wasn't that sincere after all.

A group of reporters and photographers rushed past us to the crosswalk where Ms. Melton and Mr. Jacobetti marched shoulder to shoulder across the street. Jacobetti still maintained the pontiff's posture, with his right hand held at eye level. Aside from Ms. Melton's skirt, which flirted with the top of her knees, the two of them were dressed nearly identically. They had matching, pinstriped suits; French-cuffed oxfords, and ties. Penny's was red, Jacobetti's crimson. They both whisked past the gathering, hardly offering a statement, barely stopping to pose for a photograph. The officers opened the doors, and the two attorneys disappeared inside.

As we glanced their way, I asked Jim about the odds of their offering a plea bargain.

"You never know, Derrick, they might have already."

Jim was toying with me, and I'd had enough of it.

Instead of trying to settle the score, or engaging in any more speculation, I decided to part company.

"Thanks again for the breakfast," I said, "good luck, today."

Jim raised his cup as if to say, "Adios." He was cordial enough, but a little too smug for my liking.

The crowd was getting restless as more and more people were jamming into the waiting area. In a twisted kind of way, it reminded me of the time I went to Iowa and saw the hogs waiting outside a slaughterhouse.

A block or more away from the gathering, church bells chimed, and I figured it had to be after eight o'clock. Judge Brewer was undoubtedly stewing inside his chambers, wondering what happened to his jury.

Instead of being dropped off at the front of the courthouse, the jury was delivered to the rear doors in four different squad cars. Two of the vehicles were unmarked state police cruisers, the third belonged to the marshal's office, and the fourth, to the Genesee County sheriff's department. What should have been a twenty-five or thirty-minute drive down I-75 had turned into quite an ordeal.

At nine-thirty, Judge Brewer fell into his high-backed leather chair, pointed the handle of his gavel at the prosecutor's table, and the trial of the Ivey brothers resumed in earnest. I thought for sure His Honor would belabor the point about maintaining the jury's integrity, but he chose not to. After all, the jury wouldn't know about "Every verdict has a price," the fliers on the windshields, or suspect that the fire alarm was anything but legitimate.

Henry Rush wondered if Robert Gilbert's ride in the back of a police car brought back memories of his brushes with the law. Gilbert looked quite fine; Yoder, on the other hand, glassy-eyed and sallow. What's worse, he wore the same outfit that he had the day before.

Dr. Ong kept his views about the jury close to the vest.

Colleen questioned the merits of TV3's reports.

And I, frankly, was losing interest.

Instead of listening to the testimony of LeBeuf's supervisor at the Arenac County sheriff's department, I decided to sneak out the back door of the courtroom and head across the street to the deli. The place was packed with cameramen and employees of the television stations who had just filed their morning reports. They laughed and sipped their coffee and told stories about incidents behind the lens. A couple of them recognized me from the time I did mouth-to-mouth resuscitation on a suspected felon on Mackinac Island. I shook their hands and we chatted for several minutes about the business of reporting the news, and what was going to happen in the trial.

The owner of Abrihim's Delicatessen was holding court with a group of employees behind the counter. All the employees were young and wholesome looking; their uniforms looked like a cross between a golf shirt and a rugby shirt. I didn't hear a lot of what was taking place with the employee meeting, but judging by the fliers in the owner's hand, he must have wanted the staff to pass them out when the trial broke for lunch. He was hungry for business and it showed.

From what I could gather, he already had a nice crowd. The place was abuzz in chatter and conversation, laughter and "Hey, how are you's?"

As I made my way to the men's room, I spotted an Amish man reading a dog-eared copy of the *Flint Journal*. An elder. He recognized me about the same time I recognized him.

I sputtered to a stop. It seemed like the most unlikely of settings for an elder.

"Morning," I stated.

"Good morning to you," he said, cordially.

"What are you...?" I couldn't think of what to ask, or how to say it.

The elder didn't make it any easier on me. He barely cracked a smile.

"I came over for a cup of coffee," I said, "would you like one?"

The elder raised his eyebrows and nodded his head. "Yah."

"Ok, great. You want cream or sugar?"

"Both."

"Very well. I'll be right back."

The elder nodded again as I walked away.

I felt a little relieved that I would have someone with whom to talk. After all, I was facing the prospect of a long day ahead, with very few urgent matters that needed attention. Even though the elder had every right to be there, and I was grateful for the company, his presence seemed a little odd.

When I returned to the table with our coffees and a couple of pieces of baklava, the elder's eyes warmed.

"Thank you," he said.

"You're welcome," I smiled back at him. "It's baklava. Ever had it?"

"Nooo, never," he said.

"It's a Turkish dish. Kinda nutty. Rather flavorful."

The elder didn't wait to hear my explanation; he dove into the square of pastry as if it were a swimming pool on a warm summer afternoon. Except for two or three crumbs in his beard, he made it disappear.

"Glad you liked it," I said, half-thinking that he really didn't take time to relish the flavor.

He nodded, as if to say, "I'm glad I liked it too."

I watched him tear the top off a container of cream and pour it into his cup. The little packets of sugar weren't far behind. It was like he couldn't focus on anything but making sure his coffee was just right before speaking to me again.

"Ever see a leaky dairy cow?" I asked him.

The elder looked up from his spoon, and glared at me. It was a dumb question, I know, but it had the potential to be the perfect ice breaker.

I flipped the little creamer packet on its top, and poked holes in the bottom with the tines of my fork. When I turned the container over and squeezed, the creamer inside came squirting out the bottom, just like a leaky dairy cow.

"Moo," I uttered, softly.

The elder smiled half-heartedly.

He watched me tend to my coffee, and took a sip of his own.

"You know," I said, generically, "I really don't even know your name."

The elder looked down at his cup of coffee. His fingers were thick and weathered, flecked with little gray hairs between the first and second knuckle, a trace of dirt trapped beneath his fingernails. "Ivan Petershwim. That's my name."

I nodded, but was slightly hesitant to fire more questions at him. Instead, I tried to find some common ground between us.

"I don't know if I ever told you this, Ivan," I said, "but I'm really thankful that you let me hunt turkeys on Eli's farm."

Ivan nodded.

"Have you seen the white gobbler lately?"

He shook his head, "I tink all dah turkeys are in dah corn."

"It's hard to see them when everything is lush and green."

"Dat's right. But I did find a pile of white feathers about a month ago."

"Oh?" I prodded.

"Between our farm and dah neighbors."

Now it was my turn to nod my head and listen.

Ivan took another sip of coffee; I finished the last bite of my pastry.

"How do I get in touch with Zachariah?" he asked.

"Who?"

"Zachariah Yoder. He's supposed to be here."

It seemed like a relatively naive question to ask: *Doesn't everybody know that the jury can't be bothered?*

"Well," I started, "I'm not sure you'll be able to. He was selected to be part of the trial."

Ivan reached below his chair and pulled out a paper grocery sack. "I know of dat. He needs a change of clothes."

"That makes sense. You should be able to give his belongings to the guards across the street."

Ivan shook his head. "Don't really want dat. I have to converse with him."

"That might be a problem. The jury is sequestered. They can't talk to any—"

"That's not what I want to hear," he said, interrupting me.

I nodded in his direction. "It's just the way that it is, Ivan. How are the children doing?"

"Which ones?"

"The Beiler boy, and the other one."

"The Beiler child is going to be okay, I tink, but I'm not so sure of dah other one."

"Some day I'd like to take the Beiler boy turkey hunting."

Ivan sighed and I wasn't sure if it was because he didn't want to get involved in such trivial matters, or if he had more important things on his mind.

I upped the ante and asked him about the cost of the children's' medical care.

"What about it?"

"You have insurance, right?"

He shook his head and sipped his coffee.

"No, we don't believe in it."

"What are they going to do? They're going to have thousands of dollars in medical bills. The helicopter ride alone is going to cost a pretty penny."

Ivan shook his head. "The Lord will provide. Sundays we take up a collection from dah entire community for such tragedies. All dah Amish do dah same ting in Pennsylvania, Michigan, Ohio and Indiana."

"How does that work?" I wondered. *It's not like you can send out an e-mail to everybody in your address book.*

Ivan shrugged off my question. It must have hit too close to home. "I really need to talk to Zachariah," he pleaded again.

"He can't talk to anybody."

"Never?"

"Maybe if there's a family emergency of some kind…"

His eyes were glaring a hole right through me, his hand firmly on the crinkled grocery sack. It seemed like the thoughts in his head were raging wild.

"What is it?" I asked as sympathetically as possible.

"He shouldn't have even been here," Ivan sighed, "I told you a long time ago dat we don't go along with dah ways of dah English."

"What does that have to do with Mr. Yoder?"

"He shouldn't even be on ah jury."

"Why do you say that?"

"It's our religion. It says it right in dah Bible."

"Where, Mr. Petershwim?"

"Matthew Seven-One. 'Judge not, that ye be not judged.'"

His words swirled inside my head. I thought about rebutting his point, but it wasn't the time, or the place, to do it.

"If you're on a jury, you're not following dah Bible," he added, "and if Zachariah wasn't on dah jury, we wouldn't have dah trouble at home."

"It's not his Belgians, is it?"

"Noo," a second or two passed, but it seemed like ten or twelve, "it's his daughter," he sighed.

"What is it, Mr. Petershwim?"

He raised his Styrofoam cup to his lips, and I heard his gray whiskers rub against the side. They were long and bristly—tough and humble, just like the man.

He looked up at one of the wait staff, who held a coffee pot in her hands. "You gentlemen ready for a refill?" she asked.

"Sure," I said, smiling.

When she stooped slightly to pour my cup, I glanced at Ivan who was staring in the direction of the woman's chest. She was eighteen or twenty years of age and her breasts bulged outside her bra and camisole. Even though I tried not to take notice, they were rather freckled and smooth—perhaps pursed with suntan oil or baby lotion—and each mountain carved out a deep, splendid valley. They seemed like fertile ground for the devil's workshop.

Good thing I didn't notice.

When she slowly filled Ivan's cup with coffee, the look of amusement on his face runneth over.

The diversion temporarily stalled our conversation so I had to reel him back to reality, "What's wrong with Mr. Yoder's daughter?"

He swallowed.

"She's gone."

"What do you mean, 'She's gone'?"

"They took her," he whispered.

"Who did?" I demanded.

"We don't know, but they left a note."

"What did it say?"

"I brought it with me," he said, unfolding a piece of paper from his shirt pocket.

He tried to hand it to me, but I refused. "Mr. Petershwim, you shouldn't be carrying around a ransom letter like that. It's…it's evidence. The police can get the DNA, or fingerprints from it."

"I have no knowledge of those things."

"Neither do I, but if you're just carrying it around, you could diminish the chances of finding out who did it."

He was melting.

"Can you read it to me?" I asked.

He looked down at the paper. The creases were worn thin, as if he had folded it and unfolded it a thousand times.

"*Set the Ivey boys free, give us $125,000, and the girl comes back alive,*" he said.

"Holy hell…is that it?"

"Yah. That's it," he shrugged.

"We've got to call the police," I suggested, looking over my shoulder.

"No, no. Dah note came in an envelope that had '*No Cops*' on it."

"Where's the envelope?" I asked.

"We burned it."

"You burned it?" I asked, surprisingly.

"In dah burning barrel with the rest of dah garbage."

"Why would you do that?"

"That's what we do," he said, emphatically. "We don't pay for garbage service like dah English."

I rolled my eyes and asked, "Mr. Petershwim, how old is the child?"

"She's twelve."

"And when was she taken?"

"Last night."

"And you found the note last night, too?"

Ivan shook his head. "Nooo, they found dah note dis morning, then realized that little Grace was missing."

"Where was the note?"

"It was wrapped around a brick."

"Really?"

"Yah."

"Was it on dah front porch?" his dialect was wearing off on me.

"Yah. That's what Zachariah's wife said."

"What are you going to do?" I thought aloud.

Ivan shook his head. "I don't know, but I tink Zachariah ought to know about it."

I leaned back in my chair and thought things through. Ivan did the same. We folded our arms and scratched our chins like wise men.

"Are you sure you don't want to call the police?"

He shook his head. "Nooo. Dah elders agreed dat we wouldn't."

"Well, what are you going to do?" I implored.

"I don't know."

"If you tell the police or the court, they'll pull him off the jury."

"Dat will be the death of little Grace." Ivan had an odd arrangement to his sentences.

He had a point. A good one. I needed a break. "I'm going to hit the men's room."

"I'll go with you," he suggested.

We were just like a couple of women who wanted to make the most out of our time together, even if it meant going to the restroom at the same time.

Ivan pushed his chair away from the table, and followed me.

"You know what we could do," I suggested as we walked, "tell the court about the kidnapping and the letter."

"What good would that be?"

"The court could delay the proceedings, which would give the police time to find little Grace."

As we entered the men's room, Ivan shook his head. "I don't know much about such tings as dah courts, but dat doesn't seem likely."

"What do you mean?"

"It doesn't seem like they'd delay dah proceedings just because one of the jurors' children has disappeared," he said, firmly.

As we addressed the urinals, I realized that Ivan's homemade jeans didn't have a zipper in front. He wiggled out of his pants like a small boy, and his suspenders dangled near his ankles.

Ivan made a good point. "You're right, Ivan," I conceded, "and how are you going to come up with dah money?"

"We don't have dat kind of currency. We're lucky enough to pay dah bills."

Ivan grunted while he stood there, which made me wonder if he should have been sitting down instead of standing up.

"What are you going to do?" I asked.

"I don't know," he snorted, "if I can't talk to Zachariah, I was hoping you'd be able to help me."

He made me think. As we stood there side by side, elbows nearly touching, and our junk exposed to the twinkling wet porcelain, his plea for help touched something deep within me. I wanted to give the Amish a hand after we put away our private parts. After all, I'm a helpful kind of guy.

But I didn't just want to whip out my checkbook and fork over that kind of money; after all, that was only half of what the kidnappers demanded. If I could kill two birds and be guaranteed of an acquittal, it might be something I'd entertain. In my head, I had already begun to think about how many loaves of sourdough all that money would buy. Then again, if I kicked in half and the Amish forked over the other half, I'd still be a sourdough millionaire for life.

Can you ever tire of good bread?

"How can I help you, Mr. Petershwim?" I asked.

Ivan grunted. "I don't know how, but I consider you a go-between between us and dah English."

"I don't mind that, I'm just not sure how we're going to go about making things happen."

Ivan hocked up his pants, slipped beneath his suspenders, and made his way to the sink.

"If we tip our hand to the wrong person," I continued to think aloud, "and he or she tells the wrong person, little Grace could be dead by the end of the week."

"Yah, but if the jury gives dah wrong decision, she's dead anyway. There must be some way to reach Zachariah."

We finished our business in the bathroom, but when we returned to our table, four people had jumped in our seats.

"Come on," I told Ivan, "let's go outside."

Ivan grabbed both our coffees from the table, and we slipped past the patrons, the waitresses, the cameramen, and eventually into the warm, August air.

Once there, I asked Ivan how he was supposed to hand over the money.

His blank face said it all: "I don't know."

"So whoever took little Grace has got to get back in touch with you, right?"

"Yah," he said, "I guess so. We can't just leave dah money on dah porch."

"That's right," I smiled. "Whoever they are will be touch with you, that's for certain."

Ivan sipped the last of his coffee and tossed the cup in a trash can.

"If you're not going to call the police, we've got to work on getting that acquittal."

"How do you suppose we do dat?" he asked.

"Come on," I waved to him, "let's walk across the street. There's somebody I want you to talk to."

Twenty-Six

I NEVER REALLY THOUGHT ABOUT what an Amish elder keeps in his homemade jeans until Ivan unloaded his pockets into the little plastic bin inside the courthouse doors. There must have been three or four dollars worth of coins, a miniature tape measure, a wad of currency folded into a flimsy money clip, a tiny jackknife, lip balm, a mangled granola bar, and a small, red apple. What was rather disturbing, however, was that he also had fifteen or twenty packs of sugar, and a half-dozen single servings of jelly that he must have stolen from the deli across the street.

He told the guards monitoring the metal detector to keep the knife safe until he returned.

Even though I trotted up the stairs, Ivan took his time. Several minutes later, we slipped into the back door of the proceedings.

The jury wasn't there, but Chitwood and Jacobetti were bickering back and forth about whether the prosecution's witness should be able to testify.

"Your Honor, the spike strips used by the defendants were purchased from the same manufacturer whose tear gas canisters were found inside the gymnasium," Jacobetti pleaded.

"Judge Brewer, the prosecution can't prove that," Chitwood explained. "It's just wild speculation on their part. The spike strips didn't have any identifiable markings on them, nor did the canisters of tear gas."

Judge Brewer leaned into his chair, wrapped his left hand around his right fist, and propped his elbows on both armrests. He was thinking about how he should decide.

When Jacobetti piped up again, Brewer held up his arm, and extended his palm as if to say, "talk to the hand."

Jacobetti stopped.

Despite the crowded courtroom, it was amazingly quiet. Mr. Chitwood stood at the defense table, one leg bent in front of the other, fingers pressed into the hardened mahogany. His pose was a lot like a professional golfer—the way they lean on their putter before it's their turn to play. The court reporter sat upright in her chair, fingers poised to flail away at the keys. Jack Jacobetti checked and re-checked that his cuff links were where they belonged.

"I'm going to take this situation under advisement," His Honor finally decided, sighing in the process. He glanced at the clock on the back wall, and said that he was going to work on his decision through lunch. "It's almost eleven now; we'll convene at one."

He was in such a hurry to get started on his research that he forgot the part about banging the gavel.

"All rise" was lost in the gallery's chatter and the clip-clop of soles. Most of the television reporters rushed out first, eager to gather their notes and prepare their noon-hour report. They'd be the first people to receive a flier from the deli's employees across the street.

Colleen was in the middle of the Heretic Fringe, and as they shuffled in our direction, I realized that maybe I should have let her drop me off a block away from the courthouse instead of the other way around. She'd still have her car keys, and I would have been the one to walk through the hood. It made me happy to see that she was okay, and when she winked in my direction, I knew that she was in full control and everything was going to be just fine.

I introduced Ivan to Henry Rush, who wanted to know if we were going to have a cup of coffee and a sandwich.

"Maybe," I said, "we've got a little business to take care of. You'd better go on without us."

Henry accepted my answer graciously, but added, "You didn't miss much this morning. I still say that the prosecution is on the ropes."

I nodded my head, but dismissed his evaluation.

Besides, it seemed that everybody that walked past us had an interest in saying "good morning" to Ivan. I might as well have brought a unicorn or a mermaid to the proceedings because of the curiosity he attracted.

Even Mr. Jacobetti said good morning as he marched out of the courtroom. Penny Melton—on the other hand—never made eye contact, never took her foot off the gas.

After about ten minutes of waiting, James Ong finished his consultation with the Iveys, Mr. Chitwood, and his junior assistant. They all strolled to the exit, and when they did, I couldn't help but notice the gold dripping from the women and the perfectly pressed suits worn by the men in the Ivey family.

As they walked past, I raised an index finger as if I was hailing a taxi. "Dr. Jim? Dr. Jim?"

He glanced in my direction and stopped his conversation in mid-sentence. "I'll meet you at the restaurant. Go ahead without me." The small collection of people kept moving, through the doors, and out of sight.

As he stepped in our direction, I introduced Ivan Petershwim.

"Is there someplace we can talk?" I asked.

"Of course," he said, extending his hand to the doors. "There's a conference room across the hall."

Ivan still had the brown paper sack in his hands as we followed Jim to a rather lifeless little cubicle complete with an ancient table and chairs. "Please, sit down," Jim suggested.

At first, I took control of the situation and explained who Jim was and why he was at the trial. When I asked Jim if I had forgotten anything about the jury consulting part of his practice, he responded, "I think you've covered just about every detail."

"What we're about to tell you has to be held in the strictest of confidence, Jim," I warned him. "Mr. Petershwim and the other elders do not want to call the police."

Jim looked a little concerned. "What are you getting at?"

"Go ahead and show him," I said, looking in Ivan's direction. For a second or two, Ivan didn't know what I was talking about.

"Show him the note," I said.

"Are you sure?"

"Yes. Doctor Ong is a professional and can be trusted."

Jim looked at me with a rather concerned look on his face.

"Here you are," Ivan said as he slid the note across the table.

Jim wasn't the least bit timid about picking it up, and his eyes raced across the page.

I added, "Juror fifty-five has a twelve-year-old daughter," I said, rather seriously. I didn't need to explain who juror fifty-five was. Jim knew everything about them.

"Jesus," Jim mumbled.

"Nooo, her name is Grace," Ivan said, even quieter.

Jim looked up from the note and glanced at Ivan, then at me. This was serious.

"They took her last night and left a note on the front porch this morning," I said.

"But you don't actually know who 'they' are, or how to go about getting 'them' the money," Jim said, somewhat agitated. "What kind of a rinky-dink outfit are these guys?"

Ivan wasn't sure what to say.

Neither was I.

"Why don't you want to call the police?" Jim asked.

"Because dah envelope said not to call them."

"The envelope was destroyed with the trash," I said. "There's no evidence or a chance at getting any DNA."

Jim crossed his arms and listened to me.

"This is the Amish group from Gladwin I've been telling you about, who've had a string of bad luck. First it was the shooting, then an accident at the school's building site, and now one of their own has been kidnapped."

Ivan watched me.

"They don't have any money, Jim."

We were all doing a little brainstorming.

Finally, after thirty or forty seconds, Ivan piped up and said, "I wish to converse with Zachariah."

"You can't," Jim said. "Nobody can, unless you want to get the police involved."

Ivan shook his head. "I have hiss belongings," he said, clutching the paper bag and his straw hat at the same time.

"We can do that," Jim said, "but don't you think we ought to come up with a plan?"

"That's why we're here, Jim."

"Here's what I think," Jim said. "If the guys who wrote the ransom note are really legitimate, they'll be back with detailed instructions on how to drop the money in exchange for the girl. The timing is going to be critical, however, because the prosecution is almost done presenting its case."

He cleared his throat, "Depending on how the judge rules on the witness with the army surplus shop, and the other witnesses to follow, Jacobetti could rest his case later today. Quite honestly, this whole thing could be wrapped up as soon as tomorrow."

"What if the jury decides guilty before dah kidnappers say something?"

"That's the risk," Jim said, stating the obvious, "If you're going to round up some cabbage, you had better do it soon."

I looked at Ivan who had a confused look on his face. "Jim doesn't mean 'cabbage' like you grow in your garden..."

"We got some...cabbage," Ivan said, "but not in dat quantity."

"How much cabbage do you have, Mr. Petershwim?" I asked, rather reluctantly.

"In dah community, almost ten thousand. If we didn't rebuild dah school or have dah medical bills, it would have been more."

Ivan was breaking my heart. The Amish could do glorious things with that kind of money, and stretch it a hundred times further than most. There was no time to take up a collection.

"What are the odds that the prosecution will offer a plea bargain, or that the Ivey boys will be found not guilty anyway?" I asked.

"Good question," Jim nodded. "I mentioned that there's a wildcard on the panel, but overall, I think the defense is well-prepared, extremely convincing, and present an excellent case for acquittal."

"Dat's only half of what dah nappers desire," Ivan said.

"You're right, Mr. Petershwim," Jim countered, "it's all about the money."

Jim slid the note back across the table, and I thought for a second that our meeting might be over. Ivan picked up the note and said, "Didn't Mr. Twitchell say that you were working for dah defense?"

"Yes, he did."

"Aren't you hopeful dat your customer is not guilty?"

"Of course."

I wasn't exactly sure where Ivan was going with this line of questioning, but he did have my attention.

"What would your customers pay for derr freedom?"

Jim scoffed at the notion, but as long as Ivan sat there—stoic as an Easter Island relic—the more his idea took hold.

"What would dey pay, Dr. Ong?"

"I have no clue," he laughed, nervously.

"How much are dey paying der barristers?" Ivan was on a roll.

"That's really none of anyone's business, is it?" Jim was getting defensive.

I smiled half-heartedly, but I realized that Ivan did have an excellent point.

"Mr. Petershwim makes a lot of sense, Jim. We're two days

into this trial already; if Judge Brewer declares a mistrial on account of jury tampering, your clients will be out a great deal of money if they have to start over with a new jury. The government may find a new place for a trial, which would add more expense."

Jim was still dismissive, until I put the concept into high gear.

"Mr. Petershwim, would you mind waiting outside?"

"Nooo, I don't mind."

He left, but forgot the paper sack on the chair between us.

As soon as the door closed, Jim shook his head, no. "I'm not going to do this," he said.

"Do what?"

"You know, ask my clients to contribute to this...scheme."

"Why not?"

"'Cause I've never done it before, that's why not!"

"You've never tried to influence a jury before?"

"No, never."

"Never?"

I had him on the ropes. "Jim," I said quietly, "I saw you yesterday at lunch time across the street. Remember those napkins at the deli? You had those napkins stamped with a special message on them, didn't you?"

"I did not."

"Yeah, you did. In fact, I looked at the napkin dispensers today, and the one up front, near the cash register is completely different from the other ones in the deli."

"That's a coincidence."

"You thought nobody was looking when you swapped out one napkin dispenser for the other."

"I did not."

"Jim, I saw you. And I wasn't the only one who witnessed it."

I backed him down.

Even though I could have implied my next step—talking to the judge about what I had witnessed—it wasn't a necessity. My threat was sincere and Jim understood.

"You son of a bitch."

"What?"

"How dare you come in here and blackmail me!"

"It's not blackmail, Jim."

"What is it, then?" he demanded.

"You know what, Jim, I'm into happy endings—"

"Don't give me that psycho babble," he interrupted.

"Okay, fine. Just talk to your people, Jim, that's all I want you to do. I know that the Ivey brothers have money. They've hired the best defense lawyer in the state. I checked them out and their family owns thousands of acres over there in orchard country, and now they're remodeling or building a new canning facility in Traverse City."

"What about it?" he wondered.

"Continental Foods? That company processes more canned blueberries than any other facility in the state. They're in every Meijers, Whole Foods, Wal-Mart and Podunk grocer in the Lower Peninsula. I know they've got money, Jim. You know it, too."

"So?"

"So, they'll do anything to get their sons out of trouble."

"Why do you care what happens, Derrick?"

I didn't need to think about a response; I had already said it once. "I told you why. I'm into happy endings."

Jim didn't respond, so I kept rambling. "I'm trying to get better, Jim, and I have to tell you that I really have grown close to those people. If I can help them get over this final hurdle, I will feel like I've done all I can."

Jim sat there, soaking it all in.

"They're not quite like family, but I feel like I owe them something because of all the grief they've had."

"What do you mean?"

"First, it was the lawsuit with Yandle, then it was the shooting, they burned the schoolhouse, the accident at the building site, and now one of their own children has been kidnapped."

Jim wasn't in the counseling mood. "If you feel so bad about it, why don't you contribute?"

"Maybe I will," I said, "but I at this point I don't know who's responsible."

"It's the Heretic Fringe, Derrick."

"How do you know? It could be the Tea Party. They're the ones who threw bricks and notes at the jurors' houses."

"You're wrong."

"I am?"

"Of course. The Tea Party wants the Iveys to be found guilty."

"They do?"

"They don't want congressmen getting murdered. They think it's bad for our country to have people getting away with it. Why would you think otherwise?"

I thought for a second, "Because Capp's vote was so unpopular among the Tea Party."

"A yes vote on a poor piece of legislation is one thing; murder is a whole other matter."

"So all those people out there in front of the courthouse protesting are on opposite sides of the verdict?"

"Exactly."

"Who would have sent the tweet to Channel 3?"

"Who knows?" he asked. "Who put the fliers under the windshields in the parking deck?"

I sighed. "Well, what the heck do you want to do?"

Jim thought for a second.

So did I.

Seconds passed, but they felt like minutes.

"One thing is for certain," I said calmly, "we both agree on a number of things. First and foremost, we both want a not-guilty verdict, correct?"

Jim nodded.

"We both know that your clients' family has money, correct?"

More nods.

"I don't want to see that little girl killed, and I'm sure you don't either."

"Right."

"We have a number of common causes, Jim. How can we make this happen?"

"More importantly, how do we get word to Mr. Yoder that the verdict has got to be not guilty?" he asked.

"Right here," I said, pointing to the paper bag.

"What are you going to do, leave a note in his pants pocket?"

"Amish men don't have pants pockets, Jim, only shirt pockets."

"Whatever," he said dismissively. "Are you going to leave him a note?"

"No, you are."

"I am?" he asked, somewhat confused. "You're the writer."

"You've got the Ph.D. after your name."

"Just do it left handed," he said, handing me a pen. "That way they'll never figure out who it came from."

"What if he can't even read?" I asked.

"Of course he can read. Here's some paper."

It felt a little odd holding the pen in my wrong hand. "Well, what do we write?"

"I wouldn't ramble on about the weather. Just get to the point."

It took me at least sixty seconds to write, *Dear Mr. Yoder.*

Jim looked a little perturbed, but added, "*It has come to our attention, that your little girl has been kidnapped.*"

"Wait a second," I said. "What if he has more than one little girl?"

"He doesn't. One girl, four boys," he said, without batting an eye.

I resumed my writing.

"*The people who took her want a not-guilty verdict,*" he said.

Amazing how awkward it feels to write wrong-handed.

"*If you value your child's life, return a not-guilty verdict,*" Jim continued.

I finally caught up to what he was saying.

"Don't you think we ought to say something about not telling the police?" I asked.

"Oh yeah. He can't tell anybody."

Between my messed-up printing and the way I followed the teacher's instructions, I felt a little like a grade-school kid.

In a little more than ten minutes, we had our letter.

Jim stood up, locked the door, and opened the paper sack. Instead of reaching inside and pulling out a clean shirt, Jim dumped everything on the table. Homemade jeans. A couple shirts. Toothbrush, but no toothpaste. A small hymnal that had only words, no music. The boxer shorts were completely shabby, the elastic band frayed and spent.

I felt a little creepy, rummaging through someone else's belongings, but Jim didn't have any trouble at all. It was like Mr. Yoder's personal items were the layers of a client's life experiences, and they all deserved to be probed, prodded and analyzed.

"Look at these undies!" he said, holding up a pair of threadbare boxers.

"Come on, Jim," I urged him, "can we get back to business?"

He laughed. The guy was giving me the creeps.

And when he held up a pair of one-piece swimming trunks, complete with the horizontal stripes and suspenders, he just about busted a gut laughing.

"Will you shut up?"

"What's wrong? These are hysterical."

I didn't think it was all that funny. Then again, I very seldom make fun of other people. It was a little disconcerting to see this kind of behavior coming from a person I was supposed to be able to trust. It made me wonder if he talked about me behind my back, too.

"What do you suppose that is?" Jim asked, pointing to a square, less than half the size of a brick. "It looks like gauze. Do you think it's plastic explosives?"

"Heck, no, Jim. That's cheesecloth, and I bet there's cheese wrapped inside."

"Where should we put the note?"

"In a pocket. A shirt pocket," I clarified.

Mrs. Yoder had packed two shirts, one powder blue, the other a dingy white. Both were short sleeved.

Jim folded the letter five or six times. When he reached into the shirt pocket of the dingy white shirt, he pulled out a separate sheet of paper. Written on it were the words *Nicht Schuldig.*

"What do you suppose that means?" I asked, rather seriously.

Jim shrugged his shoulders. "It looks like German…'night' something. Let me check."

He pulled his phone out of his sport coat and thumbed the keys.

"I didn't think you were supposed to have phones inside unless you were an attorney."

"You're right, Derrick," he said, rather distracted.

"How'd you get yours in here?"

"It's irrelevant, don't you think?"

He was right.

While we waited for the Internet to give us the answer, I put Mr. Yoder's belongings back in the bag. I almost felt sorry for him. He wasn't poor, but he chose not to spend much money on what he wore. It was all about function; clothing and possessions had no relevance.

"Son of a gun," Jim said, smiling, "we don't need that note after all."

"What is it?"

"Your buddy Ivan out there is one step ahead of us," he snickered.

"What is it?"

Jim looked up from his BlackBerry and calmly said, "'*Nicht Schuldig*' has nothing to do with night. It means '*not guilty.*'"

Twenty-Seven

BY THEN IT WAS NEARLY NOON, and Ivan was patiently waiting for us outside the conference-room doors. I handed him the paper sack, and the three of us made our way down the stairs to the guard's post near the front door. Ivan picked up his miniature jack-knife, and left the grocery sack with the guards.

"Dis belongs to Zachariah Yoder," Ivan said.

"Juror fifty-five, in the Ivey trial," I clarified matters.

The guards nodded, took a brief peek inside the bag, and that was that. They saw the honesty written all over Ivan's face, and never doubted the innocence of what might have been contained inside.

Dr. Jim was talking on his cell phone outside the courthouse doors, but had the wherewithal to hand me a business card with his cell number on the back.

Ivan was temporarily stuck in no man's land. He had accomplished his first and second objectives—deliver the overnight bag, and the secret note—but he really didn't address the kidnapper's monetary demand. It occurred to me that without any way to communicate with the Yoder farm, our hands were tied.

"Mr. Petershwim, how are we going to make this happen?" I asked.

"Make what happen?"

"The exchange…the money for the girl."

"I do not know."

"How do we reach the Yoder farm?"

He shook his head.

"Maybe the kidnappers have already given Mrs. Yoder instructions."

"What you say could be factual."

"This is why people get cell phones, Mr. Petershwim. Do you think in a case of an emergency, you could make an exception to Romans verse eleven?"

"It's twelve," he corrected me. "Chapter twelve, verse two."

"I remember…the business about rejecting what takes place in the outside world."

Ivan just listened, but he didn't necessarily want to hear what I had to say.

I stopped.

As we waited for Jim to finish his discussion, Ivan spoke. He sounded just like an elder.

"Mr. Twitchell, I recommend you read more of dah Bible," he said sternly beneath the rim of his hat. "It will give you great peace. I tink *you're* more concerned with today's trials and tribulations den we are."

"I am concerned. It seems like you folks are going to be trampled by today's busy, cutthroat society and I just can't let it all happen. Don't you care about little Grace?"

"Of course I do, but if you walk in faith, everything will be okay."

"Everything?"

"Everything," he nodded. "It is God's will."

When Ivan put it in that context, who was I to argue? Then again, if God helps those who help themselves, I was up for trying to save Grace's life even though her safety appeared to be quite tenuous.

"How are you supposed to get home, Ivan?"

"I did not figure that out."

"Do you want a ride?"

"Yah."

"Okay, then. Let's go."

I gestured to Jim that I'd call. He waved nonchalantly, as if to say, "So long."

As urgent the setting we were in, I still couldn't hurry Ivan. He was rather bowlegged and I'm sure he had enough aches and pains to fill an hour's worth of conversation. Maybe that's part of being an elder: take your time; weigh each step; tackle the issues of the day, little by little.

Me, on the other hand, I'm like a whirling dervish. Every day is an opportunity to get as many things done as I possibly can. I try to make the most out of every minute. Some days I get a lot accomplished; other days not so much. One thing is for certain, patience is not one of my strong suits.

"Ivan," I said, "why don't you wait right here, and I'll pick you up."

Ivan agreed, and after racing up the parking deck, finding my car and paying the woman in the booth, I pulled onto the sidewalk. Ivan was there, chitchatting with a bum who had wedged himself into the corner of the parking garage and the stairwell.

I didn't need to honk. Ivan knew I was in a hurry, and I watched him reach into his pocket and place something in the bum's plastic cup.

The man made a peace sign and smiled, even though he had very few teeth.

Ivan made his way to the car, and sat inside.

"You know, Ivan," I said, "a lot of those people just take the money you give them and buy more alcohol."

"I can imagine."

"Why did you give it to him?"

"I didn't," he said, rather defensively, "I thought that maybe he could use some jelly."

"Oh," I said, apologetically, "I'm sorry."

Ivan never batted an eye. "It doesn't smell so good in here," he said, "like rancid meat."

"I'm sorry, Ivan; it's leftover steak from last night."

He nodded.

"The leftovers are for my dog at home. He's pretty much spoiled."

"We have ah blue heeler," he said. "It helps out a lot, especially when it's time to bring in dah herd."

"Of course. I don't think there's anything prettier than a dog doing what it's been bred to do."

Ivan buckled his seatbelt and crossed his arms.

Before we made it back to I-475, he buried his head in his chest, and drifted off to sleep.

Colleen's car galloped along at my standard ten miles an hour above the speed limit. In my head, I was already planning the afternoon's schedule. If I hustled, I could be in Gladwin by two or two-thirty, then return to Flint to pick up Colleen by the time the day's proceedings ended. Even if I wasn't at the courthouse at the exact instant the trial ended, I'm sure she could find a safe place to wait. If nothing else, the deli would be open for business, and she could chill out there.

For a second, I thought about the vehicles in the Twitchell household. I was in Colleen's, and mine was at the bar in Montrose. I looked at Ivan sitting next to me, and thought about letting Ivan drive my car from Montrose back to Flint. That way, Colleen would have her car available to her, and Ivan and I could take our time getting back to Gladwin.

Even if I gave Ivan a fifteen-minute crash course on how to drive, it was still a recipe for disaster. Besides, Ivan had a lot on his mind; at least that's what I presumed. Despite his unflappable faith, Ivan embraced a frustrating tactic of inactivity. Like all the other Amish I have known, Ivan let life's circumstances push him around. It's like he cared about the missing child, but if she were never to return, it would be okay: God would bless the group with a new baby girl soon enough.

My heart bled for all the Amish and their troubles. If my family was in dire straits, and things were out of my control, I'd ask for as much help as I could get. And I was happy to lend a hand, drive the Amish here or there and even consider a financial contribution to the cause.

As I put more and more miles between us and the trial in Flint, I began to sift through my personal finances. Dad had left quite a bit of money to me and my sisters when he died and I poured my share into the purchase of the newspaper. Although it was very solvent and rolling along with decent subscription rates, it never really was the money maker that I had hoped for. Still, though, the paper wasn't doing that badly: last time I inquired, it had thirty-five or forty thousand collecting dust in the checkbook, waiting for a new roof on the building, a new piece of equipment, or an upgrade for the presses. At home, our house was paid for, and although it really wasn't very big or exceptionally furnished, we had a nice, comfortable place for living. I had a savings account, a retirement account, a rainy-day fund, a vacation fund, and last but not least an education IRA for Elizabeth. My Suburban was old and needed new tires; my car wasn't new, but it was almost paid for. Life was good, and I was blessed in a number of ways.

Wouldn't it be great to share some of those blessings?

The renovations at the paper could wait. The money collecting dust could be used to save a little girl's life.

God would approve of that.

And who knows, maybe I'd get my money back.

Once little Grace was returned home safely, and she identified who had kidnapped her, the cops would surely find the money. Even if I lost it all, it would have gone towards a worthy cause. The money would seem like a small price to pay if she was safe and sound. I could close this chapter of my life, knowing I had did all I could to make matters right.

And besides, I trusted Ivan, Mr. Yoder, Eli and Rebecca as if they were my own family.

Although I really didn't know Jim all that well, I trusted him, too. Despite that little incident in the conference room, and another with the napkin holder, his caring mannerisms in our two therapy sessions put my mind at ease. He may have been a little sideways, and not the straightest arrow in the world, but I think his heart was in the right place. He'd be the perfect person to broker a deal.

I reached into my pants pocket and pulled out the note Jim and I had written. It was all mangled and crooked and should have been destroyed long before now. Despite all our college degrees and Jim's subsequent letters after his name, we couldn't come up with a better letter than the one written by an archaic man with an eighth-grade education. Ivan's letter was perfect; ours wasn't even close. Before he woke up, I refolded the letter and stuffed it in my pocket.

As we raced past Saginaw, I realized that my phone was still under the driver's seat where I had left it. Six people had called, but not Colleen.

I needed to talk to her, but I couldn't do that while Ivan was sleeping next to me.

For a few seconds, I beat myself up for not calling her when I was all alone inside the parking garage in Flint. It was just another example of the way I fail to plan ahead. If I could eliminate half the dumb things I do in a day, I'd double my smartness quotient. Now it was close to one o'clock, and she may have been on her way into the courthouse. Maybe she didn't even have her phone. Where would she keep it?

Doing almost eighty miles an hour, I scrolled through thirty-seven new e-mails. Most of them were forwarded jokes from friends or relatives. Honestly, if an e-mail joke is longer than about two sentences, I just read the punch line and that's good enough for me. A couple of other e-mails were pleas for prayers, or admiration for members of our armed forces. Walter Claety sent me two that he must have received from his right-wing pals, who were stirring the pot of angst against Capp's liberal replacement.

I wished I would have been more insistent with Colleen when it came to which e-mail address she wanted me to use.

When I scrolled to her name in the address book, I had four or five e-mail addresses for her.

While Ivan continued his hibernation, I pressed the "select" button. All four addresses appeared in the "to" box.

My car drifted out of my lane and onto the "rumbly bumps" on the left side of the highway. I collected myself, slightly, and realized that maybe I should add her *39andholding* address to the carbon-copy section of the e-mail. It seemed like a good idea; after all, this was a very important matter and I wanted to make sure that whatever e-mail address she was monitoring, she'd receive it.

As we passed over the Zilwaukee Bridge, and I glanced at the huge marsh on the north side, I typed the words: *we gotta talk* in the subject line.

The body of the e-mail wasn't all that complicated. Perhaps I stole the idea of brevity from the man sleeping next to me: *It's about the jury.*

I pressed the send button and that was that.

When we stopped for gas on the outskirts of Midland, Ivan chipped in ten dollars. It seemed that he and Eli were under the same naïve impression about how much it costs to run an automobile. What's worse, when we stopped for a burger, there was never any doubt that we were going Dutch. In a way, the Amish frugality was wearing thin. It was one thing for both Eli and Ivan to be appreciative; it was a whole other matter to take advantage of the generosity of others. If I had more guts, I would have been more insistent that they pay their fair share. Instead, I bit my tongue and figured that I was doing a good deed for the day.

Silly me. Silly, silly me.

Forty minutes later, we pulled into the same farm where I witnessed the pig slaughter earlier in the summer. Nobody appeared to be home but the chickens and a pair of gray-colored geese that weren't far from a morbidly dirty, miniature swimming pool. The geese hissed in our direction, squatted slightly, and splashed a foul-looking grease on the lawn.

"Wait here," Ivan said as I put the car in park. "Let me go find Mrs. Yoder."

Ivan waddled up the stairs and knocked on the side door. A middle-aged woman with curly gray hair and a hamstrung dress let him inside. She didn't hug him, or shake his hands, or express any signs of emotional hardship over the kidnapping. It's like the knock on the door interrupted a casual game of checkers, or, with Grace's siblings, the preparation of shoo-fly pie.

I pulled out my cell phone. It was twenty-five minutes after two, and Colleen hadn't responded to my e-mail. Dr. Jim didn't call, either.

Court was still in session.

Good news.

If I left right now, I could probably be back to Flint in time to pick up Colleen, I thought.

The longer I sat there, the more anxious I became. We were burning daylight, and I felt like I was wasting time on account of Ivan's lack of courtesy.

After three or four minutes, I turned on the radio. Colleen must have been a fan of talk-radio, too, because I didn't need to adjust the knobs.

"It's the biggest money-laundering scheme in the country: the union bosses send union dues to Democratic candidates. Once the

candidates are elected, they negotiate contracts with the union bosses. What a scam! It's no wonder the UAW supported Democrats Don Ringle and Floyd Capp: the health-care law gives the UAW two hundred million dollars of the taxpayers' money. It's legalized money laundering, folks, and it's beyond repulsive."

America still held a grudge against Capp, against the health-care debacle, and the schlubs who rammed it down our throats.

With each passing second I became more and more anxious. The clock was ticking towards my appointment with Colleen. I really had to go.

Instead of waiting any longer, I scribbled my cell phone number on the back of a business card, and wrote: *Call me.* I opened the car door, put a small pebble on the card, and got the heck out of there.

I really had had enough of Ivan Petershwim and his insolent ways. All he had to do was poke his nose inside the door, and ask, "Any ransom notes?" and report back to me. Mrs. Yoder could have been consoled after I had left. He didn't need to go inside and chitchat, fix her leaky faucet, or sample one of her pies while I was outside, going bananas. It's like I had nothing better to do but dote on him and his family.

The way I left might have been just the impetus he needed to get himself into the twenty-first century. What the heck, phones aren't bad, people are.

A minute or so later, I approached Eli's farm and remembered that he still had my machine gun. Instead of carrying on to Flint, I decided to wheel inside, and pick it up.

Business must have been good for the Beilers. The UPS man had a dozen crate-sized boxes in his truck and Rebecca had six or eight others labeled, taped, and ready to go.

"Go ahead inside, Mr. Twitchell, Eli's in there somewhere."

I knocked half-heartedly on the door jamb and stepped inside, past the rows of jackets hanging on the hooks, and the assortment of shoes and boots on the floor. Little Angus Beiler was lounging in a hospital bed near the kitchen table. He was all alone, three of his four limbs covered in plaster.

"How's it going?" I asked him.

He barely acknowledged my presence, and continued his game of paddling a small rubber ball on an elastic string. I'm not sure if Angus was right- or left-handed, but he wasn't very good at it.

"Mind if I give it a try?" I asked.

Angus handed me the paddle and I tried my best to make it work. In relative terms, I was successful. He laughed at my antics and cheered half-heartedly as I danced around the kitchen, rhythmically thumping the ball against the paddle.

"Good!" he cried.

"Thanks," I said, "I've had plenty of practice."

"Me, too," he smiled.

Poor kid. I felt sorry for him lying there in all that boredom. Rebecca had him dressed in suspenders, but I wasn't sure why; his homemade jeans were cut off at the thigh; each cast stretched to his ankles. In other words, poor Angus wasn't going anywhere.

Nonetheless, Angus maintained a positive mental outlook. He reached for his bedside tray, sifted through the coloring books, and handed me a copy of *Field & Stream* magazine. On the cover was a pair of strutting gobblers—all puffed up and proudly displaying their beards. I looked at the mailing label on the front of the magazine, *Gladwin Community Library*. Someone wanted to make sure Angus had something fun to do while he convalesced.

"How about that, huh?" I said, rhetorically. "Do you like to hunt, Angus?"

His eyes lit up. "Oh, yeah. Never shot a turkey before, but I'd like to."

"We'll have to try it next spring," I said, just as the sound of footsteps came down the stairs. "Between now and then, you've got to get better, okay?"

Angus nodded, and a few seconds later he was surrounded by his brothers and sisters, who said something to him in German.

Eli wasn't overjoyed to see me, but he was cordial enough. He crossed his arms and leaned against the handle of Rebecca's ancient stove.

"I was in the neighborhood, Eli, and thought I'd pick up my AK."

Eli wasn't sure what I meant, so I explained a little further, "My firearm."

"Oh yes," he said, somewhat surprised, "it's out in dah garage."

Just as Rebecca finished her paperwork with the driver and said, "See you tomorrow," Eli and I entered the garage.

"I've been trying to keep it oiled," Eli said, glancing into the rafters. "About once a month I take it down and give it ah spray."

"Thank you, Eli," I said, calmly, "for everything."

"No problem," he said. "I figured if you didn't come back for it soon, I'd put it on EBay."

I laughed and watched him pull a step-ladder off the wall and set it up in the middle of the garage.

"Your son looks like he's doing well," I said.

"Yah, dey took great care of him."

I watched him peer over a toboggan, smiling the way he always does. First, he handed me the bulletproof vest, followed by a metal case of ammunition, which was quite heavy. Last was the gun itself, uncased, unloaded, but intimidating as hell.

By then Eli's kids had gathered around the opening to the garage, with four or five cats wrapped around their legs.

Eli said something to them in German. They said "Yes, Papa," and ran away.

As I picked up my belongings and headed for the car, I couldn't help but say again, "Thank you, Eli."

He smirked.

"It's not dat big of a deal."

"I just wanted you to know how appreciative I am."

"No problem. Everyting will turn out just fine."

At that point, I wasn't exactly sure if Eli was aware of what was taking place with the Yoder child. He hinted that he knew she was missing, but I didn't really want to take the time to ask. If Ivan wanted to fill him in on the sordid details, that was fine. As for me, I had to hustle.

"I'm sure you're right, Eli. Everything will be fine."

I tossed the gun and gear in the back seat of Colleen's car and asked Eli if his dog would like some table scraps.

"Of course," he said.

I handed him the little bag from under the seat, started the engine, and was on my way.

Eli waved. When he did, his children came running back to him in their homemade outfits.

As I drove away, I wished more and more that the court case was over and all the Amish were going to be okay. The Beilers were a great family. So were the Yoders and the Petershwims. They didn't deserve to be thrown into this mess that I felt partially responsible for creating.

The trial was in its second day and I knew it wouldn't be long until it was finished. When it was complete, I knew that I'd have a great sense of relief. It would be the perfect time to take the family on a late-summer vacation. Maybe we could go to Mackinac Island and become fudgies for several days, and eat whitefish plucked from the Great Lakes. Ludington, Manistee, or Frankfort sounded like fun destinations, especially if the salmon were close to shore and willing to bite. There's nothing quite so much fun as battling a giant, angry fish on a long, whippy rod.

I wanted to take my dog for a long walk, and spend quality time with my daughter. Heck, I missed my wife too and the way her eyes light up when I bring her breakfast in bed.

Church sounded agreeable; maybe I should have listened to Ivan when he suggested that I read the Bible.

The possibilities were endless.

All we had to do was save the Amish child and spring the Ivey boys, which wasn't out of the realm of possibility.

For now, though, the ball was in the kidnappers' court. They were the ones who needed to explain where the money needed to go and when it was supposed to happen. Once we knew that, Jim, Ivan, and I could come up with a way to meet their terms.

And honestly, we weren't talking about a ton of money. If the kidnappers had asked for a million dollars, they weren't going to get it. They seemed to know how much we could handle, and tailored their ransom to fit our collective budgets. If the Amish and I kicked in a share, and Jim's clients did the same, we might be able to pull this off. Maybe they'd take less than their original demand.

Although there were a number of variables that still needed to work themselves out, at least we had a plan. Instead of taking the Amish tack and patiently waiting for life to come at us, I was confident in taking the bull by the horns. We had the money, the connections, and a jury that appeared to be tilted in our direction.

All we had to do was close the deal.

What in God's green earth could possibly go wrong?

Plenty.

Twenty-Eight

I T WAS ALMOST FIVE BY THE TIME I made it back to the Federal Courthouse in downtown Flint. Ivan Petershwim didn't call, and neither did Colleen or Dr. Jim. I was beginning to think that maybe my phone was broken.

The mounted police had given up their vigil outside the rotunda, and were undoubtedly cooling their jets back at the police barn several miles away. A fresh set of troopers was staked out in front of the courthouse doors, their bright, blue cruisers parked curbside, near the caravan of media trucks. I caught a whiff of something delicious in the afternoon humidity—perhaps a barbeque or a mouth-watering beef brisket—as I waited for the trial to recess.

The streets of Flint were alive with the busyness of humanity. It seemed like every minute or so a young person with a loud stereo would drive past the gathering, rumbling to the beat of some toxic rap music.

Instead of selling newspapers, the boy with the girly voice had a red wagon hooked up to the back of his bike. Inside the wagon was a medium-sized cooler, taped to the side was a sign that read, *ice water…$1 each or 3 for $4.*

Not only was the kid an entrepreneur, he also wasn't afraid to show the world that he had a sense of humor.

I bought a bottle, and the boy stuffed the dollar neatly into the front of his fanny pack.

The troopers at the doors of the courthouse had water bottles too, and were nonchalant as they sipped their drinks and talked to each other behind their sunglasses.

Instead of fiddling with my phone, I decided to strike up a conversation with the troopers. At first they were rather stand-offish, but when I asked them if they were the two that broke up yesterday's skirmish inside the courtroom, their eyes lit up with joy.

"Yeah, that was us," they confessed.

"Good job, gentlemen," I smiled. "Did the court get its van towed off the edge of the road?"

The troops seemed to lose their smiles. "How'd you know about that?"

"I saw it on the side of I-75 this morning."

They looked at each other rather oddly, and one of them pulled a small pad of paper from his breast pocket. Next thing I knew, they wanted to know everything about me...where I lived, my driver's license number, the whole ball of wax.

I was beginning to regret taking action on the urge to socialize. The troopers were taking all the fun out of it. The last thing I wanted them to do was follow me to Colleen's car and arrest me for having an uncased machine gun in my possession.

"Can you help me understand what the problem is?" I asked.

"It's the van," one of them said. "It was vandalized."

"You're kidding?" I suggested, "While it was on the side of the road?"

"No, it was the engine. Someone poured sugar into the gas tank last night, and it fouled the motor."

"Aw, that vacuums, doesn't it?"

The troops glanced in my direction as if they had never heard the term before.

"It's a polite way to say 'sucks,' without offending anyone," I said.

They seemed to realize that I wasn't the one who vandalized the court's property, and became rather forthcoming in what was taking place inside.

"They've had people on the stand all afternoon," one of them said.

The other verified that it was the prosecution's witnesses who were doing the testifying.

"One of the reporters just said that the momentum has swung in the prosecution's favor."

"Is that right?" I asked.

"They gave their report right there, ten minutes ago," one of the troopers said, pointing to the sidewalk. "I overheard the whole thing."

"Oh, I believe you," I confirmed. "How long are you guys stuck here?"

"Till it's over, whenever that is."

All at once, the courthouse doors burst open, and the people poured into the late-afternoon sunshine, thankful to be relieved of the cramped quarters and stuffy air. The troopers and I didn't want to get trampled, so we held open the doors and let the masses file past. There was great chatter and conjecture, and I heard bits and pieces of the trial's details by way of the people's comments.

"That Chitwood is going to have his hands full..."

"Those Ivey boys are toast."

"Did you see the looks on their faces when the judge allowed the testimony?"

Colleen waltzed past twenty seconds ahead of Henry Rush. Neither one of them saw me.

I wasn't exactly sure of what I should do next. Colleen was going to need a ride home, that was for certain, but I couldn't just crash her party. She was engaged with the crew from up north, but I couldn't do anything about it. I really wished we had planned things differently and had set up a place to rendezvous. Heck, I bet she didn't even have her phone.

As I watched her mill around on the sidewalk, I felt slightly helpless. Jealousy gnawed inside my head, and insecurities ran rampant. I bit my tongue, held my breath, and pretended like I was engaged with the troopers. The longer I lingered at the doorway, the church members left her side. I figured that most of them were anxious to get to their vehicles and eventually back to the campground.

Little by little, forty church members became twenty, and shortly after that, ten. Colleen held her ground and deflected their dinner invites, the chance to fellowship, and the smothering closeness, I was certain.

I glanced at my watch. It was almost six. The television reporters were poised to give their reports and they primped themselves in the sideview mirrors of the trucks, their reflection in the windows, or the hand-held mini-mirrors in their purses. I thought that some of the reporters took themselves way too seriously when they covered their head in hairspray. It made me realize that I was a lucky guy for being able to cover the news in a golf shirt and a two-day growth of whiskers. Unlike those people, I needed time to think things through and sort out the details. Those spontaneous reports are a thing of beauty—at least that's what I believe—because the reporters very seldom trip over their tongues, omit anything relevant, or ramble on about things that are immaterial.

If Mr. Chitwood and the prosecutors didn't get outside in the next thirty seconds, they would miss their chance to be the "live" lead story on the nightly news. I'm sure that was the least of their concerns, however; they were doing whatever lawyers do when the trial is underway and the stakes are high. Publicity is great for any business, and free publicity is even better. Mr. Chitwood never missed a chance to toot his own horn, and it must have been something important that kept him indoors.

Secretly, I hoped that Chitwood, Jacobetti, and Melton would reach a plea bargain, which would effectively take the ammunition out of the kidnapper's hands. Without an acquittal as a possibility, half the kidnappers' demands would be off the table. With half as much leverage, I would think that the ransom would be half as much, too. Maybe the kidnappers would return little Grace, and figure that it was a bad idea after all.

Make no mistake, though, the ball was still in the kidnappers' hands.

They were the ones calling the shots; we really didn't have any way to expedite the situation.

What's the proper way to negotiate with a kidnapper?

How does a kidnapper deal with the Amish?

My head was swirling in possibilities, jealousy where Colleen was concerned, and wonderment at the reporters' abilities.

James Ong interrupted my thoughts as he stepped out of the courthouse doors. Instead of saying "Hey, how are you?" he casually took off his blazer, and in the process, handed me his card. I figured that he must have seen me through the window.

On the back he had written: *Braveheart's Pub.*

By the time I had looked up, he had brushed past Colleen and was crossing the street, headed for the parking garage.

There was only one Braveheart's Pub that I knew of, and that was in downtown Alma.

Dr. Jim remembered where I lived, and realized that Braveheart's Pub was on my way home. How thoughtful. What's more, he wanted just the two of us to meet, making me think that he had something important to review.

I leaned against the metal railing near the front steps of the courthouse. The troopers were on my right, Colleen on my left. I glanced at the row of television reporters on the sidewalk not far away. They were under the blaring lights, microphones in hand, delivering the news straight into the cameramen's cannons.

The Tea Party had disassembled, and the Heretic Fringe went on their merry way. Casual observers didn't hesitate to leave, and car after car paid their parking fee and pulled onto the one-way street.

The little entrepreneur with the girlish voice used a pair of bungee cords to strap his cooler to the wagon, and the wagon handle to the rear wheel fender. He sped away, smiling a satisfied smile. I never did ask his name or age, but I guessed he wasn't that far away from Angus Beiler.

Colleen ditched the last of her clingers, and I watched her drift to the rear of Channel 3's truck. That was my cue to approach—at least that's what I thought. I felt like a tom turkey in the springtime that wasn't really sure if the hen was real or just a decoy. Colleen must have understood my reluctance, and lifted her chin as if to say, "Come here."

As I approached, she smiled secretly and said, "Go get the car."

When I passed she added, "I'll walk down the street."

It was rather fun to think of her as an undercover agent; even more fun to be part of the facade.

I skipped across the street and met James Ong exiting the parking deck. He nodded at me from behind the wheel.

With all the secret signals and nods, head shakes and half winks, I felt a little like a player in a baseball game when he looks to the third base manager on whether a hit and run had been called.

Instead of plain old nodding at the private security guard in the darkened gallows of the parking deck, I simply had to go out of my way to be cordial. The guard welcomed my overzealous greeting, and the next thing I knew we were having a conversation about whether he had fought the good fight against crime in the community.

The conversation didn't last long, but it was long enough—I figured—for Colleen to walk a block or two from the courthouse.

When I emerged from the parking deck, the troopers were loading the jurors into their cruisers, two in the backseat, one in front. Two other sedans were there, too, and I watched the people disappear behind the tinted windows. It took four government employees, all that gas and time, just to keep the jurors safe and free of any outside influences.

As I waited for traffic to clear, the gentleman who received the jelly earlier in the day had risen to his feet and was watching what was taking place across the street. One of the man's colleagues was near the jury pool, undoubtedly asking for a helping hand. The panhandlers were out in force, and the competition was keen.

I didn't have time to dally. Colleen must have walked a block from the courthouse in the time it took me to get the car. The last thing I wanted her to do was have to linger on a street corner when the boys in the hood are on the prowl. Looking back on our decision about where to meet, Colleen and I should have picked a different place. Liquor stores have a way of attracting the seedier side of life.

Colleen was waiting for me on the same street corner where I had dropped her off earlier in the day.

There were four or five street thugs standing around her, undoubtedly making inappropriate remarks about the goodies she was packing beneath her dress. It made me mad just thinking about it.

Instead of casually driving up to the curb, I screeched to a halt, threw open the car door, and held the machine gun in the crook of my elbow. It made a nice little ornament.

In my best street lingo, I asked, "Was'sup, G?"

All four gentlemen backed away, flat footed, hands in the air. "Just mindin' our business," one of them said.

"Das cool, das cool," I said smiling. "Ready to roll, Mama Twitch?"

I didn't have to ask. Colleen dove into the passenger side and screamed, "Get the hell outta here, will ya!"

Those were marching orders.

I tossed the gun inside, slammed the door shut, and buried the accelerator.

Colleen and I took off like a rocket, past the bums and hoodlums, and the tricked-out cars with the bass pumping.

"What took you so long?" Colleen demanded.

"I'm sorry, Babe," I said, breathlessly. "Whew!" I exhaled, "Always wanted to do that."

"Why do you have a machine gun in here?"

"It's mine, silly. Don't you remember?" I asked, as I turned the corner and headed for the expressway. "I'm just glad that you're okay."

"Those punks probably thought I was a prostitute," she said, as she took off her red wig and huffed the huffs of escape. "They wanted to know how much for a trick."

"What did you tell them, something about dinner first at the Bavarian Inn?" I laughed.

She slapped me on the arm. "You jerk."

I laughed, then patted her on the knee. Colleen composed herself somewhat.

"What a day," she uttered.

"Why do you say that?"

"The trial. The witnesses' testimony. Everything with having to keep up this mirage."

"Somebody told me that the momentum has swung back to the prosecution."

"You bet. They ran up about four or five witnesses this afternoon. Each one of them drove a nail into the Ivey brothers' coffin."

"Figuratively, right?"

"Of course." Colleen ran her fingers through her hair, ridding herself of the wig's memory. "Who was that Amish man with you?"

"Ivan Petershwim? He's one of the elders from Gladwin."

"Why was he inside the courtroom, another long story?"

"You could say that, Colleen."

"Why don't you tell me?"

"Let's see, where should I start?" I thought aloud.

"In the beginning," she mentioned.

I thought for a second. "In the beginning, a mass of ice covered North America, gouging holes in the earth that eventually became the Great Lakes…"

Colleen slapped me again. "Get to the point, Derrick."

"You're not going to believe this, but the Amish guy on the jury has a twelve-year-old daughter who was kidnapped."

"Serious?" she asked.

"Serious-lee, Colleen."

She smirked.

"The kidnappers want a hundred twenty-five thousand, and a 'not guilty' verdict in exchange for her safe return."

Colleen exploded, "What did the police say?"

"The Amish haven't told the police."

"You're kidding. Are they stupid?"

"I don't think so. The note said 'no police' so the elders decided not to."

We had made it to the expressway, and were steaming our way north to my vehicle in Montrose. Colleen reached behind her seat and retrieved her purse.

"So what's going to happen?" she asked.

"Got me," I said, shrugging my shoulders. "I want to know who kidnapped the Amish girl."

Colleen rummaged through her purse until she found her phone.

"Don't you want to know?" I asked.

Her attention was somewhere else, but I couldn't help but wonder, "Did the Heretic Fringe kidnap her?"

Colleen looked up from her phone. "Of course not. I'd have known about it. And besides, the members who aren't in jail are really good people."

"Good people, but a little extreme, right?"

"Right," she sighed, "far right."

"Then who did it?" I asked.

"I don't think there's any doubt," she said, "it's the Ivey family."

I nodded my head in agreement.

"It has to be them," she added.

We were galloping along, thinking aloud, poring over the trial's developments and the angles that might affect the outcome.

Colleen thumbed her phone and eventually asked, "Looks like you sent me an e-mail about the jury. Is the kidnapping what you wanted to tell me?"

"Yes."

"Who's *39andholding*?"

"You, isn't it?"

Colleen acted surprised. "No, it's not."

I bit my lip, but didn't want to say anything.

"Who is it?" she jabbed me again.

"I thought it was you, but I must be mistaken."

Colleen let it go.

Minutes passed.

"I want to tell you something," I finally said.

She turned her head in my direction. "I really feel bad for what's happened to the Amish. They've endured so many horrible things. In some respects, I feel partly responsible."

Colleen held my hand, but didn't tell me how I should feel. All she could say was, "I understand."

We were glued to each other for ten or fifteen seconds.

"What would you think about contributing to the release of the Yoder girl?" I asked.

"What do you mean?"

"I mean, what if we gave the Amish a check for the ransom?"

"A hundred twenty-five grand, I don't think so!" she roared. "Besides, you don't write a check for something like that. They'll want it all in cash."

"Who?"

"The kidnappers!" she almost yelled. "I've seen enough TV shows to know that they'll want it in unmarked bills."

I sat there, driving.

"Who else knows about this?" she asked.

"Dr. Jim. That's it."

"He's probably rooting for an acquittal too, right?"

"Oh, yeah. He's going to talk to his clients about contributing to the ransom."

"The Ivey family?"

"Yes."

"I guess that rules them out as suspects, doesn't it?" she asked.

I nodded slightly, but added, "Not necessarily."

"What do you mean, Derrick?"

I shrugged my shoulders. "Just because Dr. Jim approaches them about contributing to the ransom doesn't mean that the Iveys didn't have something to do with Grace's disappearance."

"You're right. That would be the ultimate irony, wouldn't it?"

"Oh yeah, paying your own ransom."

Colleen and I were laughing together; I saw the love in her eyes.

"I bet it's the Tea Party," she said.

"That's what I thought too, but Jim says that they want a guilty verdict."

"Why's that?" she asked, "I thought they hated Floyd Capp."

"You're right, they hated him, but they don't believe in murdering somebody just because he didn't vote a certain way."

Colleen made a funny shape with her lips.

We exited I-75, and made the left turn towards Montrose.

"So, it sounds like this Jim has got every angle covered."

"He's really, really thorough," I said. "In a very modest way, I think winning is really important to him."

"What are you getting at?" she asked.

"What if we chipped in some of the ransom?"

Colleen raised her eyebrows and listened to me speak.

"Baby, we are blessed in so many ways…our health, our daughter, the paper's doing just fine. Eventually things will turn around in Michigan and then we'll be in even better shape."

She didn't interrupt me.

"We've got a big start on Elizabeth's college fund, and the house is paid for. We've got a rainy-day account, everything."

She put her phone back in her purse and listened to my heartfelt speech.

"How many times do we get to save a little girl's life?"

She stared out the windshield, and I caught the edge of her lips form the beginning of a smile.

"Besides, we might get our money back. You know how these things work themselves out. Once the girl is safe and sound, the police get involved and the money is recovered."

Finally, Colleen said something. "That seems unlikely to me."

"You never know, Colleen."

We were almost back to the bar in Montrose.

"How are you going to guarantee a not-guilty verdict?" she asked.

"That's the thing. We haven't figured that out yet, for certain, but we do have the inside track."

Before she asked me how, I gave her the Paul Harvey on Ivan's note, and how Jim and I were going to meet at Braveheart's.

"How much are you thinking about, Derrick?" she asked.

"I don't know, maybe twenty thousand," I finally said. "I think it would help me get over the tragedy at the schoolhouse. It'd be better than any counseling, and more helpful than all the drugs in China."

"Oh, Derrick," she sighed. "I think you messed up. It should be 'all the tea in China.'"

I pulled into the parking lot of the bar in Montrose and smiled in Colleen's direction. She smiled back, which puckered the dimples under her eyes.

"I won't be late, Babe," I told her. "Don't let Elizabeth go to bed, okay?"

She nodded.

"Great. I want to tuck her in and say goodnight."

Twenty-Nine

ALMA WAS ONCE A BOOMING LITTLE TOWN in the heart of mid-Michigan, but when the refinery closed years ago, it sucked the financial lifeblood from the community. In a lot of ways, I feel sorry for this little town where I live. The storefronts are old and tired, and the shops that don't have "for lease" signs taped to the windows are boarded up, awaiting renovations.

It's no wonder people from Alma and across the country are frustrated.

I figured that Braveheart's Pub wouldn't be very busy when I pulled open its heavy wooden door and peeked inside. It wasn't busy, and it probably wasn't going to be until Memorial Day weekend when the town has a homecoming of sorts. James Ong was seated way in the back, past the bar, and adjacent to a set of billiard tables. He didn't wave or tip his hat; in fact, he barely acknowledged my presence.

"What took you so long?" he asked.

"Nothing. I just drove."

"I was beginning to wonder if you had lost your nerve," he pried.

Thankfully, the waitress interrupted Jim's inquisition. "What do you want to drink?" she asked me.

I ordered an iced tea and lemonade, mixed together.

"Oh, an Arnold Palmer, then?" she confirmed, placing the menus on the table.

"Yes."

"Very well, I'll be right back to take your order."

Jim glanced at her skirt, which was actually a kilt made from Scottish plaid. Aside from the male bar owner, every female employee in the pub was wearing an identical outfit. Even Mel Gibson was pictured wearing a kilt, taken from the movie *Braveheart*.

"So, what did you think of the trial?" I asked.

He jiggled the ice in his drink. "Well, I'm not surprised with what I'm hearing," he said.

"That the prosecution's on a roll?"

"Right," he raised a finger as if I was supposed to wait. "But I've been through things like this before. It's always darkest before the dawn, and when we get those defendants on the stand, I'm sure the tide will change."

"What's your strategy?"

Jim gulped his drink. "I guess you'll find out soon enough," he said, "but I can assure you that Mr. Chitwood knows what he's doing."

"What do you mean?"

"I mean tomorrow will be here before you know it."

"Well, yeah, but I'm not so certain I'll be there," I admitted.

"Why not?" he asked.

"Because I have a paper to run, and I don't like to be away from the office for too long."

Jim shrugged his shoulders as if he didn't agree with my logic. "What if I need you?" he asked.

"For what?"

"For our plan," he said, quietly.

"I didn't know we had one," I admitted.

"We need to come up with one," Jim confirmed, just as the waitress brought my drink.

"Are you gentlemen ready to order?" she asked.

Jim nodded, and asked for the special, along with a fresh cocktail.

"And for you, sir?" she asked, pointing her pencil in my direction.

"Quesadillas, *por favor*."

She almost curtsied at my request, then went on her merry way. A couple of men wandered up to a pool table, stuffed a dollar's worth of coins in the dispenser, and released the billiard balls. As they brought each ball to the felt, I heard them talking and joking among themselves about who would break. Their quandary seemed quite trivial compared to what was taking place between Jim and me.

"So what's your plan, Doctor?" I asked.

"Just a second," he said, rather harshly. "I need to know if you're going to be a part of this."

"I'll do what I can, but I won't if it means I have to break the law. What are you getting at?"

"You may already have broken the law, Derrick."

"When?" I demanded. "How?" I asked rather loudly.

"Back at the courthouse," he said angrily. "The letter from Ivan Petershwim. You'd be an accomplice to jury tampering or at the very least, obstructing justice, but I don't want you to worry about that."

"Easy for you to say."

"Listen to me," Jim demanded, softly, "There are fourteen jurors on the panel, but only twelve will decide the case. That means we've got to get rid of two."

"And how do you suppose we do that?"

"We've got to be careful, that's for sure. If we get rid of two jurors, and the judge or prosecution finds reason to get rid of another, then we're looking at a mistrial."

"So, you're saying that we want to keep Mr. Yoder, but need to get rid of two others."

"Exactly."

"How are we going to make that happen?" I asked.

He sighed thoughtfully. "Derrick, the question is which two jurors are we going to get rid of?"

His question was underscored by the crack of the billiard balls on the table. They scattered around the felt rectangle, at least one dropping into the leather pockets. A man holding a pool stick snubbed the end with a chalk thimble.

"Do you have an answer?" I asked Jim.

"Yes," he said, leaning into me, "Oscar Haynes and Rick Nills."

"Who?"

"Oscar's the bald, kind of roly-poly fellow, and Rick Nills is the auto executive in the back row."

"Why those two?"

"I did some checking on both of them. Nills has a reputation for being a back-stabber and a coward," he said. "The people I talked to at the plant hate him."

"Geez."

"Besides, they're both hard-core conservatives."

I thought for a second while the waitress brought Jim his cocktail. "What does that have to do with it?"

"Those hard-core types don't see anything other than in black or white." Jim sipped his drink and eased into his booth. "They don't believe in second chances or compassion for their fellow man."

I glanced at the pool players, but Jim kept speaking. "We want liberals up there: people who will be sympathetic to our cause."

"How do you know they're hard-core conserva—"

My phone interrupted our conversation. I didn't recognize the number, but answered it anyway.

"Dis is Ivan Petershwim in Gladwin Michigan."

"Yes, Ivan," I said, pointing to the phone. Jim's eyes lit up, and he was tuned into our conversation.

"Dey sent us a picture of da Yoder girl."

"Who sent you a picture of the Yoder girl?"

Jim's eyes bulged.

"I don't know," Ivan sighed.

"What do you mean, you don't know? Wasn't there a note with it?"

"Noo, just da picture, and dey sent it to da Beilers' around da corner."

"Hmmm," I answered, *why the Beilers?*

"I don't know what we should do," he said, somewhat sorrowfully, "We don't really trust da English."

"I know you don't, Ivan."

Jim nodded.

"At this point, I don't know that there is much you can do," I added. "Jim and I are working on it, okay?"

"Okay, bye."

I hung up the phone and wished I'd have asked whose phone he was using, or how I was supposed to reach him.

"So the only thing in the envelope was a picture of the Amish girl?" Jim asked.

"That's it, and they sent it to the neighbor's house."

Jim sat there and thought. "Look at the timing of all this," he said, "Whoever is doing this really couldn't have mailed the picture of the girl, because she wasn't missing until this morning."

I nodded.

"You should have asked him if the letter was postmarked or just stuffed in the mailbox."

"Sorry," I lamented, "I can call him back."

"No, don't do that; we might have other questions."

"Like what?"

"Who knows?"

"I've got one for you," I started. "Who kidnapped Grace Yoder?"

"What do you mean?"

The waitress temporarily stunted our conversation. The quesadillas were first, then the fish and chips.

"Anything else I can get you gentlemen?"

We politely dismissed her.

"I've been thinking about this," I started, "and I can't figure out who would want the Ivey boys acquitted." Jim drizzled ketchup on his fries, but he didn't interrupt me. "At first I thought it might have been the Tea Party, but from what you said, that's not true. The most obvious group is the Heretic Fringe, but I'm not so sure…"

"Keep going," Jim urged me, counselor style.

"An extension of the Fringe would be the Ivey family themselves," I said. "They certainly have the motive."

"That may be true if it wasn't for the money. Why would the Ivey family demand money if they were going to pay themselves?"

Jim made a very good point.

"You really never know who could be involved, Derrick." I watched him devour his fish. "If I were you, though, I wouldn't get the cart too far ahead of the horse."

"What do you mean?"

Jim didn't reply, so I asked him if he had talked to his clients about contributing to the ransom.

He nodded.

"How much are they willing to chip in?"

"Not enough."

"How much are you short?" I asked.

Jim pulled on his cocktail, then fished a small bone from his teeth. "About twenty-five."

I nodded my head, *I can do that.* The men playing pool distracted my attention. It appeared as if one of them had sunk the eight-ball while there were still others on the table.

"Let's make this thing happen," I said.

"How?" he asked. "We can't do anything until the trial is over and we get our acquittal."

I sighed, impatiently. He made a very good point.

"If I decide to contribute, what do you think the odds are that I'll get the money back?"

"What do you mean?"

"I mean, the bad guys always get caught, and the money gets recovered, doesn't it?"

"Maybe on television, or in Hollywood, but I wouldn't count on it, if that's what you're thinking." Jim wiped his lips with a napkin. "Besides, you never know who you're dealing with."

"You make it sound so…clandestine, Jim."

He rolled his eyes slightly. "I'm serious, Derrick. Anybody who kidnaps a child has got to have a few screws loose. Don't forget that in my profession I've seen all kinds of nutcases and whack jobs. The road to a criminally insane defense goes through me."

Jim wasn't necessarily scolding me; he was merely stating the facts.

Neither one of us knew who kidnapped the Yoder girl. I doubted if the person or people responsible were mentally ill, or a pervert, or even an opportunist. This was the work of a bully, union thugs, or some operatives associated with Congressman Capp.

At the end of the day, I felt a little like my dog Jacque when he's on a neighborhood squirrel hunt. The dog knows that he's quick, but the closer he gets to a squirrel, the better the odds of catching it. I've watched him stalk his prey, step-by-step, using the available cover to hide his approach. What's more, Jacque seems to know which direction the squirrel is going to run and takes an angle that gives him the upper hand. The intensity etched across his face is deliberate and undeniable. When it comes to hunting squirrels—and equally important, birds—his instincts command his behavior.

In a lot of ways, I felt like a Brittany on the warpath. I knew that the case was almost settled, and could smell that the end was near. The closer we came to a conclusion, the more and more I wanted it to be finally over.

I was ready to be free, and anxious to get back to a normal life with Colleen, Elizabeth, and my dog, the neighborhood menace.

Thirty

A T A LITTLE AFTER EIGHT THE NEXT MORNING, Mr. Jacobetti called Louise Capp to the witness stand. Every eye in
the courtroom was upon her as she rose from the back aisle
of the gallery, slid through the thigh-high swinging wooden
doors, and found her seat adjacent to the jury box. She was
maybe fifty-five or sixty, but could have passed for ten years
younger. Her makeup, the clever outfit, the perfectly groomed
hair, helped create the impression that she was full of life and
vitality. It didn't take much to imagine her in a sweatsuit or an
athletic skirt, whaling away at golf balls at the driving range, or
taking her pet dog for a walk among the mansions in northern
Michigan.

Mr. Jacobetti asked for her name and where she was from.

"Louise Marie Capp, Harbor Springs, Michigan."

"And what was your relationship to Floyd Capp?"

"He was my husband."

"How many years were you married to him?"

"Seven," she sighed, "seven wonderful years."

"What made him so wonderful?" Jacobetti tried his hardest
to wear an understanding smile.

"He was a great man. I just loved him."

"Why?"

Mrs. Capp didn't hesitate, "We traveled a lot, and not just to and from Washington DC. We have a beautiful home up north, and a condominium in Florida."

"Keep going."

"He bought me all kinds of wonderful gifts and took me on great vacations." It appeared as if she was wearing a great deal of those gifts. They twinkled beneath her earlobes, and were wrapped around her broomstick wrists. "Last winter we went to Cancun to celebrate our anniversary."

Jacobetti's intent, I believed, was to create sympathy and yet he didn't want the jury to forget the reason everyone was gathered in the courtroom: a murder had taken place, and the people who were allegedly responsible for it were on trial.

"What kind of congressman was your husband?" Jacobetti asked.

"I guess you could say that my opinion was a little skewed because I saw him work so hard."

She took a second to swallow; perhaps it was her pride that had knotted her esophagus.

"In every given week, he received over a thousand letters and half as many e-mails."

Jacobetti stood still, and listened to her testimony.

"He took great pride in answering those letters," she said.

My mind flashed to Henry Rush. Mr. Capp didn't answer all the letters...

"Floyd used to attend the funerals of the servicemen and women who died in the line of duty."

Jacobetti clarified her statement. "You mean the servicemen and women who were from his district?"

"Yes, of course. If he had to be in Washington, he sent flowers, a heartfelt letter, and a giant American flag."

More swallows.

"I think that Floyd felt like everyone in his district liked him."

Mr. Jacobetti skated to an easel near the judge's bench, and removed the cover from a stack of Styrofoam displays. The first picture was Mr. and Mrs. Capp dressed in short-sleeved shirts and sunglasses. They were sipping something fruity from a pair of carved-out pineapples. In the background, several palm trees barely masked the setting sun. Without even being asked, Louise piped up, "That was from our trip to Cancun. We had a glorious time."

Jacobetti removed the first display and showed the jury the second. It was the two of them again, arm in arm, dancing. He had on a black tie. She wore a sequined gown. Their smiles were gloriously poignant. "That was a state dinner, held at the White House," she said. "It was held a week before he went home to Standish."

"What was the occasion?" Jacobetti asked.

I glanced at Chitwood and could see the muscles in his jaw flex.

"A diplomat from India or Pakistan was there, can't remember which. What I do recall is that the White House served ribeye steaks, baked potatoes and creamed corn. After dessert, the band started playing. We danced until midnight."

"Your Honor," Chitwood interrupted, standing at attention, "this all sounds like a fairy-tale evening, but I don't understand how this line of questioning is relevant to the case."

Judge Brewer agreed and asked Mr. Jacobetti to move it along.

"If it pleases the court," Jacobetti said, "I just have a few more items to show the jury."

Chitwood was still on his feet. "Your Honor!?"

"Sit down, Mr. Chitwood," Brewer said; "you'll have your chance."

Chitwood slumped in his chair. Dr. Ong tapped him on the shoulder, then pointed to something written on a legal pad. They nodded heads while Jacobetti revealed the next image.

"That was Whistler, British Columbia," Mrs. Capp rejoiced. "It was last summer. We were on a golfing and whitewater rafting trip."

Jacobetti smiled along with Mrs. Capp as she gave us the details about her excellent trip to the Canadian Rockies.

"What's it like to be a congressman's wife?" he asked.

"I think it's exciting, and quite prestigious. There's never a dull moment."

"What do you mean?"

"I worked in his office and kept track of his schedule. When he wasn't in session, or a committee meeting, he had to go to luncheons or dinner engagements." Mrs. Capp was smiling wistfully. "Floyd took me everywhere."

Four months after her husband had died, she still looked like a trophy wife.

"Did you ever think it would end?"

"Floyd always joked about retiring someday and becoming a professor of government affairs. As it stood, the deans at Harvard and Berkeley were in contact with him. Then again, there were lobbying firms all over DC that wanted his services too."

Jacobetti had his opening. "All those wonderful dreams ended in the high school gymnasium in Standish, didn't it?"

"Yes," she sniffled.

I glanced at the jury panel. The woman from the north side of Flint held a tissue to her nose. The laid-off auto workers in the back row crossed their arms in unison. Oscar Haynes and Rick Nills were nodding their heads. Dr. Jim's hypothesis was probably correct: they had already made up their minds that the Ivey boys were guilty.

Mr. Jacobetti approached the witness box, placed his palm on the wooden rail, and pointed a remote control at a television not far away. He pushed a button on the remote, and the television came to life. One button later, and we all watched in horror as the images of Congressman Capp's murder came to life.

"Shut up, you friggin' liar!" the voice on the television ranted. Months had passed since I had seen the hooded bully make a fist and bury it in the congressman's face.

"In one hour, thy judgment come," came back to me in streaming reality.

Jacobetti pushed the pause button just as Yandle dropped the axe.

"Is this, Mrs. Capp," Jacobetti asked loudly, "how you expected your whirlwind love affair to end?"

"Heavens no," she wailed.

Jacobetti gave Mrs. Capp the chance to cry. He plucked a couple of tissues from a box on the clerk's table, and kindly passed them to her. Between her sorrowful sobs and the image plastered on the court's television, the jury couldn't escape the vivid sadness percolating throughout the courtroom. Everywhere the jury looked, every sound they heard, were reminders of why we all were here. After a minute of more of deafening silence, Jacobetti pushed the power button on the television's remote. "I have nothing further, Your Honor."

Judge Brewer nodded. The court reporter scribbled notes on the scroll of paper that had spit out of the top of her machine. Everyone in the gallery turned their attention to Mr. Chitwood, center stage. Without being introduced, without Judge Brewer's clearance, Chitwood rose to his feet, buttoned the top button of his suit coat and asked Mr. Jacobetti if he'd like some help disposing of his props. It seemed like a nice gesture on Chitwood's part, and together they put away the easels and enlarged photographs. Mr. Chitwood rubbed one hand against the other as if he was removing grass clippings from his fingers. "Mrs. Capp, we're all sorry for your loss. Believe me, our hearts ache for what you're going through and the pain that you've endured," he smiled, grimly. "And we appreciate your being here this morning."

Someone in the gallery blew his nose. It sounded like the honk from a goose.

"I just have a few questions for you on behalf of my clients, Peter and Russell Ivey." He smiled slightly, extending an open palm to the table behind him.

Mrs. Capp had composed herself somewhat, and managed to nod.

"Did you and Mr. Capp have any children together?"

She shook her head, but didn't say anything.

"May the record reflect that the witness is shaking her head, no."

"Mrs. Capp, how many husbands have you had?"

"Four."

"I see," Mr. Chitwood nodded. He mashed his lips together tightly, then raised an index finger, as if he was testing the wind. "And how many times was Mr. Capp married?"

"I was his third wife, but I don't understand why that is relevant."

Mr. Chitwood paused slightly, smiled again, but this time he was rather dismissive. "If it's okay with you, Mrs. Capp, I'll ask the questions."

Mr. Yoder seemed to like the way Chitwood put her in her place.

Judge Brewer looked up from his Sudoku puzzle and glanced Chitwood's way over the upper edges of his spectacles.

"I want to clear up a couple items in your testimony," Chitwood added. "Just a few minutes ago, you said that you worked in Mr. Capp's office, is that correct, Mrs. Capp?"

"Yes."

"I see. Would it be safe to assume then, that you knew a lot about the people who came to see the congressman and the reason for their visits?"

"Yes, that's true. I handled most of the scheduling."

"Can you help me understand, Mrs. Capp, why the people who worked in the government unions would have paid so many visits to see Mr. Capp?'

"There weren't *that* many," she said defensively.

"Oh?" Chitwood asked, letting the question linger. "How many times would you say?"

"I don't know, maybe twenty in the past year."

"Twenty, Mrs. Capp?"

"Yes. That's what I said."

"Your Honor, I would like to enter into evidence the official docket used by Congressman Capp's office. May the record show that there were ninety-seven visits made by people on behalf of their unions in the last year alone." Mr. Chitwood handed a stack of paper to the bailiff. "Ninety-seven is a lot more than twenty, wouldn't you say so, Mrs. Capp?"

"Yes, sometimes I underestimate things."

"I see," Chitwood smiled, almost as if he understood, "are there any other parts of your testimony that you've underestimated?"

"No," she said, doubtfully.

"Why were the government unions in to see Mr. Capp?"

"I'm not entirely sure why."

"Why don't you tell the members of the jury what your hunch is, relative to the unions' visits."

"They liked him," she said, bashfully.

"'They liked him?'" Chitwood repeated.

She nodded.

"Mrs. Capp, you have to speak into the microphone so the court reporter can document your answer," Brewer directed her.

"I'm sorry," she said. "I just get a little nervous." All of a sudden, Mrs. Capp sounded a bit incompetent. That must have been Chitwood's intent. "Yes, I think everybody liked Floyd."

"They loved Mr. Capp, didn't they?" he asked.

"Yes. Everyone did. Well, almost everyone."

"Didn't Mr. Capp love the unions in return?" Chitwood asked.

"I can't say for sure."

"I see, but the unions certainly had access to him. Do you think it had anything to do with the fact that the unions were his second-highest campaign contributors?"

"I never really got involved with the finances." She shook her head.

"Your Honor, I'd like to enter into evidence the campaign contributions made to Congressman Capp by the state and federal employee unions. They gave more than two million dollars to the Friends of Floyd Capp campaign fund."

The bailiff met Chitwood halfway to the judge's bench.

"Mrs. Capp, did you ever consider who paid for your trip to Cancun?"

"No."

"Well, it wasn't your husband."

Jacobetti and Ms. Melton put up a fuss, claiming that Mr. Chitwood needed to ask a question, not use the courtroom as a soapbox for his political viewpoints. Brewer agreed with their argument.

"Very well, Your Honor, I'll rephrase that," Chitwood obliged. "Were you aware that the Traverse City chapter of Federation of Local Government Employees paid for your trip to Cancun?"

"No!" Mrs. Capp cried. "I didn't know that."

Mr. Chitwood let her squirm for several seconds. She wasn't the one on trial, but I figured that attacking the legacy of Congressman Capp was Chitwood's strategy.

"Did you know that the unions who helped widen I-75 just north of this building were the ones who sent you to Whistler, British Columbia?"

"I did not."

Mr. Chitwood raised his voice, "Did you know that it was the same unions who contributed more than seven hundred fifty thousand dollars to the Friends of Floyd Capp?"

Ms. Melton jumped to her feet. "Your Honor, the defense is badgering the witness."

"Overruled," Brewer answered, "the witness will answer the question."

"I did not know that the unions contributed that," Mrs. Capp admitted.

Mr. Chitwood casually moved to the defense table. He picked up his legal pad and flipped a page. Those theatrics made everyone in the courtroom believe that he was about to drop a bombshell.

"What about Fayette Pappas?"

Mrs. Capp unfolded her hands and placed them on the armrest. In a cool, almost simmering kind of way, she asked, "Did she give the congressman seven hundred fifty thousand, too?"

"That's not what I meant, Mrs. Capp," Chitwood smiled along with the snickering in the gallery. "What do you know about her?"

Mrs. Capp was lying. "Didn't she kill herself?"

"Is that all you know about her?"

"That's basically the extent of it," she sighed. "Other than she was a prosecutor of some sorts."

"Don't you think it's a little peculiar, Mrs. Capp, that a federal prosecutor should kill herself at the same time she was investigating your husband?"

Mrs. Capp stuttered. "Like, like I said, I really don't know a lot of what was going on outside of the office. People kill themselves all the time."

Mr. Jacobetti threw her a life ring. "Your Honor, I believe the witness has clearly established that she merely handled the decedent's schedule and not much else. The defense is belaboring a point that has no bearing on the case."

Mr. Chitwood countered loudly: "With all due respect, Counselor, the defense knows what we're doing and we don't need any unsolicited advice from the prosecution."

Judge Brewer picked up his gavel and in his Yooper accent

warned, "Gentlemen, please. Mr. Chitwood, dah prosecution makes ah valid point. Are you almost done with dis line of questioning?"

"Yes I am, Your Honor," Chitwood admitted, "I just have a two or three more questions."

Brewer sighed, "Very well."

"Mrs. Capp, can you please tell us what Mr. Capp told you about the health-care bill?"

She sat up in her chair and said confidently, "He said that it's not the perfect bill, but it's a start in the right direction."

"I see," Chitwood smiled.

"Did you know what the residents of northern Michigan thought of the bill?"

"Of course. We had constituent surveys and a team of pollsters. Our field offices called in every day and reported tallies from the phone calls they received."

"And what were those results?" he asked, palms clenching his lapels.

"About sixty-five percent of our constituents didn't want health care overhauled."

"But Mr. Capp voted for it anyway. Is that correct, Mrs. Capp?"

"Yes, that's correct."

"Help me understand, Mrs. Capp. How he could do that?"

She sat back in her chair slightly, but her hands still clung to the ends of the armrests. Smugly, she said, "Because we know what's best for our people."

Chitwood didn't say a thing. He drifted to the far edge of the jury box, leaned against the wooden rail, and waited several seconds. Only after the jury panel looked in his direction, he said he didn't hear what she had said. "I'm sorry Mrs. Capp, I didn't hear what you just said. Could you repeat that?"

Mrs. Capp leaned into the microphone, "I said, 'We know what's best for our people.'"

Chitwood scoffed, "I thought that's what you said."

Oscar Haynes was shaking his head slightly. He either didn't agree with Chitwood's line of questioning, or he couldn't believe that Mrs. Capp could be so arrogant. Mr. Chitwood would reserve his commentary for the closing arguments; for now, he wanted to impugn the witness.

"Is that what the congressman told you, or is that what you believed as well?" he asked.

"That's what we both thought."

"Why are you so much better at deciding what's best for the people than the people themselves?"

"Education. Life experiences. We just know better."

"I see," Chitwood acquiesced half-heartedly. "So, we should feel thankful for the brilliance of you and the congressman; is that correct, Mrs. Capp?"

"Yes," she nodded.

"Did it ever occur to you that the invitation to the state dinner at the White House might be the payoff for Mr. Capp's vote on the health-care bill?"

Jacobetti and Ms. Melton jumped from their seats.

"Never mind, Your Honor, I'll withdraw my question," Mr. Chitwood said as he strolled back to his table. "I have nothing further."

Judge Brewer glanced at the prosecution's table and asked if they'd like to redirect the witness. Jacobetti and Melton huddled for almost a minute, whispering to each other and pointing to the notes on their legal pad. Finally, Mr. Jacobetti stood, buttoned the middle button on his suit coat, and declined further questions.

"Then call your next witness."

"Your Honor, there are no more witnesses. We rest our case."

At one o'clock of the third day, the defense rolled out their first witness—the man in charge of the Standish High School's video surveillance system. He was the one who captured what had taken place on the evening Mr. Capp was kidnapped. Naturally, the shot of Capp being pushed into the back of the state police's cruiser turned out the best because the camera was so close to the action. With a little narration, however, it was relatively easy to see the Ivey boys at the outer edge of the camera's effectiveness. They were at the end of the driveway, hidden behind the rows of parked cars. Every cop car that raced past them hit the curb of nails and almost immediately became immobilized.

Mr. Chitwood didn't deny that it was his clients who put down the spike strips; their defense was based on a statement Yandle gave them before the mission was underway. Both brothers testified that Yandle told them that the state police and the sheriff's deputies wanted to kill Capp. The Ivey brothers' job was to stop every cop car but the first that drove past their location. They didn't waver in their testimony. Their stories were water-tight and lock-step with one another. Try as he might to get the brothers to point the finger at the other, or another member of the Heretic Fringe, Mr. Jacobetti couldn't get them to crack under cross examination.

When they were arrested, they maintained their innocence, and held fast to the notion that Yandle had lied to them. Their testimony was remarkably similar, as if they had rehearsed what they were going to say, how they were going to say it, and what they were going to deny. Mr. Chitwood was remarkably smooth, extremely thorough and wonderfully convincing.

Both brothers seemed rather naïve, but they each said that Yandle was lying to them. Since Yandle was dead, they could have made up just about anything. Mr. Chitwood timed their testimony so that the one brother finished testifying at the end of day three, and the other brother at the start of day four.

After the second brother finished testifying, Mr. Chitwood introduced the boys' high school counselor, who had come all the way from South Haven to be a character witness on their behalf. He said that the Ivey boys were fair students at best, and were susceptible to practical jokes and bullying by the other students. The Ivey boys often went along with the crowd and periodically got into trouble for performing sophomoric dares encouraged by the other students.

Little by little Mr. Chitwood was painting the picture of his two clients as being gullible.

The Ivey's personal physician testified that when the boys were younger they had multiple broken bones; not just from sporting activities, but from dares and stunts gone awry. When asked if she could give the jury an example of those accidents, the doctor said that the Ivey boys sledded down a relatively busy street after a late-winter ice storm. They didn't get hit by a car when they sailed through the intersection, but Peter slammed into a tree and broke his leg. Six months later, Russell jumped off the second story roof of his parent's house onto a trampoline that was tilted on a forty five degree angle. "His intent, I believe," she said, "was to carom off the trampoline onto a swing that was attached to a limb of an oak tree."

"I guess you could say it didn't work out so well, is that correct, doctor?" Chitwood implied.

"You could say that," the doctor said. "Little Russell broke his arm in four different places."

"And how old was little Russell at the time?"

"I'm not sure," she said. "It was just about four years ago."

Chitwood smiled.

We all did.

He was crafting a quite convincing personalized defense.

Before the witnesses' chair had the chance to grow cold, the person in charge of Kalkaska County's economic development took the stand. He testified that the Ivey boys were good, honest businessmen, but six months ago they really didn't possess much business acumen.

"What do you mean," Chitwood asked.

The man at the witnesses' chair shrugged his shoulders. "They really didn't know about easements or right of ways, tax incentives, building codes or safety updates."

"What did you think when you spoke to them?"

"I thought that the factory they were building was a pet project from mom and dad."

"You mean, like a way to get them out of the house?" Chitwood asked.

"Well, yeah."

"That was last winter or spring, wasn't it?"

"Yes, but the two boys or the Ivey family haven't given up on the factory idea even with all this going on. They've stayed with it, and they're working on it now, just in time to process the apple crop this fall."

"Has your opinion changed about the Ivey boys?" Chitwood asked.

"Yes it has. Six months ago, I would have said they were being led around by their parents, now it seems as if they've matured quite a bit."

"Thank you."

The last witness of the day was Channel 3's meteorologist, who testified how much snow Standish had received on that April evening. Her testimony was relevant because the snow contributed to the wet grass, which kept the police vehicles from driving across the lawn. She also testified that the congressman's bullet proof vest would have kept him somewhat warm, since the temperatures that evening were in the mid thirties.

And why would Capp be wearing a bulletproof vest?

It seemed that maybe Chitwood missed out on a glorious opportunity when he had Mrs. Capp on the stand. She would have known why he felt the necessity to wear it.

And that issue—of why Mr. Capp wasn't safe in his own district, combined with the Ivey boys' ignorance—became the backbone of Mr. Chitwood's closing argument.

He did a masterful job of combining the two elements into a patriotic, yet heartfelt plea for the boys' innocence. He said things like "We've already endured the tragedy of a murdered congressman, don't compound the issue by sending these two young men to jail." Mr. Chitwood had a very comforting style that reminded me a lot of Colombo, and the way he scratched his chin and thought out loud.

"Didn't it seem a little odd to you that the congressman's wife said that 'they knew what was best'?"

He stood on his toes slightly, making himself an inch taller than he actually was.

"That's not why we elected him, is it?"

Chitwood paced back and forth, an arm's length away from the jurors in the front row. They watched him slide past, spin on a dime, and drift past them again. The ideas poured from his lips and sometimes they were spoken so softly that it was hard to tell exactly what he was saying. He had the jury right where he wanted them—in the palm of his hand, clinging to every word, listening to the thoughts that pursed his lips. No note cards were needed; he had memorized the strategy, the game plan, the highlights of the case. Chitwood's late nights in the office reviewing the case, and forming a strategy with Dr. Ong was paying off. It was no wonder he and his team of lawyers were in high demand—he was prepared and convincing as if it was his own sons on trial.

Henry Rush whispered to me that Mr. Chitwood had stolen a page from his defense team's playbook. He also said that Mr. Jacobetti was sure to offer a lesser charge because he has to realize that the jury was leaning in the defense's direction.

I didn't want the Ivey boys to take a plea if it was offered, because I really wanted the Amish girl to be saved. The whole scenario was out of my control. The charge of murder seemed way too harsh. Aiding and abetting was just as severe. In my mind, the boys were guilty of malicious destruction of property, but that seemed like a slap on the wrist, when compared to the fact that a United States congressman was dead. There had to be some sort of middle ground that would satisfy the prosecutors and the Ivey boys.

Chitwood was playing it "all in." So was Jacobetti. He was just as passionate, just as convinced of the jury's correct decision. Everyone in the courtroom was witnessing a heavyweight battle, and had no idea of the jury's decision.

When His Honor finally turned the jury loose at the end of day four, Dr. Ong got half of his wish. Oscar Haynes was selected as an alternate, as was the dean from Saginaw Valley. Mr. Yoder was still in, so was his roommate, Robert Gilbert.

I figured that Dr. Ong had lost his nerve when it came to dismissing two of the jurors. The threat of a mistrial or worse yet, a charge of jury tampering must have been enough deterrent to keep him from acting on his urges. He could have discussed the scenario with Mr. Chitwood and realized that it probably wasn't worth the risk. Besides, he and Mr. Chitwood may have realized that regardless of who was chosen as an alternate, they had an excellent chance of winning the case. Further, they may have considered waiting to see who was an alternate and then they'd decide if they'd accept a plea bargain.

What was going on behind the scenes was a mystery to me. A major trial like this one has all sorts of angles, tentacles and perspectives that capture the attention of the American public.

The jury deliberated inside the courthouse until seven that evening, at which time they ordered three large pizzas and two-liter bottles of pop from the deli across the street. By eleven that evening, they were still mired in a deadlock. Judge Brewer held them there until midnight, then recessed for one last evening at the Bavarian Inn.

Colleen and I hardly spoke about the trial that evening. We were home, catching up in family activities, planning a vacation, and playing with Elizabeth. I paid some bills and cashed a check for twenty-five thousand, just in case the verdict was not guilty and we had to get our hands on some cash.

Whatever decision the jury came up with, we would be okay with it.

At eight Friday morning, Colleen and I arrived at the courthouse together, unafraid and unashamed of what was about to take place. I introduced her to Dr. Jim, and we talked for quite a while about what was going to be the jury's decision. He was confident in an acquittal because of the way the jury looked at Mr. Chitwood.

"Experts will tell you that eighty to ninety percent of communication is non-verbal," he said. "I can tell a lot about the jury and the way they looked at Mr. Chitwood. Almost all of them looked straight at him and nodded their heads. That means they liked what he had to say and how he said it."

"Didn't they do that to Mr. Jacobetti, too?"

"To a lesser extent," he said. "They were like this," Jim said, as he crossed his arms.

"Sounds like you liked the jury after all, Jim." Colleen suggested.

"I really do," Jim said. "There's a difference between having carpenters on the jury and cabinet makers."

We looked at him slightly confused.

"Carpenters can visualize how things fit together but they don't need to know every fine detail."

We still were confused, so he explained things even further.

"I'm speaking metaphorically now," he said. "For a cabinet maker, everything has to fit together perfectly."

Just before noon, we didn't have to wonder any longer.

Jacobetti and Chitwood never reached a plea bargain. Both were going for broke.

The courtroom was as packed the last hour of the trial as it was on the first day when all the potential jurors were present. The buzz of conversation filled the steamy air, and people waved folded up newspapers in front of their faces. Mr. Chitwood sat on the edge of his seat and faced his clients and the mass of onlookers. He enjoyed the limelight, and the chance to show off his face, his suit, and the confident smiles to all that glanced his way. Jacobetti and Melton sat at their table—backs to the crowd, speaking to themselves.

I introduced Colleen to Henry Rush, who proceeded to tell us why the Iveys would be found not guilty. Henry was an expert on body language and he pointed out the way the two teams of lawyers were waiting for the jury. The defense was confident, while the prosecutors looked like they had just lost their best friend. Colleen listened politely, but not all that attentively. And besides, it wasn't long before Judge Brewer was introduced, who in turn pulled in the jury.

"Guilty!" Henry cried, quietly. "They're going to be guilty," he said. "I can see it in the jury's eyes."

I held up a finger for him to wait.

"They don't make eye contact with anyone," he said. "They're ashamed of their decision."

"Shh," I whispered.

A man in the row ahead of us glanced over his shoulder. We were being too loud.

The court had plenty of cops at the ready. They stood between the jury box and the door leading to the darkened gallows. I had a hunch they were sizing up the two Ivey boys and whether they'd come peacefully after the guilty verdict was read.

Judge Brewer asked the defendants to rise. When they did, both tables of attorneys did too.

This was it. The trial's grand conclusion.

"Ladies and gentlemen of dah jury," Brewer started. "Have you reached ah decision?"

The jury froze momentarily, until the auto executive in the back rose to his feet. *Maybe Henry was right,* I thought. *They're going to throw the book at 'em.*

"We have, Your Honor," he said.

Brewer didn't miss a beat. "On dah charge of capital murder, what say you?"

"Not guilty!" Nills said.

The crowd gasped. Chitwood put a limb around the closest Ivey and squeezed. Jubilation was in the air.

Brewer blasted his gavel. "Order!" he warned them all, "order!" The chatter simmered, just long enough for him to ask, "On dah charge of aiding and abetting, what say you?"

"Not guilty!" Nills cried even louder.

Henry Rush jabbed me in the ribs, and whispered loudly, "I told you so!"

Colleen heard him too and rolled her eyes.

The reporters left their seats and started down the aisle. Some of the cameramen beat them to the double doors.

Brewer banged his gavel. Jacobetti and Melton hung their heads. They Ivey boys turned to their parents and hugged them all.

"On dah charge of malicious destruction of property," Brewer growled. "What say you?"

"Guilty!" Nills announced emphatically.

"Ladies and gentlemen of dah jury," Brewer started, "on behalf of dah United States government, dah city of Flint and dah citizens of dis great nation…" His dismissal was drowned by chatter and gleeful musings. I saw Bob Gilbert hug his little Amish buddy, who seemed totally oblivious to the peril that had eclipsed his family. Others within the jury box shook each other's hands or waved goodbye. Penny Melton and Jack Jacobetti gathered their papers, put away their writing utensils and zipped their attaches. They couldn't hide the disappointment scribed across their faces, but they weren't too proud to shake Chitwood's hand.

Dr. Ong was in the middle of the Ivey family, shaking hands and back slapping his clients. A guilty verdict on destruction of property was a negligible offense, a mere misdemeanor with an even smaller fine.

"Wow!" Henry Rush exploded. "That was something."

I didn't have to ask Colleen if she was ready to go. She had already turned away from us and was marching single-file with the other spectators toward the exit. Henry Rush was right behind me, carrying on about the Ivey boys and how their sentencing wouldn't be for another month. Tea Party members were huddled on the prosecution's side of the courtroom, the Heretic Fringe on the other. I didn't care if they saw me or Colleen together. I didn't care to hear the grandstanding by Mr. Chitwood, or the alibis from the prosecution.

All I cared about was saving the little girl, otherwise known as Grace Yoder.

Thirty-One

Early the following morning, Colleen and I drove her vehicle up the heart of mid-Michigan towards the little town of Clare, where we made a sweeping left turn on US-10, then a right on 115. Elizabeth was in the back seat, and Jacque, his kennel not far from the van's caboose. The smell of cash filled the cockpit and it all stemmed from a small athletic bag filled with currency way in the back. It felt a little odd to have twenty-five thousand just lying around, but then again, I have never been in this position before. When we stopped for gas in Cadillac, I unzipped the athletic bag, and pulled a crisp hundred from the stack of bills stuffed inside. A hundred bucks wasn't enough to fill the tank, so I peeled another off the stack and hoped the kidnappers wouldn't know the difference, or have time to count it all.

When I went inside the gas station, and briefly looked over the supply of newspapers from around the state, every one of them had the same emblazoned headline: *Ivey Brothers Acquitted on Murder Charges*. I snickered for a half second, knowing that while the state woke up on a Saturday morning to read about what happened in Flint, I had a ring-side seat to all the action the day before. As I glanced at all the different headlines, and observed a version of the same photo—Jacob Chitwood sandwiched between his two clients—I also took note of an accompanying story: *Inside the Heretic Fringe, a glimpse into the radical right and the group that killed a congressman.* It was written by Colleen Beyer, the alias my wife uses for clandestine writing assignments.

I snickered even louder. Colleen's picture next to her byline was ten or fifteen years old.

The lady behind the counter must have thought I was a little odd for having purchased so many newspapers, but that didn't bother me; it's not every day that your wife's hard work makes it to the front page.

"I'm surprised you didn't mention it," I said to Colleen when I returned to the vehicle.

Colleen smiled. "I was going to surprise you," she said, wryly, "with a paid vacation from the money I'd make off these stories. The AP will pay me next week for everything."

"That's cool," I said. "I'm looking forward to reading it."

"Me, too," she said, pulling her reading glasses from her purse. "I just hope we don't run into any of the Fringe."

"That would be bad."

By the time we crossed the Manistee River in northern Wexford County we had finished explaining to Elizabeth about the story Mommy had written. Of course, we didn't give her all the details. Little Elizabeth didn't need to know that the reason why we were going on a family vacation on such short notice, was to deliver my portion of the ransom.

The end of August is a great time to be in Traverse City, when wine tasting is in full swing, concerts near the water's edge are rocking and rolling, and the season's first salmon get a taste of the Boardman River's fertile currents.

Our instructions were to meet Dr. Ong with the money in the parking lot of Menard's lumberyard at the south end of Traverse City. At nearly nine that morning, he took my athletic bag to the rear of his vehicle and opened the trunk. Inside, was a metal toolbox the size of a suitcase.

"What's that for?" I asked him.

"Let me show you," he said.

He opened the hood of the toolbox, and I looked to see piles of cash stacked like cordwood. Tons of it.

"Holy hell," I said. "You weren't kidding that the Ivey's were going to pony up most of the ransom."

"I told you, Derrick. These guys are serious."

"When did they give it to you, before or after the verdict was read?"

"Before," he said, grabbing a bundle of money from my duffle and dropping it on the pile within the toolbox. "If I waited until after the verdict, I wouldn't have any leverage, right?" Jim asked.

I looked around for security guards or the police. We were safe. "Right," I said, somberly.

Jim loaded the last stack of my hundreds onto his pile. Mine were bound with blue belts, the pile in Jim's, red.

"What's the plan?" I asked him.

"Come on with me," he said, seriously.

"Where are we going?" I urged him.

Dr. Jim didn't respond. He snapped the lid on the toolbox, handed me my empty duffle bag and asked: "are you sure you want to do this?"

"Yeah, I'm sure," I said, seeing my reflection in the lenses of his sunglasses. Jim pulled a small padlock from his shirt pocket, and threaded the clasp of the lock through the snap on the box.

"Once I lock it, we can't open it again," he said.

"It's for the little girl, right?"

"Right," he said. He didn't look up at me. He lifted the tool box onto a flat bottom, metal cart and began pushing the cart towards the front door.

I waved goodbye to my family and followed Jim into the establishment.

"Why can't we open it again?" I asked him.

Jim didn't even hesitate, "those are our instructions."

As we entered the store, I had to ask, "Who gave us the instructions?"

Jim didn't respond, but nodded to the man at the customer service desk who was engaged with another guest.

He was on a mission: past the garden supplies, the plumbing, electrical, and floor-covering aisles, to the back corner of the store. Without batting an eye, he pushed the button for the overhead door and we were on our way to the vast expanse of lumber, shingles, and plywood, outside.

"Where are you going?" I asked.

"You'll see, Derrick," he said. "Now come on."

A man driving a forklift truck beeped at us. We let him pass, then followed in his wake.

"Come on," he said.

Jim didn't hesitate or waffle in the slightest.

"What are our instructions, Jim?" I demanded.

"Here we go," he said. "That's our truck, number seven."

I tried to stop him, but there was no use. A few steps later we were at the truck's flanks, which was loaded with assembled trusses, rolls of insulation, and eight-by-eight inch pilings. The truck was a big one and had an oversized cab.

"You must be Norm," Jim said, looking up at the driver.

"You got it," the man said, flicking the ashes from a cigarette.

"Great," Jim smiled.

Jim slid past me to the other side of the cab, opened the passenger side door, and heaved the toolbox inside amidst the ashes, fast food bags, and discarded clothing.

"Thanks a lot," Jim barked.

"No problem."

Jim backed away from the truck. The guys on top of the cargo were wedging a hot water heater into the nooks of the trusses. Others were securing the load with the help of some oversized straps. It was a rather hectic situation, but I didn't care. I had enough of Dr. Jim.

"Are you ready to talk, counselor?" I said, clutching his elbow in the process.

He looked at me rather concerned, as well he should have. I'm sure the veins in my neck were bulging, and my face was turning beet red.

"I've got a lot of money up there," I gestured Norm's way. "If you don't tell me who gave you those instructions," I said, taking a half step his way, "I'm going to pound the piss out of you, right here, right now."

"Whoa, whoa, don't get so…hasty, Derrick," he backpedaled. "We don't have to get violent."

"Are you going to tell me?"

"Yeah, here," he said, handing me a folded up paper from his pocket.

It was a printout of an e-mail, dated yesterday afternoon. From *doodledandy@gmail* to Dr. James Ong.

Bring the money to the loading dock of Menard's lumber yard, Traverse City, at nine tomorrow morning. Give it to Norm, in truck seven.

Jim was eyeing me up—analyzing the way my eyes darted across the page.

"When I got home last night, the toolbox and padlock were on the front porch," he said. "Inside the toolbox was another note that said to put the money inside and lock it with the padlock."

I thought for a second. "That's all you know?"

"Yeah, that's it."

"How are we going to get the girl?"

"I don't know, but she might be in the store," he said, glancing left and right.

Jim had me looking around too. I thought for a second about shouting her name, but decided not to.

Norm opened the cab of his truck and stepped out of his rig. Jim and I stayed near the passenger-side door and made sure that nobody walked away with our loot. Ten seconds later, Norm appeared from the back of the flatbed, checking and double-checking that the straps were secure.

"All set?" Norm yelled to the crew.

The foreman jumped off the truck bed, removed his gloves, and tore a yellow sheet of paper from the clipboard. "Thanks a lot," the foreman said. "You've got everything. I'll radio to the security guard that you're good to go."

Norm waddled around the front of his rig, hopped in the cab, and pressed the gas pedal several times. When he did, a plume of thick, black smoke erupted from the overhead stack. A group of house sparrows didn't care for the intrusion, and they dashed away, to calmer conditions near the outdoor nursery.

"Where's he going?" I asked Jim.

"I don't know, but we'd better follow him."

Norm put the truck in gear and the truck lurched forward.

"We'd better hustle," Jim said, briskly walking away.

I never thought to scribble down the license plate of Norm's rig, or waving goodbye to my hard-earned stash.

All I could do was keep up with Jim as we made our way through the busy store and into the parking lot.

Colleen wanted to know what was going on, naturally, but she wasn't as mad as I thought she'd be.

"This will be fun," I told her. "We're going to save the day!"

Norm pulled out of the lumber yard and onto US-31, which was relatively busy.

Jim was ahead of us in his Chevy Impala; the Twitchells hot on his tail.

Elizabeth wanted to know what was going on, so we told her a therapeutic lie.

"All we have to do is keep an eye on that truck and see where it goes," I told her. "Can you help me?"

She was agreeable to that, and as we made our way through town, around the shore of East Bay, and the turnoff for M-72 at Acme, the allure of keeping up with truck number seven had worn thin. "I'm ready to start our vacation," Elizabeth sighed.

"Me, too," Colleen said.

"How much farther?" she asked, naturally.

"We'll be there soon," I promised, even though I had no idea how long we'd be behind the windshield.

Together, we drove past Grand Traverse resort, a schmaltzy new casino, and just when I thought we were about to enter the city of Kalkaska, Norm turned into a bustling construction site. There were trucks everywhere, just like his. I noticed the pickups, lined up in a row, adorned with stickers that featured contractor logos, or various hunting company insignias. Testosterone was in the house.

"What's this?" Colleen asked.

"I don't know," I said, "but all I want to do is follow that truck."

Norm kept driving towards an old, rather large building, which had been stripped of its outer shell. The roof was still intact, but the sides bore the metal skeleton from its distant past. In front of the old building was a cement pad, which was outlined by surveyor's stakes flapping in the breeze. Above the cement pad, a crane lowered a triangle-shaped truss to the wooden frame. Whoever the crane operator was had his hands full as the truss wobbled in the dusty breeze.

I looked closer. Men clung to the frame, and the previously placed trusses. All were ready to nail it into place, and begin the process of laying the plywood on top. The closer Norm drove towards the building, the more I couldn't deny who the men were. Amish.

"Holy hell," I mumbled.

"Daddy!" Elizabeth scolded me.

"What is it?" Colleen asked.

"Look," I cried, "the Amish."

"What's wrong with that?"

"Nothing," I thought for a second, *this must have been the project they were talking about at the school-raising a few weeks ago.*

I wondered what Jim was thinking. It made me wish that I had his cell phone number.

Norm pulled into the parking lot, then backed his truck to the edge of the building site. Jim stayed with him. So did I.

We were going to find out who had kidnapped the child, who demanded the ransom, and dashed the prosecution's hopes in Flint. My heart was beginning to race again, the way it always does when the chips are down and an explosive situation is ready to unfold.

We were walking a tightrope of anticipation, teetering on the brink of wonderful discovery.

Colleen looked at me and I looked at her. Elizabeth was still in the back, patient as ever. Somewhere beyond her, Jacque was balled up in his kennel, chasing squirrels and pointing game birds in his dreams. What a wonderful life dogs live, not a care in the world.

We must have idled there for five minutes. Norm was next in line to drop off his payload, it appeared. He hopped out of the cab and began loosening the heavy straps from the sides of his truck.

Just then, a rather squat man wearing a yellow hardhat walked up him and began issuing directions. Using a clipboard as a prop, the foreman gestured right and left. Norm understood. He hopped back in the cab and the truck lurched ahead. The Twitchell gang followed Norm around the back of the building.

The Amish had set up camp in the shade of some nearby trees. Tablecloths flapped in the breeze. Children rode their bikes or played jump rope. They were at peace with the world and making the most out of a busman's holiday.

Norm pulled into the building, out of sight, behind another rig.

This was it.

I jumped out, and told Colleen and Elizabeth that I'd be right back.

"Be careful, Derrick," Colleen said.

Jim didn't want to go inside and I didn't have time to find out why.

I ran to the edge of the building. There were men everywhere in their hard hats and their work belts, loaded with tools. I smelled the exhaust from diesel motors and the dust from a cloud of dirt.

Just as I was about to enter the building, I heard a woman yell, "Hold it!" I glanced in her direction. It was Penny Melton, coming right at me.

The men were unloading Norm's hot water heater. Others were peeling sheets of metal siding from the adjacent truck. It was hard to see inside with all the dust and people and bustling activity.

Penny marched toward me, a hardhat of her own covering her bronze mane. "What are you doing here?" she demanded.

I wasn't sure what to say; she caught me way off guard.

She was dressed in blue jeans and a Daisy Duke kind of plaid top tied at her waist.

"You're going to blow my investigation," she said.

I was still mute. Barely. "What investigation?"

"About the unions," she said sternly, "We're investigating them for intimidating non-union workers on government-subsidized projects."

"Oh," I said, rather bland. "On a weekend?"

"Heck yeah," she said, "This is a prime example of it. The government is subsidizing this venture, but the owners don't want to use union workers. Don't you remember what I told you about Fayette Pappas?"

"Yeah, I do," I said. My mind was flailing between two storylines: the trial that had just concluded, and the ransom just a few yards away. "Why didn't this union conflict come up at trial?" I asked.

She didn't even hesitate. "It wasn't going to help our case."

I was trying to stay focused. Seems like Penny should have presented what she knew about Congressman Capp and the unions at the Ivey boys' trial, regardless of whether it was going to hurt her case. Perhaps it was just as well the Iveys were acquitted if the prosecution was withholding evidence that might have helped their case.

Norm's passenger side door was open. Somebody was inside the cab. "Listen, Penny," I said. "I gotta go."

"Are you okay?" Penny asked me.

"Yeah, I'm fine. I'll talk to you later."

Three steps later I was inside the building, on the concrete floor.

At that instant, I heard Colleen scream, "Der...rick!" Her plea sounded like a lonesome hen yelp in the May turkey woods.

I looked over my shoulder.

Colleen was surrounded.

Men had her by her arms. Women in her face. Their Howdy Doodie kind of outfits gave it away: Heretic Fringe.

Holy hell, I thought.

I looked back at Norm's vehicle. There was a pair of legs standing at the passenger side of the cab. Blue jeans. Work boots. It could have been anybody, and they were only thirty yards away.

I heard Colleen's cry again.

The situation had boiled down to saving my family, or solving the mystery.

What a decision.

Even though there was a great deal of loot just lying there, I chose my family, of course.

Colleen was maybe fifty yards away from me, which was plenty enough room to build up a head of steam. I passed Penny

Melton in a blur, but refused to take my eyes off my wife. One of the men held a newspaper to her face, and was yelling something inaudible. She was doing her best to break free of the confines, but she couldn't. And dear old Jacque, my faithful companion, was humping an unsuspecting Amish child in a blue denim dress. It was terrible.

At twenty yards, I centered my attention on the man holding a newspaper to Colleen's face. My blood was boiling, but I was racing faster and faster towards the conflict. Nobody disgraces my family and gets away with it. There was hell to pay, and I couldn't wait to deliver it.

When I was five yards away from the man with the newspaper, he turned around. I caught him under the chin with my shoulder. His head snapped backwards and I heard the air depart his lungs with a guttural heave. Together, we plowed into one of the men who had a hold of Colleen's arm. All three of us fell to the ground, and as former announcer Ernie Harwell used to say when the Tigers turned a double play, I got "Two for the price of one."

"Hold it right there," Penny screamed.

Colleen wriggled free and ran twenty yards to the open van. "Don't cry," I heard her say.

The men that I tackled were slow to get up. As they brushed the dust from their jeans, I felt like burying my fist in their face, Yandle-style.

"Derrick, stop," Penny yelled. "All of you. Break it up!"

Some of the Fringe weren't quite ready to give up the fight. "You're the guy who killed Marshall Yandle!" one of them yelled.

"Yes, I am," I said proudly, "and I'd do it again if I had the chance."

The Fringe wasn't sure what to think. I think they thought I was a madman. Maybe I was.

Penny wasn't for a loss of words, "Move it along," she ordered them.

Fifteen or twenty of them lingered in the dust and the commotion, in the tension-filled setting.

The uproar attracted the attention of the Amish women and children who had gathered around the uprising. I didn't recognize many of Amish, but I know I saw Rebecca, Mrs. Hooley, and Mrs. Yoder. Some of them were older, and I figured that they could have been the spouses of the elders. They all wore genuine smiles on their wholesome, natural faces.

One of the girls emerged from the assembly and handed me Jacque's leash.

"Thank you," she smiled.

"For what?" I asked.

"For everything you have done," she said, calmly, a slight accent in her voice. I looked into her eyes. They were bright blue and framed by tawny bangs that hung beneath the edges of her bonnet. She could have been ten, or twelve, but I didn't want to ask.

"That little mongrel pulled free!" Colleen yelled from the vehicle, "Just as those jerks came at me."

"You're welcome," I told the girl. She almost curtsied before she turned to join the clan.

"Can we get going now, Derrick?" Colleen demanded. "Or do you want to go another round with the boys in the Fringe?"

Penny said "so long" as I put Jacque in his kennel.

I waved in Penny's direction, and hopped inside the van.

Colleen had the motor running and the air conditioning on full tilt.

"You know," I said, buckling my seatbelt, "I think that girl who handed me Jacque was Grace Yoder."

Colleen glanced out the window. The Amish were walking away from us, back to their enclave at the edge of the construction site.

"Well, good," Colleen said, somewhat relieved. "Maybe we can get on with our vacation."

"Yeah!" Elizabeth chipped in. "I'm ready to go to the beach."

I laughed, "Me, too."

As I put the van in gear, two big trucks pulled out of the building. One of them was Norm.

Colleen glanced my way. She put her hand on my thigh and said, "Let it go."

I watched Norm back his truck into the front entryway, near the skeleton of joists.

"You mean, like water off a duck's back?"

Colleen knew what I was talking about. "Yes," she smiled.

She was right. It was time to move on.

I looked in her direction, back at Norm's truck, then at last, Jim's Impala.

Remarkably, Jim had disappeared.

Thirty-Two

SEVEN MONTHS HAD PASSED since the trial of the Ivey brothers had concluded. I'm sure Peter and Russell were on the family farm over in South Haven, pruning their trees, applying fertilizer, or doing whatever fruit growers do in the early weeks of spring. Then again, they could have been up in Traverse City at the Continental Foods factory, preparing the machinery for a busy season ahead. The parents of the boys would never speak of the trial again, and in due time, everyone in the community would have forgotten about the mistakes they had made. In Michigan, life goes on in the busiest of cities and the quaintest of societies.

I hardly gave the trial much thought as I drove the old Suburban north in April's pre-dawn darkness. The relics of the refinery in Alma reminded me of times when gas was relatively cheap, and hundreds of people found employment. Now, gas is expensive, and the people who haven't moved out of Michigan can't find work.

There were hardly any cars on the road that morning, and it seemed like there were very few people alive. Strange though, while most of America slept, AM radio was alive with chatter. When I pushed the "scan" button on the truck's radio, I picked up radio stations on nearly every click of the dial. Virginia, and Iowa, Chicago and Milwaukee; almost all of them had the same format: weather and sports, traffic and a never-ending supply of commercials. For a brief time, I listened to a right-wing talk-show host, who decried the liberals in Congress for their wild spending habits. "They vote yes for piddling spending cuts, while the deficit continues to skyrocket.

"Ladies and gentlemen, they're destroying the fabric of our country. We're getting buried in debt and snowed under in deficits."

I turned off the radio and listened to the sounds of my truck tires galloping over the cracked pavement. *Our roads are terrible,* I thought to myself, *but we hate paying higher taxes. We've made our bed when it comes to blacktop and deficits, now we sleep in it.*

About half an hour later, I rolled into the driveway of Eli's farm. The robins were singing their little hearts out from the tops of nearly every tree. I love this time of year, this time of morning. For just one day, I want to be a robin and be able to fly, to sing, to feel the warmth of the countryside on my flanks as I dash from treetop to treetop, searching for the perfect place to sing. It would be so much fun to trot through a stand of grass—pausing every six or eight feet, listening to the earth be-low—and pulling a nightcrawler from its hole. I longed to be the bird most associated with "a sure sign of spring" and cradle a bundle of eggs such a delightful shade of baby blue; it would be the inspiration for nurseries everywhere. Never mind that there might be hawks lurking in the bushes, chemicals in the lush grass, or my offspring might get hit by a car. Today—this day—it would be good to be a robin.

Or a cardinal.

But, definitely, not a wild turkey.

It was opening day of gobbler season, and I had made plans to take little Angus Beiler turkey hunting.

At first I had to wonder if little Angus had made it out of bed. The farmhouse was completely dark when I first arrived, but little by little the house warmed to the delightful hues of propane and kerosene lights. It made me wonder who was upstairs turning the lights on, Eli or Rebecca. Amish farmhouses seem to glow in dawn's inky darkness. Propane lights have a warmth about them that reminds me of a campfire, or candlelight. It's no wonder Amish communities are bound so tightly, when their families are basked in the wholesome goodness of propane.

Rebecca peeked out the side-door window and gestured for me to wait.

After three or four minutes, she opened the door again and told me that breakfast was almost ready.

Maybe her conscience was bothering her, and that big hunters like me need breakfast too.

Either way, when I stepped inside the kitchen, I was overwhelmed by the smell of breakfast. Rebecca had the sausage cooking and the pancakes nearly made.

"There's a cup on the counter there," Rebecca whispered, "help yourself to the coffee."

"Thank you," I nodded.

It was just the two of us in the kitchen.

"All week, Angus has been talking about going hunting," she said, smiling. "He's been practicing, too."

"What has he been practicing, his shooting or his turkey calling?"

"Both," she said. "I think those chickens in the barnyard are a little nervous with him shooting those arrows. I must hand it to him—he's pretty deadly inside of twenty yards."

I poured a cup of coffee and heard footsteps sneaking down the wooden stairs. Little Angus limped into the kitchen, dressed in his homemade jeans and a new camouflage hunting shirt.

"There he is, the man of the hour," I greeted him.

He smiled at me, but couldn't wait to ask his mother where he had left his new hunting boots.

"They're by the back door, right where you left them," she said. "Come on now, you'd better eat. Mr. Twitchell, find your place."

Rebecca pointed to the same end of the table where I had eaten a delicious lunch during the previous summer.

In a way, I felt like an old family friend. Maybe I was.

Rebecca seemed at home and at ease in the kitchen, despite the early hour. She stood in front of a giant, eight-burner range and flipped buttermilk pancakes as thick and heavy as home-made potholders. And the sausage wasn't links, but an enormous patty that covered the entire bottom of a cast-iron skillet.

"Are you ready to kill your tom today?" I asked Angus.

He nodded.

"Are you going to shoot the first one that comes into range, or are you going to hold out for a big one?" I asked.

Angus shrugged his shoulders and kept eating. His arm was bent awkwardly, and I wondered how the plates and bolts installed in his elbow would hamper his growth.

We ate pancakes and sausages and washed them down with glasses of milk and a cup of coffee. There's something remarkably satisfying about a big breakfast on the morning of a grand adventure. I love the smell of the sausage, the stickiness of the syrup, and the feeling of being full, but not stuffed. A good breakfast should fuel the engine, not bog down the momentum.

Rebecca wished us "Good luck," as Angus pulled his boots from the box and slid his stocking feet inside.

We loaded up our gear and started the big walk to the pasture in back of the barn. Angus walked with a limp, and I guessed that he'd have that for the rest of his life. Instead of traipsing through the barnyard and disturbing the inhabitants, we decided that it might be a good idea to walk around the front lawn of the farmhouse and down the east edge of the property.

We'd be hunting the opposite edge of the pasture where I had the encounter with the white gobbler the previous season. Even if the gobbler had forgotten about the close call from the year before—and somehow made it through the winter—I still felt much more confident on the other side of the pasture.

Dawn was in full tilt when we wandered up to the fence-line that would take us to the woods at the back of the pasture. Angus settled in behind me and carried his crossbow in a safe manner.

A cottontail rabbit dashed out of the copse of bushes in the fenceline. It wasn't especially scared of the intrusion, but it didn't give us long to check him out, either. He darted back into the cover and we never saw him again.

We slowed our pace and took in the sounds of spring. Some distance away, Angus and I heard the roar of a gobbler. It was a little like pulling the obscure dirge of a foghorn from the splashing clabber of children playing on a beach in the summertime. We both heard it, but we weren't exactly sure where it came from.

That was okay; we really didn't have a lot of options when it came to places to hunt. Our only choice was on a small rise where the fenceline met the woodlot at the far edge of the property. The closer we stepped in that direction, the louder and louder the gobbles became.

In my head, the hunt was taking shape. We had a bird on the roost, a beautiful day ahead of us, and a brand-new hunter in the making.

How the hunt would unfold was yet to be determined.

The previous spring's hunt had a lot of drama. Today's might or might not. One thing was for certain, however: Angus Beiler would remember it for the rest of his life. Hunters always remember their first hunt, which is why I wanted it to be so special.

Angus' dad, Eli, would just as soon take out a gobbler with

a high-powered rifle and skip the challenge of calling it into range. It'd be quick and easy. Over and done with. On to other things; there's not much sportsmanship in that.

Never mind that using a rifle is also illegal.

I wanted to give the kid a chance to hunt turkeys the way they were supposed to be hunted—by calling them into range. If he wanted to take them illegally after that, it wasn't up to me to decide.

And honestly, we had a reasonably good chance of killing a bird. The tom was gobbling up a storm by the time we arrived at the corner of the woodlot, and he didn't see or hear us setting up the portable blind that looked like a camouflaged version of a tent. Angus and I opened our folding seats and settled into the theatre that is mid-Michigan in the springtime.

I was glad I brought the portable blind, because I knew that if Angus was like most ten-year olds, he might fidget and fuss, which is bad news if you plan on fooling a wary tom turkey. The blind had four little slits for windows, which would conceal Angus' movements, yet grant him enough space to raise his crossbow and fire.

We had a perfect view of the pasture. As his head bobbed from one slit to another, I couldn't help but wonder what it would be like to have a son of my own and teach him how to hunt, to shoot, and to make memories of our own. We didn't speak at all during those few minutes, which was fine; there's nothing worse than a jabber jaw when the setting called for stealth and cunning.

"Don't you think you ought to load that thing?" I whispered, quietly.

He smiled, as if to say "Oh duh," then proceeded to crank the handle that cocked the drawstring. With great care, Angus pulled a little arrow from his backpack, and slid it into position. While he did, I noticed the way his tongue worked the inside of his cheek. All that wrestling inside his head seemed to contort his tongue muscles. He was a cute boy with adorable traits and an appetite for adventure.

I felt sorry for what he had to endure, for all the pain he had to overcome. The little guy was as cute as cute could be.

An adorable kid with a killer's instinct.

He wasn't afraid or intimidated, reluctant, or apprehensive about taking down a wild turkey.

And when the first hen turkey waltzed into the pasture and took a look in our direction, little Angus Beiler sat on his folding chair as if he was cast from stone. The lady bird was maybe forty yards away, glaring in our direction. I hated to blink, to breathe, to think about addressing the itch on my calf. Angus understood the urgency, too, and he watched intently as the first hen was joined by three others. The three might have been sisters for all I knew. They sneered at each other with their necks outstretched as if to say, "Move it along, sis-tah."

Even though there were many more members in the group than there were last spring, the hens were going to dictate which way the flock was going to go.

Try as I might to bend the group in my direction with a couple of lonesome hen calls, the lead hen would have nothing of my impersonations. Angus tried it too, but the results were just as bad. The five hens and three toms in the group made a giant figure-eight in the pasture, and backed out the side door of the field without as much as a *sayonara*.

What's worse, the white tom wasn't part of the troupe.

Angus was glued to the turkeys' every step. He had borrowed my binoculars and watched the flock with great interest as they ambled farther and farther away.

"That happens a lot in the early season," I whispered.

Angus put the binoculars in his lap, and took a sip of hot chocolate.

"The hens lay an egg a day in their nest before they begin sitting on them," I whispered. "Till that happens, the hens are out wandering around. It's almost impossible to pull a tom away from them."

Angus understood; any kid with a farming background would.

He also understood the notion of being patient.

When I suggested that we hang out in the blind for a while and munch on candy bars, Angus was all in favor.

"Maybe they'll come back around," he whispered.

"Do you have any chores to do?" I asked, quietly.

"Not yet."

"What about school?"

"That doesn't start for a while," he whispered.

"Did your older brother make that arrow?"

Angus nodded.

"How cool is that," I said; "aren't those turkey feathers for the fletching?"

"Yeah."

A pair of deer trotted into the far edge of the pasture, swishing their tails behind them. Angus raised the binoculars to his eyes and watched them for several seconds. They were fat and plump, and I wondered how many more weeks till they dropped their fawns.

"Have you ever shot a deer?"

"No. I think you have to be twelve to do that."

The deer looked over their shoulders as if they were expecting danger.

"Have you seen the white gobbler at all?"

"Not lately, but I seen him last winter down the street."

"Oh yeah?"

"Yah. He was in the neighbor's feed bunk. No telling how much weight he might have gained."

"He was a big bird last spring. I hope we get a crack at him today."

"Me, too."

I reached into my pocket and handed him a candy bar. Angus looked up at me like he wasn't quite sure I could be trusted.

"Go ahead. Go ahead," I encouraged him.

"Thank you."

"You're welcome," I smiled. "How's your arm feeling?"

"It's okay. Same with my legs. The doctors say that I won't be able to run."

I nodded.

"Are you okay with that?"

"Yah. It's okay. The Lord will provide. He always does."

I smiled. Gradually, the kid was opening up to me.

"My doctor says that it's good to have faith."

"What doctor told you that?"

"My head doctor."

"Is there something wrong with your head? I thought it was your arm and your legs that were injured?"

Angus raised his eyebrows, and swished a moth that had flitted into the blind. The deer were too far away to notice, and really, I didn't care if they did.

"My dad calls Dr. Jim a head doctor, because he deals with the thoughts in my head."

"I see." Little Angus was singing like a canary, but I had to make sure who exactly he was talking about. "Is Doctor Jim a psychologist?"

"Yah. From Mount Pleasant."

I nodded my head in agreement, but my heart was starting to beat like mad. "How long have you been visiting him?"

"Oh, I don't know. Since last summer."

More nods.

"My mom really likes him," he munched. The kid was in heaven, doing what he loved doing, eating candy bars and sipping hot chocolate.

"Why's that?"

"Because he bought her a new kitchen."

"He did?"

Angus nodded. "We had a little celebration. Mom got her new kitchen, Papa got a new set of Belgians, and I got these special boots…"

I was laughing under my breath. His story became more and more incredible.

"Where did Doctor Jim get the money?"

Angus smiled. "He got two hundred from his customer, thirty from his lawyer friend, and twenty-five from some rich guy."

"Oh, wow." *Now I was some rich guy.*

"Dr. Jim paid off the hospital bills and had extra."

I tried to control the anger galloping through my veins.

"Who had extra?"

"Dr. Jim. He bought himself a Harley Division."

I felt Angus' eyes upon me as I buried my head in my hands. *All that money, down the drain.*

"Don't you mean, Harley Davidson?" I asked.

"Yeah, yeah. Are you okay?" he asked me, extending the thermos my way. "You look like you could use a drink."

Laughter came out of me, sympathetically so.

"I could use a drink, that's for certain."

Angus' confession was a dandy, but I really didn't want to make him think that he was doing anything wrong by telling me.

When the hot chocolate hit the back of my throat, I wished it was a Bloody Mary.

"Are you going to be okay?" he asked again. "You look like you seen a ghost."

"I'm sorry," I said, "I just get choked up when it comes to happy endings."

"Me too," he said, craning his head from one window slit to the other.

The deer had wandered off, and aside from a pair of robins in the baby April grass, the pasture was completely lifeless. In those few moments I had lost all interest in hunting, in being a nice guy and in the Amish culture. I had been double-crossed by Dr. Jim and the Amish to gain an acquittal and save one of their own.

At least, though, I could hang my hat on the fact that I helped save little Grace.

"How is the Yoder girl, anyway?" I mentioned.

Angus turned in my direction and asked, "Who?"

"Grace Yoder. Zachariah's daughter. She'd be about twelve or thirteen…"

"The Yoders down the street? The folks who own Buster and Billy?" Angus interrupted me, shaking his head, "Oh, they don't have no kids. Papa says Mr. Yoder got kicked by a horse when he was real young. Now, he's startle."

I glanced at my little hunting partner and laughed. He may have mispronounced his words, but he didn't mind telling me the truth.

"Don't you mean, *sterile,* Angus?"

"Yeah, I guess so," he said, a glorious hot-chocolate mustache above his crooked teeth. "I don't care what Papa says about you. For an English man, you're pretty smart."